Nice to be so Naughty

Andre,
Be good—
or else!

Dahlia lay

Adapted from *Nice to be so Naughty*, screenplay © Dalila Caryn 2018

Cover art and interior decoration by Yenthe Joline.

ISBN: 978-1-7338845-6-3
Ebook ISBN: 978-1-7338845-7-0
LCCN: 2022920308

Evil Goddess Press
Grand Terrace, CA
92313

Evil Goddess
—— Press ——

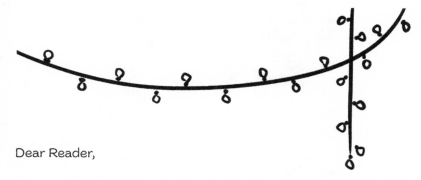

Dear Reader,

Nice to be so Naughty is a large departure from my usual work. Full of sarcastic humor, zany characters and a ton of references to movies songs, and books. It also employs a ridiculous style of narration that I really enjoyed writing! I truly hope anyone who picks it up is entertained.

That being said, any time an author picks up their pen (or more likely opens their computer) to write they run the risk of unintentionally harming someone with their words. In an effort not to do so I would like to inform my readers that this book contains themes of exclusion, grief and anxiety. Including pranks, workplace politics, interpersonal disputes, and some reference to Christmas themed violence.

There is also one character specifically who is neurodivergent. They are in no way meant to represent all neurodivergent people, but only themself alone. I went through several versions of this story. Some in which everything was named, and catalogued and gone into with great detail, others where things were glossed over, but both failed to capture the heart of the story, which is to love and accept people as they are. So in the end I chose to focus on moments in this character's life and how they were affected by them.

There is also a strong Christmas theme running through the book, but hopefully written in such a way that even people who do not celebrate might enjoy the fun!

If these warnings have yet to scare you off, please, read on!

With much love,
Dalila

Nice to be so Naughty

Merely Mortal Men Myth
Book 1

Dalila Caryn

Evil Goddess
— Press —

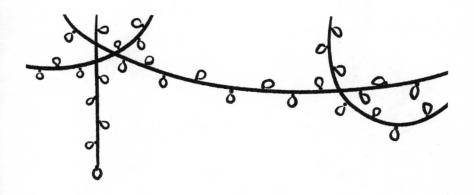

For everyone left out of the party. You are seen, and you are wanted, and you are loved.

Eight Tiny Reindeer

"There were, in fact, *nine* tiny reindeer on my desk when I left work for Thanksgiving weekend last Wednesday; now there are only eight!" Gabriella Anjelica Cruz, one of Santa's very favorite helpers, strives for a light tone as she responds to the film crew behind her.

Gabriella was not exactly on board with the concept of this film when emails came in from her company's CEO saying a group of college students would be doing a documentary about the doll company. Nope, she was decidedly opposed to it and sent a flurry of emails to the human resources department about the sensitive nature of the work done in IT. Until the company, in what they considered a great show of consideration, *gifted* all the IT workers with protective screens so their work couldn't be filmed.

It was about then while researching the film crew on her own time that Gabriella realized she was in over her head trying to get out of it. One of the "producers" of the piece—Kristen Kringle—was the only daughter of the company's CEO. Not being one to bite her nose off to spite her face, Gabriella gave in and threw herself firmly behind the documentary. But deciding to be helpful and professional has yet to make her comfortable with cameras following her around or the sense that her every secret is being exposed. And now, to add to that discomfort, *someone* is playing pranks on her. It's too much. Politeness can only extend so far.

"So fine," Gabriella sighs dramatically, resisting the urge to roll her eyes, but just barely. "Some people think a full week before Thanksgiving is too early to decorate for Christmas. But that is no excuse for theft. And he did it so blatantly too!"

"He?" Kristen inquires blandly; she knows full well who he is: Jack Hilary Drummer. The man on the opposite side of Gabriella's cubicle wall.

This interview came up because Kristen saw the pair arguing. But she needs to lead the conversation back where she wants it. This is the most promising sign of life in this office so far. She knows there is workplace tension. There has to be, and she is here to capture it, but no one has opened up about anything in the two weeks she's been here. If she doesn't get something soon, this project won't even be worth a C, and she's after an A. She won't settle for less than an A.

If she has to create the drama herself, she will have her A!

Gabriella rolls her eyes at the younger, but really not that much younger woman, well aware of Kristen's manipulative intents. It annoys her to be sure, but in later moments, away from *perfect* Kristen's *perfect* teeth, perfectly smooth skin, bright, vapid smile, condescending laugh, and *BMW,* really a BMW! Anyway, in later moments, she will admit she sort of respects the girl's drive. Gabriella also never settled for less than an A. Well—once. But she still considers it unfair that any grade in a college class can be weighted that heavily on a group assignment.

"Yes, *he.* I'm about ninety percent sure the thief is Jack." Wisely, Gabriella restrains the comment that the other ten percent of her would bet Kristen stole the deer herself to stir up conflict.

But the smile on Kristen's face might lead one to believe that she reads minds.

This is not accurate. However, Kristen is entirely able to extrapolate the remains of Gabriella's calculations from her facial expressions alone.

Kristen would do it too. She just didn't have to. All she had to do was flirtatiously complain to Jack after wrapping up for the day last week that everyone was too nervous about the cameras to do anything but work stiffly. And she wished she could see the real people. *Really, men are so easy.*

"It's always Jack," Gabriella finishes. "He's like a five-year-old."

At this exact moment, the five-year-old in question, Jack Hilary Drummer, chronologically aged twenty-nine, though it has been remarked before that men are allowed to mature much slower than they age, is eves-dropping with a broad smile. A playful smile. An *imps* smile. With the sort of immature thoughts running through his head that have landed many a more mature man on the naughty list before.

Jack looks into the eyes of the pilfered reindeer and places a finger against his lips. Then, apparently unsatisfied with the *complete* silence of the figurine, Jack takes things a step further. Shaking with silent laughter Jack places a tiny sliver of scotch tape across its mouth assuring that the inanimate object won't give him away.

It is worth wondering if he would have done the same had he known that Santa was indeed watching. And that Santa does not forget. But Jack, rather sure of his own maturity and thus having long since decided Santa is not real, does not know. And is far more concerned with his own amusement than he is with the consequences of his actions. Thus he continues to bask in the entertainment he has provided himself by riling Santa's model citizen.

"It's not as if he stole Rudolph, who wasn't a part of the original octet, so I might not have noticed right away," Gabriella continues to the film crew. She feels internally, but does not stop to examine, the strangeness that is how much more comfortable she is with the film crew today— while angry. She is more herself. Concerned, but less so, that she appears at all times *normal.* She speaks with passion and playfulness even a bit of self-deprecation and feels very much herself, all because she can't really focus on anything other than her missing reindeer.

Were she to have a tech call come in right now, even if it were a challenging one, half of her mind would be focused on her missing reindeer. She would be shuddering from the invasion over her walls, literal and metaphorical. She would be fighting off the urge to clean the desk. The walls, her phone and all her decorations. She would be fighting the need to kick Jack Drummer in his little drummer boys as if that would drive into his thick skull that it isn't okay to invade other people's space! But instead of doing any of that, she's talking about it. Trying to make light of it.

"Nooo!" She goes on, managing quite well, she thinks, to sound playful though she is, in fact, *angry*. "He stole Vixen!"

Kristen giggles softly, a giggle she knows annoys *sweet* Gabriella. And she is just as sweet as a gumdrop. Too sweet. So Kristen riles her in the hopes of finding Gabriella's bitchy side.

"You know their names? Their order?" Kristen knows those answers. But she is quite pleased and amused to know that Gabriella knows them as well. And even more pleased when she watches the other woman's eyes narrow and all but feels Gabriella clinging to her friendly smile with sharp, angry teeth.

"Of course, I know their order. It is *basic* logic. Santa speaks English, so presuming an English education, he would call them from left to right," Gabriella says instructively, with a condescending smile of her own. "Starting with the deer furthest from his sleigh! The perpetrator stole the second furthest deer on Santa's right. Vixen!"

Kristen has never liked her better. And to think she expected this assignment to be no fun at all. But ooh, look how perfectly prepared Gabriella is for her upcoming job title shift.

This, you see, is the story of Gabriella Anjelica Cruz and what she made of her world in the twenty-five days in the year two-thousand-and-eighteen when she became, for lack of a better name, and with a few limitations, Santa Claus.

However, this magical transformation has yet to occur. This is likely why, at this same moment, on the other side of the cubicle, unaware of what lessons the remains of the year have in store for him — dangerous lessons —Jack couldn't be more pleased than he is upon hearing the bite in Gabriella's voice. He only wishes he could be looking right at her as Gabriella gets downright snippy. Not to worry; eventually, he will be.

Dom. Dom. Dooooom!

*Wink.

It is unsurprising that Jack is fearlessly riling Gabriella because up until the exact moment in which she receives the power of Claus, she displays no other magical ability. Nor much compulsion to steal cookies and milk from homes she has broken into. Nor even any interest in housebreaking at all.

If one were to ask her friends, coworkers, or family members what warning signs they had witnessed, they might remark that she did appear to enjoy Christmas a *scooch* more than most human adults. Or perhaps that she was known to be quite generous. But surely, no signs of magic were ever detected. And certainly nothing as extreme or worrying as a belief that she is Santa Claus. She is simply—good.

So while Kristen and Jack are basking in having brought Gabriella closer to their, sometimes called *naughty* side of the list, Gabriella is feeling bad. Gabriella—having not yet received the magical gift which will empower her both to reward the good and punish the bad—being only herself is thinking about being the bigger person. She is thinking about spreading kindness without even one thought of retribution—yet.

She doesn't know exactly what it is about this young woman that sets her off, but she won't let it rule her. Kristen is just trying to do her assignment. She isn't trying to be rude about the reindeer. She simply doesn't believe the way Gabriella does, specifically the suspension of disbelief in order to embrace the wonder.

Breathing out, Gabriella smiles and gives a little laugh at the intensity of her annoyance. "I guess you can call me a Who. I like

Christmas—*a lot*." She laughs at her own joke and is a bit surprised when Kristen as well laughs in genuine amusement.

"But I'm not rude about it. At least I try not to be. I don't play my music so others can hear it. That's what the ears are for." Gabriella proudly indicates the elf ears she has added to her headset, a combination of headphones and Bluetooth connection to her office phone. "I don't try and get other people to decorate or sing random Christmas carols in the break room. But if someone still has a problem with me, they should come at me." She slaps her chest, intending it to appear as playful thug-like intimidation. Unfortunately, being the model citizen she is, the attempt fails. Striking herself a bit too hard in the chest, she starts a coughing fit that makes her eyes water and her cheeks turn red.

Being good is such a trial.

"Not the deer," Gabriella finishes the statement with a few tears still in her eyes and a strained voice. She is thoroughly embarrassed as she watches Kristen's eyes dance in amusement, and her lips press together to resist a laugh. Gabriella fists her hands tight to fight off the urge to tap her pointer finger against the desk on film. Digital? On *camera*, she decides will do.

One might think she is an overly precise young woman. Too orderly, some have said. Too intense many have said. But Santa holds a special place in his heart for the believers who must fight to hold onto wonder and are willing to struggle just to be kind. Even when they sit next to immature nonbelievers, who simply must be entertained every moment of every day. And in some cases, *in this case,* Santa is inclined to remind this very good person that it is okay to be *less than kind* in the face of intentionally inconsiderate people.

Goody-Goody Gumdrop

Kristen Poppy Kringle fights off her—very smug—amusement, as, sweet as a gumdrop, Gabriella smacks her own chest a bit too hard and causes herself a coughing fit. Strictly speaking, riling Gabriella is not any part of Kristen's assignment. Neither one, the school project she wants an A on, nor her secret family business assignment. But it is so much fun!

Why oh why does Santa always attach to the goody-goodies? To Kristen's way of thinking, the goody-goodies have it easy. Everyone loves them; they are naturally perfect. Why should anyone like that be rewarded? But it isn't up to her.

Over the wall of Gabriella's cubicle, a head appears with a finger pressed to his lips, calling for silence from the documentary crew. It is a request Jack did not need to make. As intrepid young professionals determined to prove themselves in their chosen field, not one of the documentary film crew would do anything so amateur as involving themselves with their subjects or taking sides.

So it is, with a darted look at the object of all his immature attentions, that Jack snares yet another deer, Cupid this time, and disappears over the wall.

Kristen bites her lip to keep from pointing it out just for fun. But she cannot resist seeing if she can get Gabriella to notice.

"Can't you move Rudolph to the other deer's place? It was Vixen, right?" Kristen prods.

"No. I can't move Rudolph to Vixen's place. For one thing, he leads the sleigh."

Kristen giggles. *He.* All the reindeer are female. *Ha. I know something you don't know,* she thinks; jealous of one of Santa's favorite humans. Not that she could ever admit this, even to herself.

"For another, he didn't even come with this set, so he doesn't match exactly." Gabriella is turning around, reaching out for the deer, about to notice.

Kristen leans forward, eyes flashing with excitement, waiting for that moment. Waiting for the explosion. Only to be thwarted by a ringing phone.

Ugh.

Ever the good girl, *perfect* employee, and eager beaver that she is, Gabriella hits the talk button hidden beneath the elf ears on her headset.

"I.T. department, Gabriella speaking. How can I help—Oh. Good morning, sir." It is barely possible, so straight is her posture already, but Gabriella manages to squeeze some more length out of her spine, acknowledging the authority figure on the phone.

Kristen rolls her eyes. Uncle Coleman hasn't noticed the posture of an employee a single day in his life. And certainly not over the phone.

"Of course anything," Gabriella says politely with her back to the camera crew. Her fisted hand uncurls under the desk and begins to tap against her thigh.

Kristen notices the exact moment when Gabriella spots the new theft. Gabriella shakes out her hands to stop them from crawling across the table toward the rest of her deer. Her posture stiffens and her breathing becomes audible. Ooo. This really bugs her. Interesting.

"Well...that's not exactly an I.T. assignment," Gabriella tries to decline the assignment as politely as possible.

Kristen, knowing full well what the assignment is, agrees wholeheartedly. It is not an IT assignment. It's a gift. But as is usual with special gifts, it won't feel that way at first.

"Maybe... No. No. It would be my pleasure. Five minutes. Yes, of course." Gabriella sighs as she pushes the side of her headset again. "Of course. Of course." She says twice more after hanging up, her tone precisely the same as if she were still on the call. She breathes out heavily and slowly swivels to face the camera, her hands clenched tightly.

Kristen looks over Gabriella's very precise desk set-up. It is easy, with all the decoration this desk has, which others in the room lack, to miss out on how orderly it is. Everything from the phone, to the mousepad, to the computer and post-its are at the same angle. Her pens are held in a flat rainbow array in a pouch on the wall of her cubicle, and all her decoration is out of the way of any work.

An undecorated, mini pine tree on the left, next to a snowman mug with candy canes sticking out the top. A strand of snowflake lights that appear to double as a cellphone charger is plugged into the computer and strung across the top of the monitor. To the right of the monitor stands a beat-up old nutcracker and a framed family photo showing Gabriella, her mother, and what must be her sister Maria. Nearly all of the decoration is behind the monitor, far out of the way of work. Santa and his sleigh sit between the keyboard and monitor. Again out of the way and very precisely arranged.

Kristen looks between Gabriella's slightly shaky hands and her neat desk and nearly rolls her eyes. Trust Santa to send Kristen to help one of the tragic perfects. Ugh. Not at all her style.

Gabriella, meanwhile, is fretting not over annoying assignments (though she will be presently) but rather over missing deer and the camera having caught her repeating things, and now that she has to go to Mr. Colman's office, her attire. All those memos about the documentary film suggested wearing colorful clothes, patterns, and things that would pop on camera. Taking time with make-up and hair. So now, predictably, because she is too obliging for her own good, she is dressed in a Christmas sweater with a llama in a Santa hat and jingle bells. She slides the headset off her head and lays it neatly to the left of her keyboard.

"When I first got this job, I was in a full business suit or dress every day. Trying to prove techs aren't sloppy and unprofessional." Gabriella sighs, her neck jerking slightly as she forces herself not to look at all the very sloppy boys in the department. "I got teased mercilessly for it and never left this basement. Like three-hundred-and-sixty-five days a year, I don't even leave this cubicle. I mean, I've never even met our COO, that's who was on the phone, Mr. Coleman."

"Three-hundred-and-sixty-five days a year?" Kristen teases. "Do we keep you chained to your desk even when the offices are closed?"

"Ha ha, very funny. No, they don't keep me chained to my desk. I can leave for weekends and vacation days. It was hyperbolic." Gabriella stands and, holding onto her blouse with one hand, pulls the sweater over her head. "If you want to know my exact number of working days—ask an accountant."

Gabriella folds her sweater as she turns around to check her hair using the computer camera. She straightens a few stray hairs, but by and large, her no fuss, shoulder-length hair was undisturbed. She looks neat and efficient in her slacks and loose blue blouse. She stands up and makes her way around the camera crew, with fully four minutes available to her to make it up two floors—on an elevator.

"Wish me luck," Gabriella says brightly. In the wild and unfulfilled hope that her brightness of spirit will conceal her awkwardness. But really, how would she know how one departs from a documentary film crew?

Goody-goody, Kristen thinks as she watches her go, smiling all the while. Why can't she dislike this woman?

It is not a well-known fact, but true nonetheless, that Santa keeps more than just a naughty and a nice list. There are degrees. A very best of the best and a very worst of the worst. Jack Hilary

Drummer, while never yet having been listed on the worst of the worst list, has frequently made a home on the naughty list. This is perhaps why Kristen is ever so slightly attracted to him. She has not once in her twenty-one years of existence been attracted to a good boy.

Slight attraction aside, she has no interest in pursuing any sort of involvement with him. But he might be a good...playmate for Gabriella. He certainly seems to think so. Though getting him to admit it will be a challenge.

Both of these, frequent visitors to the naughty list, watch Santa's model citizen until the doors of the elevator close in front of her awkward self.

Jack leans back in his seat, dancing the stolen reindeer across the air, and waiting. He knows where Kristen and her camera crew are headed next. Kristen smirks as she crosses to him. At least this part of her assignment will be fun.

Kristen's family business is not limited to her father's doll company but also includes its parent company, Santa industries. Which extends around the globe involving toy, clothing, game, and recreational equipment manufacturing, sales, and distribution. It also employs every child, grandchild, great grandchild and great great grandchild of the original, the man, the legend— Santa Claus. Well, every child they can find anyway, but that's another story. Kristen, as a fifth-generation Claus has only this year been entrusted with a high-level assignment for the good list department.

Gabriella Anjelica Cruz has been on the good list every single year of her twenty-six years of life. In fact, in that time, she has only ever had two single checks against her on the bad list. One in the fifth grade when she pulled the hair of a younger boy who insulted her sister. And the second just a week after her mother died, when she threw a mug through her first floor apartment window while arguing with the landlord over her refusal to pay back rent for the months they'd lived with a leaking tub. This second incident resulted in Gabriella losing her security deposit, and the landlord needing *three whole Bandaids.* There were a few small incidents before she turned eight, but Santa doesn't count such things against children, but rather against their parents. So it is only the post-preschool check marks that count against her, and both incidents were properly apologized for, learned from, and the result of high emotional turmoil and thus, expunged from her official record.

Kristen had to dig those up with the help of Santa's head archivist, Aunt Ginger, when she was given this assignment, as it was personally offensive to Kristen that anyone could be *that good.* Kristen herself has only been on the good list eleven times, and most of those before she hit puberty. And she's a Claus!

But not Gabriella. And more importantly—offensively—she is on Santa's honor list and has been twelve times, nearly one-third of her life. It is a list reserved for those special souls who are not merely good but also kind, generous, or selfless. Only one blood Claus outside of Santa himself ever made the honor list more than once. But this isn't about Santa's golden child, Holly Kringle; this is Kristen's assignment.

She is here to bestow Santa's very special Christmas gift on Gabriella. It isn't romance. Though if Kristen gets her way, she might get a bit of that as well. It would do Gabriella some good to have some naughty fun! The gift is nothing that Kristen would have given. She's here to grant Gabriella the honor above all honors. Something, not even family have experienced. A brief, highly limited, but nevertheless euphoric taste of the power of Claus.

Kristen is fond of saying that the power of Claus amounts to two things, a euphoric certainty that you are morally superior to all around you and an ineffable ability to find the perfect gift to make other people agree with you. A better description might be happy; the gifts make people happy. It is a fairly simple word and thus might make one worry about her vocabulary, but to be fair to Kristen, happiness is not something she's had much of since she was a small child.

But she has also forgotten one aspect of the power or was perhaps too close to it to ever know it. The power of Claus is a call to reach out, to connect, and to leave the world better for that connection. Even were she to have recognized this part of the power, Kristen would not have cared.

She sees this as a very boring, very annoying assignment. Holly would have loved it, poor girl; no one ever lets her leave the north. But it's Kristen's burden, or she will be cut off from her allowance and have to actually work at one of the family businesses. So she'll do it. She'll do exactly what she was sent here to do. But...she plans to have a bit of fun with it. And maybe, just maybe, ever so slightly, corrupt one of Santa's golden children.

Prologue
Which ought to come before the body of the story or be titled differently, but it is what it is.
Also, it's about characters you won't see again.
Want to skip it yet? *Wink.

F ar in the north, on an island known as the North Pole, which is quite hard to find intentionally as it lays amid the ice-frosted waters of the Arctic Ocean, in the office of none other than Santa Claus himself, at approximately eleven-fifteen, on the morning of October tenth, in the year of two-thousand-and-eighteen Holly Kringle bursts in with her usual wide smile holding up a file in one hand and a single sheet of paper in the other.

"Grandpa, wonderful news!"

Santa laughs softly. It always makes him happy when Holly bursts in with good news. And she knows it too. His other fifth-generation grandchildren all think Holly is the favorite, perhaps the older generations do as well, but it just isn't so. Santa loves all his children, grandchildren, great-grandchildren, great-great-grandchildren, great-great-great-grandchildren and great-great-great-great grandchildren in their own special ways. It is only that Holly... makes such an effort to make everyone happy, so it is hard not to smile in her presence, basking in her joy.

"What is that, precious one? Come up with a new jam recipe for me to try?"

Holly pauses in the doorway, working to hold onto her smile. Everyone loves to keep her in the kitchen. And she does quite enjoy baking, but it isn't all she loves.

"No, I'll have to work on that, but this is about the good list, I was helping Aunt Ginger c—"

"Now Holly, what have I told you," Santa says in a voice he considers quite patient, and Holly considers quite condescending. It is a tone that says no, and before she has even asked a question.

But Holly is used to this tone, and not just from Santa. *Everyone* thinks she is so delicate, unable to navigate negative emotions. Of all of them, she really thinks she has had to navigate the most negative emotions and come out of it stronger, so why they persist in doubting her, she cannot say. Nevertheless, having been doubted so often in the past has taught her how to hold onto her smile.

"The nice and naughty department is no place for you. There are things seen in there—"

"Grandpa, I wasn't in the naughty department, but the nice. And I promise Aunt Ginger is very concerned with protecting me"

"My precious child, it is only that you have never been off the island. The rest of the world holds things that...you shouldn't have to see." Most people living or dead could pick up on the inherent condescension in that statement, and Holly is no exception. But she merely smiles as though she hasn't understood.

Behind her bland smile, her thoughts are these: *What precisely do you think the world holds so much worse than what I've witnessed first-hand here? This island is not devoid of badness.*

However, what she says aloud is this: "Of course, Grandpa, thank you. But please, just listen one moment. I was helping her with the honor roll," Holly says lightly, fingering the honor roll pin she wears on the lapel of her jaunty white blazer, with an orange pattern (the fruit, not the color, well, also the color, but only because the fruit is the color of their namesake).

Holly always wears it, as she finds touching it and drawing one's attention to the fact that she is one of the rare Claus' with such a pin to be quite effective in certain arguments. Like this one. Holly lets her hand slide away and flicks out her high-waist suspender skirt of deep blue; she settles into one of the seats before her grandfather's desk without invitation and launches into what she came in to say before he can send her away.

Not that Grandpa doesn't love her or isn't willing to listen to her, but Holly has begun to suspect that he doesn't quite respect her, not like he does his other descendants.

"It is about Gabriella Cruz! She has been on the good list every year that she's been alive! Such an achievement! I'm a little jealous. But... it's not only that, Grandpa, she will be on the honor roll for the *twelfth* time this year!"

"Not consecutively?" Grandpa asks in shock, holding out his hand for the file.

Contrary to what many people believe, Santa is not omniscient. He doesn't know what every person is doing every moment. When he is in the presence of a particular child, the basics of their file comes into his head, but away from them, he relies on the files.

"No. She has been struggling since her mother's death. Her mother was ill for sometime before her death, and Gabriella took on extra work to help pay for the medical bills. But after her mother died she just stopped." Holly stops at the words. Stops speaking that is, but her heart is beating harder. She feels...connected to Gabriella. Feels drawn to her story. She so wants to meet her, and tell her she understands.

But Holly is well aware that saying this is not the way to get through to Grandpa. She has to keep this conversation all about Gabriella. "She stopped working, or planning, or doing much of anything. For several months she didn't really leave her home at all. But! She has worked so hard, Grandpa! She is putting her life back together, and it is beginning to pay off. Well, not monetarily; she works for Uncle Coleman at the doll company. Do you know what he pays employees? I haven't left the island, as you pointed out, and even I know it's low."

Grandpa chuckles softly, a puff of air, shaking the papers before him, but he doesn't look up from the file. Santa is well aware of what the doll company pays its hourly employees. And there is purpose behind it, but Holly doesn't need to know it yet.

My Best Friend Doll Company is a way station for most of its employees. A place for people in situations exactly like Gabriella's to take the time they need before they are ready to pursue their passions. A place to just be. True, some employees find they quite like it there and stay on, and their pay is raised accordingly. But those are few and far between.

"Anyway, this year she's been going out of her way to help people again," Holly continues undeterred by Grandpa's lack of response. "And stretching herself. I think she deserves a *very* special reward. And I have an idea of what that should be."

Finally, Grandpa looks up with a puffy white eyebrow sloped like a snowy hill. "I take it that is what is on that last page?" Grandpa asks in a conspiratorial voice.

Holly nods but is nearly too excited to hold out the sheet; slowly, she stretches it forward.

Grandpa takes the sheet and reads silently. Both his eyebrows arch now. And a twinkle like mischief settles around him.

"The power of Claus, to a mortal? And one under the age of fifty."

"Hear me out," Holly says, and rushes the rest of her words out before Grandpa can interrupt. "She works so hard, Grandpa. Harder than half the people on the good list, and that is only how hard it is for her to do regular good, and she has gone beyond that, helping others and constantly trying to improve herself. She deserves to feel some—*power*, and excitement and—euphoria. She is not the sort of person who has ever felt such a thing. She should, please."

Grandpa leans back in his chair. His round cheeks have a bit of cherry red peeking out beneath his white facial hair. And his eyes twinkle like Christmas lights. He's going to say yes! Holly can feel it. Yay! She's halfway to getting her full request honored.

"You know, Holly, sometimes I think you would make a very *good* Santa Claus."

Holly laughs, shaking her head. She knows Grandpa didn't mean that as an insult, but *really* are good, or sweet, or precious, the only descriptors anyone thinks apply to her? Half the reason she wants what she wants for Gabriella is because of all the similarities Holly feels between them. Both are used to putting on a bright smile over anger, pain, and struggle, making other people more comfortable in their presence. The power of Claus isn't just a thing of goodness. Elves have playful, naughty sides, loud and angry and retaliatory. Sides that Holly wishes she could embrace just once.

And since she can't. She wants that for Gabriella.

"It is a good idea, Holly. I will have to put some limitations, confine it to her immediate area, and not let the deer or other elves be drawn to her and such. But that is an excellent suggestion. And I know just who should deliver the gift."

"Me?" Holly jumps forward, accidentally shaking Grandpa's desk, so excited is she with the mere thought that he sees her worth without even having to be talked into it.

"Oh, no, Holly," Grandpa says with patient shock. He could never have imagined such a thing. "You've never left the island," he repeats. I cannot send you to L.A. the first time you leave! The very idea is horrifying."

"It's Burbank, not L.A.," Holly begins.

"Holl—"

"And I'd be at the same company with Uncle Coleman. I'd be perfectly safe."

"Holly," Grandpa says again. In *that* tone. The patient, careful tone, so concerned by any show of emotion but her sweet smile. The same tone he uses every time he says no to one of her ideas. Work in the Naughty-and-Nice department, *no, my precious one, that isn't for you.* Train with the elvish guild to be a master craftswoman, *oooh, no that is much harder work than it seems.* Respond to the letters angry with Santa or disbelieving, *goodness no, that department is so very wearing, such a positive light should join the sweet works, or answering silly letters.*

No. It is always no.

"It's a very simple assignment," Holly tries one last time, already swallowing the acidic sting of this latest rejection.

"It only seems that way," Grandpa says firmly. "Wait your turn; we'll find the perfect assignment for you. I know it. But this one belongs to Kristen."

"Kristen?" Holly demands in a tone of anger and disbelief.

Holly loves every one of her cousins, and Kristen is no exception. But she doesn't know that she *likes* this particular cousin, not at all. Not since she was about twelve anyway. When she came home from boarding school with a mean spirit, picking at Holly all the time. And not about anything normal; most people pick at Holly's weight or her childish spirit. But no, Kristen picks at the things Holly has to work at, like being kind, being on the Honor Roll, or not acting out. Kristen is just mean.

She'll be mean to Gabriella! Holly wants to shout. But she doesn't shout. She never shouts. Not since she was very small, not even for joy. She is enthusiastic, she babbles, and she always wears a bright smile, but she never raises her voice. And she always surrenders an argument before it can get too heated.

So she smiles. "Yes, I suppose that makes the most sense. She is...already in the area after all, and it is her father's company."

"Don't be too disappointed. I promise we'll find something for you."

Nodding, Holly stands to go, a bright smile fixed in place.

"You've not been baking as much lately, my dear, not one new dessert for me to try in months. Are you all out of inspiration?" Grandpa probes carefully as Holly approaches the door. So carefully.

She looks back, shaking her head with a smile. *With a smile.* It might as well be her motto. Everything she does is with a smile. No, she supposes she hasn't made anything new recently. But really, there are only so many combinations of sugar and spice in the world;

DALILA CARYN

surely, she's found most of them by now. Sugar plumb cider biscuits and chocolate cinnamon muffins are all delicious and very exciting the first time they're made and shared, but...

An angry fire begins to burn in Holly's chest, wondering if this was her very last hope that Grandpa had just crushed. Wondering if he really thinks she is so unobservant that she doesn't see that he keeps her here because he thinks she's fragile and bound to break completely apart in the rest of the world? Wanting to look him in the eye when she says that he ought to start listening to his descendants or Mistletoe won't be the last of them to run away.

But angry as she is, she smiles. "I've been having this idea for a chocolate pumpkin muffin with Cheyenne pepper in it!"

"Sounds frighteningly good. I cannot wait to be your taste tester."

"Always, Grandpa." Holly wears her smile of acceptance. The one that all of her family mistake for agreement. "Thank you for giving Gabriella the gift I suggested." *One of us ought to have some fun!* She adds internally.

Santa watches her go, feeling badly. He knows Holly wants to be loosed on the world, just like her father did. He won't fail her the way he did Dash. And anyway...this assignment might be good for Kristen. She could stand to be around a good girl for once.

Two Naughty Children

"So, Jack, are you bored out of your mind? Flirting?" Kristen winks. "Or do you actually have something against Christmas? Are you on Santa's bad side?" She whispers provocatively.

Jack laughs. "Nah, I have nothing against Christmas or even decorating early. At home." He says, striving for a lighthearted, fun guy attitude as he pointedly ignores several of Kristen's questions.

Jack is, in his own opinion, an easy-going man by nature. In reality he isn't nearly as *easy-going* as he believes and his attitude has a fair amount to do with nurture as well. It has *more* to do with nurture. Were you to ask his parents, they would say that as a child, Jack was very shy and anxious. He much preferred individual pursuits like reading and playing video games. But as he aged, he developed friendships and hobbies that stretched him, and he became much more social. He was born quite solidly in the middle class, had a happy home life and supportive parents, and never had to deal with any unfortunately alienating aspects of his person or personality. As an only child, he was bestowed with all the love his parents had to offer. As such, he has rarely experienced enough strife to cause him to develop a toughened or bitter nature.

However, in recent years, following a *traumatic* end to a romantic relationship, Jack has been reverting ever so slightly towards his childhood behaviors of preferring books to people, *singular*, keeping all romantic relationships casual, compartmentalizing his social interactions so as to keep work friends, relatives, and workout friends separate, and not sharing any of his deeper self.

That being said, he is generally a friendly person, game for a good laugh, willing to work hard, but *never* eager to do so. Intelligent, and unfortunately, or fortunately, depending on your perspective, *quite* good-looking. And there is one skill he has that he has put great effort into perfecting, self-preservation.

There is no smart way to answer *are you bored out of your mind* to your boss's daughter. So he isn't about to touch that one. Nor is it wise to tell a, by all appearances, spoiled young woman who is flirting pretty hard that, *yep,* you are flirting with another woman, but really just for fun. As for being on Santa's bad side, if the guy were real, Jack would likely have gotten on his bad side once or twice, but it hasn't been an issue as far as he remembers.

"I like screwing with Gabriella. She's too intense about everything," Jack says playfully. Making a clicking noise with his tongue and teeth, he sets the reindeer cantering across the sky.

It should not be lost on anyone that Jack has not been doing an ounce of work thus far this morning. He answered one call earlier, in the middle of his argument with Gabriella. Just before the camera crew descended on her and stole her attention. But that call came from his good pal, Cory, another tech who saw the fight and decided to rescue Jack from Gabriella. Various men in the basement have done this various times since Jack got *stuck* being desk buddies with Gabriella, the department's only female.

A few of those times, Jack quite appreciated the save. But...well, sometimes, today, for instance, he was intentionally riling Gabriella and didn't mind the results. She looks so *dangerous* when she's annoyed. He enjoys watching that.

Jack's lack of professional stimulation is not at all lost on Kristen, and she would mention it, but she doesn't care. Also, it doesn't fit in with her plans to have some fun at his expense.

"Have a little thing for her, do you?" Kristen asks, putting on a pout.

"No." Jack shakes his head, looking anywhere but at Kristen.

"You sure?" Kristen probes flirtatiously. "She's not bad looking."

Both Jack and the remains of Kristen's camera crew, Terrance and Andrew, raise brows at this. Gabriella does not have Kristen's doll-like perfection, no, but she is warm, enthusiastic and real. When she smiles, it is genuine and wide and infectious. *Not bad looking* doesn't begin to describe her. But Jack isn't sure if Kristen is fishing to see how interested he is because she is interested in him? Or if she is trying to bait him into spicing up her boring documentary with a romance.

He already spiced up her film with the prank. Jack is well aware of the look Gabriella gets when she is annoyed. Her fists ball up, her shoulders get tight, and her brow wrinkles as she resists, with her full body, the violence she holds inside. It's seriously fun to watch. Exciting. He can't wait for the day when she finally gives in and chooses violence. It's bound to be entertaining.

But not knowing what the *CEO's daughter* is after, Jack isn't about to raise to the bait of correcting her description of Gabriella.

It was actually Gabriella who told Jack who Kristen was. On her first day of filming, Jack was chatting with the girl in the parking lot as Gabriella walked by. When Jack made it inside with Kristen—a few minutes late, but no one should have needed him—there was an IM on his computer from Gabriella that said "careful" and had a link. The link led to a tiny article about the company, from eleven years ago, about the "family in mourning." It showed the CEO, Don Kringle and his daughter Kristen.

Jack had been nearly finished reading the article when Gabriella sent another IM: *she's the CEO's daughter, if you hadn't put that together.*

Gabriella could be so annoying *if you hadn't put that together.* Jack is perfectly capable of reading. But before he could get too annoyed with her smug way of saying things, he realized she must have a real thing for him to try and warn him away from other women.

She was always flirting with him. Sending him IMs with little emojis they used to indicate different coworkers while he was on tech calls, guessing who it was by how needless the request was. Sure, he'd started it, but she'd kept it going. And she'd bring in candy she knew he liked and leave it in a basket that hung off the outside of her cubicle. But this was the first indication that she had a real, serious crush. He likes it.

"No. I'm not interested." Jack lies, resisting Kristen's baiting.

"If you say so," Kristen agrees. "But you know what they say about boys pulling the pigtails of girls they like."

"Gabriella doesn't seem the pigtails type." Jack jokes. No one laughs.

Kristen thinks back. She doesn't have a photographic memory or anything, but she has Gabriella's file at home, and you don't get to be a straight A student by refusing to do your homework. So she's been through that file a time or two. And if memory serves, there is a picture of Gabriella with pigtail braids.

"I can picture her in pigtails," Kristen says to be perverse. "Maybe wearing those onesie Christmas pajamas like an elf or a snowman, all curled up by a fire with her hot cocoa watching *Frosty the Snowman.*"

Kristen holds back a giggle as Jack shuts up, caught in the image. Kristen would bet top dollar that Gabriella has exactly such a set of pajamas, and if she doesn't, Kristen would be happy to gift them to her. And from the look of him, so would Jack.

What is it with bad boys and always being so obsessed with good girls?

Jack looks up, suddenly realizing that he's been quiet a bit too long.

"Seriously, *no*. I'm not into...that. I mean, can you imagine." Jack forces a laugh. He doesn't want to have this conversation. But he

NICE TO BE SO NAUGHTY

can tell from Kristen's smug grin that she isn't going to let this go. *So, play it light, man*, Jack tells himself.

Jack pulls a terrified face. Lifting the reindeer in front of him, he plays it up for the cameras like no one else seems to know how to do. You don't have to be yourself, just the character they cast you as. He's been cast as the class clown. He has been before, though not that often. There is usually someone funnier than him around.

"This is the level of intensity she puts into a holiday—at the office!" Jack shakes his head. "She has twinkle lights, candy canes. A candy she says she doesn't even like, by the way! And she has a mini tree, a Santa and," Jack chuckles, enjoying his own joke, "*seven* tiny reindeer."

Kristen laughs appropriately. Andrew, for all that anyone can tell, hasn't heard a word of the conversation since Kristen called Gabriella *pretty enough*. And Terrance chews on his tongue to keep from rolling his eyes. But none of it matters because Jack made the joke mostly to entertain himself.

"And as of yesterday," he goes on, his tone growing in volume and amusement. "While on a tech call, she made and decorated a chain of elves." He shakes his head, smiling fondly.

"Don't get me wrong, she's a nice girl. Maybe too nice. When she first came to work here, she told everyone that she didn't like being called Gabby, but everyone calls her that, and she just smiles sweetly. And when Maya accidentally synced her home calendar with the whole office and lost all the other appointments, Gabriella not only fixed the calendar, she also spent hours comforting Maya and showing her how to run her phone."

Jack is quiet for a moment, looking at the reindeer in his hands like he's talking to them. It's hardly any time at all. Just long enough for the elevator doors to open behind him, without his noticing. And long enough for him to notice time passing once more in silence and for his pulse to race imagining how Kristen will cut this. Long enough for Gabriella to approach unseen by anyone but the slightly smirking Kristen. Barely any time at all. Just enough for Jack to realize he won't come back from being recast as Gabriella's romantic interest if he doesn't make a joke—fast.

"But she can't relax. I mean, is she on speed or something? And this whole *I like Christmas like a ten-year-old thing*." Jack shakes his head. "Can you imagine *dating that*?"

Andrew and Kristen are the only people not to jump as Gabriella leans into the shot and yanks both reindeer out of Jack's hands. The camera jerks a little with Terrance. He needs to pay more attention to his surroundings; that's bad form.

Terrance Pine has been handling a camera for a while now. Ten years, minimum, he is sure he made use of his parent's camera before he was able to buy one for himself. He is much better than this. He is well used to finding a sort of zen place inside where he can follow energy and light and capture a story without actively listening to what is going on. Without getting invested in it. But...this Jack guy is so annoying, and Kristen eggs him on. And just then, as Gabriella leaned into the shot, Terrance jerked not so much from the shock but from the angry, hurt look in her eyes. Damn, his mom's right; men are jerks.

"Imagine all you want," Gabriella snaps. "It isn't going to happen."

Gabriella glares at Jack for a few more seconds. Until the camera crew showed up, Jack was not this big of an asshole. Yeah, he picked at her a little. But she honestly thought it was just that he was bored. He wasn't mean. He would just do things to make her laugh or annoy her when days were slow. Some days he was even casually nice, bringing her a bag of Cheez-It's when he went to the vending machines or getting the other techs to include her in their games.

IT is an all-male department aside from Gabriella, and she has never been one of those female techs featured on TV shows who know how to kick back and hang with the boys. She doesn't play video games, she doesn't socialize, and she cannot stand a mess. She is intense, focused—talented. More talented than anyone else in this basement. And that isn't ego. It's a fact.

She wouldn't have called herself and Jack friends before the documentary, but she would have said they were friendly. It's why she warned him about Kristen being the CEO's daughter when he was flirting with her that first week. She wouldn't have done the same for Cory or Michael. But Jack was the least condescending of the techs. He was just...lazy and entertained by immature antics. But now, he is going out of his way to be mean. All so he can flirt with Kristen.

Which is a fairly ill-advised choice. She is the daughter of the CEO; there is no way that ends well. And it seems like a bad choice for Kristen as well.

Gabriella gives it another second, with an eyebrow raised, waiting for Jack to have the decency to apologize for calling her a thing. Or for stealing her possessions. Any contrition at all will do. But he just stares like a deer in headlights. Reindeer in hand, Gabriella jerks out of the cubical and marches to her own. Settling into her seat with studied calm.

Terrance zooms out, trying to encompass both desks in the shot, trying to take in Jack's red face and sunken shoulders, as well as Gabriella's straight back and overly calm motions as she replaces her stolen deer.

"Fuck," Jack mutters under his breath, seeming to bite his own tongue as he looks at the wall of his cubical.

Kristen smiles evilly. She has a weird, bubbly feeling that she's going to be on the naughty list again this year. But ohhhhh, what fun she is going to have!

Call me Claus

A **bout** two and a half hours later, Gabriella is much calmer about everything. While everyone was at lunch, she cleaned her desk. She knows that there are stationary camera's around the office that almost certainly caught it, but she doesn't care. It eased half the tension in her body. And now that all the deer are in order, back in their homes, and the *glue* from the tape is cleaned off of their faces! *Jerk.* She is much more herself. So when Kristen asks to do a private interview that is set up in the break room, Gabriella goes along positively.

"So, *Gabby*," Kristen says in an overly bright, overly leading voice. "What was your meeting with Mr. Colman about?"

Terrance stands behind the tripod fighting hard not to roll his eyes. She called her Gabby intentionally. This girl is determined to make their documentary into a reality tv show, with screaming and love connections and lots of drama. It's annoying that she may actually get what she wants. Kristen is diabolical. If he never has to work with her again, it will be too soon.

Presently Gabriella is thinking similar things. Wondering if the girl honestly thinks Gabriella cannot tell she's called her Gabby intentionally. Wondering if Kristen likes making people around her unhappy. And wondering, with a good amount of anger but a nearly equal amount of pity, how sad this girl's home life must be to make her so insecure she has to lash out at everyone.

Gabriella is never one-hundred-percent secure in herself, but she clearly isn't as insecure as this girl. So she smiles softly at the attempt to goad her and just answers.

"The meeting with Mr. Colman was nothing special. At least nothing special about me." Gabriella gives a small self-deprecating shoulder slouch. "Mr. Coleman wants me to run the office Secret Santa this year because last year was such a disaster. He basically ordered me to data mine the office for gift ideas."

She pauses, laughing, though inside she is frankly offended. But she can't say that. The more research she did on Kristen, the more interesting stuff she found out about this company. Gabriella has worked for My Best Friend Doll Company for two years, but it is only now that she realizes Mr. Colman, the COO, is something like a third or fourth cousin of Mr. Kringle, the CEO. And Mr. Coleman replaced Kristen's mother as COO after her sudden death from an aneurism. So Gabriella really shouldn't go around insulting any of them. But Gabriella isn't comfortable rolling over and saying nothing when she is opposed to something. Damn. She has like zero self-preservation instincts.

"I am," Gabriella says with a small laugh, trying to sound playful as she expresses her displeasure with the assignment. "Slightly opposed to the invasion of privacy. But we do sign contracts that give the company access to everything we do on our office computers." She reminds herself, it is something she does once a month whenever she participates in usage checks. "So no one should be that upset. Still, I really think he should let the whole Secret Santa thing go." She rolls her eyes.

"What?" Kristen laughs, delighted.

Ohhhh, she wants this to get back to Santa. The man loves anything with his name on it! He'd hate that one of his favorites wants to do away with a tradition to honor him."You love Christmas. I would think you'd be excited about a Secret Santa exchange."

"Oh, I love Christmas! I love decorating my desk and my house. I even have magnetic Christmas light reflectors on my car. But that doesn't mean I think there should be a company-wide *mandatory* participation in a holiday function." Gabriella puts special emphasis on the word pulling a seriously offended facial expression.

Kristen could kiss her! Of all Kristen's relatives, she is particularly lacking in fondness for Great Uncle Coleman, Santa's little brother. She has frequently made the joke that he chose the name Coleman (i.e., Coal-man) when interacting with the human world because he wanted to make it clear he was stingy with his good nature. He is a bit bored of the near eternal life thing and very old-fashioned. Doesn't like that employees get entire weekends off sort of old-fashioned. He didn't even want a Secret Santa, but in the family, it's hard to avoid, so the man did the worst job of it in the entire family history. And it is awesome to finally not be the only person willing to say it! Everyone else pussyfoots around dark, sad, angry, or unpleasant subjects in desperate bids to stay on the nice list. Everyone else fights their elf nature hard.

Most elves tend towards mischievous impulses and wild urges to grab attention. One doesn't deliver gifts worldwide wearing a bright red suit riding a sleigh pulled by *flying mammals* if they aren't after attention. But the rest of the family tries to pretend they have put such traits behind them. Kristen has never been able to do the same.

Now Santa's favorite of the year is saying things Kristen might, on camera! *This is everything.*

"He should just give end-of-the-year bonuses and leave it at that," Gabriella says, getting too comfortable again. She just asked for money on camera. But what the hell? It's done now. And a *mandatory* Christmas celebration annoys her. As much for the people who don't celebrate as in Christmas's defense. If someone doesn't want to celebrate, they shouldn't have to.

"Hasn't it ever struck you as strange that a country with 'separation of church and state' written into its founding documents makes a *national* holiday out of what should be a religious one?" Gabriella says, only to be met with silence.

Kristen loves this woman. Yes, that has struck her as odd, but she rarely mentions it, as she is not *technically* an American citizen.

She was born in the North Pole, which is not on anyone's maps as a country. She lets people assume she is one of them and, thus far in life, has not been questioned.

Kristen is grinning from ear to ear, but to Gabriella, that could mean either that she agrees or is pleased with how deranged she can make Gabriella look on camera. But Gabriella doesn't need anyone to agree with her. She thinks it's weird. But she ought to get back to the point.

"I'd much prefer money to the kind of gifts I got last year," Gabriella says, intentionally playful. "I only got one on the last of the twelve days, and it was a box of Bic pens. I'm pretty sure they stole it from the supply closet."

Everyone in the room laughs as Gabriella makes it out like she is only complaining about the quality of her presents.

Good as she clearly is, Gabriella is also funny. And not nearly as unaware as she seems with her Christmas decoration and elf ears added to her headphones. Maybe she isn't naive. Maybe she is just... authentically herself. *How novel,* Kristen thinks.

"Well," Kristen tries to regroup. It suddenly occurs to her that this doesn't have to be a useless assignment. This can get her an A and maybe, just maybe, make people listen to what she's been saying for years. That the younger generation should be running the family enterprises. The older generation, despite or because of their long, long lives, isn't up to running things in a modern world. Maybe, using Santa's favorite to highlight a bit of that, she can drive the point home.

No longer only in it for the laughs, Kristen sits up straighter. "It still must be flattering to be singled out for this job?" She probes, hoping Gabriella is aware enough to say what Kristen wants to hear.

"No." Gabriella shakes her head.

From the narrowing of Gabriella's eyes, it's clear she feels Kristen leading her somewhere in particular. Also, she might be weighing the logic of answering honestly.

Kristen supposes she wouldn't blame Gabriella if she chose job security over integrity. Kristen herself has merely a passing acquaintance with objective truth. But she is...perhaps *hopeful* that the woman in front of her will choose honesty.

Gabriella observes Kristen critically. She is suddenly alert. Odd, Gabriella hadn't noticed before, but everything Kristen's done since starting this project has been done with such boredom. She is used to being the smartest person in the room, isn't she? Used to manipulating people to entertain herself because she doesn't know how to connect. But not so now. Now she sees some opportunity. Why does Gabriella like this manipulative, spoiled girl better, realizing that Kristen is secretly, perhaps *tragically*, socially impaired? Gabriella thinks to herself with just a bit of sarcasm.

Gabriella doesn't bother examining it. She has a feeling she knows what Kristen is after. And Gabriella has never been very good at lying.

"It's not flattering to be singled out for this job. I'm the most junior member of the department, so I cannot say no." Gabriella holds up a finger as she counts out the unflattering reasons she was chosen. "And I obviously love buying gifts and giving them since I'm female. The only one in the department. Which by the way is weird." Gabriella grows steadily more agitated the more of the truth she expresses. "At least a third of my graduating class was female. Why are they so under-represented in the workforce?"

There is a long pause in which Gabriella waits for Kristen's next question, but it isn't coming. She only grins. "That's quite the impassioned speech. I wish we could have gotten it with the llama sweater on."

"What? You think that just because I smile and decorate for Christmas, I'm incapable of viewing the inequity around me and being offended by it?" Gabriella snaps. *Ugh, this girl.* Just when Gabriella was starting to like her better, she has to turn around and snipe at her like a pissy cat.

Kristen opens her mouth to correct Gabriella. She actually wasn't teasing this time. She thinks it would be nice for once for levelheaded females to be portrayed in all their weirdness and quirky fun. Also, she feels that the Christmasy attire would be more effective with the old school family members.

But Gabriella is done being needled.

"You listen to Jack too much. What did he do, call me an airhead before I came back?" She asks snidely as her agitation grows.

Kristen grins. Her devilish grin. Her *ooooh, this could be fun* grin. Because even though she now has a practical reason to like Gabriella, she still loves the basic fun of manipulating people into doing what she wants.

"Did it bother you to hear him say he didn't want to date you?" Kristen asks in a far too innocent voice.

"Of course!" Gabriella snaps. "Not in an *oooh my poor broken heart* sort of way. I'm not into him either." Gabriella says quickly, a bit too quickly. "But the way he was talking, like dating me would be a form of torture or something. It was offensive! You'd be offended too." She shrugs. "Maybe even hurt."

Kristen can't decide if she should goad her a bit further about Jack. Or about the inherent sexism at the company. Maybe neither. Everyone in the family knows how manipulative Kristen is. The glory of Gabriella is that she spit out what Kristen wanted to hear without having to be manipulated much. Maybe Kristen should use the medium to its highest effect and step back. Observe. This is her third documentary-specific film class, but the first one in which she is realizing it might have an actual value.

"So, do you have any plans?" Kristen lets the words hang in the air until Gabriella looks up. "For what to do with Secret Santa?"

"Oh," Gabriella is shocked by the question. She expected to be goaded about Jack. Now that the new subject is raised, Gabriella sits back and thinks.

As she's thinking, Kristen does the main part of her job for the family. She reaches into her pocket for an old-fashioned handkerchief. Great, great, great, great, great Grandma's handkerchief, to be specific, embroidered with a sugarplum fairy.

Faking a sneeze, Kristen shakes out the handkerchief to let loose a bit of magic; it falls through the air around Gabriella, and tiny flecks of light glow on her skin, as the magic sinks inside her.

"Do I have plans for Secret Santa?" Gabriella repeats the question for the camera as everyone has been asked to do so that the producer's voices can be cut out more easily. She starts to smile a bit, and as she speaks, it grows into what can only be called a *jolly* expression. "Mr. Coleman gave me a lot of latitude, so I'm gonna have fun with it. Not everyone celebrates Christmas, but that doesn't mean they don't all have something they want or need. So—" She is really grinning now. It nearly looks devious when she pops her eyebrows and bites at the right corner of her lips. "I'll figure it out. This year—just call *me* Santa."

Kristen laughs. She is almost glad now that she was given this assignment. She's going to have fun seeing where this bit of power goes.

As Gabriella walks out of the break room, she feels something strange. Something electric. It is as if a breeze is tickling up her arm hairs and her fingers are soothing them back down. It goes on like that beneath her skin, tickle, soothe, tickle, soothe. And the rhythm of it begins to sound like music. It becomes sleigh bells shaking and a chilly breeze waking her up to a world of possibilities.

Jingle Bells

T he thing about magic is that most people expect it to look a certain way. They expect explosions, wild weather, boiling potions, and magic wands. They want to see frolicking creatures of small stature but long ears, or giant stature but paper thin frames, green-colored skin and pointy teeth, spindly fingers, or giant eyes, some sort of altered feature that will set them apart. And some magic looks that way. When magic beings are in their own realm, more than a few of them look that way, and many more exciting and beautiful ways too. But when moving within the *human* realm, in an effort not to overly frighten the locals, many magic beings disguise themselves and their magic. Which isn't too hard as humans are wont to dismiss anything they cannot explain.

Take, for instance, the massive storm systems that shook Oklahoma, or more specifically, one small town in the state six years ago. In a two-day period, Unforgiven had multiple small tornados, two category five tornados, a precisely localized rainstorm that flooded a dry lake basin, and several earthquakes that clocked in at over four on the Richter scale. This was not, as some meteorologists called it, "weird-ass natural phenomena," nor was it "the hand of God angry over declining birth rates"—*really, Oklahoma?* Imagine a despairing head shake here.

That event was, in fact, a magical showdown involving natural force guardians, a group of kelpies and a few other magical beings, and a fourteen-year-old witch, but that's a different story.

*Wink.

The point of this illustration is: in the "real world," humans ignore magic. Or write it off as imagination or symptoms of stress and exhaustion. So it is not all that strange that, at first, Gabriella Anjelica Cruz did not realize she had a magical power.

On Monday, after she was gifted the power, Gabriella noticed but dismissed it as mere imagination that Kristen Kringle has a certain twinkle about her skin. When the light hits it, she looks almost like she is very lightly dusted with glitter, and her ears seem to—*hook*—a bit at the uppermost ridge. But having dismissed this, she promptly forgot about it. And since she makes an effort not to look directly at the snotty young woman, she hasn't had occasion to see it again.

On Tuesday, while data mining her coworkers for gift ideas, she began to hear shaking sleigh bells in her head whenever she found out something, shall we say *good,* about her coworkers. Like how Stan and his wife had been fostering his nephew and recently started fostering another child of no relation. Or how Debbie regularly volunteers at homeless shelters. And Gloria rescued two shelter dogs. Nice things, possibly innocuous, possibly good, but things that compelled her to list them on the good side of the Naughty-and-Nice list that she had started, really just so that she could put Jack on the bad side of the list. But even as she heard the jingling, she dismissed it as having Christmas music stuck in her head.

When Wednesday rolled around, and she noticed the slightly greenish-tinged skin and very purple irises on her barista, she briefly wondered if there was a fantasy convention going on but didn't ask as she sees no reason people can't dress in fantasy costumes and colored contacts whenever they feel like it.

All told, there were a number of small signs of the power that she might have noticed earlier, but they were so spread out and different in nature that it is not all that odd that it took Gabriella well into the weekend before she began to notice that there was something out of the ordinary going on in her life. But even then, she had no immediate explanation.

The first realization came on Saturday, December first, while pulling out more boxes of Christmas decorations from the basement storage locker in her apartment building. That's right *more* boxes. Her apartment is already fairly decorated. Lights hang around the window; her pine tree has been up since Black Friday, November twenty-third. It was lit that weekend and decorated with balls and tinsel. But some decorations had not come out yet, like the window clings she just now found, the old Christmas card collection she likes to display, or the tiny decorations for her office tree.

She is humming a slower, heavy version of "I'll Be Home For Christmas" as she closes her locker, thinking morosely how disappointing it is that she still can't find Mom's buñelos recipe. It apparently got lost when she and Maria moved into this apartment after their mother died. They always used to eat buñelos at Christmas time, but Gabriella has tried some recipes she found online, and none was exactly right. Mom must have had a secret ingredient.

She was so sure it was in one of the Christmas boxes, but she's taken them all out twice, smoothed out packing paper in case it got caught up and dug through old books in case it is tucked between one of the pages, but she can't find it. It doesn't feel the same without it.

It will never feel the same. She knows that, but she wishes there was more of Mom in her Christmas. Mom used to make it all so sp—

The thought is cut off as a neighbor she doesn't recognize bumps into her running down the basement stairs and sends Gabriella spinning into the wall. She manages to snag her box out of the air and yank it to her chest, but a few things escape the merely folded shut cardboard box. What looks like a small stocking and definitely a set of bells as she hears them jingle loudly.

"Ooh!" The young man blurts out in a sweet, almost cartoonish voice. "Sorry!"

He darts down the stairs at a speed that might have raised eyebrows if Gabriella had noticed. But she is busy trying to catch her breath, maintain her footing and hold onto her box. So it is only as he stretches out a hand returning her dropped possessions that Gabriella even gets a good look at him.

He has a big bright smile and skin that twinkles like it's dusted with glitter, and ears that...hook. Gabriella startles and tries not to stare as the sight fills her with a slightly tingly feeling.

"You dropped this." The boy remarks.

Gabriella tears her eyes away from his face and looks at what's in his hand. A string of seven swans with big red bows around their necks and a mini stocking with a bit of paper sticking out. Gabriella's heart leaps, and she reaches out for the stocking, entirely forgetting the box. Somehow the boy manages to grab the box in one arm and hold out Gabriella's decorations in the other, but she barely notices.

Breath held, she tugs at the slip of paper and releases an elated gasp. Sleigh bells jingle in her mind, and a tingly sensation dances through her veins as she sees her mother's recipe.

Gabriella returns her slightly teary gaze to the boy again and opens her mouth, though no sound comes out.

Grinning, the boy carefully puts the now empty stocking and the strand of swans into the slit between box folds and holds out the box. "Gee, I'm sure sorry I bumped you. Better hold on tight, so this doesn't get away from you."

Gabriella nods, taking the box back in one arm and gripping the recipe in her free hand. She wants to say thank you and wants to ask if he is an elf or an angel. Wants to cry with joy! But words are still lost to her. She makes her way out to the basement, suddenly very certain that magic is real and that it is in her life. It leaves her wondering about different things she's been noticing lately and if it was all magic. And why? Why now? Why her?

She searches the ground and the stairs for the bells she heard falling through the air, but she sees none. And she isn't surprised at all. She didn't even expect to see them...that music is magic.

Rushing up to her apartment, she very nearly throws her box onto the couch and rushes into the kitchen to see if she has the necessary ingredients. Again, she isn't surprised at all to find she has every—single—thing she needs.

By the time Maria has returned from an early morning grocery run, the dough is already resting for the second time.

Gabriella takes two bags from her sister and starts putting away the groceries with her back to Maria.

"You'll never guess what I found today! Never." Gabriella challenges excitably.

"No point trying then," Maria mutters, annoyed already just from the traffic and other people at the—

"Buñelos." Gabriella interrupts her sister's pouty thoughts.

"You found another contender, eh?"

"No," Gabriella latches onto her sister's arm and drags her behind the kitchen counter. "Look."

Opening a cabinet door, Gabriella shows off the recipe she has closed in a Ziploc bag and taped onto the inside of the cabinet door with blue painters tape.

"You found it!" With a burst of happy energy, Maria jumps, spinning around to give her sister an excited hug. "You actually found it. How? Where was it?"

"It was like magic, Maria! I swear I've been through all of those boxes a hundred times, but today...I tripped, and the recipe just...fell out of the box. It had been stuffed inside a tiny stocking. It was just... there. Like a magical message from Mom.

Maria rolls her eyes and shakes her head at her sister, but she is still clinging onto her arm in wonder, so one might not be remiss in believing she is just as awestruck as her sister by the Christmas miracle.

A while later, when they've completed the buñelos and syrup together, the sisters curl up on their couch, eating, laughing, and basking in the sweet cinnamon-flavored memories of their mother. And Gabriella is quite sure that this will be a very magical Christmas indeed.

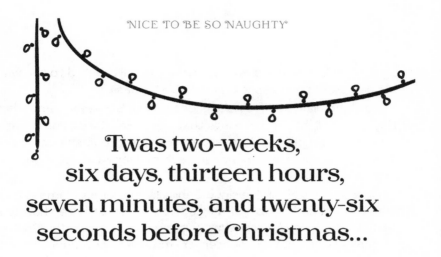

Twas two-weeks, six days, thirteen hours, seven minutes, and twenty-six seconds before Christmas...

Many a desk is now decorated for Christmas in the offices of My Best Friend Doll company. Today is Tuesday, December the fourth, a mere twenty-one days from the big event, and many people are growing in excitement. But at the desk of the, quite certain he is mature, *immature* Jack Drummer, nothing is altered. His walls are the same manila color they were before, boasting only a calendar and a few haphazardly stuck-up notes on old tech calls and assignments.

Beyond this grinch-y corner of the basement, Stan has a three-dimensional Rudolph-the-red-nosed-reindeer ring toss on the outside of his cubicle. Cory has a small tree decorated with various Nintendo game character ornaments and a bowl of Christmas candy. And even Jay, who does not celebrate, has a strand of multicolored cone-shaped lights attached to his monitor.

Gabriella's desk is growing steadily more decorated. The tree has ornaments, mostly related to The Nutcracker Ballet: there is a Clara with toes pointed holding up her nutcracker, a Drosselmeyer with his distinctive cape and eye patch. A mouse king, a sugarplum fairy, and even a nutcracker in a leotard caught mid-leap. But there are also a few more playful ornaments a small reindeer with a blinking nose, a cup of cocoa with marshmallows and a mini replica of Nikky, the company's first doll, that she bought from the online shop when she got the job. There are even snowflake decals pasted to the walls of her cubicle. No one's space is more Christmasy.

And Gabriella herself is no less decorated. She wears a necklace of tiny glowing lights and earrings that jingle. Her Christmas sweater of the day is bright red (actually a sweatshirt, but she counts it) with three rows of three reindeer, each making faces over squares with their names.

In the six days of filming since Gabriella got her assignment from Uncle Coleman and her bit of magic from Kristen, Kristen has been hanging back. Trying to see what this medium has to offer. She has not manipulated one encounter or force-fed anyone lines. And frankly...it's getting annoying. On the one hand, people are loosening up a bit. She's gotten more people to insult last year's Secret Santa on camera! Which she is quite pleased with. But Jack and Gabriella are not cooperating.

Jack has been milder, as if he thinks waiting long enough will make her forget what happened. *Really?* Has he watched any television? Participated in any pop culture? Has it not been well established by now that women do not *forget* insults? They might forgive, but that requires the event to be addressed and moved past. Not ignored.

Kristen might have to intervene. But damn it, she doesn't like to give up on a course once she's started it. She told herself that she would see where this medium took her. So she isn't interfering. *She isn't!*

All she asked Jack was how his day was going. That is all!

"*Gabby* over there us still pouting," Jack says, intentionally baiting Gabriella when he should own up to what he did.

Kristen shakes her head at this behavior, though if he wanted to, Santa could point out to Kristen a number of times when she behaved exactly the same. But if she wanted to know what Santa thought she did wrong, she could easily ask. And not once in her life has she.

"She hasn't said more than three words to me in like a week."

This is a bit of an exaggeration. Gabriella said hello and goodbye to Jack every day. When he asked for a pen on Thursday, she replied, "sorry, I'm all out." Which was a lie but was also four words. When he rifled through the candy in her basket, asking where the KitKats were on Friday, she answered, "sorry sir, if you don't see them on the shelf, we don't have any." A tiny sarcastic joke of fourteen words that actually made Jack smile.

Gabriella regretted his amusement at once and forced herself to double down on her proscribed punishment of behaving as if he doesn't exist, and thus refused to respond when he IM'd her about her tech call with emoji to represent different coworkers, guessing first that it was the big-eyed smiley face (Angelo), then the snoring smiley face (Fred) or the blushing smiley face (Cynthia) or the nose blowing smiley face (Martin). That last designation never made sense to her; Martin had only been sick once since she's worked here and didn't even sneeze. But she didn't respond to Jack. It would have been faster to get rid of him by answering that he was right with the first guess, but that would be giving him too much attention.

But the point is, she has said a few things to him. It's only the last few days that she has avoided even saying hello. And if he wants it to change, he needs to grow up and apologize.

"I mean, it's not like I mutilated the reindeer or anything," Jack says in an overly loud voice to be sure he is heard by the object of his affections—sorry! *Attention.* The object of his attention. Goodness, don't know how that happened. *Wink.

Meanwhile, on the Christmasy side of the cubicle, Gabriella is tapping her toe impatiently and making dirty looks at her computer screen as Jack talks. When he makes his joke, she smirks with angry superiority and pretends to hit the button on the side of her headphones.

"I.T. this is, Gabriella." She uses her bright, work voice, then invests it with even more excitement. "Is that you, Santa? Wow! I can't believe you're calling me personally."

Jack quiets on the other side of the partition leaning near to listen in amusement. At last, he has her attention again! *Boys.* Imagine an eye roll here.

"Oh, you've taken Jack off your nice list." Gabriella continues brightly. She's not speaking to him, but she can still drive a point home. "Yeah, that makes sense. I did hear him mention reindeer mutilation like it's okay."

Jack's face bares a wide grin of achievement. He knew he could annoy her into acknowledging him. Kristen, meanwhile, is feeling quite successful herself, all she had to do was ask how his day was going, and she got such excellent results. She knew Gabriella had a fun side. Although it is equal parts amusing and annoying for Kristen as she thinks of how much more likely Gabriella is to get the Claus on the phone than Kristen is. Oh well, she is supposed to be fading into the background. Such a struggle when one is as bright and compelling as Kristen finds herself.

But she knows this story is not about her. If anyone asked her, she would say that no story is about her. When she was at boarding school, the story was about an ensemble of unhappy girls. When at the North Pole, she was merely the cousin everyone rolls their eyes at. When she was first finding herself on the naughty list, even that wasn't about her. It was about how it reflected on her father. Somewhere around four years of no change, it ceased to be a story at all. And *even her mother's death* when she was ten was all about her father's grief and his withdrawal from the world.

No story is about Kristen. But she's used to it. And anyway, when Gabriella is being herself, her playful self, Kristen is at least slightly entertained by this story. So she can fade—for now.

"Yep, Santa. I'll keep you posted. Happy Holidays!" Gabriella finishes her bit with a pert grin.

"See what I mean?" Jack says to the camera. Though nothing Gabriella did, proved any point he'd been trying to make today, i.e., that she was ignoring him. But people will see what they want.

Gabriella's a bit annoyed with the man on the other side of her wall, but honestly...not much. She has not felt nearly as annoyed with him since Friday, but on principle, she didn't want to let him know. And the weekend made her even more forgiving. So now, in a playful mood all her own, Gabriella decides to do a little goading. She stands up, lifting a walnut from the bowl of nuts that sits beside her nutcracker, and pulls up the nutcracker as well, fitting the nut into his mouth.

"Walnut?" She inquires sweetly. Then precedes to crack the nut open, so its shell sprays all over Jack's desk and a bit on the man himself.

"I'm good. Thanks." Jack shakes a bit of nut debris off himself, chewing on his own grin.

Gabriella, with a breezy smile she does not feel because of the mess she made, pops the walnut into her mouth. Carefully replacing her mother's nutcracker on the desk, she backs away with a smug expression. Comforting herself about the mess with a reminder that Jack is a slob anyway and very likely won't even notice the shells.

Ugh. Then they'll be there tomorrow. No. Cleaners come tonight! She can wipe down his desk before she leaves, and the rest will be vacuumed up. Yeah. No problem. She comforts herself as she walks to the break room where she's spotted Maya, who only comes down here when something is wrong upstairs.

Not that she comes down to talk to Gabriella. Although, maybe she does. Maybe Gabriella simply hasn't noticed it before. Anyway, Gabriella is making an effort.

The truly unfortunate thing about the proud, driven Gabriella's of the world is they simply cannot do a job by half measures. And after finding Mom's recipe, she got an extra boost of Christmas spirit, and she wants to spread that magic around. Thus she is trying *very* hard with this whole Secret Santa thing. She's done research on the religious beliefs of almost everyone in the company. Looked into their social media profiles to see what sort of things they are into and even went so far as to, sort of without permission, look into the group complaints to HR over last year's Secret Santa debacle.

Now she knows plenty about everyone she works with; she just needs...a personal touch. Something that makes them feel the way she used to when she would find one secret special gift from her mother. Something she hadn't even asked for, usually something really small, but something that made her feel seen. Made her feel like magic existed. The way she felt as she bit into those buñelos like she'd gotten one more present from Mom, to remind her she is loved.

No small order. She's probably setting herself up for failure, but... what if she can do it?

The Mystery
of Gabriella Cruz

Jack grins as he watches Gabriella leave. "She is totally acting suspicious. This whole week," he volunteers unprompted.

Honestly, it's getting weird how easily he is adapting to saying what he's thinking aloud. It's bad, actually. The other day he was in the grocery store and started, out loud, discussing with himself the value of the healthy cereal he knew he wasn't going to buy.

"No, it's longer than that." Absentmindedly Jack lifts a pen and taps it on the edge of his desk, drawing nearer a pad of paper, and brushing walnut shells off it. "And I don't just mean with me. No. This isn't about me saying I would never date her."

Kristen is tempted to interrupt his soliloquy and point out that those aren't the words he used. But right now, he looks like a villain plotting his ultimately doomed plan, and it looks so good on camera. She catches Terrance's eye and smirks; for once, Terrance relaxes his 'this is important' work attitude enough to smile back. Yeah, Jack is looking really outrageous; otherwise, Terrance wouldn't unbend. Someone other than Jack has a thing for Gabriella.

"It's ever since her meeting with Coleman," Jack says. At the top of his notepad, he writes: Gabriella Cruz Observation Notes and makes an arrow mark below it for bullets.

It is at this moment important to note that Jack Hilary Drummer erroneously believes himself to be a very observant person. It would not be entirely unfair to say that he is observant for his sex. But still, *very,* seems a bit generous. However, he was raised first with Nate the Great novels before graduating to Encyclopedia Brown and the Hardy Boys, followed by Sherlock Holmes, Hercule Poirot, and Sam Spade. Until eventually, it was any mystery novel he could get his hands on. Like all amateur sleuths, he possesses a great deal of interest, so much so that he often sees mysteries where there are none. And also a total lack of murders to solve.

Now we shall return to observing him as he makes a great discovery that had he truly been a "very observant person," he could have made days earlier.

"Instead of what she usually does: actually working between tech calls, which by the way, is redundant." Jack breaks off, looking guiltily up at the daughter of his employer. "Sorry."

Kristen shakes her head. "I'm not even here."

Jack pretends he believes that as he continues. "Gabriella hasn't been doing her redundant work. No, she's been leaving her cubicle to chat with people. She's never been chatty before. Add to that she took on the usage reports, which anyone can see she hates."

"Could you explain usage reports for us laymen?" Kristen prompts.

"Oh, usage reports are random spot checks we do to see how employees are using their computers. You know, how much time does Daniel spend on minesweepers or Tiffany on Facebook? That sort of thing." Jack shrugs. "No one cares about them until they want to fire someone, then they use them as ammunition. Gabriella dislikes them because she feels like she's invading people's privacy. But technically, they have no privacy on work computers." Jack's gaze trails Gabriella through the break room door.

"She gets too involved," he says thoughtfully, and his fondness for the woman in question sneaks into his voice. "Once last year, when she ran the reports, she found out that Frank was spending all this time on medical sites, and she dug deeper to see what he was actually looking at. Turns out his wife has ovarian cancer. She got all worked up about it. Hasn't liked doing them since." Jack breaks off a moment.

He is occupied, remembering that was the first time Gabriella talked to him, *really* talked. She was too stiff before that, but when she'd seen what Frank was looking at, she got so upset she shoved back her seat, shut off her computer and marched out of the building looking like she might cry. Jack had followed her with a full-sized KitKat from the vending machine. He found her in a bit of shade in the parking lot. It sort of became their spot later on, it is only a bit of curb with a tree shading it, and they would sit there when they had to get out of the building. Anyway...he'd sat next to her, offered her the KitKat and asked what was up.

"Sorry," she apologized for nothing at all, accepting the KitKat. "I just...just...just." She shook out her hands, looking ready to scream.

"Seriously, what? Was someone looking at creepy porn or something?"

"No." She said morosely; then, ever the most honest and accurate woman, she corrected herself. "Well, Brandon. But it was sort of normal porn, really."

Jack had laughed at that, and Gabriella looked up, softening a bit.

"I don't think it's right to get someone in trouble for looking up their spouse's cancer while at work. I mean...do you know how hard that is to do with the person in the next room?"

Jack shook his head, wanting to shift away, wanting to go back inside. He didn't want to know about his coworkers' real problems. But Gabriella looked so...intense.

It really was, is, and will always be the best word to describe her. But intensely vulnerable and yet fierce at the same time. He couldn't leave.

"So don't get anyone in trouble for it. Don't report it."

Gabriella snapped the KitKat in half, and not the way the sticks were made to break. Right through the four rows. It looked unintentional. A physical response to her mind's refusal to break the rules.

Jack wanted to laugh. But...he wasn't even sure she knew she'd broken the candy. And he got a sinking suspicion about why this bothered her so much.

"Who was it you knew that had cancer?" Jack asked softly. He knows it wasn't a spouse. He researched her slightly when she started working here, just a quick social media sweep, and she was nowhere close to marriage.

"My mom. She died from Lymphoma."

"I'm sorry."

She nodded. Looking down, she realized how she mutilated the candy and held half out to Jack.

"How about farming some of your work out to me," Jack said around a mouthful of candy. "I don't have much to do today. Can I take anyone off your hands? You know what a diligent worker I am." He said with a very exaggerated wink.

And Gabriella—defeated the sun with the massive, incandescent loveliness of her smile.

"You wouldn't mind?" She asked eagerly. It was clear she understood plainly that he was offering to find nothing at all but company business on Frank's computer.

"Nah, I was getting bored. So...who can I take off your hands?"

"Frank." She said without hesitation. Then as an afterthought. "And maybe Brandon and Cory."

Jack laughed loud and long. "Excellent. I love getting paid to watch porn."

She giggled, ate her candy and a few minutes later went back in with him, much more settled. And Jack was...charmed. She really was too sweet for her own good.

"Now she volunteers," Jack says; having returned to the present, he makes a note of this strange behavior on his page. "And she is using them to go out there and get to know those weirdos. It's very odd."

Standing, Jack nods at the break room. "Watch her."

Terrance is a professional and is not about to do any such thing. It would be involving himself with his subjects. However, he does know what entertainment looks like, so he happily pans the camera towards the break room to show Gabriella patting Maya on the shoulder. Before he pans back to Jack, following him out of his cubicle to the other, Christmasy side. Gabriella's side.

Kristen follows the boys, eating her tongue to keep from giggling, leaping and clicking her heels together.

At this very same moment, Gabriella has her back to the invaders at her desk. She had launched into what she felt was an innocuous conversation with Maya about Christmas traditions and which were her personal favorite. Only to have Maya break down over her boyfriend and how he promised to come home with her for Christmas but is backing out.

Gabriella blinked fully seven times, wondering what the hell she was supposed to say to that. It never occurred to her that real-life people took this 'bring home a boyfriend' thing as seriously as movie characters. She supposes never having actually left home has something to do with that disconnect. She lived with her mother through college. Mom knew every one of Gabriella's giant number of boyfriends, three. She dated other guys, but none became anything close to a relationship; most ended after a few dates.

Additionally, Gabriella's mother was much more concerned that her daughters be happy, healthy, and in pursuit of their dreams than that, either one have a romantic partner. So as Maya bawls about how much grief she is going to get from her family about this, Gabriella can at first only come up with platitudes to comfort the woman.

"And that's not even the worst of it," Maya exclaims when Gabriella doesn't seem disturbed enough by her tragedy. "He's been lying this whole time. Not only is he still married, but he also lied about having kids."

"Wow. Liars." Gabriella says, honestly. She isn't at all fond of liars, but how is she supposed to comfort Maya over something like that? They aren't close. She has no idea how long Maya even knew the man was married. "That really sucks."

"I know! He's completely ruining Christmas for me," Maya sobs.

"Oh, come on now," Gabriella says with a bit more energy, feeling a buzz of understanding build up inside her, not for Maya's exact problem, but...for her deeper need, to be seen, and loved. "Don't let him ruin it for you. He can't be the only thing that makes the holidays special." Gabriella tries for motivational and upbeat.

And fails to bolster her subject. "He wasssss!" Maya wails.

Gabriella allows Maya to turn into her shoulder to sob. "It's okay," Gabriella reassures her gently. "I'm sure you had nice Christmases before you ever met him. Times when you weren't with family to show off all you've achieved, but just because you love them. There must be someone, or something that made you feel special, a family tradition, or a favorite dish maybe." The longer Maya clings on, the more Gabriella's tone softens as her heart reaches out to help her as she would her own sister. In her arms, Maya quiets, looking at Gabriella in a bit of surprise.

In the past, if someone was clinging onto her this way, she wouldn't have been able to think past getting them off of her. But in this past week, Gabriella's assignment has functioned like a shield. Making her more comfortable around people and willing to actually interact with them. Not even just willing, she wants to connect.

"Focus on those times," Gabriella suggests, offering up one of her own therapeutic techniques in hopes her experiences can help this woman. She has never considered before that her struggles might help her to connect with other people, but everyone needs help sometimes, don't they? "Recreate them in your mind. It's hard when we're hurting, for any reason, but we can't let the pain steal our chances for joy," she says, pleased with how peaceful she feels even while being touched, totally unaware of what fires of discomfort are shortly to blaze inside her.

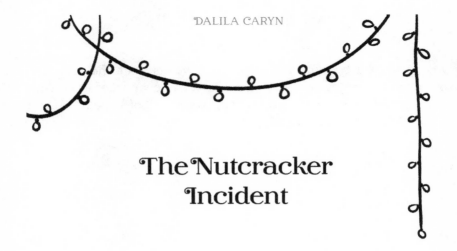

The Nutcracker Incident

Whilst Gabriella comforts, Jack investigates. He is not the tidiest of detectives, nor the most subtle. But his methods are proving useful to his way of thinking. Ends justifying means and all that. In this case, the ends being: keeping Jack entertained. And the means being— for lack of a better term— breaking and entering.

"You guys gotta see this. No one likes Christmas this much." He points at the screen that the camera cannot pick up due to the protective covers. "Oh, yeah." he remarks when the blank looks of the film crew alert him to this fact. He sets about, attempting to pull off the screen. "Just wait. You'll see. She's like a reverse Grinch. What would you call that?"

Kristen snorts, but resists giving the very obvious answer.

Andrew, on the other hand, with an eye roll and a low, incredulous mutter replies, *"Santa Claus."*

Jack appears not to hear, busy at his task. But, in fact, he has heard, and is attempting to hide his shame. He knew that. He just doesn't seem to be thinking clearly at the moment, as is evident in his struggles with the relatively easy removal of the protective screen.

One has only to lift up the clamps at the bottom of the monitor, and up it goes. Jack, however, is a bit frazzled and the easy solution has escaped his notice. His eyes dart furtively towards the break room, and he grows desperate to get to the bottom of the mystery that is Gabriella Cruz before she notices him.

"These are her fault, you know?" He says as he struggles with the privacy screen pulling from the right side when anyone can see that it won't work. "She didn't want to be in your documentary. Sorry." He throws an *'oops, did I say that'* face at the doc crew, none of whom are anything but entirely amused by his hysterical loss of control on the camera. Goodness, such *extreme emotionality*, how embarrassing. *Wink.

"She complained that we deal with too much sensitive information to take part," he continues, his voice showing the strain of exertion that, once again, was entirely avoidable if he took the time to—*observe*. "We don't deal with anything remotely important. We're a doll company, not the NSA. But they caved and gave everyone these truly annoying covers. I think she was just nervous about being on camera. Ah-ha!" He shouts, finally managing to yank off the privacy screen, but so violently that he falls backwards and knocks the snowman mug over, spilling candy canes across the desk and floor.

"Oops!" Jack says, clearly unrepentant. He yanks up a random candy cane and, breaking the seal, shoves it into his mouth. He moves aside slightly, shoving the keyboard off angle and pointing at the screen Vanna White style.

On the screen is really a rather average computer wallpaper, considering the level of intensity he expressed in trying to show it. Merely a young girl ice skating around a Christmas tree on a frozen lake, holding up a nutcracker.

There is, to be fair, also a Christmas countdown clock in the corner of the screen that breaks the time down into weeks, days, hours, minutes, and seconds.

But if one is bothering to have a countdown, it is so much more satisfying to see the seconds tick by.

Jack is quiet, staring at the screen with a look so delighted you would think he were a Christmas fanatic.

"She did this thing last year," he says with a smile in his voice. "Every time she turned on her computer, she'd start singing. Really quiet; it wasn't annoying or anything, just...weird. She would like whisper it, snow, over and over again, going up an octave every time. You know, like in that Christmas movie, Singing in—no. White Christmas! That was it." An especially tickled expression lights his eyes. "*Snow.*"

Terrance annoyed though he generally is by this man, zooms in on his face. Kristen said in one of their strategy meetings that should the opportunity present itself to spice things up with a workplace romance or a prank war, they were going to point their cameras right at it. And he has to admit, it does spice up what has been a fairly boring project thus far.

"Let's see what she's up to." Jack grabs Gabriella's seat and settles in, poking around her computer.

It is at about this time that Gabriella notices the commotion around her desk. Immediately her insides are set alight with the fires of rage. And the lovely tingle of magic that had begun to dance under her skin becomes a sparking open wire biting at her from within. However, as she is a *genuinely* nice person, she cannot abandon Maya as she cries. She jerks back but does not leave the woman's side.

But oh, how rage eats at her. Oh, how much she will make Jack pay! He will be made to suffer. How dare he invade her space?

Again!

"Maya," she says using more snap than she has up to now. Her rage toward Jack informs the tone. "You can't let some lying jerk come in and ruin your good time. Do something for you."

"I wanted to share the holidays with someone," Maya protests.

"So do that. Just not with him. Share it with family, with friends. Buy yourself a puppy. You know," Gabriella's tone sharpens further, her eyes narrowing on Jack as her body is beset by a thunderstorm of barbed nerve endings. Throughout her body, she feels edgy. Her space has been invaded.

She has techniques. Breathing. Mantras. Stepping away. But right now, all her body wants is violence. Why is it okay for everyone else to break the rules? "Maybe it would help to go find him and give him a good swift kick in the hazelnuts." She bites out what she knows is bad advice.

But she cannot seem to stop seeing Jack curled up on the floor, sobbing and gripping his balls in pain. She's got to get ahold of herself.

Honestly though, knowing how wonderful it will feel to kick him, can it really be called bad advice? Gabriella wonders.

The answer to her query is yes. The answer is always yes. Violence is never the solution. It is, however, *much* more entertaining than taking the high road.

Kristen is on tenterhooks waiting for a confession, an explosion. Something. Jack is looking unhinged. She knows why he's doing what he's doing. And she hopes her audience will too. But if nothing comes of the romance, it might never be clear. The trouble with documentaries is that without a plot to reveal character intents, one sometimes must prompt them into speaking their reasoning aloud.

"Why is this so important to you, Jack? I mean, what difference does it make what jobs she takes on?" Kristen prompts.

"Either she's up to something. Or she's acting weird intentionally to make me curious. All because I said I wouldn't date her. Ah-ha! I've got—"

"You *never* said you wouldn't date her," Kristen can no longer resist pointing out.

"I most certainly *did,*" Jack says in an offended tone. A highly defensive tone. A slightly frightened tone. Largely because he has a sinking—*accurate*—suspicion that he might not have said it. "That's why she's so upset. Look, would you just be a pal and watch her?" Jack asks.

Terrance shakes his camera slowly from side to side like it is his head. Kristen bites her lips, smirking as she shakes her head as well. This is fun! Who knew Terrance had fun in him, but look at him delighting in Jack's misery and making the camera delight in it too.

"Crap lot of help you are," Jack says, growing anxious and embarrassed. Very embarrassed. "How can she work with all this clutter?" He demands violently, pushing everything *he has knocked over* off the desk and knocking over the nutcracker in the process.

Jack's eyes widen as he watches it bounce onto the desk and tip forward, over the edge, crashing slowly towards the floor. Damn. The nutcracker hits the ground with a loud crack. That makes even Kristen jerk a little in shock.

Jack stares down at the mess as the fullness of his crimes hits him over the head. *Shit. Shit. Double Shit.* This is all his fault. He knocked over her candy, and now he's basically had a tantrum over the film crew saying he has a crush on Gabriella, and he's broken her nutcracker. And all of this on camera. Is there a way to come back from this?

"Quick, get me some glue," Jack says, reaching out for the broken toy. "There is no way she won't notice."

"Seriously!" Gabriella's voice reaches a pitch most humans cannot muster. "What is your problem with me?"

Gabriella, having finally extracted herself from Maya's tears, has marched over to the desk in time to see *her mother's nutcracker* break on the floor.

She feels tears welling in her eyes and fists forming from her hands, and every part of her feels like it is on fire. Her nerve endings dance electrically under her skin, making her muscles clench one moment and shudder the next. It's all she can do to keep from striking out. So it's only fair that her voice is loud and enraged and her attitude less than understanding.

"I've been leaving you alone. I don't stick my stuff on your side of the partition. Or make childish noises when you're on calls," she snarls. If it was not obvious, this is in reference to an actual event in which Jack made the noises of an airplane fire fight while Gabriella answered a tech call on Monday.

"If you want to decorate with the swimsuit issue of Sports Illustrated or the skulls of dead bunnies, I won't bother you. Why can't you leave me alone?" The last is said with a bit of betraying sadness in her voice. A bit of breakage, not unlike the nutcracker on the floor with its cracker lever split in two. Her right-hand jerks, punching her thigh. Hard.

"It was an accident," Jack says with a tone still far too defensive to do him any good.

"Oh, you *accidentally* walked to my side of the partition, ripped off my privacy screen, made a mess of my desk, and broke my mother's nutcracker?" Gabriella demands her voice fully acidic now. Her hand jerks, three rapid strikes against her thigh.

"Just the last bits were accidental." Jack tries for cute at exactly the wrong moment. Gabriella raises an unimpressed brow, and up rise Jack's defenses again. "Look, if you like the thing so much, why was it here?"

Gabriella punches her thigh once more, hard. "I like having it around. I like using it. What's it to you?" Gabriella says, taking a step forward in a threatening manner she doesn't entirely intend, but one she isn't resisting either. She cannot back down. Cannot. She was *invaded.* And he *laughs* as he destroys things. Wants you to pinch his cheeks and call him cute. He...

"I'll buy you another one. That one was a piece of crap anyway." He offers defensively and again uses the very worst words possible.

Gabriella's eyes tear all the more as she glances down at the piece of crap on the floor. She can see her mother laughing as she breaks open a walnut, and its shell sprays all over the kitchen table.

"You found one that works! A real proper nutcracker! Thank you mija! It's perfect!"

A sudden numbness falls over Gabriella's entire being. On her tongue, she tastes burnt cinnamon and sugar, the pain of this moment corrupting the memory she had only just recovered. Her right hand continues to punch the same rhythm, but the rest of her quiets. She thinks perhaps this is what hatred feels like. She no longer has any desire to kick Jack. It wouldn't make a difference if she did anyway. He would never see his guilt. He would always feel like the wronged party for having been caught mid-crime.

He will never learn. Not with violence anyway.

"Just move." Gabriella orders. "This is my space. Get out of it."

Jack swallows but moves to obey. Still red-faced with his—less than righteous —indignation.

"What did you even need here?" Gabriella demands.

"I was doing a spot check on your usage," Jack fumbles for a lie and should have simply kept his mouth shut as no one believes him. It only makes him look puerile.

Gabriella waits with a brow raised.

"Fine, I wanted to know what you were up to. You're acting weird."

"And that's unusual how?" Gabriella demands. She waits for an answer. "That's a concern of yours why?" She continues when he has nothing to say.

"I really will buy you another nutcracker," Jack says in a sudden attempt to make amends. His tone closer to apologetic. "It's my bad."

"You can't. They don't make working nutcrackers anymore. They're all decorative. And anyway, that *piece of crap* was my favorite because it belonged to my mother." She lets the words sink in, watching Jack begin to look slightly contrite, but not caring at all. "But...whatever." She shrugs with an angry smile on her face, and truly vindictive plans form in her mind. "It's done now. You can't change it."

Jack, actually feeling quite regretful, now, waits a moment longer. Waits, one might observe, to simply be forgiven now that he feels bad for his crime. But if Gabriella's stance is any indicator, he can go ahead and wait until hell freezes over. She has no intention of letting him off the hook.

After a few heavy moments, Jack moves away. Around the room, all the other techs, and Maya, who have been watching with wide eyes and wrapt attention, suddenly look away. The room that was silent for so long explodes with sounds of people faking work.

As if unaware that she is the object of such attention, Gabriella crouches and begins to set to right the mess Jack has made. She neatly gathers up her scattered candy canes and replaces the snowman mug. And gently lifts her nutcracker, now in three pieces, body and a two pieced tattered cracker. She sets them gently on the table. She can take it home tonight and see if she can fix it. But she doesn't really have a lot of hope for that. And anyway, even if she can fix it—she rolls her shoulders to escape an awful pinch between them—even if she can fix it, she will still feel it. She will still hear him calling this beautiful memory a piece of crap. She will still see it, tossed to the ground like it was nothing. Because Jack Drummer doesn't have any respect for her, her things, or her space.

Calmly Gabriella lifts her bent privacy screen and shoves it under the table. She sits down at her computer, closing one window after another as she sees what he was looking through. She leaves only one window open. It's a file entitled N.N.list.doc, a document with two columns, one topped with a smiley face and another with a frowning face and a list of names in each.

An angry jangle of bells sounds in her head, pounding out a song of wild joy, a song of magic and wonder. A song of retribution. She feels the power buzzing beneath her skin, promising to be satisfied. Gabriella moves the cursor next to the name Jack Drummer, already on the naughty list and adds a check mark, along with a note in parenthesis *(may the punishment suit the crime)*.

Must Be Santa

Kristen sits back in the chair she has set up in the break room for some private chats. Thus far, Gabriella has declined to discuss the incident of the nutcracker privately. So Jack is the current occupant of the hot seat.

Kristen lets him stew, examining him objectively. He just screwed up so massively and he knows it, but he is one of those males who are unwilling to apologize. So she really doesn't see a way for him to fix this. It's too bad because he is a handsome bundle of a man, funny, intelligent enough; he could have been really fun for Gabriella. But to not only break something of hers but then act like he had a right to be offended that she was upset...well, damn, that's some really impressive lack of self-awareness.

Honestly, Kristen feels bad for not stepping in and keeping Jack out of Gabriella's space. The look on her face when she saw that nutcracker was heartbreaking. Mother presents are uniquely important things, even it seemed when they were gifts to a mother rather than from. So much memory stored up in that bit of wood and paint.

Kristen remembers the object from Gabriella's file. The very first gift she'd bought *anyone* with her own money. A milestone, obviously. But also a precious memory because her mother kept it at her office every year after and boasted to her coworkers that her daughter had bought it for her. Now, with Gabriella's mother dead these three years, it is a connection between them.

Kristen should have stopped him. Or she should use magic to fix the nutcracker. But it seems too late for that. Gabriella will never be able to unsee the nutcracker on the floor. Like trash.

An image flashes through Kristen's mind of the office upstairs where Uncle Coleman sits: her mother's office. She sees it as it once was, with cheery lavender walls, framed doll photos, and trash bags. Four trash bags of Mom's things were tossed aside to make way for the painters and decorators coming to prepare the office for a new COO.

Kristen shakes herself; this story is not about her.

"Was it worth it? The secret you discovered?" Kristen asks. Wondering if she can make this one man see what he's done and try, even if it's impossible, to make it right.

She has a feeling that this whole fiasco is going to come back at her with the rest of the family. They will blame her for Jack having been at Gabriella's desk as if she goaded him. Or outright gave him the idea. And it isn't true this time. But Kristen, for once, doesn't care if she gets credit for someone else's bad deeds. Because she knows it isn't true. She was stepping back.

But that doesn't make her feel any less guilty. The only thing that gives her any comfort at all is that note she watched Gabriella make on the Naughty-and-Nice list. *May the punishment suit the crime.* She is very excited to see what sort of punishment Gabriella meets out. Not great great great great great Grandpa's style, she'd bet.

Jack seems to be ignoring her question. So Kristen glances sidelong at Terrance; he shrugs as if to say she should move on.

Jack Drummer is not ignoring Kristen's question. He is thinking about it. He is thinking about the tears in Gabriella's eyes. And how long she stayed at her desk before walking stiffly to the bathroom and not coming back for fully twenty minutes, with her eyes red and her face puffy. She cried. Over a broken nutcracker. *Shit.* Over her *dead mother's nutcracker.* That *he* broke. And he yelled at her about it like a jerk. He knows full well he was a jerk. What he doesn't know is what to do about it. He said he was sorry. And she was right when she said what is done is done. He can't fix it now.

"So what did you find out, Jack?" Kristen tries again.

"I should have figured it out sooner really," Jack replies a bit hollowly. He is still thinking about her earlier question. But this one is much easier to answer.

"There were plenty of clues. Hanukkah started over the weekend, and when everyone got back, the people who celebrate found cards and little bags of chocolate coins on their desks. It wasn't much, but it also wasn't anything HR would have come up with."

Kristen tosses a look over her shoulder at Terrance and mouths, "did we get that on camera?" He nods and shrugs. So they must have gotten it but not addressed it. That's fine. She can go back and address it. Ha! Kristen is downright tickled by Gabriella now. No Claus, at least not one that Kristen has ever heard of, has gifted anyone for an out-of-family holiday. They are strictly in the business of Christmas. But Gabriella is using family funds to give another holiday attention! Yes. Tickled positively pink.

"Then Tuesday, they all got individual donuts on their desks; no one knew where they were from." Jack shakes his head somewhere between impressed and offended. Or maybe *jealous.* "Trust her to look up appropriate food for Hanukkah and pass it out. And she had donuts for the whole staff in the break room with a note on it asking people if they knew the significance of fried food and Hanukkah."

Kristen grins and starts making notes for herself on her phone. There is a question she doesn't know the answer to. But she will. If she has to find it out through individual interviews or internet searches. Gabriella is certainly an interesting Santa.

Grandma would love it. Grandma who always laughed the wildest of any family member, always sang the loudest, and believed the most, even more than the family members with a share of the Claus magic. Grandma who always...*forgave* the fastest.

She was a bit like Gabriella really. Sweet. Good to her core. Generous. And forgiving.

Kristen observes the man before her in silence once more. What would Grandma do with a naughty boy like him? How would she help him to improve? It was always about improving with her. Anyone could be better than their worst mistakes. Anyone could learn and change and grow. But it wasn't punishment that made them change; it was understanding.

"Why do you care what she's up to?" Kristen probes softly.

"Why do I care what she was up to?" Jack looks up from his private contemplations, remembering to include the question in the answer. "I don't know." He lies. He knows. But he doesn't want to know. Especially not now that he has screwed up so royally. It would make it worse to know now. It might ache to realize he's screwed up his chance with Gabriella.

"I don't, I guess." Jack shrugs. Playing light again, even if it means potentially getting himself in some hot water at work. "This job isn't that hard. I keep three books in my desk for the downtime. It used to just be one, but I finished a book in the morning once and actually spent the rest of the day talking to my coworkers. It was pretty rough."

Kristen is unimpressed with the attempt to deflect, but she can play along. "Why not surf the web?"

"Surf the web? Oh no, the company isn't catching me in that trap. If they want to fire me, they'll have to come up with a real cause," Jack says in a mock threatening voice.

"Funny," Kristen baits. "I don't think I saw you reading at all this week. Did we miss it?"

"I guess I didn't get in much reading this week." Jack shrugs again. Really the man needs to learn more physical expressions of disinterest. "Gabriella was the more entertaining mystery," he admits, and a smile crawls over his features. "She'll make a decent Secret Santa. Not that Mr. Coleman knew that. She just commits herself to every task like it has epic importance!" He scoffs. "Anyway, now that I solved the mystery, that's the end of it."

"Did you talk to Gabriella much, that day you finished your novel early?"

"Gabriella didn't work here yet when I ran out of books to read," Jack responds as if there is no more importance to this statement than *oh, it's sunny outside*.

There is significance. He knows it. Kristen and Terrance, and even Andrew—who is currently thinking through the best way to approach the boss sequence in his RPG—knows it. But it seems Jack will be allowed to pretend for the time being.

"Tell me, Jack, to your knowledge, have you ever been on the naughty list before?" Kristen inquires. She knows the answer. She checked into him over the weekend.

Jack Hilary Drummer has been on the naughty list, with double checks and thus no hope of getting back on the good list, seven times. Not that high, really. But if you add into it that he has had at least one naughty check against him for about eighteen of his twenty-nine years, it sounds a bit worse. It could fairly be stated that while not exclusively naughty, Jack Drummer was not an excessively good boy.

"Have I ever been on the naughty list before?" Jack laughs. "Maybe Gabriella will give you Santa's number, and we can find out for sure. Honestly though, before I broke that crap nutcracker I hadn't done anything worthy of the naughty list." Jack feels himself flinch as he calls the nutcracker crap. Seeing Gabriella's expression again when she threw his words back in his face.

That piece of crap *was my favorite because it belonged to my mother.*

But Jack cannot acknowledge any of that now, with these people. So he keeps going. He keeps it light.

They cast him as the class clown, so that's what he'll be. "Stealing the deer was just a bit of fun; she is sooo easy to goad. And what I said about never dating her—"

"That isn't what you said," Kristen points out again. Tempted, oh so tempted to make him watch the recording of himself and see his blushes. And his far-off stares as he spoke.

"Let's not get into this again," Jack snaps because he knows, he *knows* he didn't say he would never date her. But he begins to wish he had. It would be so much easier if that decision were his. "The point is...I don't mind being on the naughty list. Knowing Gabriella, she'll pass out chocolate coal or something. She's a soft touch."

Little does he know that at this very moment, that soft touch is hard at work concocting twelve days' worth of torment exclusively to teach Jack Drummer a lesson.

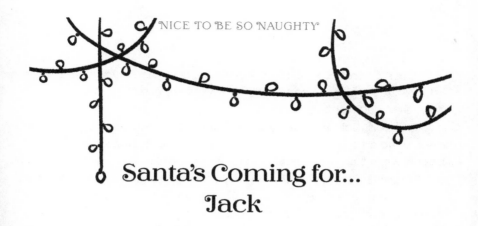

Santa's Coming for...
Jack

"**L**eaving aside Jack and what he did, the camera saw a few... interesting things on your computer before you came over. Can we talk about that?" Kristen inquires.

It is Wednesday, December fifth, at approximately ten-thirty in the morning. Kristen has convinced Gabriella to have a private chat with her and the film crew about her Secret Santa assignment. So they are sequestered in the basement break room.

"Of course," Gabriella replies pleasantly, though she is thinking how convenient it must be for people like Kristen who can just separate the pieces of their life and lay aside the ones that are disturbing or harmful. Gabriella has no such ability.

But she can answer questions about one thing and not another. She can do that. She can do that. She can do that.

"You already know about my secret assignment; what else can I tell you?"

Kristen smiles softly, not her usual smirk, showing a tiny bit of understanding for the woman in front of her. But also...because this is Kristen a guiding determination not to let understanding stop her from pursuing what she needs.

"Correct me if I'm wrong, but a Secret Santa exchange doesn't usually include a *Naughty-and-Nice* list, does it?"

"Does Secret Santa traditionally include the *Naughty-and-Nice* list? No. It's a gift exchange with a mystery person. And usually not even gifts you want."

"Did Mr. Coleman suggest a Naughty-and-Nice list?" Kristen asks, unable to entirely conceal her amusement. She's just pleased that it wasn't an outright chuckle.

Gabriella actually smirks briefly at that question. "I believe Mr. Coleman's four instructions were to: give out eleven days of silly presents and one present of around a forty dollar value," Gabriella says, holding up her pointer finger. "Stick to the budget," she adds her middle finger. "Make it good!" Up goes her index finger. "He followed this up with 'you tech people can like...see what they look at, right? What they're interested in? Use that. And," up goes the pinky. "Don't offend the religious objectors."

Kristen can't hold back a chuckle.

"Oh, my goodness! He came right out and said it?"

"Well, no." Gabriella bobs her head to the side, literally biting her tongue. The truth is he did not use those specific words with Gabriella. He was *very* careful not to. So careful that Gabriella felt those words screaming at her. Felt so uncomfortable she was tempted to try and organize a walkout. But no, he hadn't actually said the words.

"No." Gabriella shakes her head, sighing. She shouldn't have said that to his...*niece*...maybe. And not on camera.

"No. Sorry. I believe what he said was 'do not offend *anyone*. Last year several people complained that they were discriminated against.' I...I..." Gabriella breaks off breathing deeply and holds the breath inside her chest brittlely. She will say it again, but she will make it sound as ordinary as she can. She breathes out. "I...was being hyperbolic again, but that is inappropriate."

Kristen laughs. "Don't worry, you aren't under oath. *Yet!*" Kristen adds with unparalleled glee. *Oooo, that would be so fun!* "So, back to the Naughty-and-Nice list. Why did you make one if it isn't part of Secret Santa?"

Now Gabriella feels uncomfortable for a different reason. "I suppose it started out as a petty way to express my frustration at the *child* I share a cubicle wall with." Gabriella bites out honestly but strives to sound playful. "And then it seemed a good place to note down the sorts of things people liked. Like Brian is into classic cars, he goes to shows, and collects mini ones. And Gloria has an Etsy shop where she sells things she knits. That sort of thing, stuff that helps me to get to know them."

"Do you plan to punish the people on the naughty side of the list?"

At this, Gabriella smirks. She opens her mouth, her eyes practically twinkling, but at that moment, the door to the break room bangs open.

Stan jumps backwards as four pairs of eyes swing his way.

"Shit, sorry. Hadn't realized anyone was in here," He spins around glaring. "Is that why you asked me to get your refill?" He screams across the room at Jack while still standing in the doorway.

Gabriella looks out the door and across the room at the child still trying to fuck with her and glares.

Kristen is annoyed as well. *More* than a little annoyed because she really liked that look on Gabriella's face, and now it's gone.

"Was there something *you* needed, Stan?" Kristen inquires.

"No...no. I'll go to two."

"You do that," Kristen says with a touch more bite than is required. "And do shut the door behind you."

She turns back to Gabriella with a sigh and sees that again the woman has fisted her hands at her thighs when she was starting to look more relaxed. She's taking her calming breaths and fighting with all her might to keep her hand from punching her thigh. They've caught that on camera a few times now. Mostly as a result of Jack's antics.

In fact, it was *exclusively* because of him. Gabriella is generally able to hide the parts of herself she's uncomfortable with. Even that apology for correctly interpreting Uncle Coleman's words...such a death grip she has on her wilder side. Kristen stares at those fisted hands, and she starts forming an idea. A way to show off the real Gabriella, not in flashes of rage or genius, but the actual her. She'll need to get the boys to agree. But she bets she can do it. Getting Gabriella to agree should be no issue. Sweet, good girls always have trouble saying no.

"Right, sorry about that. Maybe we should make up a sign so we don't get accidentally interrupted in the future."

"That was no accident," Gabriella says, her voice low and annoyed and her eyes still trained out the small window in the break room door, staring right at Jack. Kristen would bet, and be right as she frequently is, that Gabriella has forgotten the cameras are rolling, in her anger. "There are rumors going around that 'Secret Santa is going to be just one person this year.' I know Jack is spreading it. Nosey, lazy, *nutcracker breaking*," Gabriella flinches at her own words, no longer able to resist the compulsion to strike her own thigh, though not as hard as she did yesterday when she confronted Jack. "Not at all subtle; I have to be entertained every second of the day, Jack! That's strike three." Gabriella finishes, breathing out.

"Strike three," Kristen chuckles softly.

"I know, I know. *I know*." Gabriella repeats it for the third time, smiling sarcastically at Kristen as she says it. "You want to know, *doesn't Santa only check his list twice*? Right?"

"Exactly so." Kristen grins, and Gabriella sees that sparkle on her skin and the impish tilt of her lips again. There is something...*extra* about this young woman. Something almost magical.

"Yeah, well, it's my role now," Gabriella remarks smugly. "And I'm going to update *the man, the myth, the legend*, to the woman, the evil genius. Which is why, to answer your earlier question, yes. Jack is going to be punished. I'll crush his lazy, attention-grubbing spirit."

Kristen chuckles. "Careful. Keep talking like that, and I may fall in love with you."

Gabriella grins back, not for a moment believing that this will come to pass. Kristen, she is quite sure, rather like Gabriella herself, has never been in love. They both always hold something back. And if you can do that, it cannot really be called love, can it?

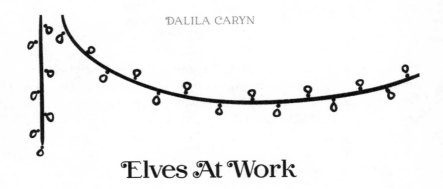

Elves At Work

Later that evening, across town, while they wait for the agreed-on time for an off-site shoot. Kristen, Terrance, and Andrew work on their project. Currently, Terrance's laptop is open, displaying footage of a talking head interview with the office receptionist.

MAYA

How did secret Santa work last year? (rolls eyes) Badly.

"That's a great cut point," Kristen says with a buzzy sort of focus. She hasn't had this much fun on a group project since, maybe ever.

"Right," Terrance responds a bit snottily; Kristen is soooo bossy. "But how about we discuss which angle you are going for *this week* before we actually start putting together footage for a project we haven't even finished."

"Sure thing," Kristen says with biting pleasantness. When she responds, her tone becomes condescending and instructive; her go-to weapons of choice. "Through the angle of the botched Secret Santa from last year and Gabriella's being singled out to do *all* the work this year, I intend to illuminate the company's failure to inhabit a modern world. Their lack of understanding of their employee needs, inadequacy to provide a positive working environment, their systemic sexism, exclusion of what Uncle Coleman likes to call 'alternative religious groups' and if the opportunity presents itself, racism."

Terrance is silent for a full ten seconds as he stares at her open-mouthed. "Last week, you were after reality show drama."

"Oh, did I forget to mention? We should throw some of that in too."

"Why? That doesn't go with your destroy my family's business theme at all!" Terrance shouts.

At this very moment, Andrew is not looking at either of his partners. He has adopted that time-honored role in group projects of the guy who just goes along. When they get to sound work, he will do his part. And as for the rest, he doesn't much care. If he gets a C, he'll be fine, and both Terrance and Kristen tend to be A students. He isn't worried. They take this *way* too seriously.

Kristen quite enjoys goading Terrance. He is too serious by half but very talented. She's been noticing it in the raw footage. Not the stationary cameras she got her father to pay for, but the ones Terrance operates as they move about the office. He has a good eye for revealing personality and telling a story with only the way he angles his lens. He can do exactly what she's asking for, and he knows it. So it's fun to rile him into resisting.

"I have no intention of destroying the family business. Merely revealing its foibles to prove the point I've been trying to make to my family for years. The old guard needs to go. It's time for new leadership."

Terrance laughs. "Who are you? Machiavelli? You're trying to use a school project to institute a coup." At Kristen's pleased nod, Terrance keeps pressing. *My God, this girl! She...she's like a whirlwind of genius ideas with anarchistic tendencies. Who raised her?* "So why the drama! Why don't I shoot it in sepia colors and get shots of the employees when they're having intestinal problems."

Kristen giggles. "Because we want people to watch. Also, because Professor Pembroke loves reality show drama. He's shown us no less than seven episodes of The Real Housewives; you have to speak to your audience. I want an A. Don't you?"

Terrance again stares openmouthed at Kristen for fully ten seconds. He's counting. Trying to come up with a way to respond and do so calmly. She has a very strange habit of making him incredibly angry when usually he considers himself fairly zen.

Terrance turns back to the computer screen. "I'll mark it here, but I'm not cutting yet."

"Natuurlijk," Kristen agrees in Dutch because she knows it annoys him that she speaks multiple languages. She knows enough to get by in eight, but all the Claus's have to learn languages growing up, so it isn't impressive to her.

"Can we see the raw footage from the break room on the second floor? You know, from when Gabriella went in on her *recon* mission," Kristen laughs. Every day she loves this particular project more.

Terrance cues it up without response. He has a new strategy; just don't talk to her. Not at all. Andrew does it, and he seems perfectly content.

The footage starts to play. Maya, Frank, Angelo, and Clara sit in the break room. Maya, the office receptionist, has a friendly smile that tends to put one at ease. Nearly her opposite, Frank, has stiff energy that gives off a constant air of being angry, the exact personality one expects of a doll designer. *Wink. Angelo is a self-appointed funny man with an infectious laugh and a bright spirit. Carol, the head of distribution, is a somewhat prim-looking woman, with a gentle presence when relaxed and all business at other times.

MAYA (excited whisper)
I hear there's going to be Secret Santa again this year, but it's just one person buying all the presents.

FRANK (angry growl)
That'd have to be Coleman, then. Unless the new limit is one dollar. I don't know which is worse.

ANGELO
Coleman! (Snorts) How is that even Secret Santa anyway? The whole fun is guessing who stole the printer toner for your gift. (Laughs uproariously)

"He has a great laugh. We may want to use that a few times," Kristen remarks.

"Yeah," Terrance agrees. "But I think we have some better shots of it later in his individual interview." Terrance cues it up on a second laptop.

ANGELO
How did Secret Santa work last year? (laughs brightly) Honestly, it wasn't that bad. Just a little (waves arms indefinitely) Stressful right in the middle of a busy time of year. So a lot of people half-assed it. You get a name that you must keep secret, and for the twelve days before the office closes for the year, you give them stuff like candy, coffee (shrug), whatever, and one big gift on the last day; the limit is forty dollars.

"Sorry, that's not it. It must be..."

"Wait, wait. I'm liking this," Kristen remarks brightly. "What if we started off with interspersed clips of all the people we asked about last year's secret Santa."

"Yeah." Terrance agrees, head bobbing. "And we could cut in spurts of Angelo laughing and Frank glaring at the camera."

"Exactly. And there are those frames when Carol is rolling her eyes and like...

"Pulling herself up with a deep breath to rein in her temper?" Terrance suggests with a laugh.

"Exactement!" Kristen replies in French this time and watches Terrance's lips nearly twitch. Was he going to smile? How intriguing. Smiling at something she was doing.

Terrance, in point of fact, had to bite down on his cheek to keep from outright grinning. She is such a show-off. And so spoiled and maniacal. He should not, now or ever, encourage her outrageous behavior by doing anything as responsive as smiling at her games. But it is getting harder to resist the longer they work together. Because whatever other insults one wants to level at her, and there were quite a few and all accurate, she is *very* good at anything she sets her mind to doing.

It just seems she sets her mind to evil far more often than good. For the next little while though, they don't talk much except about the footage, doing a rough cut of her idea, with Kristen telling him "si" *yes* or saying "perpekto" *perfect* or "ne" *no;* all her responses in various languages, but always choosing simple enough words for him to figure out her meaning. She is so annoying but weirdly cute about it. With incredible effort, Terrance manages to resist smiling every single time.

CAROL

Four of us are J. W., there are at least six Jewish people I know of, and Miriam is Muslim, and Andrew's (beat) (rolls eyes) I don't know a hippy, maybe. He doesn't celebrate because he dislikes the commercial nature of the holiday (shakes head). Really? We work for a company that designs dolls. Our biggest seller is Krissy the Christmas doll; she has a pet reindeer and is somehow the child of this (beat more eye rolling) Thousands of years old couple. Maybe she's adopted. I mean, she comes in several races. Well, three-ish. Black, white, and vaguely non-white.

Kristen laughs privately at all of Carol's complaints. And only just resists telling her workmates that the Krissy doll was based on her. Well, the white one. She loves that Carol is pointing out what Kristen, Holly, Klaus, and well, really any number of the children of her generation of Claus have. Man, she is really loving this project.

Cut to Maya.

MAYA

Then there was this screw-up because a memo went out calling it mandatory. I warned him, but Mr. Coleman never listens to me. He said, "everybody loves Secret Santa."

Cut to Angelo laughing.

ANGELO

The kicker is all these people refused to participate for religious reasons. And the boss just says fine, but doesn't adjust anything! (Speechless with laughter)

Cut to Hannah

HANNAH

Honestly, Secret Santa never bothered me. I participated the first three years I worked here. The problem was that pesky word they used in the memo: mandatory. Just because I was okay with it doesn't mean every Jewish member of staff would be. Or every member of staff, period. So I signed onto the complaint. The problem was always with the executive level of the company. And the fix was so simple (precise and disdainful) And never done. All they had to do was send out another email that said, "our bad, we meant to say Secret Santa was optional," and it would have been over. But Coleman gets very defensive, and it makes him overlook tiny details.

Cut to Frank red-faced with restrained anger.

FRANK

I bought ten days' worth of nice Christmasy treats for Carol before getting yanked into HR for religiously discriminating against her.

Cut to Carol with a heavy sigh and a forced smile.

CAROL

My complaint was always with management. I told HR that. I don't begrudge anyone else their celebrations. I just don't participate. The trouble was nothing to do with Frank. I would have continued to get the presents and left him with a thank you at the end. But I didn't want management putting me or anyone else in that awkward position again. That's what the complaint was about.

Cut to Angelo, overcome with laughter.
Cut to Frank.

FRANK

It was seriously frustrating. And! (Spittle at the edge of mouth, enraged) When I tried to sign on to her complaint with management (pokes own chest), I was called combative. Can you believe that?

Cut to Angelo, overcome with laughter.
Cut to Maya.

MAYA

I didn't get gifts. My secret Santa was supposed to be Miriam from the design team. But when she and the others opted out, Coleman forgot to reassign any of us. (Shakes head, sighs) So like fourteen people went without gifts but bought stuff for other people.

Cut to Angelo, drying the tears brought on by laughter.

ANGELO

So me and Ed, trying to be nice, stole a bunch of supplies from the closet for the people who were getting stiffed! (chuckles hard enough to bring on more tears) And you know what, we never even got thanked.

Cut to Frank glaring.

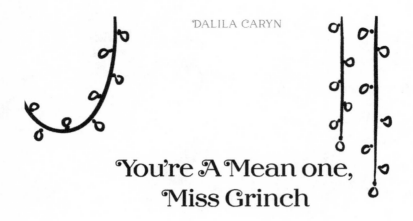

You're A Mean one, Miss Grinch

A t this very moment, still Wednesday, December fifth, the documentary film crew has made an agreed-upon visit to apartment three-hundred-and-seventeen at an undisclosed street address in Burbank, CA. The residence of one Gabriella Anjelica Cruz and her sister Maria Estrella Cruz, a student at the California Institute of the Arts in Santa Clarita. The crew arranged to meet with Gabriella outside of work, *this one time*, to do a more thorough interview about her secret project, away from some unnamed interfering persons.

It is a small but neat apartment with a very homey atmosphere. There is a couch with a snowman blanket spread across its back. A large pine tree is centered in the living room window, fully loaded with lights and ornaments. On the wall is a snowflake design made up of Christmas cards, some very worn and beat up, others clearly new. An easel is set up with a large handwritten Naughty-and-Nice list with drawings of Christmas-style cartoons decorating it. A counter separates the living room from a small kitchen. Where Gabriella stands at the counter buzzing with energy as she stirs a bowl of what will eventually be sugar cookies. A finished batch of snowflake-shaped cookies cools on the counter in front of her.

Maria stands at the easel, sketching a hunky toy soldier holding a drum with his head hanging sideways next to Jack Drummer's name, referencing a picture she keeps referring to on her phone.

Christmas music plays quietly in the background, a mix of classic renditions and modern poppy songs.

Gabriella smiles evilly as she stirs and responds to Kristen's question. "The plan is coming along quite nicely, thank you! I implemented phase one before I left work today. Like the original twelve-day Secret Santa our work set up in the past, the first few days of *gifts* are small, and it builds from there." Gabriella breaks off to cackle. The speed and intensity with which she stirs her cookies begin to grow. Here, in her home, she is less the shy, polite Gabriella the film crew has come to know and more her *unwound* self. Like a child's toy turned a bit too tightly, the release is an explosive thing to witness. *Excellent,* Kristen basks in the success of her plan.

"By the time I'm through with him, Jack will be reduced to a pathetic, regretful puddle of mush." Gabriella beams at the camera. Making Kristen gasp slightly to cover her near explosion of laughter.

But Kristen cannot draw in enough breath to ask the question she needs answered. Maria looks between her sister and the grinning film students. Her gaze refocuses on her art as her amused voice rises up to help out these young artists like herself.

"I think they meant the plan for the *nice* list. Not for revenge," Maria points out. She sneaks a quick grin at the camera and teases. "You know most people think she's sweet."

"I am sweet." Gabriella defends, entirely unrepentant for having been excited over her plans for Jack. They took a lot of work, and she always takes pride in her work. "I'm just not a pushover. Santa could really fill out his nice list if he'd put a little more focus into his punishments than coal."

Kristen fights hard not to roar with laughter. There would be no way to cut it out of the scene, and she *really* wants this scene in her documentary. What most people don't know is that lumps of coal for bad kids went out around the same time as Santa found the woman the world knows as Mrs. Claus and the family called Grandma. She was not at all fond of punishment. Not at all fond of exclusion. She believed in reform and forgiveness. Redemption. She believed that if Christmas was about miracles, then that should be the focus. The good children deserved rewards, but it was the bad children who *needed* miracles.

And though Kristen knows Grandma managed to reform Santa into her way of thinking, she is certain that little comments like Gabriella's are bound to irk his pride. Kristen loves it.

Gabriella's sister, Maria, already entirely at ease in front of the camera, glances back and winks over her sister's antics. Kristen is oddly charmed by their relationship. She has no siblings. But so many cousins, and even the siblings among them, though they love each other, would almost certainly not choose to live together in a tiny apartment. Or any size apartment, for that matter.

"Anyway, this isn't revenge." Gabriella goes on, undeterred by her sister's censure. "It's a lesson. I start with a simple, annoying reminder that he didn't need to be in my space. Even to solve his little mystery." She sets down the bowl and leans against the counter, looking intently into the camera. "I programmed his computer *remotely* to change his wallpaper to Christmas-themed stuff. Every time he tries to change it, it will get more Christmassy."

Excellent, Kristen thinks again. She knew this girl had a dark side. Kristen basks in the bright, magical lights that dance around Gabriella as she plans. Part of it is definitely the Claus magic, but not all. No. Not all. Gabriella has magic all her own.

The Claus power should make her more prone to attracting miracles or magic beings. It would certainly help her discover the secret desires of those around her and feel their levels of Christmas spirit. And being elf magic, it is bound to encourage her to enjoy things many humans frown on, like housebreaking for the purpose of spreading joy or accepting sweet offerings as an encouragement to return the next year. Or even to stand out like a bright beacon of joy and goodness. But this pride, this effort, and joy in her own skills are all Gabriella. And there is something else about her, too, some secret ingredient that Kristen cannot name that...for perhaps the first time in her life is making Kristen see the beauty in the magic.

"The first wallpaper is just a snowy forest," Gabriella explains enthusiastically. "By the time it changes five times, it's eight cats with reindeer antlers and reins made of flashing lights."

Everyone laughs. How could they not? This is *fantastic* revenge. Subtle. Annoying. And the sort of thing to drive Jack, with his *I'm too mature for Christmas* attitude, nutty.

"This isn't even her at a ten," Maria says proudly. "And she can go *waaaaaaay* beyond ten. It's actually great fun to watch if it isn't aimed at you." She smiles evilly, and the resemblance is suddenly quite obvious.

Most people, if seeing Gabriella, with her wavy dark hair and big brown eyes all dressed up in Christmas-themed sweaters over neatly pressed pants, wouldn't immediately relate her to Maria, who is somewhat shorter, with the side of her head buzz cut and the straightened comb over died black and blue, wearing somewhat sloppy attire. Neither woman is one to vanish into the background but in such different ways. But in those evil smiles, one sees sisters.

"The plan builds from there. Day two has his screen saver rotating through famous Christmas movie moments." Gabriella is warming to the subject as she rolls the finished dough into plastic wrap and puts it in the freezer of her small fridge. "And he sees his screen saver a lot. Since he makes zero effort at doing work between calls. All his punishments will serve as reminders to keep his nose out of other people's business. A few "accidentally" shared job applications and subsequent rejections. It culminates in what he'd hate the most—"

Gabriella's pause for dramatic effect is totally ruined by her sister's perfectly timed spin and sarcastic statement to the cameras. "A visit from the elves! *Dom Dom Do-oo-oo-oom,*" she finishes in a silly sing-song voice.

Terrance looks at Kristen over the top of the camera and grins. And silently, Kristen has to agree, *this house is gold!* The dynamic between the sisters and Gabriella's comfort in her own environment makes for some of the most compelling stuff they've gotten yet.

"No." Gabriella sticks her tongue out at her sister, clearly annoyed with the interruption. "An accidentally emailed clip of his ex-girlfriend turning him down flat when he proposed."

Wow!

Wow. Kristen may have to revise her up to this moment held views on her own sexuality. She has never been so turned on. Gabriella definitely has a naughty girl inside. And Kristen is *very* into it.

But it seems not everyone in the room is equally impressed. Her sister's arms drop to her side, and she looks at Gabriella with a horrified expression.

"Damn, bruiser, that's a bit mean. It was just a nutcracker. How'd you even find something like that?"

For a moment, there is silence as Gabriella takes in her sister's judgement. Then she turns away, filling the bowl with soapy water in the sink. Terrance moves to try and get a better angle on her face as Gabriella works with her back to them.

"It wasn't easy actually," Gabriella says in that same bright voice she uses at work, her false joy. As if she hasn't noticed that anything is wrong. But her motions grow steadily more jerky and stiff, betraying that she has indeed heard and taken in her sister's disapproval. "I could only find innocuous things about him. He doesn't have *any* social media accounts. He doesn't bring many personal things into the office. So I had to get creative. I backtracked through his parents' social media. His mother's account was a wealth of information about his past."

Gabriella spins away from the sink with excited eyes and soap on her hands as she explains with pride her triumphant discovery. At the easel, Maria lays down her markers, her body seeming to slow down. Her breathing evening out as she moves slowly closer to her sister.

"She'd deleted all this stuff from a few years ago," Gabriella goes on brightly. But from the corner of her eyes, she watches her sister approach. Gabriella *knows* she is getting overly intense on this subject, but she can't stop talking until she's finished saying this. She can't, and the closer Maria comes, the more the intensity builds. Maria can't stop her. She can't. And Gabriella is sure Maria won't make a thing of this in front of strangers with cameras. Will she?

"She'd gotten rid of photo albums," Gabriella explains. Her hands fist at her sides. Unconsciously her right fist begins to jerk into her upper thigh. "And all these posts that had him tagged in them. Then I found his old account!" The words nearly leap from her lips, so important are they. She feels her fist punching. "And I figured out about the fiancee that wasn't."

"Gabriella," Maria says softly. She can feel her sister's intensity growing, and it's partially her fault. She shouldn't have called it "just" a nutcracker. That's minimizing the trauma and disregarding the pain. She didn't mean to do that. But...these people have cameras pointed right at her sister, and Gabriella has already given them permission to use the footage.

Who knows how they will cut this. Look at them salivating with every bit of rising intensity from her sister. Gabriella needs to wind down. And Maria needs to help her without making too big a deal out of it because her sister has been through enough. She doesn't need rich kid strangers making her out to be the villain of their project when she isn't. She is...fucking amazing! And there is nothing at all wrong with—most—of what she has planned for Jack.

"Everyone gets upset when someone dumps them," Gabriella is saying, rubbing her left wet hand, up and down her pant legs, as her right-hand punches, trying to ignore her sister. "But he went off the grid. And he's techy—and not a slouch at it either. I mean, he only graduated cum laude, but I've seen his work. He's pretty good." *Almost done. Almost done. Almost done. Just get out these last few sentences, and you'll be fine. Just get them out. Just get them out.* Gabriella tells herself, her eyes boring into her sister, willing her not to touch.

"It didn't make sense, so I dug. And I found the clip! It hadn't exactly gone viral, but locally yeah! *Valentine proposal fail!* It's kind of sad, actually," she says and breathes out heavily. Gabriella's intensity is by no means gone, but she got the story out, the plan out, and that helps. *He'll be wrecked.*

"Gabriella Anjelica Cruz," Maria whispers and stretches out a hand.

There is no further back for Gabriella to retreat from her sister, but she shakes her head tightly, and Maria drops her hand.

Maria picks up two slightly overcooked cookies she knows Gabriella won't use and holds one out to her sister like a peace offering.

Gabriella yanks up the cookie and turns her back to the camera; a loud crunch sounds as she bites into the slightly over-baked sugar. Maria makes a big show of getting in the way of the camera, swaying back and forth as if it is an accident.

"Oh, sorry. Did you want a cookie?" She asks in a teasing voice. "Were you wanting a shot of the cookies?" She laughs, but she is glaring hard enough at the man with the camera to make it clear he isn't getting a shot of her sister right now.

Terrance backs off and lets Maria lead him to see her drawings on the Naughty and Nice list.

By the time Gabriella finishes her cookie, her punching hand has eased. She lifts a dish towel next to the sink and begins drying off the counters and the faucet, her hands returning to the same, already dried places, once, three times fast, once again.

"The trouble is you aren't leaving room for him to properly feel remorse and change," Maria says as if the other moment never happened, taking a bite of her own cookie.

Gabriella's intensity is ebbing. She folds the towel and hangs it off a bar above the sink. Her hands alternate between fisting and opening so her pointers can jab against her leg in a one-three-one pattern.

"If you go through with the whole thing, he'll feel victimized." Maria's voice is calm, coming and going in a cadence like an even tide. A steady presence to lead her sister back from the brink. "Maybe that's why Santa passes out coal. I doubt Jack intentionally broke the nutcracker. It was—"

"Quit saying that!" Gabriella snaps with her back to her sister. "It wasn't just a nutcracker, just a nutcracker, *just*" the words vibrate from her, her whole being quaking.

"I wasn't going to say that again," Maria says calmly.

Gabriella spins around and glares at her sister. Maria returns the look with a smirk and a raised eyebrow. After a bit more silent glaring, Gabriella walks forward and leans her head across the counter, touching it to her sisters. And Maria's right arm comes up to rub her sister's back.

"It isn't *just* the nutcracker," Gabriella has to say. Has to finish, intent on the object's importance in her life. "And it isn't only this incident he's being punished for. He is always needling me about being too 'up-tight.'"

"That is guy speak for *you make me feel lazy*," Maria remarks. Gabriella moves to put the cooled cookies into containers.

"I know. And I try to let it go. I was even letting it go when he messed with my deer. I know he thinks he's being cute for the camera." Gabriella pulls a face at the camera in question. Focusing her hands on her task and her breathing into a steady rhythm, and for once, since she's already had a very small outburst on camera, she tells the full truth too. "But I can literally feel it under my skin when people mess with my space." She breathes out, watching furtively to see how her words are being taken. "So I remind myself that isn't really my space." She takes a breath and holds it. "*This* is my space."

She forces herself to look around her kitchen. Around her home. She invited these people into her home, wanting to feel more comfortable when they spoke. But maybe she should have stayed uncomfortable. She is so used to uncomfortable that it's nearly normal to think about every move her body makes, to count before she breathes or stands, to brace for being brushed by strangers. But at home, she isn't braced, and the real her is coming out, and that is risky. Behind Kristen, she can see a framed photo of Mom. Mom, who would have encouraged her to invite the film crew here. Encouraged her to be herself with them. Mom, who always used to tell Gabriella that the real her was wonderful, special, and strong.

Every time she thinks of the broken nutcracker, she hears those words crack inside like they aren't real. Aren't true. Mom never saw what Gabriella was like after she died. She wasn't strong then. She retreated from the world. And here she is here trying to let the world back in. Trying to let more of the world in than before. Trying to make her mother proud, but it isn't easy. It's frightening. She is not entirely sure how to be herself, but also entirely unable to be anyone else. How can that be so? But it is. So she doesn't stop to examine it, she just allows herself voice.

"I'll think I've let it go," Gabriella says, looking not at the camera or the college students. But at her mother's photo. "And he— He didn't just mess with my space; he *invaded* it!" Gabriella feels her hands gesturing without her leave and forces them fisted to her sides. "He broke things. He made a mess. And all to poke around in my computer, which he could have done from *his* cubical!"

The room is momentarily silent with the exclamation. Gabriella's hands unclench, and she stares, waiting for her mother to move in the frame and tell her what to do. The thing is...this (actually punishing Jack) is not at all like her. She might have imagined revenge before, but never planned it. She is used to accepting things. Perhaps not letting them go, but putting them aside because there is nothing to do. She is used to writing people off rather than confronting them.

This isn't like her. But those bells in her head insist on her confronting Jack. Insist on his punishment. It is part of her...magic mission.

"So he needs to be punished." Maria bobs her head from side to side lightly. "Good and punished. But maybe not day twelve level punished," she entreats softly. "Days one through five are pretty awesome. Subtle, annoying, and funny. My favorite is the Santa memo—telling everyone to sit on his lap to deliver their wish lists!" She laughs hard.

Gabriella can't help but be pulled along in her sister's laughter. "Yeah. That one is pretty good. Though it won't exactly say that. But it could still get him into soooo much trouble with HR."

The sisters laugh evilly. And Kristen feels like she should be laughing too, but something hot and wet is slipping down her cheek, and it's all she can do to hide it. But no one notices her as her heart stretches achingly in her chest, one cautious beat after another, reminding her of when she had someone who was on her side no matter what. And longing to—maybe— let someone in again.

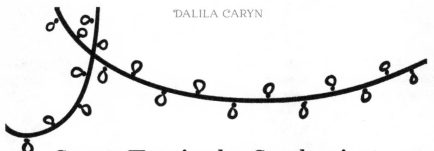

Some Fun in the Sweltering Midwinter

"**Y**ou know you are literally a genius," Maria says to her sister playfully. While Kristen is still busy recovering from the feeling of connection with Gabriella. "You don't have to be an evil one. Remember what Mom always said?"

"You have to be better than the bullies, or you are the bullies," they say in unison, Gabriella annoyed, Maria instructive.

And suddenly, Kristen is fully recovered. *Ugh. No wonder poor Gabriella spent her life being a goody-goody with crap like that shoved down her throat.* Kristen wants to vomit just hearing it.

"Yeah. Yeah." Gabriella rolls her eyes. "Fine. I won't release the video if he shows any sign of contrition before the twenty-first." Gabriella offers incredibly magnanimously both from her perspective and that of Kristen, who is, as previously mentioned, fully onboard with *Operation: Reduce Jack to a Sniveling Puddle of Regret.*

"Generous," Maria says playfully. "So, how about the good folks, Santa? Do you know what you are doing for them?"

Maria seems to be taking over Kristen's job directing this piece. Kristen shoots her a sharp, stay in your lane look that appears not to intimidate Maria. Kristen can only assume she still has tears in her eyes because that look has intimidated people of power, influence, and even occasionally, magic.

"Some of it, yeah." Gabriella latches onto the new subject with gusto. "The donuts went really well. I mean, people were actually talking about Hanukkah and the meaning and their traditions. And that got me thinking. The fun of Secret Santa is someone doing something special for you. But that doesn't begin and end with Christmas; everyone can feel it if you take Christmas out of it and make it a fun way to end the year together.

"It was really bothering me at first because I couldn't think of a way to do what Coleman wanted without excluding people." Gabriella breaks off, breathing deeply; she smiles at the camera crew. "I was excluded from a lot of things in school. And some of the most traumatic stuff happened before *I* understood why I couldn't do things like the other kids. There was this one teacher, Mrs. Stapleton, in *kindergarten,*" she says with great emphasis. "She held me back from recess a lot or forced me to sit alone at this giant table in the back instead of a desk like everyone else. When people would touch me or my things, I would feel it everywhere and...lash out! Scream, throw things, break things... we each had our own set of crayons, but the girl next to me at the beginning of the year kept taking mine.

"I kept saying, those are mine. Those are mine. Those are mine," Gabriella breaks off, realizing she is getting tense and repeating again. But she can still feel that moment. Still hear her teacher in the back of her mind, shouting at her. "Anyway, she wouldn't stop, and I felt...knotted up and explosive and like I was going to burst apart, so I screamed at the top of my lungs, 'Don't touch my things.' Then I broke my crayons in half and threw them— towards the trash can— but one of them hit my teacher, and she was so angry. I can still see her face above me, how frightening she looked as she shouted at me and told me I would sit at the back table *all alone* until I could act *normally.* She said I was *dangerous.*" Gabriella laughs softly, but there is no humor in the sound; it is heavy on the air, like a whimpering animal, and yet Gabriella stands tall, and she forces a wry smile. "I still hear her in my head. Leaving people out is not something I am okay with. A celebration is for everyone who wants to join, or it isn't a celebration. Hence the hours of baking." Gabriella says with forced cheer, trying to break up the tension that has stiffened the room.

"Tomorrow, everyone is going to arrive at work and find a few undecorated snowflake cookies on their desks with a little frosting and decorations and a note saying," she lifts the prototype and reads. "Let's end this year on a sweet note. Please decorate a cookie and give it to someone you don't usually talk to."

Kristen snorts, appalled by such utter sweetness. Such a gooey gumdrop Gabriella is. So why does Kristen adore her?

Maria gives her sister a look like she's stepped into something putrid. "How can you be so sappy and so evil at the same time?"

"I got skills," Gabriella brags, popping her eyebrows.

"So nothing individual then?" Maria asks again before Kristen can do it.

Kristen may kick this girl in a minute. But she doesn't even glare at her because...well, she saw Maria's face while Gabriella was sharing. Her rage on her sister's behalf, sadness over what she'd suffered, even fear for her with the camera's running. It is a very rare thing, though apparently not today, but Kristen is moved again and finding it hard to come between these devoted sisters. Though no amount of sympathy has ever had such an effect on her before.

"It is individual!" Gabriella sounds offended. "I heard at least three people mention how much they love decorating cookies. And by decorating them themselves, it shares their personality. It's individual and global at the same time. And not Christmas specific since they are all snowflakes. It's just winter fun!"

"Unless they're diabetic or have a gluten allergy," Maria points out, tongue in cheek.

"What do you want from me? Not every day will be about food. And I never said they have to *eat* the cookies." Gabriella throws her hands up at her sister.

Maria laughs wickedly. Well aware that Gabriella is going to send her to the store for gluten free ingredients as soon as the film crew leave. It is worth it to annoy her sister.

Kristen really isn't in the headspace to lead the film back where she wants it, so she doesn't even try. Saying they are about wrapped up, she asks the sisters for individual chats with the Christmas tree for background.

Gabriella has been dreading this, but she agreed, so she can't back out now.

Kristen can see how nervous Gabriella is about what happened earlier, and for the first time in her life, she isn't actually all that comfortable making someone more uncomfortable.

"So, tell us about Maria. Who is she? What it's like to live with her? That sort of thing," Kristen prompts because she honestly can't think of anything else.

Gabriella observes Kristen for a silent moment. There is something different about her. Faintly, as if from very far away, Gabriella thinks she may hear sleigh bells ringing sweetly.

"Maria is my little sister. She used to live with some friends near campus at CalArts, but after our mom died, we wanted to be closer together. And anyway," Gabriella says, intentionally loud and playful. "I let her live here rent-free."

"You just like having something to lord over me," Maria calls out from the kitchen.

Gabriella smiles softly. "I like having her here. I feel more grounded with her around. And I think sometimes I help her too. I hope so."

Kristen doesn't press for much more. From the corner of her eye, she can see Terrance noticing, but he doesn't say anything. Really she would have expected him to be mad if she pressed his crush for more about her outburst. Kristen might have been the only one not to mind the intensity with which Gabriella expressed herself or even her plans for Jack, so why they all act like she's the villain, she doesn't know. But she is quite used to from her own family.

Her interview with Maria isn't quite so considerate.

"You seemed to be encouraging your sister to simply forgive Jack's invasion. Do you not see anything wrong with it?"

"I encourage her to do things that are good for her, regardless of if it means being more forgiving of jerks," Maria says, not bothering to repeat the question in the answer and giving Kristen a sharp-eyed look.

"I always thought siblings were supposed to have each other's backs, not pick at them when they are down?" Kristen counters.

"Shows how many siblings you have," Maria says with a laugh. "Everyone needs to be teased. You see, the trick is knowing how to properly needle her. Asking her about gluten and diabetes is going to bug her for hours. But she won't feel it under her skin for ten days."

"Ten days?" Kristen prompts, her tone as flat as she can make it to cover her intent curiosity.

"Oh, it's no joke. Gabriella feels it for ten days minimum when people move her things. Sometimes it's months. But that hasn't happened lately. Honestly—" her voice falls away as she glances into the kitchen where Gabriella has turned up, "It's A Marshmallow World" so as not to hear this interview.

"The nutcracker is really important to her. She bought it for Mom. Now that Mom's gone taking it to the office with her is an extra special connection." Maria stops speaking briefly, and smiles around the tears. "But it being broken doesn't take away the memories, and she'll see that—eventually. Anytime between ten days and a few years. Whenever she stops feeling it break beneath her own skin. I know I was teasing her, but she's not mean." Here she breaks off and gives each member of the film crew a look that lets them know this next bit will be a pointed statement. "And if she weren't getting revenge, I'd find the jerk and punch him myself. She'd do the same for me."

That about wraps up all the film crew needed at the Cruz residence. As the boys pack up the equipment, Kristen looks around the small, comfortable room. And the decorations, some store-bought, some clearly homemade, all well loved. She looks over the framed photos of mother and daughters, of the sisters, of graduations and birthdays, and beach days.

It's a good home. When Kristen was younger, Santa had a tradition. Once every few years, he would bring one of the grandchildren along with him on Christmas Eve to deliver presents. They would go into the different homes and see what Christmas was like for ordinary people. But he hasn't done it in years. Not since Misty disappeared three months before her turn.

Kristen never got her turn. It feels like she is getting that chance now.

As she and the boys walk out of the apartment towards the elevator, Terrance comes up alongside her, and his voice drops to a whisper.

"What the hell is going on? Are you crying?"

She hadn't realized there were tears on her cheeks again.

"It's nothing," Kristen remarks right away.

"Seriously, what is it? We don't have to show...what happened if you don't want."

"Ugh, Terrance, you are so annoying. It isn't that," Kristen rubs the back of her hand on her cheek, drying the tears. "I just..." she shrugs, looking anywhere but at him. "I always wanted a sister."

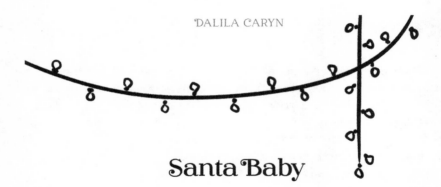

Santa Baby

At this very moment, nine-O-three a.m. Monday, December tenth, Gabriella Anjelica Cruz is basking in the glow of pure joy. She is dancing on cloud nine within her heart. She is humming, both metaphorically with the hum of joy in her heart. And aloud, "You're a Mean one, Mr. Grinch." It seems as though Gabriella has never before felt this wonderful! Euphoric. Her every muscle is relaxed, and her pulse is humming to an accelerated rhythm in anticipation of Jack's arrival. Oh, he is going to *hate* this! *Yay!*

Gabriella's Secret Santa mission commenced the previous Thursday to great success, in her opinion. After all, Jack didn't lift his mystery novel once on Thursday. Too busy trying to eradicate the incursion that was changing his computer wallpaper. And Friday was even worse. He grew so frustrated at one point that he shut down his computer and went to another terminal in the office. An empty desk in marketing. Gabriella had basked in that for a good minute and a half. Then with a gleeful heart and slightly mean spirit, Gabriella figured out what station he was at and, in only a few minutes' work, sent the same *Christmas bug* to that computer!

She could hear jaunty sleigh bell music, like the beginning of "Sleigh Ride" by The Ronettes, in her head all day!

It was glorious!

Not that her joy was only to do with Jack. It wasn't. On Thursday, she kept making excuses to go to other floors and see people exchanging cookies, really messily decorated cookies mostly, then hanging out at each other's desks and chatting. Tiffany, who'd been really down all month, took a cookie to Angelo's desk, and he had her laughing so hard she teared up.

And on Friday, she saw Frank, literally the grouchiest man in the company, grin when he got his rain slicker and the extra one Gabriella left for his wife, sure he wiped the expression away in a flash, but Gabriella had seen it. And it made her happy; the magical sleigh bell music in her head had agreed. Things were going beautifully.

And today, Gabriella burns bright in anticipation of what the day will bring.

The basement IT department of My Best Friend Doll Company is currently crowded with loudly laughing and festively dressed individuals. No, not carolers. Coworkers. A memo was sent out through a dummy account to a select few individuals who are known to be down for a joke. It read:

> Dear Office Buddies,
> Secret Santa is stumped for how to keep making this season bright! If you have any ideas, get yourself on the nice list, by whispering your suggestion in the ear of Santa's merriest helper, Jack Drummer. Head on down to IT Monday morning in your cheeriest attire and make his holiday season bright. Photo's available upon request.
> But remember, this is a workplace. Let's not be too silly, don't sit on my helpers' lap.
>
> Yours Truly,
> Secret Santa

Who sent the email? Hard to say, isn't it, with Gabriella basking in the glow of all the extra bodies? *Wink. Also, it seems so much more widely spread than the few individuals it was intended for. Oh dear, surely this was not Santa's intent? *Ha.*

Let it never be said again that this woman is a pushover.

The elevator dings and Gabriella feels bright like a red bow wrapped around a present. The workers in line by Jack's desk begin to cheer. Gabriella hunkers over her desk and snickers.

Oh, this is marvelous. Why can't it be Christmas every day?

"Gabriella!" Jack shouts over the roar of the crowd. "What did you do now?"

Gabriella makes no move to rise. Really she cannot. She has never been this overcome with laughter before.

"Santa! Santa! Santa! I got here first! Me first," Angelo calls out in a put-on childish voice.

"I don't know what this is about," Jack snarls as the elevator doors bump against his shoulders. "But unless all your email servers crashed, get lost." He still hasn't moved.

He would not have thought that he was uncomfortable with crowds, but with all these Christmas sweater and hat-wearing individuals, he has a sinking suspicion he is about to hear carols, or watch a skit. And really...he can't stand it when untalented people stand in front of him, perform and then want his opinion.

He doesn't know how much more of this he can take. At first, Gabriella wasn't talking to him. She barely acknowledged him on three separate elevator rides. And since he did brake her stuff, he figured she had a right. So he took his lumps.

Then—on the first day of the secret Santa event—Gabriella messed with his computer wallpaper. Which was actually sort of genius, if quite annoying.

He hadn't connected it with her at first and only tried to change it from the snow-capped mountain scene because it was weird that it was different from the Hawaiian beach it usually featured. Then it got worse, children building snowmen with a Norman Rockwell-style town behind them. Strange. He tried again and saw Santa's workshop with elves building toys, and suddenly he saw the hand of the prankster. He very nearly left that one. It was sort of cute. Jack isn't all that into Christmas decorations, and he honestly feels that the music should be limited to the single week before Christmas and, if people really must, the week after, but he has nothing against it. And he can see the childlike draw of pretending it is all real.

By that point it seemed like leaving it was letting Gabriella win. So he had to undo her work, and it took the better part of the day.

But he figured that was the end of it, so when it was done, even though he was more exhausted than he usually was at the end of a work day, he actually felt like he'd accomplished something, so he was fine with it his punishment.

Then—on the second day of Secret Santa—Gabriella left him that damned screensaver. *She*...ugh, there were no words for how frustrating, enraging, and...*And* she still wasn't talking to him! Sitting there snickering and talking to literally everyone else in the office. All the while, he tried to fix his screensaver without it getting worse and worse like the wallpaper had. When he finally figured out *what she'd done this time,* he realized it would never have changed.

He was so angry he literally had to leave the basement. And she sent it to his new computer.

Now this!

She is *evil.*

"But Santa, I've been good all year for this," Cory teases from the line, wearing a teeshirt with Santa chugging beers.

"You haven't even been a little good," Jack says dryly and forces himself to shove forward out of the elevator.

He can see Gabriella peeking over her cubicle, trying to be subtle as she beams. Angelo and Cory laugh as Jack comes forward. But Maya looks apologetic. As he passes her, she latches onto his arm.

"I'm so sorry about all this. I really did try to stop them," Maya says sweetly.

"It's fine," Jack says loudly, trying for unperturbed as he aims his voice towards Gabriella, but only managing strident. "I know who did this."

Behind her partition, Gabriella looks around to find the camera crew and pulls a *who me* look at the camera. Then she mouths the word "wait" and holds up a single finger. Terrance gets the drift and angles back to Jack.

"I'm so glad you understand," Maya says in a voice of much relief. "I would hate for you to get angry with me and not bring my teacup warmer."

Everyone in line explodes with laughter at Maya's rehearsed piece. Jack narrows his eyes; shaking off Maya's hand, he shoves through the others to make his way around his desk to lean over the side of Gabriella's.

"This has gone far enough, okay?" Jack says, frustrated beyond what he would have expected. Why won't she let this go? Can't she see he's sorry? "Stop. How am I supposed to get any work done?

"Work?" Gabriella says, all innocent shock. "Have you received a call already? You always say there is no point in working between calls."

"Get rid of them." Jack bites the words out between clenched teeth.

"Jack, come on, you've gotta relax," Gabriella says with pure joy. She knew this would upset him. She has practiced this. *Oh, life is sweet, and just desserts are even sweeter.* "It's just a bit of *fun.*"

Gabriella feels it the second the last word is out of her mouth in a tone far sharper than she intended. Her muscles might be somewhat tenser than she thought. She maybe should not have practiced saying that so many times. It was meant to sound playful. And she can see from the flashing in Jack's eyes that he noticed the lingering anger beneath her game, and he's going to dive on it.

And indeed, rather than *ever* being the more mature person. Jack notes her anger and feels a sudden otherworldly calm come over him as he realizes Gabriella didn't ignore him for even one day. Maybe she wasn't speaking to him, but he was her whole focus.

Jack grins because all is now right with the world. "You know. You're right, Gabriella. You're the uptight one. Thanks! At least now I won't be bored." Jack spins away, returning to his desk and the waiting coworkers. "Give me a second guys; I can't wait to hear why you're here."

Gabriella glares slightly, grinding down her back teeth. But it doesn't matter. He is bluffing. She saw his eyes. He's upset. He's enraged. And anyway. She is nowhere near done with him yet.

He'll suffer.

Across the partition, Jack is still fighting to hide a bit of his lingering annoyance. But he knows how to solve that. He'll spread it around.

"Now guys, as *loudly* as you can," Jack shouts with a bit of a bite. "Tell me what you want for Christmas."

Jack swivels in his seat to face the line, pad, and paper in hand, only to have the resident clown of the bunch plop right down on his lap.

"Angelo! What the hell?" Jack shoves the man to the floor.

Every person in the line and every tech watching from their cubicle bursts out laughing. Even Angelo on the floor is having the time of his life. Gabriella chuckles softly, booping her Santa figurine on the nose; he understands. She boops Santa again, and once more, for safety. From the corner of her eye, she catches a congratulatory wink from the Santa figurine; he gets it. Her hand slides away, and she feels some of her tension easing. Part of her brain is still disappointed at having let Jack see her lingering anger, but it is far away. Because she can feel his tension and annoyance through their shared cubicle wall. He's feeling exactly what she wants, invaded, cornered, *tormented*.

Gabriella's plan has worked, and the only person in the basement not having a great time of it is Jack Drummer, who rather wishes he hadn't gotten up this morning.

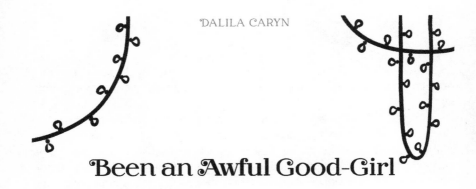

Been an Awful Good-Girl

Now that an hour has passed since the incident of the Santa's lap email, the IT department has resumed its usual quiet hum of little work. Kristen is taking this opportunity to interview individually the two parties involved, shutting herself in the break room with a sign to **KEEP OUT** on the door.

Kristen was thoroughly entertained by the events of this morning. She loved *nearly* every second. It bothered her slightly to see the one moment in which Gabriella lost a bit of her cool, and Jack gained some of his. She knows that feeling. The feeling that everything is more important to you than it is to anyone else. Honestly, she wanted to walk over and smack Jack across the face when it happened. Can't he just feel what he is supposed to feel? At the moment though, it appears to be bothering Kristen more than it is bothering Gabriella.

To say that it is not bothering Gabriella would be incorrect. She keeps seeing that look in his eyes the moment he realized she wasn't playing. There was a fiery superiority to it that made her stomach drop. But she isn't letting that one moment steal her focus. She has nine days of torture left for Jack, and that is what drives her. Tomorrow drives her. Imagining his face, his shame, his suffering.

"So, Gabriella, are you satisfied with how the plan is going?"

"I am very satisfied with the plan so far," Gabriella answers Kristen in a chipper voice. Because she is pleased, everything is going to go her way. "The gifts for today were chains of paper snowmen I got my sister Maria to decorate for everyone. Well, she didn't do them all. We made a party of it on the weekend with some of her art school friends. We drank cocoa, listened to Christmas music, and decorated seventy-seven individual chains of snow folk in unique ways to represent the recipient. Not an easy task." Gabriella says, lifting her head in pride for all she's managed lately. "For instance, Cory's snowmen are dressed as some of his favorite game characters. Ed's are all in Eagle's jerseys, and Miriam's are all based around the character art from this random indie fantasy series. I mean, I never could have done that without Maria and her friends. That art is way too special for my abilities, and none of the characters has like...scars or weird features to set them apart. I thought I was going to have to come up with something else." Gabriella breaks off, laughing as she remembers that whole day.

Gabriella has never been one to invite people over, even before Mom died. And since...well, she's pulled away from the friends she already had, in the nearly three years since their mother died, Gabriella and Maria have had almost no people in their home. So it was new and a lovely surprise to have five people over and actually enjoy it.

She loved seeing Maria with her friends, watching them play fight over artistic styles and...well, all compete to impress one guy. Maria, Rory, Alexandria, Henry, and Marco all flirting with Kai, the TA from one of their classes. And...as weirdly uncomfortable as it was, Gabriella got it; the guy is like supernaturally beautiful, his skin sparkles, and his eyes look like the ocean. And he didn't even seem offended or surprised when they all flirted with him. He just laughed and joked easily with everyone without ever actually flirting back. A week ago, Gabriella would have found it weird and assumed he was a really conceited guy who likes to have everyone chasing after him, but now...Gabriella *knows* magic is real. She feels it; she sees it. There is something magical about Kai, and other people can sense it; they just don't know it. But he seemed to know that Gabriella recognized the magic more clearly, and would sneak a smile at her when people got overly competitive for his attention.

It was so weird and special. Everything has been feeling special lately, good and bad.

"I had to get the e-books so we could see the art, and everybody was convinced they couldn't make them into snow-people. Then Kai, one of my sister's friends, is like...*I've got this;* he really liked the art; he said the illustrations made him want to read the series. So he puts the bad queen and the good queen at the opposite ends of the chain. The good queen just has her sword belt, a necklace, and her crown, but the bad queen," snickers, overcome. "She has a corset with, I kid you not, two giant snowballs filling it out, and her crown and scepter and a sultry expression. Did you know you can make snow-people have sultry expressions? Well, you can. In between the queens, there were three snow kids with similar expressions to the artwork in the book but designed out of like rocks and twigs and stuff. You really need to get a shot of those if you haven't. They're great." Gabriella beams, thinking but not voicing *it's magic.* Everything is so magical right now; she's loving every moment, savoring it, because she is sure it is going to end, but...she wants to keep the feelings with her afterwards. Like a silver sleigh bell with music only she can hear.

"Anyway, you get the idea. I even gave some to the person on the naughty list. And I only charged the company for the art supplies." Gabriella playfully puts her finger to her lips. "I let Maria keep the extra."

Kristen smiles as Gabriella expected. And hoped. Ever since the film crew came to Gabriella's apartment, she and Kristen have understood each other better. Gabriella overheard Kristen saying she'd always wanted a sister. And it made Gabriella think of all she'd learned when she researched her.

Kristen Kringle has no siblings, a deceased mother, and a father who is rarely in the country. Her mother died when she was ten, after which she'd attended a series of boarding schools. Intellectually Gabriella is aware that some people send their children to boarding schools. Rich people. But she hadn't really thought of them as places for real children. But Kristen spent two-thirds of every year away from family since the time she was a small child. While Gabriella and Maria were arguing over books and the covers of their shared bed, Kristen was in a dormitory.

Gabriella feels equal parts bad for Kristen and jealous of the wild confidence it seems to have inspired in the younger woman. There appears to be very little in the world that frightens Kristen. Gabriella cannot say the same of herself, but she also wouldn't part with herself to be a Kristen. So she is trying to befriend her.

"Well, that all sounds great! And I am thrilled Secret Santa is going well. But I was actually asking about your plans for a certain naughty Mr. Drummer." Kristen says with a smirk.

She can feel Gabriella trying to befriend her. And she is happy enough to play friendly. But it would be unprofessional to let herself get involved. She will not be allowing a breach in formality like her tears at Gabriella's house again.

"Oh, you meant my punishment for Jack," Gabriella snickers as if she didn't know this all along. "I may have sent an email from a dummy company account to a few people I knew would enjoy the joke. I think they must have forwarded the email; I only sent it to three of his friends." Gabriella grins her evil grin. She is delighted with this anticipated development that is, nevertheless, out of her direct control and, therefore, cannot be traced back to her.

"And," Kristen prompts, trying to hide her own amusement. "What did it say about sitting on his lap?"

"I decided not to get him fired," Gabriella responds like she's chatting with a friend. "So the email specifically said not to sit on my helpers' lap."

Kristen makes no remark, waiting with a brow raised. Gabriella relents, rolling her eyes.

"Okay fine, I had a feeling some people wouldn't be able to resist. I may even have been counting on this." Gabriella releases a wild laugh. "He'll be fine. But he also won't forget it any time soon."

The women share evil laughs. And after a few more questions about Gabriella's plans for Secret Santa, Kristen sends Gabriella on her way and waves to Jack with a falsely inviting smile.

Jack rises obediently, heading to the break room. Passing Gabriella as he goes, he cannot resist a big smile and a baiting comment.

"You never told me what you want for Christmas," he says, spinning around to walk backwards as she passes him without a word. "A clue for how to beat me, maybe."

Gabriella settles at her desk, smiling snidely at her nemesis. She lifts up the receiver of her phone and asks nonchalantly. "Apropos of nothing, do you know the extension for HR? There was an incident earlier I think needs reporting."

Jack shakes his head, holding onto his grin with tightly pressed teeth. She wouldn't dare.

"It would only come back at you," he teases just short of lightly.

Gabriella laughs proudly. "No, it wouldn't. You could never prove it."

Having gotten in what she wants to be the last word, Gabriella spins to face her computer screen, replacing the phone receiver and lifting her headset.

Jack has a comeback. Or the beginnings of one. Something along the lines of her not being nearly as talented as she thinks she is. The trouble is...she is definitely as talented as she thinks she is. He isn't untalented himself, though. He could prove it was her. But he has already waited too long to say any of that. So with a superior smile, she isn't looking up to see, he saunters into the break room.

Once Jack is settled in with a microphone and the lighting adjusted, Kristen launches into her interview. Jack can see Gabriella's desk over Kristen's shoulder, and his eyes are drawn there as he talks.

"Tell me," Kristen says, her tone implying she takes great pleasure in whatever line of questioning she is about to pursue. "How are you enjoying being on the naughty list?"

"The wallpaper thing was inspired. I was totally amused by it," Jack lies. Well, not lies. He was amused. At first. And he is amused again, now that he realizes how much time she was putting into pretending to ignore him. It is only that in-between those two times, he was, in fact frustrated, a little offended and perhaps...no, not sad. But disappointed to realize that he may have pushed Gabriella too far and lost their friendship.

But, now Jack would bet—in a style any shrink worth their coffee mug would recognize as projection—that Gabriella must have a real thing for him.

"I was impressed too," he goes on. "It took me some real effort to get rid of it. She's way too smart to be doing this job. And I was right; even though she's trying to punish me, she's given me the group gift every day. Pushover," Jack says fondly, his eyes trailing over Kristen's shoulder again to watch Gabriella. He notices Terrance moving and glances over. While the camera on the tripod is still pointed firmly at Jack, Terrance is using a cellphone to capture a video of where Jack is looking.

It is only at that moment that Jack consciously realizes where he is looking. Damn. They are going to start their reality show manipulations again, aren't they? He had better pay more attention to the holes he lets them exploit. He wasn't looking at Gabriella because he likes her. He assures himself, but really it feels like even he may need a bit more convincing of this.

"Today, she almost had me," Jack admits, sticking to more comfortable subjects. "I was seriously pissed. I may have to get back to pranking her. Three people tried to sit on my lap! I can't go to the bathroom without being bombarded with Christmas lists. And Cory keeps singing "Santa Baby." But—" Jack breaks off a smile unconsciously creeping over his face.

"Her face, when she was trying to tease me." He chuckles softly. "She couldn't keep it up. She always pushes a step too far. Just past fun and into..." Jack shakes his head. "I don't know. She looked like she literally wanted to take a bite out of me, and it was too much fun to resist goading her." Jack laughs at the disapproving expressions from all around the room.

"Don't look at me that way; she started it!"

"How is that?" Kristen prompts, and her tone turns biting. "When she broke your nutcracker? Or when she stole your reindeer figurines?"

"Oh yeah, that's right. I started it." Jack chuckles softly. "I guess she'll have to finish it."

A Murder of Snow-folk

Despite the lingering sense that the film crew disapproves of him, and in a blatant bid for more of Gabriella's attention, Jack has convinced the crew to follow him back to his desk to see something he considers to be epically entertaining.

In this instance, he is not wrong.

Once at his desk, he lifts his keyboard and withdraws a string of paper snowmen he'd been protecting. He holds them up to the camera with a look of absolute delight.

"Can you believe these?" He laughs.

The snowmen in question are Jack's...*gift* might be too generous a description; they are, however, what he received from his not-so-secret Santa today. All of the snowmen appear to be suffering the most gruesome Yuletide deaths imaginable.

"She may secretly be a serial killer," Jack says, seeming to take great pleasure from the prospect. "I mean, look, this one's been impaled on antlers. This one has been stabbed by really the sharpest candy cane I've ever seen." Jack cracks up.

The strand has five artistically rendered snow-people decorated with individual expressions of fear and pain built with coal or buttons. The snowman who suffered a reindeer run-in shows a look of shock at the antlers protruding through his chest. Another has a red and white striped candy cane extending through its chest. A third appears to have been the victim of a tree-cutting accident with an axe sticking out of its head.

"How does she come up with things like this?" Jack asks, snickering. "I like this guy. How do you electrocute a Snowman? Well, obviously with Christmas lights, but aside from his singed branches, is it even possible? This one is nice; she really knows how to drive a point home."

Jack indicates the final snowman with two-thirds of his body blocked by an angry and somewhat broken nutcracker. The nutcracker's missing cracker arm is jabbed upwards through the snowman's head and pokes out of its face.

Though Jack was forced to inquire, it doesn't seem all that hard to figure out where Gabriella might have gotten this last idea.

"How is she this talented at this many things?" Jack laughs. "And why isn't she running the world or something?"

In the not-so-great distance, the elevator opens and a man emerges. Jack very carefully tacks up his snowmen, determined that they not be further injured, as Gabriella makes faces at the camera, having heard the whole of Jack's snowman presentation.

"Wow! You guys are hardcore down here," Daniel Burns says in shock, stopping at Jack's desk and observing the snowmen he is hanging.

"I like a murder mystery." Jack shrugs.

On her side of the partition, Gabriella is momentarily disturbed. Did she subconsciously give Maria an idea Jack would enjoy? It was Maria and not Gabriella who decorated Jack's snowmen. Gabriella had started and mangled three sets before her sister took over, instructing Gabriella to organize and give ideas for the different snowmen and "do not do any of the drawings."

Gabriella should have felt embarrassed in front of her sister's friends, but everybody's favorite guest, Kai, joked that wrangling six artists with their own ideas sounded like a more difficult job to him. It was a sweet attempt to put her at ease. And anyway, Gabriella has always known where her talents lay. And art isn't one of them.

But even if she didn't do the work. Drawing all of Jack's snowmen dying was her idea. And he seems to like them. And what is most disturbing is that she is pleased and unpleased at the same time, realizing he is happy with them.

Daniel laughed at Jack's remark but did not move off as Jack expected. Jack raises a brow at this man, the head of human resources.

"Don't tell me," Jack says with a sigh. It has been over an hour since anyone came to tell him their list, but he supposes he was being a bit too hopeful by assuming that was the end of it. "I've already guessed your list. You want little Krissy in each race and a collectors cabinet."

"Ha. Ha," Burns says, forcing a laugh, with no idea what the joke is about nor any great interest in knowing. "Actually, I am here officially for HR."

"What?" Jack leaps to his feet. Also, to a conclusion or two.

Gabriella peeks over her cubicle with her lips pressed together, partially amused, partially concerned.

"What?" Mr. Burns takes a step back in shock. He cannot go much further with the film crew behind him.

Utterly lost as to why Jack has taken an antagonistic tone, Daniel Burns glances awkwardly at the film crew for an explanation. Kristen could easily explain the whole situation but will not do so. She's loving the amusement in Gabriella's eyes and the fear in Jack's. And anyway, this scene is going to be gold! Jack has forgotten Daniel's presence to lean on his desk to glare at Gabriella.

"This is your fault," Jack accuses, leaning in so his face protrudes over Gabriella's side of the partition. Gabriella steps back just slightly as his presence intrudes on her personal bubble of space.

"Jack, I think you have the wrong idea," Daniel remarks and is generally ignored.

Gabriella glares at Jack, hating that he is forcing her to back down physically but unable to do so in all ways. Her eyes flash with vindictive lights, and she turns to Mr. Burns with a wide smile.

"What is the complaint? Can I verify anything?"

"Okay. I don't know what is going on with you two but cool it. This is nothing bad." He pauses briefly. When met with two militant employees, he presses on. "Of course, if either of you has a legitimate complaint, my office door is open." He snorts. "Because I'm down here with you."

The poor man laughs alone. Even at home, he laughs alone. But at least there, his wife, daughter, and two sons give him the acknowledgment of rolled eyes. He is certain every time they roll their eyes, it is to resist uproarious laughter. They are just shy. But that doesn't seem to be the case in this silent room.

"Okay, tough room. Should I know something here?" Daniel asks, hoping against hope that the answer is no. Please let the answer be no. He doesn't want any more paperwork.

"Why are you here?" Gabriella and Jack demand in unsettling unison and exchange brief fiery expressions before turning all their intensity back on Daniel.

Daniel feels an uncomfortable pit open in his stomach and leans in, trying to whisper low enough that the cameras will not pick it up. An attempt that is unsuccessful. *This is all he needs*. "You two aren't involved, are you?"

"No!" The pair exclaim, again in perfect unison, seeming to belie their statements.

Though in truth, they are not lies. This pair is not involved. They are as uninvolved as is possible when kept in close quarters, mutually attractive, single, and sharing an unacknowledged attraction. Not at all. *Wink.

"Right. Well, if you're sure," Daniel says without an ounce of sincerity.

"We're sure," Gabriella snaps.

"Why are you here?" Jack says, releasing the breath he held to keep from speaking at the same time as Gabriella again.

That whole exchange was uncomfortable. But they are not involved. He isn't attracted to her. He already said he would never date her. He did! Jack implores his mind to believe him, but it is worth noting that his mind is mocking him with paraphrased lines from the bard, *me thinks thou dost protest too much.*

Giving up on anything but getting out of this room as quickly as possible, Mr. Burns simply answers. "Jack, Mr. Coleman is looking to have someone head up the IT department and do some liaising with the corporate types. Someone to travel with the sales team and do troubleshooting on the road. He'd like your resume before the first of the new year."

"Just his resume?" Gabriella demands, offended on like twenty levels.

1. She is a better tech than him.

2. Sexism.

3. Jack is lazy.

4. Jack is annoying.

5. Jack does nothing to deserve a promotion!

6. Jack, as her boss, is insupportable.

7. Jack is lazy. (Yes, she is repeating herself, but it's important)

8.—19. are all in this same repetitive vein.

Which only leaves:

20. She works harder than any tech and gets less respect.

"I've been here two years longer than you have," Jack points out, incensed.

He moves in closer to her again, making Gabriella realize only now that he had backed off a little. She had still felt his presence crowding her. Still felt the electric way he made her body tense up, longing to back away. Now it's worse again. And it makes her feel as uncomfortable with that episode of speaking in eerie unison as everyone else seemed. When in the moment, it had actually sort of amused her to think how fun it must be for Jack to finally be at her level.

"Meaning I am more familiar with current and developing technology," Gabriella responds reasonably, trying to stick to more comfortable topics.

"Are you serious?"

"Of course I am! I installed all of the new shipping software and trained half of this department on how to navigate it."

"Well, I wasn't in that half," Jack shouts back.

"True." Gabriella concedes. After all, her main complaint is that she is not being considered for the job, not that Jack is. And he knows it. Neither of them needs to hear Mr. Burns's answer to know she isn't in the running. "And you know I am more than qualified for my job or that one."

"So go get another job and leave mine alone," Jack snaps. Not because she isn't right, but...really, the gall on her. Daniel came to talk to him! She should keep her tiny button nose out of it.

"Enough!" Mr. Burns shouts.

Jack and Gabriella manage to shut their mouths and look at their...sort of boss. Gabriella suddenly notices how many heads are pointed their way. And remembers with an unfortunate skin-heating sort of embarrassment that there is a film crew right there recording everything and likely celebrating the overly dramatic fight taking place.

She wishes she could vanish. Not that anything she said was wrong.

"Gabby," Mr. Burns says a bit impatiently. "The request wasn't just for Jack. It was, however, for the senior technicians, Jack, Michael, and Stan. After their applications are reviewed, the position will be opened to the public, at which time you are welcome to apply." He shifts his gaze. "Jack, I told you first because your desk was nearest the elevator. It is not your job! Now! Do you two need to come to my office? Should I be separating you? Or can you work together like adults? Before I put notes in both your files saying you aren't management material."

Gabriella swallows her complaints and her burning shame and is the first to respond in a professionally neutral tone. "Of course, we can work together. Sorry, Mr. Burns. Things get sort of competitive down here."

Mr. Burns looks at Jack and accepts a mere nod from him before sighing. "Alright. I'm going to tell the others. Try not to kill each other."

Gabriella and Jack are still staring at one another. By no means as murderous, but in no way friendly. But as Mr. Burns passes Gabriella's desk, he stops.

"What happened to your privacy screen?"

Gabriella's eyes widen, and her color, already a bright shade of red, turns even cheerier, though she doesn't feel at all cheery. "I...It broke. Sorry." Gabriella looks down, anywhere but at Jack as she speaks the absolute truth, but omits a few details. She ought to tell. But it really should be Jack to confess. Or she should have told immediately. If she tells now it will make her sound like a child blaming someone else to get out of being punished. She doesn't do that.

"You were the one who insisted on them. Maybe you should get it fixed." Mr. Burns points out in a disappointed-principal voice.

That tone has Gabriella's stomach churning and tears pressing at the back of her eyes. Of course.

"Of course. I will," she agrees in a small voice and sinks into her seat. "Of course."

"Good." Seeming to catch onto having thoroughly chastised Gabriella, Mr. Burns makes a rather paltry bid to lessen the blow. "Cute desk! I love all the..." he waves his fingers around, "decoration. No snowmen for you?"

Gabriella's mouth falls open. Her nails are literally gouging holes into her palms to keep from crying. Perfect. Just perfect. This day couldn't get any worse, could it?

"I...have them in my drawer for safekeeping," she lies with a strained voice that may just reveal how close to tears she is. Yep. Of course, it can get worse.

"Good, good. Mine," Daniel laughs before getting out any funny information. "Were seeing, hearing, and speaking no evil, with the two at the ends filling out forms about it." He chuckles alone.

Jack is watching with something close to regret visible about him. And the film crew are experiencing varying degrees of annoyance. While Gabriella, always one to be polite, manages a slight nod and a forced smile, despite her own inner turmoil. Mr. Burns backs away so awkwardly one would think he'd never spoken to a person before.

Gabriella, trying in vain to pretend that she is invisible, bends down and attempts to replace her bent privacy screen on the monitor. All the while reconciling herself to always working for people who aren't as driven, knowledgeable, or committed as her. To always, every second, for the rest of her life, hearing in the back of her mind. Sit at that table alone until you can behave normally.

She chews on her tongue until it really ought to be shredded. And manages to stick her privacy screen on at a bit of an angle that is going to eat at her forever but is the best she can do right now. Then, still feeling all the eyes in the room on her, under her skin, making her burn, making her ache from muscles coiled too tightly, making her feel at once like the smallest, most worthless being in the world and also the biggest most obvious bumbling giant. When she can no longer take it, she slips away down the hall, never once lifting her eyes from the ground, but managing still to see Jack open his mouth as if to stop her.

But she doesn't stop until she is outside of the building. In fact, she doesn't stop until she has driven two blocks away and parked in a hardware store parking lot.

There she buries her head in her hands. There, all alone, she utilizes one of the oldest therapeutic techniques she was ever taught. She screams into her hands as if no one could possibly hear her. Screams out her rage and her shame and sadness and fear.

Screams until she runs out of voice, even if not out of feelings she wants to expel.

Not Like Christmas at All

Gabriella Anjelica Cruz was absent from the office building for precisely fifty-three-minutes-and-nineteen-seconds. Just six-minutes-and-forty-one-seconds short of her full lunch break. In that time, Jack checked his computer's clock twenty-nine times. Jack Drummer is unaware that he has been checking the clock every few minutes until Gabriella returns. But the film crew is.

All Jack noticed was that he really didn't mind the cartoon woodland creatures decorating a Christmas tree that is now his computer wallpaper. Even once he managed to stop Gabriella's code from changing his wallpaper, he left that last one on his screen. It's sort of cute. It occurs to him that it might be fun to change his wallpaper up every now and again for a different view. And as he's thinking it, his eyes slip once again to the time. It is then that the elevator opens, and Gabriella walks back into the room as though nothing has happened.

Despite Jack's apparent concern over her absence, the minute Gabriella walks in, he makes a great show of not looking at her. Gabriella isn't looking at him anyway, so she fails to notice his lack of interest in her person or the plastic bag she is carrying.

She returns to her desk, fully aware that people will have rightly assumed that she left because she was upset over the incident with Mr. Burns.

People's minds are predominantly selfish. Usually when we're worried about what people must be thinking of us, they are busy thinking about themselves.

It's not quite a mantra, but her mind frequently replays those words from her therapist, Dr. Hearth. It seems however that repetition of the words has not convinced her that they are correct. Not in the moment, at any rate. So as she heads to her desk, pretending nothing at all is wrong. Her fingers tap her thigh in a one-three-one pattern.

Once seated, she removes her purchases: a pair of needle-nosed pliers and a thin roll of duct tape. She shakes out the plastic bag they were carried in and folds it in half on the side of the table. Carefully removing the privacy screen, she attempts first to use the pliers to bend back the lip of the screen that will no longer grip the bottom of her monitor.

She is having more success than anticipated. The screen is fairly malleable. Which is good because if she has to tape it onto her screen, she will wind up buying a new one. She won't be able to work with it taped on.

Logically she knows that no other tech in this basement would be in the least bit worried about something like this. They would tell someone their screen had broken and receive a new one as though it were an extra pen from the supply closet. But logic doesn't exactly apply to the only female in the department. She stands out. And as Mr. Burns put it, Gabriella was *the one who insisted on* the privacy screens.

The fact is Gabriella did no such thing. She only pointed out that pointing cameras at screens with people's passwords was a mistake. The privacy covers were the management's idea. But nuance rarely matters in workplace drama. And if Gabriella keeps being the squeaky wheel, she'll be labeled needy, emotional, a detriment, not a team player.

Oh, how she wishes that being a team player would have stopped being so important once she was out of grade school.

To be quite fair to Gabriella, which *she* rarely is, while she does not give the social appearance of teamwork, she does the *work* of a team player. She is happy to help her coworkers with any project she knows how to handle. Even a few where she must do research. And though she was not fond of the assignment, Gabriella has embraced the role of Secret Santa with a gusto not even shown by many party planners.

But she is not thinking any of this. She is thinking only that she can always use a roll of duct tape at home. She is even somewhat pleased with herself for having fixed the screen with minimum fuss and barely more than a scuff on the bottom edge to show it was ever broken. That is what she is thinking until she sees the shadows of the approaching film crew fall over her.

"Gabriella," Kristen says politely. "When you aren't too busy, can we steal you away for another short interview?"

Gabriella has been expecting this. She planned for this as she sat in the office parking lot for twelve minutes. So it is silly that her stomach drops, and she can see again, playing out in her head, the whole scene from the moment she playfully offered to report Jack to HR to the moment Mr. Burns backed away from her like she was unhinged. Nevertheless, she looks up at Kristen and nods.

"I'm not in the middle of anything now, if that works." Gabriella offers.

And indeed, that works very well. Kristen leads her away to the break room and sets up for another interview.

"Can you tell me anything about the incident with Mr. Burns?" Kristen asks in a tone that sounds all too similar to her original leading tone for Gabriella not to notice. Kristen is back to wanting a specific answer. But her question is so vague Gabriella wonders if the girl is trying not to lead or if she is afraid to be too obvious.

"The incident with Mr. Burns...got heated. Unnecessarily so." Gabriella tries for a neutral tone.

"Why do you think that is?" Kristen asks hungrily.

NICE TO BE SO NAUGHTY

Gabriella, generally a fairly observant woman, occasionally too much so, takes in Kristen's tone and her eager expression and comes to the conclusion that Kristen is looking for some sort of love affair angle. She wants to equate Gabriella and Jack's battle with little boys pulling on little girls' pigtails. Gabriella is not amused by this comparison and is angry enough to answer with a bit more truth than she'd practiced sharing when she imagined this interview in the parking lot.

In this case, however, Gabriella's assumption is incorrect. Kristen saw the whole exchange, and rather than focusing on the battle between Jack and Gabriella, her senses honed in on Daniel Burns. On the manner in which he spoke to Gabriella, like an errant student, and to Jack like a peer. An exasperating peer, but as a peer all the same. Kristen doesn't want to lead Gabriella because then her answers will seem stilted. But she would just as soon ignore Jack altogether and focus on the bigger issue.

"So look," Gabriella says, a bit defensively. "I didn't want Jack to get fired for my prank. That's why I only sent the email to his friends. But." Gabriella cannot help a shake of the head and a slight incredulous snort. "He's getting a promotion. Really? Jack as my boss. That's too much to ask of anyone. He'd fit in perfectly with the other managers." Gabriella is warming to the subject, her tone annoyed but far from heated. "*Liaise* with them. Ha. Drink beer and do nothing more like. He has that 'I'm so handsome,' 'I'm so popular,' 'I'm so charming' thing going on." Gabriella says and pulls a childishly disgusted face.

"Do you think Jack is handsome and charming?" Kristen asks lightly.

Gabriella shrugs. "Me thinking it or not wouldn't change the fact that he *is* handsome. That doesn't mean me liking him." She rolls her eyes, perhaps overly annoyed for the person who brought it up, to begin with. "As for charming...I don't know. When he wants to be. But that is very rare."

Gabriella smirks at the camera, but when she speaks again, her tone has dropped. Flattened. And it is clear where her mind is really focused at the moment.

"And that comment Mr. Burns made about my desk and the *decoration*," She says with air quotes. "It felt like I was on one of those reality singing contests, and I'm the girl they wanna let down easy. 'You look so pretty,'" she mocks, growing more agitated and animated. "Who cares? Is this a beauty pageant? No. Just give me your damned critique. I'm female, so we know I can take it. Like ninety-three percent of being female is taking criticism."

It is important to note that Gabriella is basing this figure on her own personal experience and has not done the research to back up her findings. Were she to do so, she would discover a figure not entirely dissimilar, ninety-seven percent. A depressing figure if one is female and has yet to work this out, but precision is important. *Wink.

"And ugh! I can't believe I forgot myself for the Secret Santa gifts. I did it every day." It is with this comment that Gabriella looks truly offended because, as previously stated, she is not often fair *with herself.* So the person she is most angry with today is Gabriella Cruz.

"If someone else had noticed and figured it out...it would have ruined the magic. When it has been going along so well. People loved the cookie exchange! And on Friday, when I gave everyone one of those fit-in-your-pocket type rain slickers with a note saying to dress warm for the So-Cal winter, they seemed to get a real kick out of it. I heard a bunch of people laughing over it. And I forgot myself every time!" Gabriella pulls in a deep breath, leaving a quiet lull in the room. "I need to quit focusing on Jack's punishments and put all my energy into the nice list," Gabriella says as if she is making the decision in this moment. When she has really been thinking about it ever since she stepped out of her car, with tears still dampening her face, and walked into the hardware store.

"What about everyone else? What will you do with the other naughty listers?"

"That's not a problem. No one else made the naughty list. I was going to add Frank since he's been so snappy with Carol all year, but —" Gabriella shrugs, "sometimes when things are going rough in your life, it's hard to face what's really bothering you. So I actually gave him a few extra treats. More cookies and a set of snowmen for his wife."

Kristen laughs softly. "Of course you did."

Gabriella looks up, straight at the girl interviewing her. Usually, really at any other time, if she heard Kristen laugh and say those same four words, she would think she was being mocked. But she doesn't think she is today.

And in this instance, Gabriella is correct. Kristen and Gabriella regard one another quietly, sharing one of those moments of silent affinity, Kristen wondering again if life would have looked different with a sister, and Gabriella realizing there is more to this girl than meets the eye.

A while later, as Gabriella returns to her desk, Andrew goes to see if they can get Jack for an interview. Terrance, from his spot behind the camera, and without ever looking at Kristen, puts in his two cents.

"You don't need to keep pressing her to verbally acknowledge the inherent sexism. Trust the medium. We're showing it."

"In my experience, the people who can grasp things when they are merely shown are not the people who need to see them. It's the ones who have to have things spelled out."

"Gosh, I wonder what you meant by that. Could you spell it out for me?"

Kristen chuckles, throwing a smirk over her shoulder. "I meant that men have to be told in clear, simple sentences."

"Ooooh, ahora entiendo," Terrance replies, *now I understand,* in Spanish and is rewarded by the loudest and indeed warmest laugh he's ever heard from Kristen.

She is still beaming and laughing loud, her heart burning with delight as Jack walks in. Terrance, *who knew he had a playful side?*

A great many people know Terrance has a playful side. His sister and brother. His mother, his father, his cousins, and close friends. But rather, like the girl he is teasing, Terrance does not go out of his way among his classmates to make friends. He goes to class to learn, graduate, and pursue the career of his dreams. He's never spent this much time with another classmate before. And is every day surprised that it isn't just the subjects of the documentary that he is coming to know and maybe, relate to.

By the time Jack has a microphone, Kristen has both her pleasure and her earlier annoyance well in hand. She smiles at Jack like he is a perfect stranger she wants to dissect and launches pleasantly into the endeavor.

"Why don't you share your side of the incident earlier? You seemed awfully upset when Gabriella put herself forward for the same job as you. Is she unqualified?"

Jack rolls his eyes, appearing instantly annoyed. For a self-described easy-going guy, he does seem to be out of sorts today.

"Gabriella is the most annoying, conceited...ridiculous woman I've ever worked with. I can acknowledge that she's good at her job. Hell, she's excellent. She goes way beyond her job description. She is—forgets this is just a job, would probably die at her desk in an emergency—level committed." Jack says fully annoyed, but seeming to see that he's boxed himself into a corner, he goes on. "But there is such a thing as *seniority*. And she is too eager to work in management. Look at the way she jumped to fix that screen."

The devious elf in Kristen wants to be the one to point out that it was Jack who broke that screen. But she holds her tongue. She glances back at Terrance and finds herself determined to do as she'd already been trying to, and he thinks she should and trust the medium. She stays quiet. She waits.

Kristen Kringle has *never* been good at waiting. She skips to the end of books because she has to know it ends how she wants before she can commit. She used to sneak into her parents' room and unwrap her presents so she would know what she was getting. She has only ever taken assignments she knew she could ace, and she has already bought herself a BMW as a graduation present, though she has two semesters left before she will have earned it.

But she is waiting. And it may be paying off.

"And the way she took all the blame for it when she didn't have to. No one in management does that." Jack shakes his head. His tone has gotten a little calmer, a little quieter, and a little more thoughtful. And above all, much more real. "I should have confessed to breaking it. Did you see her face? It was like...she honestly thought he wouldn't believe her if she said I broke it. How could she even doubt that? I mean, of the two of us who would you believe had broken work equipment?" Jack says like it's a joke, but his tone is far heavier than usual. He pauses a moment, his mind muddy with regrets over Gabriella's earlier expression, and his part in bringing it about. He should have spoken up. He shouldn't have broken it in the first place. But he doesn't know how to fix any of it.

When he pulls himself back into the moment, Jack glances at the film crew and rallies, getting back to Kristen's question. "But she had no business being offended that they want me over her. And what am I doing? I'm sitting here feeling sorry for her. With her sad puppy look when Daniel shut her down and her horror because she'd forgotten to give herself the snowmen." Jack laughs, a sad, hollow thing, and his eyes slip past Kristen to look out to the office where Gabriella works.

Kristen watches Jack reveal some of the real, perhaps almost sweet person beneath the show he's been putting on for the cameras and wonders if it might not be good to take an even bigger step backwards. She's been trying not to force things, not to manipulate outcomes, and just observe. But maybe she should spend some time behind the camera. Terrance is gifted with it and has a natural eye and great instincts. But...maybe Kristen should spend more time observing and less plotting. Because she wouldn't have expected this man to have any depths. And it appears he does have them.

"Do you know I think forgetting the snowmen may be what she was most upset about," he goes on quietly. "And she needn't have worried. No one was going to notice," He says, with his voice utterly devoid of tone. "No one notices her."

Checking It Twice

Right at this moment (eight-thirty-three a.m. on Tuesday the eleventh of December) Gabriella Anjelica Cruz is the only worker present at the offices of My Best Friend Doll Company, Burbank, CA. She was given special, limited access to the building to prepare today's surprise for the staff. Although no other employees are present, Kristen Kringle, having been alerted to Gabriella's plans by her uncle, is on-site with the rest of her film crew.

Gabriella is looking particularly festive today with a jingling colorful headband made of tiny sleigh bells pushing back most of her shoulder-length hair but for a few strands framing the sides of her face. She is also sporting a pair of drop earrings with three different color gift bows. And her sweater has a tree with lights that blink on and off. She is in a calm, positive mood as she moves around the office, laying out envelopes with snowflake seals.

As she passes Jack's desk, she tosses the letter in with much less care than she has taken at other desks and, smirking back at the camera self-deprecatingly, waves another envelope.

"Okay, so I've remembered to bring a *gift*." Gabriella makes air quotes as she emphasizes the word. "To my own desk today. Check."

As she places the envelope on her desk and moves on, Terrance widens the angle of the camera to take in Gabriella's whole desk. Lingering on key spots to highlight the many missing decorations.

Santa, along with reindeer and sleigh, are gone. The strand of lights is gone, and the elves that lined the monitor are gone. And even the elf ears have been removed from the headphones, and all glue gunk cleaned off. All that remains of her Christmas decor is the Christmas tree, shoved now into the furthest back corner of the desk, and the broken nutcracker.

Kristen stands behind Terrance, watching him work. Watching the world through his lens. She hasn't decided yet if she wants to ask to take up the camera. But she really does want to try standing even further back. It's an odd, very new concept for her. All her life, Kristen has tried to stand out. Tried to be the best student, the wittiest conversationalist, and the most popular girl. She always tried to shine the brightest of anyone in the room. But suddenly, she doesn't want to anymore.

"You know this is all sort of weird but fun. I was upset about the assignment when I first got it." Gabriella volunteers the information without any prompt from Kristen. "Offended to be picked because I was the *only female* in the department. But..." Gabriella grins softly. "People were play arguing over whose snowmen were the best yesterday. They're loving it; I know it! I can *feel* it. It's Christmas adjacent with all the Christmas fun. And I think everyone is enjoying the suspense of coming to work to see what today's surprise will be. Even I like the suspense, and I always know what's coming." Gabriella giggles, making her appear younger and more relaxed. "I can't wait to see what each day brings out in people."

With her last envelope delivered, she moves into the break room, where she has already left a bag of supplies. There she begins lifting what appears to be largely crafting supplies and laying them out neatly on the table.

"It's the big gift at the end that is troubling me." Gabriella continues with her focus on her task; her expression has a lovely seriousness about it that looks strangely suited to her festive attire. "I mean, forty dollars wouldn't make much of a year-end bonus, but I get the feeling people would still prefer the money. I should have bought all the gifts by now, or at least know exactly what I'm getting, but I don't. I hope that's not what Mr. Coleman wants to see me about later." She pauses in her work and glances up at the crew with a slightly apprehensive expression. "His secretary Debbie sent me an email saying she would call when he was ready to see me. But she didn't give a reason."

The table in front of Gabriella is neatly ordered with: tee-shirt paint, stickers, glow bracelets, glitter, faux flowers, mini sleigh bells, ribbons, sequins, and colorful pipe cleaners. She sets out a small cardboard sign with a bright red train engine on it, held up with a cup. The sign reads: Decoration Station.

Since Gabriella seems a bit lost in thought, Kristen prompts her softly to share information that could be helpful to the scene. "So, what are all of these art supplies for?"

Gabriella flashes Kristen a quick grin, then sets about organizing, answering in an informative voice as she goes. "Today's event is to make your own ugly rain slicker." She smirks in pride at this idea she's come up with. "Like an ugly sweater, but So-Cal appropriate. People will get to use their breaks and half of the hour before the end of work to decorate. The last half hour will be the voting and award giving!"

Having finished at this table, Gabriella lifts the bag and nods out of the room, heading to the elevator with the film crew.

"Using the slickers I gave them on Friday and the various supplies I'm leaving out, they each make their own ugly slicker. Then we have a short break to view and vote. I wasn't sure everyone would participate, so I pushed for something special to make sure everyone interested gets involved. I...It is very important to me that even if people opt out, no one *feels excluded.* I don't even sign the notes as Secret Santa. Well, none but the prank email."

The elevator doors open on the second floor. The desks are a bit more widely spread out here. And there are a few offices along the walls. Gabriella lays out cards as she heads to the break room to set out supplies of the exact ratio and arrangement as the ones in the basement.

The first floor of the building has no break room. Housing only reception, a few conference rooms, and a small "museum" for guests to learn about the company. With displays of every doll ever made, from design to prototype to production, and a few shelves worth of "gifts" that can be purchased.

"Second and third prizes are a coffee gift card and a desk cactus respectively," Gabriella explains as she works. "Nothing awesome. But the grand prize winner will get one extra paid vacation day!" She nearly does a dance; she is so pleased with her prize. "And no one gets to vote for themselves, so...I think everyone is going to get involved and have fun. I had to really push for that vacation day. My aim was to get one for everyone and to give the cactus to the winner, but Mr. Coleman prefers a *healthy* competitive atmosphere." Gabriella shakes her head but tries to maintain a neutral expression. He is, after all, her boss. And while she is entirely certain she can get another job, she doesn't have one lined up, so it's smart not to rock the boat too much.

There is a lull in the conversation as Gabriella sets out another train sign and heads back towards the elevator. And Kristen has to prompt because it is becoming too essential to the documentary not to.

"So what do you have in store for Jack's punishment today? Should we be expecting more fireworks?"

Gabriella takes a careful breath as she hits the up button. "Actually, there won't be a punishment for Jack today." The doors open, and everyone loads in. "He hasn't shown anything remotely like contrition, and I don't think he was thoroughly punished to have learned his lesson," Gabriella says with her back to the crew. She hits the button for three.

"But I guess I have," she says calmly. "Mr. Burns was right. I was behaving childishly. This is a workplace. My personal disputes don't belong here. I even took home a bunch of my decorations. None of it needs to be here." Gabriella's light dims ever so slightly as the elevator doors close.

Ugly Sweaters

It is now eleven-fifteen on this same Tuesday, December the eleventh. Kristen has, in a moment of reckless determination, demanded Terrance's extra camera, informing him, "we should get more detailed footage of all the break rooms than the hidden cameras will capture."

Terrance, who has been noticing, ever since the visit to Gabriella's apartment, a change in Kristen felt that he should most certainly address it. He should see what's going on because every day, she is in a different mood. He should ask, right? For the sake of the project. He should know what's going on in her mind. Shouldn't he? But because of this uncertainty in his being, and also because really, as much as he's coming to understand her, she can be a bit much when she wants to, he simply hands over the camera and heads up to the second floor where the majority of the funny people work.

This is why Kristen alone is in the basement break room, slowly moving about in the background, adjusting angles and getting a seriously invasive knot between her shoulder blades as she tries to look at this world through a glass window.

"Quit hogging all of the glow bracelets," Cory snaps at Michael.

"Come up with your own design. Mine needs stripes," his older coworker says, with his hand firmly trapping all the glow bracelets before him. Apparently, he is one of those oh, so rare individuals that never learned to share.

*Wink.

"So use the paints!" Cory's complaints grow in volume.

"The paints don't glow," Michael says and literally sticks out his tongue. A sight not unseen in forty-six-year-olds but one not often expected of them.

Kristen feels strange. Usually, she would be laughing at such antics or egging them on. She would almost certainly be egging them on. And though a part of her feels like it is probably good for her not to for once, another part of her feels like she is now trying to deny who she is. And up to a week ago, she never thought there was anything about herself that she did not like. Being behind the camera is...not what she expected.

"This paint glows," Jack informs his coworkers. He has painted a reindeer on his slicker and is now, with meticulous care embellishing the beast with a glowing icicle of a booger. You will recall that this is the man who considers himself *too mature* to celebrate Christmas.

Michael casts a derisive eye over Jack's creation. "Only in the dark. The contest takes place indoors."

"How dare you belittle my masterpiece. I'm wearing this baby everywhere," Jack says proudly.

Michael rolls his eyes. Cory laughs but also takes this moment of slight distraction from Michael to try and steal a few glow bracelets. He is unsuccessful, gaining only a slapped hand.

"Seriously man, I want some of those glow bracelets," Cory says with a sharp tone.

"Only losers whine, loser!" Michael says, displaying for all his own *very deeply seeded* maturity. "I'm getting another vacation day! It's just good strategy to steal all the best supplies."

Jack snorts. And Cory angrily sorts through the other supplies as he contemplates violence. Contemplates stealing all of the glow bracelets out from under Michael's hands and running away with them. He's younger and faster. The only thing stopping him is the camera. How badly is he willing to embarrass himself to get this vacation day?

"I still don't believe management actually offered up both a half-hour to do this and one vacation day. Last year they denied me sick pay for my third day with the flu because I would no longer have been contagious," Michael says, blissfully unaware of Cory plotting beside him.

Jack laughs. "Oh, management didn't offer it. This was *all* Santa's doing."

Kristen tightens the shot on Jack's face. He is angled slightly away from the round table spread with art supplies. Stepping slowly, one foot over the other so the camera is focused on Jack but also through the open break room door behind him, views what he is watching out of the corner of his eyes: Gabriella. She is at her desk, looking intent as she types into her computer.

"Yeah, about that," Cory says, momentarily distracted from plotting his great glow bracelet heist.

Kristen widens the angle on the camera, thrilled to find she can show Gabriella and all three of the men. She lifts the camera higher and angles down, trying to get a nice shot of their work and Secret Santa behind.

"You said Coleman picked one person to do the whole thing this year. Is this all you?" Cory's tone and his disbelieving expression imply he would never accept this answer.

"Santa never reveals his secrets," Jack answers easily.

"That's a magician," Michael says, with a distracted voice, as he very precisely lines up his glow sticks and holds them deep in the glue until it begins to harden. "Santa revealed his secrets long ago: magic and slave labor."

Kristen swallows a laugh. Grandpa won't like that. Neither will the North's hundred-and-thirteenth, the labor union for the toy makers of the North Pole. Having the most coveted and time-honored jobs in the North, those elves are anything but slaves. They tend to be more highly revered than Santa.

In the North Pole anyway.

All the same, Kristen is amused in the extreme. It's the first thing beyond quiet and intrigue with camera angles that she's felt since she picked up this machine.

"Wow." Cory inches away from Michael, disturbed. "You're a terrible person. The elves aren't slaves; they're magical helpers."

"Like house elves?" Jack suggests, tongue in cheek.

"Slaves." Michael drives home the punchline of Jack's joke.

"Or Fairy godmothers?" Jack cracks a wide smile.

"Voyeuristic judgmental slaves." Michael points out.

"You guys are the worst," Cory says, but it is worth noting that he is laughing as hard as either of his coworkers. "Santa is definitely putting you on the naughty list."

"Eh, Santa is a big softy," Jack observes.

And were his coworkers at all observant themselves, they might have noticed that again, Jack's eyes have strayed to Gabriella. However, even were they to have observed it in this moment, neither man would have thought much of it. It has not been at all hard to see that *someone* has a little crush. And that *someone's* eyes often stray to a certain serious young tech. *Someone* has been teased mercilessly behind his back. *Someone* is Jack Hilary Drummer, not to put too fine a point on it.

"Right. Well, whoever is running it this year is doing a good job. This is actually fun." Cory laughs. "Maybe the best year ever."

"Oh, it's going to be. When I win. Ta-Da!" Michael lifts his slicker and turns it around, hoping for applause that isn't coming.

Kristen steps around the table to take in the slicker alone before stepping back to take in the men observing the masterpiece. Michael's creation sports diagonal stripes made of glow sticks, interspersed with a sequined pattern of stars and hearts.

"Dude, it's supposed to be ugly," Cory says, shaking his head.

"It has glow bracelets and sequins!" Michael shouts a bit to be heard over Jack's laugh.

"In a pattern, Mr. Rogers would wear," Cory argues. "What do you moonlight as a seamstress?"

"It pays to be neat. And it's gonna win."

"I'm going to three and steal some of their supplies," Cory says petulantly, throwing down his barely touched slicker. Some people don't have artistic ideas, and that is okay if they can accept it about themselves. "I bet theirs are better than ours."

"I'd bet my winning slicker that they have exactly the same things." Jack winks at the camera. "Exactly."

Cory's eyes narrow on Jack. "You ought to know, Santa. Hey! Do you have extra glow bracelets stashed somewhere?"

"Oh, most definitely." Jack laughs, fully glancing at Gabriella. "Email the dummy account, and I'd bet they show up magically on your desk."

"Special slave delivery," Michael teases, touching up a few loose sequins because it pays to be neat. Cory rolls his eyes and exits without another word. "Are you going to submit your resume for the promotion?" Michael asks Jack when they are alone but for the camera and the girl behind it.

"Dunno," Jack says sarcastically. "You know I really hate to travel on other people's expense accounts."

"Well, it's not like they'll be going cliff diving in Costa Rica or anything. It's probably just to Cincinnati to meet distributors. But it is a pay raise."

"So you're doing it?" Jack says absent-mindedly. He is busily adding a contrasting color as a border around his glow-in-the-dark booger to make it pop.

"Are you kidding? I already had my resume out on three headhunter sites. I emailed it to Coleman thirty seconds after Daniel left my desk." Michael pauses, looking Jack over in a clearly intrigued manner. "What was with that shouting match between you and Gabby? It's like the third time one of you yelled at the other this month?"

"I thought she had prank reported me. And she thought it was unfair that no one wanted her resume," Jack replies and again, his eyes dart away to glance at the woman in question.

"Gabby in management?" Michael laughs dismissively. "She's a good tech, but she can't handle people."

"She is incredibly skilled and committed." Jack shrugs, feeling his shoulders tighten slightly at Michael's dismissive tone. "They don't need half as many techs as they have, and she'd tell them. Unlike either of us." Jack looks up and playfully fakes shock at seeing the camera. But he doesn't sound or feel playful as he continues speaking. "She'd probably crack down on waste in a lot of ways."

"She's too meek."

"*Meek*?" Jack demands with a disbelieving laugh. "She about took off Daniel's head when he didn't ask for her resume."

"Okay, sorry." Michael holds up his hands in surrender. "I forgot you have a little thing for Gabby."

"No!" Jack all but shouts. And has to strangle the laughing voice in the back of his head. "I just...I work next to her. She isn't someone to underestimate, that's all."

"No one is doubting her skill or commitment. She's out there right now fixing a glitch on the website,   even though the website has its own techs. All because Carol complained that the website techs weren't getting back to her. Gabriella is committed," Michael concedes. Then goes in for the kill, eviscerating her reputation. In his opinion, anyway. "Too committed. Management won't let go of a worker like her, it's counterintuitive. She hasn't even taken a break to join the contest."

"Yeah." Jack laughs, falling back on his old standby position: *the boy who cares for noting, Pierre who did not care,* if you will. "I, on the other hand, have taken an extra twenty-five-minute break and look at the results."

Jack's reindeer is a bit wobbly, and there is a lopsided tree behind it with sequin decorations. But the booger shows great attention to detail.

"Well, it's certainly ugly," Michael says brightly. Both men laugh. "See you in the salt mines," Michael says and, without any effort to make the table as neat as his slicker, heads out of the break room, grabbing a bag of chips off the counter on his way.

Jack starts to straighten things, but about halfway into his task, he stops. Lifting a thick piece of white paper, he fan-folds it five times and lifts a pair of scissors, cutting around the edges to form three large attached circles.

Kristen smiles over the top of the camera as Jack starts making a chain of snowmen.

"You seemed a bit disturbed by what Michael was saying." Kristen comments. There is a sort of calm rightness to the way her body moves with the camera, and her mind tells her the moment when she needs to speak.

"He was just saying things that I had. Some of it to Gabriella." Jack doesn't even lift his head from his task as he begins to add sequins and bubble paint decorations to the individual snowmen. "But hearing it from someone else, I sort of heard her point. She's good at her job. She works harder than anyone. Why exactly wouldn't they want that?"

Kristen lets the words hang in the air, feeling no further internal push to speak. He works in silence, and so does she. Kristen steps sideways until, once more, Jack and Gabriella are lined up in a pleasing diagonal in the frame.

My Kingdom
for Some Mistletoe

O n this very same Tuesday, December eleventh, at precisely three-forty-one p.m. Gabriella at last fixes the glitch on the website, for which she is not the technician. It's been a busy day. But she quite appreciated the challenge. The software she tends to work with has small, annoying problems that she can fix but bring her no pleasure. This was fun. Well, not the part where she had to speak with the annoyed website techs, all upset that Gabriella was doing their job, even though none of them wanted to do it. But it's done now, and all she is up to is writing a quick email to Mr. Coleman in case this comes back to him, explaining what she did and why.

Debbie has yet to call and say they are ready for Gabriella, and the longer she waits for the meeting, the more it's bugging her in the back of her mind. But also, she's excited to see the contest judging. She was too busy to take breaks and go see people's slickers earlier. But she heard laughter all morning. As she was closing a bunch of windows on her computer, she noticed the Naughty-and-Nice list open though she didn't recall opening it. Michael had a check by his name, on the naughty side. And August, from the mail room, had a new check as well, but his on the good side. And both of them had notes in glowing font that said *sharing*.

Gabriella is absolutely tickled to realize she must have elves spying for her! She always thought of Santa looking at a list and knowing who was bad and good, but this is excellent! She wonders if

NICE TO BE SO NAUGHTY

she'll get to know who the elves are. And if every Secret Santa gets this sort of magic? And why she isn't more weirded out? But she isn't weirded out at all. She's having fun!

While Gabriella is checking over her email for typos, Jack Drummer decides to lean over her cubicle wall, lifting a Hershey's Kiss from the candy basket that hangs outside it. He leans on the cubicle, an action the flimsy bit of cork and thin metal is not up to. But Gabriella does not rise to the bait. Forcing her attention forward.

Jack, like a two-year-old without attention, begins to flick the balls on her tree until he has knocked the tree off its proper angle. Unconsciously Gabriella reaches out her left hand to fix the tree's angle while simultaneously using her mouse to delete half a sentence that wasn't needed.

Jack smiles fondly at the top of Gabriella's head. He knew he had her attention. He bets she is dying to tell him to get off her cubicle. It really is a great deal of fun watching her resist.

"Where did Santa and the reindeer go?" Jack inquires.

"I'm gonna bet, to the north pole. Gotta get ready for Christmas," she replies and hits send on her email, only realizing at the last second that she should have kept it to have something to focus on.

Her hands flex uncomfortably. And her right pointer finger taps against her mouse pad in a one-three-one pattern.

"Makes sense," Jack says with laughter in his tone. "Did he need the elves that used to stand on your monitor too?"

"Huh. Looks like." Gabriella has to argue with herself to keep from clenching her teeth. "What do you want?"

"Thought I should remind you to work on your slicker," Jack leans over the wall, so his face is right next to hers to whisper. "Before someone else gets a clue to Santa's super secret identity."

Gabriella rolls her shoulders slightly but notches her thumb behind her, indicating the slicker on the back of her seat. "I did work on it."

Jack steps around the cubicle wall and lifts the slicker away from the back of her seat, holding it out so the camera can get a better look. The film crew is back together now, having joined forces after lunch. But Kristen, though no longer holding the camera, has remained entirely silent.

The slicker has a random arrangement of glued-on bells around some, not terribly neatly written, words in puffy paint, and a puffy paint drawing Jack cannot make out.

"*Get me*," Jack reads off the slicker. "*I'm givin' out*...what is this supposed to be? Christmas trees?" He guesses.

"Wings!" Gabriella throws a dirty look over her shoulder as if Jack is intentionally trying to offend her.

He isn't, but he feels like she *intentionally* made the drawing too ambiguous for people to recognize.

"It's from *It's a Wonderful Life*. That's why the bells." Gabriella snaps. "Get it?"

Jack shakes his head.

"You haven't seen it?" Gabriella demands incredulous.

"I have," Jack smirks. "But I didn't take notes. I didn't realize there would be a quiz."

Gabriella jerks her head away, annoyed and pretending to ignore him. Jack chuckles, holding the slicker out a moment longer and examining it closely. She writes much neater than this. And doodles better too; he's seen her draw pointy little flowers while on tech calls. This isn't even close to her best work. No attempt whatsoever has been made at artistry, nor even Gabriella's usual precision. To be honest, it looks like the work of an impatient child who didn't like the assignment and wants the world to know it.

She did it on purpose, he realizes.

Gabriella is muttering to herself. Well, not muttering, that implies that her vocal cords are moving, only her mind is moving, but it is talking to her in a snide little voice pointing out that no one seems to remember that line, she's been looking for a sweater, or card or anything with that quote on it for years and has yet to find it. No one appreciates details like her.

Jack leans near Gabriella, shaking with laughter. One of his hands settles on the back of her seat, brushing her shoulder as if unintentionally. But it seems well established that even if he doesn't think he does these things intentionally, some part of him certainly does.

"You can do better than this. Aren't you even going to try? Someone will notice," Jack points out, his voice low, but his humor still apparent.

Gabriella tries to turn the seat to face him fully, thinking he'll get the hint and drop his hand. He does not take the hint, so all she manages to do is turn partway towards him and push her shoulder more firmly against his hand. She tries not to focus on the point of contact. But it is uncomfortable with Jack right there, staring right into her eyes full of amusement and...intensity. Not a word that is often used to describe him.

"Not to sound conceited," Gabriella begins a bit quieter and, unfortunately, *breathier* than intended. "But how would it look if I pressed and pressed to get that prize, and then I won it?"

She does sound conceited. A point Jack is about to make.

"You do sound conceited."

See?

"And I've never liked you better." Jack laughs. "Honestly, I'd bet the big guys would respect that sort of move too."

Gabriella stiffens now, not from his nearness but from his words and from that pounding home, again and again, that the world doesn't respect people who put effort into being kind, honorable, and ethical.

Well, not the "real" world anyway. The magical one seems to appreciate her style. Otherwise why give her magic? Why help her find Mom's recipe, or give her new ways to spread joy? There is magic in the world, and it likes Gabriella.

"Well, I wouldn't respect it. And there is nothing wrong with that." Gabriella stares at Jack's hand with a brow raised.

Now it's Jack's turn to be uncomfortable. Because he supposes there isn't anything wrong with Gabriella's way. In fact, he supposes there is a lot right with it. But she won't get ahead that way. Not ever. And she deserves to get ahead.

Jack pulls his hand away as she clearly wants and straightens. Awkwardly he nods at the nutcracker in the back right corner of Gabriella's desk. "Were you able to fix him?"

"No." Gabriella bites out the word sharply. "Even glued, the cracker handle kept breaking off whenever I tried to use it. But I like having him *here*."

"I am sorry about that. Seriously." Jack scuffs his foot on the floor, backing away a bit. "I got defensive when you were upset, but I shouldn't have, you know..." he fumbles for the words.

Gabriella is not so hindered. "Broken him? Been in my cubicle?"

"I was going to say shouted at you. But sure, whatever you need an apology for." Jack fights back a grin, but just barely.

"Whatever I *need* an apology for? Are you kidding me?" Gabriella stands, crowding forward with her hands fisted at her sides. "You *broke* my property. After *invading my space*. Now you want to make it out like I'm unreasonable for expecting you to take responsibility for your actions?"

Jack shakes his head, no longer able or even willing to fight off the smile on his face. "Not really. I just wanted to see how long it would take me to piss you off again." He laughs at her narrow-eyed, nostril-flaring expression. "Oh, by the way, Debbie called. Coleman wants to see us both in his office."

"When?" Gabriella demands like an overwrought librarian.

Jack shrugs, chewing on his laughter. "When she called probably."

"And you wasted all that time?" Gabriella marches around Jack towards the elevator impatiently.

Jack follows along casually. "Not wasted. I used it exactly as I meant to."

"What, to make me look as lazy as you?" Gabriella demands a bit meanly, but she is distressed. And if Jack can break her property and feel no remorse, she shouldn't feel remorse over insulting his work ethic. *If you can call it that.*

Jack takes it in his stride; after all, it is not an entirely inaccurate description of what he was trying to do. "I'm not lazy; I'm just not desperate to be noticed. But, yeah. I was slowing you down. So you don't look so hungry." The elevator opens as Jack is getting in his last shot. "Coleman's the sort you should play hard to get with."

"I have no intention of being gotten," Gabriella snaps as she enters the elevator. Only as she turns to the front does she remember the film crew behind her. It is a moment quite evident on film as she jumps and her eyes widen. Jack, beside her, steps aside for the crew to enter, smiling wide.

It is immensely pleasing to adult men and very small boys when they can so agitate the people around them that they forget where they are and what is going on. Jack is in no way immune to this sort of wild delight. It all but eclipses the slight offense he took earlier when Gabriella was so determined for him not to touch her.

The elevator doors close, and Jack's pleasure makes him into a very easy conversationalist. "Sure you do. If you ever want a promotion. Which honestly I don't get. You've gotta be bored here. And that promotion would only mean less of the work you like best. The code you wrote to change my wallpaper, was *way* above this place. I had to unravel it one line at a time like…"

"Knitting. Yeah. I know." Gabriella says with unmitigated pride in her work.

One might hear her pride and think it a thing of arrogance. But Gabriella has never excelled socially. Never quite fit among her peers. A rather large number of things that other people do not even have to think about, take her mountainous effort. She has spent her life being judged against other people and subjectively found lacking for a different reason every time. There is no winning. But at a computer, writing code, her every ability is objectively measured. She is not the greatest tech genius the world has ever known, but she knows she is great. She can prove it. So when she speaks of her work, it is always with pride, for here is a place where her value must be acknowledged.

Jack laughs. Only Gabriella would describe code as knitting and notch her head up with gangster-style pride. "Why aren't you at a tech firm or opening a cyber security company? Or something?"

Gabriella tries to open her mouth, tries to answer. But her jaw feels goopy, like she's crammed half a bottle of peanut butter inside her mouth, and can't chew through it to find her tongue. And it is just as well, because she doesn't really have an answer.

What would she say? *I had a challenging job that I loved, but my mother died and I stopped loving that job, or much of anything. And I couldn't do the work anymore. So now I'm here, just wasting hours.*

No. Not the truth.

Before Gabriella can respond the elevator doors open. Gabriella charges out, woman on a mission style.

"Hurry up," she calls over her shoulder.

Jack snorts at the camera crew, most of whom are laughing. Andrew, though, was barely paying attention. His mind was trapped in one of those images he often contemplates for no apparent reason but has learned not to tell anyone about, lest they "worry" about him. On this occasion, the image was of the elevator doors closing around his outstretched arm and amputating it. Logically he knows this wouldn't happen. But he can see it. And it makes for an interesting image to add to the horror film he is writing in his spare time.

This, however, has almost nothing at all to do with the story at hand. One simply wants to feel fair to poor, often forgotten Andrew. Gabriella would want it that way.

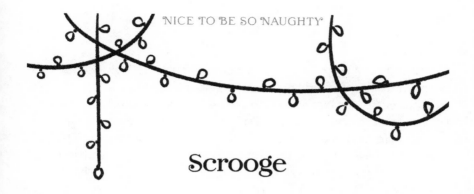

Scrooge

Zooming ahead briefly, several moments have passed to bring us to this exact moment. It is nine p.m. Terrance and Kristen are editing in Kristen's apartment, and Andrew has run out for some pizza. They've been at playing around with a rough cut of a scene Kristen is calling "Scrooge" for some time now and are now waiting for Andrew to watch it back. Even though he has *fully twelve times* told both his partners that he really needs to go, he trusts them to do this one scene without him.

Let it never be said that either Kristen or Terrance is especially good at listening.

"Are you sure you want to call this scene Scrooge?" Terrance asks, truly uncomfortable, though Kristen seems to be fully at ease. "I thought you said he was your cousin."

"Great Uncle," Kristen corrects. "We aren't that close. Anyway, haven't we established already? This is a coup."

"You don't think it will put you on the outs with your family."

Terrance is truly disturbed by this prospect. He has a number of relatives he fights with, hates to spend more than an hour with, and would rather die than tell if he ever wins the lottery, but he's never disliked any of them enough to set out to make enemies of them.

This is not the case for Kristen. Not at all.

"None of the ones I care about."

"Won't it..." Terrance hesitates. Kristen is in high spirits. She hasn't once mentioned the hours she spent with the extra camera. And has yet to let him even upload the footage. It can't be that bad. He wants to press, but...ever since they filmed the scene with her *great uncle,* she has been back to her old Kristen self. The self Terrance doesn't like at all. And yet, now that he knows the other Kristen, he finds himself more sympathetic for this Kristen and doesn't want to upset her any more than she clearly already is.

"Won't it what?" Kristen asks with a casual nothing-bothers-me laugh that no one is buying. She didn't like being back in that office. Mom's office. And seeing nothing of Mom in it, as though the entire company, like her family, simply moved on and forgot Mom ever existed.

And she doesn't like that condescending game Uncle Coleman used on Gabriella, manipulating her, so she won't insist on doing things her way, all because he knows if she insists, he'll have to back down. Kristen hated the look that Gabriella wore after that interview. It was a near thing because Kristen really wanted to leap out from behind the camera and attack her uncle or tell Gabriella the truth. But she didn't. And she is fine. Kristen is always fine.

"Won't it bother your parents?" Terrance asks softly but pointedly.

"My mother is dead, and she never liked my great uncle anyway, so it shouldn't bother her any," Kristen says with a laugh. "It might bother my father, but only in as much as it drives home that he should either pay attention to his holdings or let someone more suited to it be in charge."

"And you think he'll disagree with how your uncle is running things?" Terrance asks in an attempt to cover his absolute shock at anyone speaking so of their father. His attempt was unsuccessful.

Kristen grins dangerously and shakes her head. "Of course not. But if the footage gets out, painted in the light, we will paint it. It might mean he gets opened up to lawsuits. Or, at the very least bad publicity. *Jack can help you with anything too difficult.*" Kristen quotes her uncle shaking her head and her eyes narrowing sharply.

"To her face, he used that condescending tone, and I have it on video! Does he think it wasn't apparent on camera that the only reason we were allowed in that office was to let him get on camera and blame Gabriella for the whole people sitting on Jack's lap thing? He was covering his ass and throwing Gabriella under the bus *while he condescended to her!*" Kristen laughs.

"People tend to see their own perspective as the only perspective," Terrance remarks, without any deeper meaning.

Men do tend to say things they think are quite straightforward. And Kristen, in a rather unusual display of solidarity with often termed "feminine" traits,   reads much deeper meaning into the words.

"It was...interesting," she says. Having judged Terrance's words to mean he wants to know about her time behind the lens. Her new perspective. "I don't know that it is something I would want to do often, but...it did help me to understand better how you can tell the story without the voices and the words at all. But." She smirks catlike in her certainty that what she is about to say is correct. "When you were alone getting footage, you didn't ask any questions, did you?"

Terrance was at first a bit confused by the subject change but, being fairly clever and possessed of a sister, managed to follow without assistance. He was even interested to hear how things went for her. But now she's turned the tables on him, and for the life of him, he can't think why.

"No. Why would I?"

"Because I think it would be just as useful for you to see how a properly timed question or prompt can help you to reveal the deeper person in your subjects."

"You can do that with the camera."

"Somewhat. But they always know the camera is there. They have a character in their mind, a version of themselves that they are willing to display for you. And yes, the longer you are there, the more their real self will emerge. But sometimes, antagonizing them and forcing them to answer uncomfortable questions helps them get there faster. Think of Gabriella and that explosive scene in her kitchen. Once she'd done that, on camera, she was never as awkward with us again. She volunteers her feelings now and shares deeper things she's been trying to hide. That's what the questions do. You ought to try it sometime."

Terrance, who is currently quite at a loss to come up with a response and a little baffled to realize she might have been paying more attention to him than her dismissive attitude suggests, is saved from having to come up with something intelligent to say by the arrival of their third partner and a pizza or two. Once everyone is settled in with pizza and drinks, Terrance, in the middle seat on the couch, hits the space bar on his laptop and the rough cut plays.

Black screen. Drop in white titles.

SCROOGE

Fade to Jack seated in the break room grinning.

JACK

I was disappointed not to get pranked today. That's why I was riling her. And because it's fun! She gets this hungry, sharklike expression when she snaps at you. It is so much fun to watch. Dangerous. I really wanted to see how far she would take the pranking. It was bound to be an intense ending.

Jump cut.

JACK

Yeah, I want that. (laughs)It's like walking right at the edge of a cliff. You know you shouldn't. You know it's dangerous but damn, isn't the view so much better when you're that close to being completely ruined?

Cut to a richly appointed office. The camera is angled at a diagonal to catch Mr. Coleman and his two employees.

MR. COLEMAN

You're doing a great job with Secret Santa, Gabby. Everyone is happy with it. I knew you were the perfect choice.

GABRIELLA

Thank you, sir.

MR. COLEMAN

And roping in Jack as a helper was great. A real hoot. (forced laugh)I trust it worked out how (emphasis) *you* hoped.

Gabriella's mouth hangs open.

JACK (spin style)

Oh, it worked wonders. Everyone got a kick out of it. And now I know everyone's Christmas wishes. (winks)

Gabriella shuts her mouth.

MR. COLEMAN (fake enthusiasm)

Terrific! That's why I want the pair of you to take care of the party as well.

GABRIELLA

Party? I didn't thin—

MR. COLEMAN (interrupting)

Krissy's sales are terrific. We're gonna have a small bash on the twenty-first, the last three hours of the day. Come up with another of your *cute* little Christmas games. Jack can help you with anything too difficult.

Gabriella is astonished, eyes wide.

JACK (lightly)
Like sitting around looking pretty while everyone tells me their wishes.

MR. COLEMAN
Exactly.

GABRIELLA (professional and bright)
Sir. This is great, of course, but I really think the staff might prefer getting that half-day off with pay, or—

Coleman holds up a hand. Gabriella stops speaking.

MR. COLEMAN
Let's not start again with talk of bonuses. You're not an accountant, Gabby. We really can't afford to give out money right now.

GABRIELLA (cold and professional)
Of course, I'm not an accountant. I agree. But a party is going to cost extra, for food, decoration. And you'll be paying everyone to be there. A half-day off *seems cheaper.*

MR. COLEMAN (grinding teeth)
Work on the assignment you're given, Gabby. Stop getting *ahead* of yourself, alright?

Gabriella nods tightly. Begins to leave.

JACK (bro to bro)
We're just passing along the number one request whispered in my ear. Over and over, it was "I want more time off," "I want a bonus." Thought you should know.

Gabriella looks at Jack in shock. Coleman forces an entirely false smile.

MR. COLEMAN (sharply)

Consider the message received. And officially rejected. Debbie will give you the budget and the number of caterers we prefer. Get me some plans by Friday.

Cut to break room. Gabriella is seated, looking into her lap as she picks at her nails.

GABRIELLA

Don't get ahead of yourself, (nods heavily) So Mr. Burns told him I asked about my resume. Guess that was my official rejection. Anyway, I got a different promotion (fake enthusiasm). I'm the company party planner! (laughs brokenly) As long as it's easy stuff.

Cut to the interior of the elevator. Jack and Gabriella stand against the railing, Gabriella looking downtrodden. Jack smiles like a camp counselor.

JACK

You know—

GABRIELLA (interrupting)

Look, thanks for sticking up for me. But (whispers), Please don't say it yet.

JACK (playful)

Don't say what? You don't even know what I'm going to say.

GABRIELLA (snide)

That you told me so. That I should "lighten up." That I'm trying too hard, and I shouldn't take it personally when he treats me like a child.

JACK

All really terrific points for me to make. I agree with me. But actually, I was just going to say how happy I am that you've stopped worrying so much about your wardrobe in front of Coleman.

Long beat. Gabriella shuts her eyes, breathing heavily. Opens eyes and looks down at her Christmas tree sweater with blinking lights. She sinks in at the shoulders.

GABRIELLA (defeated)

Perfect.

Cut to break room, Jack seated, quietly smiling into the distance.

JACK

She is sort of creepily perfect. But I don't think she sees it any better than Coleman does. And everyone calling her *Gabby* is really starting to bug me. It's like they use it to make her feel immature while they're knocking her down. She ought to be in their faces about calling her by her actual name! And about respecting her work. Not about getting bonuses for the rest of the staff who don't even notice her enough to realize that she didn't get the first three gifts. Do you know no one brought her a cookie on the cookie exchange day? Really? No one.

Several silent beats. Jack groans, rubbing a hand over his face. He glances at the camera and shrugs, smiling wryly.

JACK

Okay. Fine. I might have a *little* thing for Gabriella.

Cut out.

Kristen stares at the screen, twisting her lips. There is something—

"Cut the last twenty-three seconds," Andrew says out of nowhere.

"What?" Kristen demands, not because she disagrees. That would cut out just after Jack says Gabrielle didn't get the first three gifts, just before he started to show signs of warmer emotions than annoyance. It's a good cut point for Kristen's aims. So it isn't the cut that has Kristen questioning Andrew, but she is shocked to hear him venture an opinion. She thought he was with them to coast to an A.

Andrew shrugs. "You want to point out mistreatment, not give them reasons to ignore it. If he likes her, his opinions are as easy to dismiss as hers."

Kristen stares, brow raised and slight respect growing at Andrew as his pizza flops on the way into his mouth, spilling his sprinkle of red peppers all down his shirt.

"He's right," Terrance says with a laugh. "He shouldn't be. But he is. We only left it because we liked the budding romance. We have to decide who our audience is and what message we want to show them."

Kristen leans back. She agrees with everything they are saying. Every word. She just doesn't like it. If it comes down to deciding between potentially losing her A by alienating her professor or failing to impact her family by focusing on the cute romance, she's going to have to choose her A.

"Ugh. I wish we could make two documentaries. The one that will impact people the way we want and the one that gets us an A. I still think there is a way." She is quiet for a moment and both boys eat in peace. They know Kristen likes to talk and she has a solution to everything. They should just eat and let her plot.

Kristen is thinking about herself and what she wants from this film from week to week. She liked this cut, this scene, but she is concerned that part of what has left her uncertain has little to do with the scene itself and everything to do with what they recorded after; that footage of Gabriella and Jack in the basement they aren't sure they are willing to touch.

This is a nice scene. It has compelling workplace drama, a touch of romance and a satisfying break point to pull the story forward. But what happened in the basement later...that was special, but it would change the direction of the piece irrevocably to include it.

"For now, I say we mark it to cut, but leave it. Keep the cameras rolling in all directions. Maybe, just maybe, the answer will present itself."

Christmas Ghosts

Having enjoyed that brief glimpse of the future, please, do join our protagonists back in the present, for that moment that so moved Kristen. At this exact moment, Gabriella and Jack are exiting the elevator and returning to the basement after their brief visit to the rarified air of the building's fourth-floor executive offices. Gabriella is a bit crestfallen. It is telling that the man beside her and all his jokes at her expense are the things bothering her the least. She knows he thinks he is being funny. Thinks he is teasing her out of a funk. Thinks such a thing is possible.

Gabriella has lived with herself long enough to know that it is not possible to tease her out of a funk. Because it is never *just* a funk. But she isn't exactly in one right now. She feels a bit like the pitiful child Mr. Coleman seems to believe she is. And she is annoyed that she had started to feel like maybe Mr. Coleman hadn't only selected her for Secret Santa because she was female and the most junior member of IT. As the events kept going so well and she saw more and more magic spreading around her, she'd thought that maybe he chose her because he saw something in her. Maybe he was a part of the magic. Now she knows that was misguided. That man sees nothing in her. Not even her name.

Jack stays right next to Gabriella, even after exiting the cramped elevator, allows them more space. He is close enough that she can feel his warmth, feel when he will move, feel his breathing;

she can nearly feel his pulse. *People's brain waves sync up when they are this close;* the thought comes and goes in her brain. Reminding her without conscious thought that it is an unconscious reaction that leads to people falling into step and matching breathing, not deeper inner workings of their matched souls.

Gabriella enters her cubicle and sinks into her chair as the film crew is asking for quick interviews. Jack is still up, so he goes first, leaving Gabriella alone with her thoughts. She looks around the empty department realizing that everyone must be up at the contest on the third floor to vote on rain slickers. She had been really excited to go up and see it earlier. Now she feels drained of energy and interest. She straightens her desk and shuts down her computer, preparing to go home after the interview.

It only takes a few minutes for Jack to come out of the break room, smiling. "Your turn." He winks.

Gabriella nods and walks silently out of the room, leaving Jack staring after her. He hates seeing her like this, so morose, defeated. She is usually so full of energy, bright and positive, or fiery and angry; either way, she is never at this low a power. It's hard to see. He knows he should probably go up to the contest, but he waits. He wants to—No, he needs to try and cheer her up.

When her interview is done, Gabriella walks to her desk without looking Jack's way. She sits again, reaching under her desk for her purse, but then just sits there with it in her lap. Jack has followed her to her cubicle unnoticed, or at the very least unremarked upon.

He leans over her cubicle wall with a bright smile. "Come on. Grab your contest losing slicker and let's go join the fun."

"I think I'll skip the contest and start work on the party," Gabriella says.

"And you think wrong," Jack responds authoritatively.

Gabriella looks up with a brow raised and has to bite her tongue to keep from telling him he isn't her boss yet. But he is grinning as if he knows the direction of her thoughts and continues speaking.

"You keep missing all this great stuff you're doing for everyone. You have totally improved the moods of everyone in the office, but you're still at your desk, missing out. Take a break, enjoy it. Even Santa stops long enough to have a few cookies." Jack winks.

Gabriella says nothing for several long moments, staring at Jack. There was a sort of glowing warmth in her chest as he spoke. Pleasure that at least someone recognizes what she's been doing for the staff. That at least someone values it. But she still feels some...resentment towards him. And not just for the things he's done to her. But for all of that *ease*. Everything is so easy for him that he thinks it is easy for everyone.

These are the sort of feelings she generally keeps to herself. Bottles up. Shoves aside. Because what is the point in sharing them? They won't change anything. He will still be easy. She won't.

But something about these past few days. Something about following the magic, and doing things that she would usually resist has made her realize that there might be a point to saying these things. She's just never seen it because it has nothing to do with changing the world, or even changing him. The value in saying these things is in allowing herself to be heard.

Gabriella has spent, nearly, her entire life trying to be inconspicuous. Trying to be quiet, and small. And she has done *so* well. Almost no one notices her. Not really.

But the magic noticed her. And the magic keeps nudging her, urging her to be bold, to be loud. To be dramatic. And while she may never be easy, the magic has shown her that she can be forceful, open, and loud. And that that can be a beautiful thing. And that more people should see it, on her terms.

"It's not a choice, you know? I mean, not going up to the contest is," she admits, not because she thinks she needs to concede that point, but because she is sure he would argue it if she did not. And he certainly would have.

"But I don't wake up every day and say to myself, 'how intensely can you commit yourself to your work today?' Or 'make sure you think about it for hours when someone slightly bumps your pens.' Who would? I get that it seems strange to you, and you poke fun at it to see if you can get me to be more *normal*."

"No, I don—"

"But you can't." Gabriella interrupts, not waiting to hear what he is trying to say. "And quite frankly, you have no right to try. It is okay for me to say, *don't touch my things*. This intensity, this...rigidity that you see is a part of me. Sometimes it is a part that I love. Sometimes it is so like breathing that I honestly forget about it. And sometimes it gets in my way, and I hate it. But it is not something that can be teased, or corrected away. It will always be a part of me. I *cannot* relax."

If one perhaps needed proof that Jack would indeed argue any point in her speech, buckle up; here it comes.

Jack—who has been nodding along and feeling bad for occasionally, *alright frequently*, nudging her pens, or her coffee cup, or outright stealing her things to get her attention—suddenly feels less guilty. Which he really should have felt for longer than seven seconds. He grins.

"Maybe you can't relax completely. But you can lighten up a bit."

Gabriella pops both brows, shaking her head and wearing a —this is exactly what I expected from you—expression.

Jack, undaunted, grins and speaks on. "When you were pranking me, you were much more relaxed about other things."

"What, now you want me to prank you?" Uptight Gabriella demands uptightly.

Yes, you are correct, uptightly is not a word, but she heard it in her head with a bit of a bite, so it's only right that you do as well.

"Absolutely!" Jack's eyes spark with unmistakable excitement. "I don't tease you because I want you to change. I tease you because...I like having all of your attention," he says quiet and playful. "I was bummed not to be pranked today. Every day was an adventure."

Gabriella sits up straighter, growing frustrated. And though she cannot acknowledge it at the moment, part of what bothers her is

NICE TO BE SO NAUGHTY

this thing she hasn't felt in years: hope. No one is comfortable with the real her. They tolerate her; they make an effort. But he's looking at her and saying things that make it seem like he...*likes* this side of her. This loud, forceful, retaliatory side that the magic is exposing. And she knows it isn't true. So she has to make him admit it. Now. Before she does something reckless, like believe him.

"That wasn't relaxed. I was escalating, every day more." Gabriella makes no attempt to hide her intensity as she speaks. She may even let it loose a bit, leaning up, investing every word with power. "I mean, it was fun, but even then, I was *intense*. I spent the better part of my weekend writing code to screw with you. And the more fun I had with it, the more I wanted to do. I have a twelve-step plan. It gets mean."

"How mean?" Jack says, leaning near and seeming nothing if not intrigued.

Gabriella blinks several times. Bites the insides of her cheeks. Entirely unaware that her right hand is at her leg, fisted, and tapping one-thee-one, every time a bit harder. She shouldn't tell him. Look at him, even now leaning near with those bright eyes and that easy smile. She's going to tell him and ruin all of that. It will take the wind right out of him like Coleman took it out of her. And anyway...if he knows in advance—

Step twelve won't mean as much if she tells him before hand.

Though some of her earlier thoughts were very nearly considerate. It should be noted that one of the deepest and strongest considerations stopping her tongue is entirely selfish. As well it should be, for once. She needs that last step. She needs to know that she has the ability to destroy something in him like he destroyed something in her.

It's just a nutcracker. Or it should be. But it's a part of her. It lived in her, and he broke it, mocked it, and even today didn't really apologize. He cannot go on unpunished and unapologetic believing his own actions to be endearing despite how deeply they have wounded her. It isn't right. Everything cannot always be easy for him!

"Come on, tell me." Jack goads, blissfully unaware of the inner battle Gabriella is waging. "How big a bite were you going to take out of my skin?"

Gabriella clenches her teeth as she prepares to give him the answer he wants. She feels her fist now; she'll probably be bruised on her thigh when she gets home. She has been before. After Mom died, she was bruised there for...months.

"Valentines' proposal fail," she bites out and doesn't have to wait long to see him bleed.

Jack falls back a step, then two, his eyes fly wide and horrified. He doesn't seem to have the ability to speak. Gabriella has never seen him without the ability to speak. He stares at her like she is a monster. And she feels like one. Though she hasn't done anything to him, and he has to her. This is her biggest trouble, she always feels more for people than they feel for her, or for anyone at all really.

"I'm not...going to show it," Gabriella says, unsure if she is trying to reassure him or herself. But she knows she doesn't like the look on his face. Even the part of her who wanted to see it. Even the part of her that is shouting his pain is not vindication enough. "I already decided not to show it. But...this isn't relaxed." Gabriella feels like she might cry. She yanks her hands away from her legs and shakes them out, trying to shake out her fist, but it isn't working.

She should remove herself. She knows she should. She should go to the bathroom and play her soothing song, probably flick the light switch; it is that sort of day. Just remove herself from the stress-inducing situation. But she can't leave him looking this way. She is the soft touch who pulled over to help a very dirty homeless woman get out of the street when she was already late to work, and she knew she'd have to go home and shower only to still feel uncomfortable in her own skin all day long. But she stopped anyway. Because people were honking and cursing and treating the woman like an animal because they didn't *want* to understand her struggle.

Gabriella can't stand watching other people feel alone. Or shut out. Neglected. So she opens her mouth, even when every muscle in her body is tense, and she is fighting with everything in her not to start punching her leg. She needs to punch her leg; she needs to feel the force of her energy being broken apart. But still, she opens her mouth, speaking as much to that part of herself that is empathizing with him, as she is to Jack. Vocalizing her struggle so that the person who has always been hardest on her—herself—might throw a bit of empathy her way.

"You broke my mother's nutcracker, so I needed to destroy a piece of you," she says and a tiny pocket of inner tension loosens.

Jack laughs. It doesn't sound amused. Shocked. Maybe appalled? Even hurt. But not amused. But Gabriella doesn't know another word for that sound but laugh. And it doesn't matter how, these words simply need to be spoken.

"When I'm pulling a prank, and you're upset, I feel refreshed in a way I haven't before. Even if you're only a little upset. Then it gets quiet." Gabriella tilts her head sideways sadly, apologetically. The *kind* part of her, and the part that is always trying to contain the bits of self the world might find wanting, like her envy, selfish desires, and resentments. Those parts are apologetic. Those parts need to be understood.

"I feel it materializing beneath my skin. I feel that nutcracker break, over and over like a ghost that lives inside me, so I escalate. As if destroying you would kill the ghost. It feels right when I'm doing it," Gabriella admits. Then her tone falls flat, and her hands suddenly unclench as her being just feels...sad and tired from fighting that vengeful force within. "But when I say it aloud, I can hear that it's not—*normal*.

"Normal people don't need that kind of revenge. It's not proportional. I'm not in control; the ghost is." Gabriella looks down. Looks up at Jack, then down again, and up again. Unable to tell where she should be looking, what she should be doing, or why—

Why he hasn't left?

This Frightful Blizzard Inside

There are several moments of silence between Jack and Gabriella, and even the doc crew in the background watching with bated breath. *You broke my mother's nutcracker, so I needed to destroy a piece of you.*

That's intense.

Everything about Gabriella is *so* intense. Jack's eyes take her in, even as his mind is reeling. He watches her rocking her head up and down, watches her shudder as if something is attacking her from within, watches her tensing further for every second of silence. *Normal people don't need that kind of revenge.* Fuck normal! Why would she want to be normal? Normal disappears normal runs. Normal…normal ditches you in a restaurant after you've publicly humiliated yourself. Gabriella wouldn't do that. She might yell at you, might refuse you, might drive you to distraction by being so intense that she expends more energy than the sun, but despite her intensity, everything in Gabriella is…good, Jack thinks as he watches her trying to apologize for a hurt she hasn't caused yet; though he hasn't even properly apologized for the hurt he caused.

While Jack's assessment of Gabriella is not *far* from the truth, it is worth noting that no one is all good. And there are many parts of Gabriella that have quite delighted to see him suffer. As well they should! But Jack is unaware of those parts in this moment and is caught magnetically in the intensity of the woman before him.

Kristen Kringle is well aware of those angrier, vengeful parts of Gabriella, but even she, is finding it hard to remember them. Her hand is pressed over her lips to keep from making a sound. She is biting on her tongue and imagining an anvil holding her in place to keep from rushing forward and shaking Jack, making him apologize properly or...hug her. He should hug her. Look at Gabriella rocking there. Can't he see she needs someone to hold her and tell her everything will be alright? Kristen feels a brittle sort of stillness, wishing for those arms, or to be those arms...wishing.

"Whenever it's quiet?" Jack asks Gabriella softly.

Gabriella, whose eyes were on the ground again, looks up in shock. "What?"

Jack smiles softly at Gabriella, this bundle of nerves that has caught fire. She is so certain she is about to be hated. He watched her pounding her fist against her leg as she spoke and kept feeling it in himself. Feeling her rhythm, her desperation. She works so hard. At everything, apparently. Even pranking.

Of course, it was work for her. She's too nice naturally for that sort of pranking to have come to her easily.

"The ghost," Jack explains his question. "It haunts you whenever it's quiet? Like when we were in the elevator, it was bothering you? And when you're working? Forever?"

Gabriella considers carefully before replying.

"Not every second. And not forever." She shrugs her head sideways. "At least not as prominently forever. But sometimes I'll think I've gotten past something like this, then suddenly, years later, it..." she waves her hands, unable to finish.

"Materializes again." Jack finishes for her, nodding. "Do you always take revenge?"

"Never." Gabriella shakes her head, her voice growing quieter with his every question. How is he just...talking about this?

Jack has nodded several times. He looks older when he isn't laughing and playing pranks. Gabriella isn't sure if she likes seeing it. Then he steps forward and gives one more casual nod.

Jack feels...odd. Different. He thinks back to that day in the parking lot when he offered to take over the usage reports, and Gabriella...glowed, her tension dissolving and the most beautiful smile transforming her face. That day, when he helped her like that, he felt stronger and happier and more himself than he had in years. Because she was happy. And now, well, he wants to see her happy again.

"So do it. Do your worst. See if it kills the ghost." Jack says boldly.

"Are you crazy?" Gabriella demands in a dismayed whisper.

"Nah. But you say you can never escape it. And I at least—"

"What? You're just so well adjusted that nothing bothers you?" Gabriella demands, advancing on him as though this is the most offensive thing anyone has ever said to her. It might be. And she has been privy to many an offensive statement.

Jack smiles as she advances on him, with those dangerous lights flashing in her eyes, angry and offended, and trying to convince him to defend himself from her monster-self.

"Not even close," Jack says seriously and watches the words fall over her, calming some of her terror at being the craziest person in the room.

"When Lauren dumped and humiliated me, and that video was everywhere, I ran. I quit my job. I stopped talking to our friends. I completely erased my social media accounts. I *thought*. " Jack can't help a laugh, grinning at the woman before him. "I ran away, and it worked out fine. So what I have that you don't is a certainty that I can escape if it comes to that. So." He shrugs. "Humiliate me. If I can't take it, I'll run away again and hide out for a few more years."

She is right before him, frozen and wide-eyed. No more than ten inches are separating them, and Jack cannot resist leaning a little bit closer.

This really isn't the moment to do it. And he has no idea why he wants to do it right this second. But he is imagining diving in those last few inches and feeling her lips. *There must be something perverse wrong with me, right?* Jack thinks as he has to fight against his every instinct not to kiss a woman who just confessed plans to *destroy a piece of him.* Yes. There is definitely something wrong with him. Because really, right now, he's enjoying having one hundred percent of Gabriella's attention.

And Gabriella is—*riveted.* She thinks along the same lines as Jack. That there is something wrong with him. That he likely needs professional help. Or that he is maybe, somehow, though she cannot think how, playing a trick on her. Or perhaps he didn't hear her right. She was speaking in English, right? She's been known to slip unintentionally into Spanish, but usually only with Maria. He makes no sense.

But stranger than any of that is the fact that he keeps getting nearer, and she...isn't bothered by it. More even than that. She feels oddly quiet inside and no part of her is reliving the nutcracker's death. She is just *quiet.*

She recalls a conversation with her therapist about adjustments that would make Gabriella more comfortable. And Gabriella fought her every step of the way.

"When you refuse to address your needs with people, you cage yourself. It forces you to live in a constant state of tension. Share your needs with people, ask them to make adjustments that help you feel more comfortable, that make you feel safe."

"When you ask people to change for you, they resent you," Gabriella argued.

"I'm not suggesting that people bend over backwards for you. But they can make small adjustments that will in turn make it easier for you to recognize when you need to remove yourself from a situation. Or do you think it's better that you be the only one forced to adjust? Better that you be the one resenting everyone?" Dr. Hearth had challenged.

Gabriella has no answer to that sarcastically rendered question. She doesn't resent adjusting to other people. Well...that's not true at all. But...but no one else feels this all the time. No one else *has* to. And Gabriella doesn't want to be the cause of anyone feeling like she does inside.

Now she wonders if perhaps Dr. Hearth had a point.

"Hell, I'm pretty sure you are one of a kind." Jack grins. "So I could probably hide forever next time. But the ghost, I wouldn't be able to escape," he says, drawing away slightly as he feels the shock of the words coming out of his mouth. "Would be knowing that you were out in the world hating me over something *I truly am sorry for.*" He pauses. They stare, locked in on one another, unable to move. Until Jack smiles, his lovely, easy smile. "So take it as far as you need to. Just promise not to hate me at the end."

"There is something wrong with you," Gabriella whispers. Anything is better than doing what she feels like and kissing him. Or running away. Or maybe slapping herself across the face so she can wake up.

Jack shakes his head. "Let's go to the contest." He holds out a hand. "You can prank me tomorrow."

In something resembling a state of shock, Gabriella takes Jack's hand, her free hand falling to the slicker hanging over the back of her chair. She follows Jack without a word as he retrieves his own slicker and leads to the elevator. The doc crew does not follow; Kristen has put out a hand to stop Terrance, but she needn't have bothered. He, too, sees how lovely this scene is without their presence invading it. They watch in silence, Terrance tightening the angle as the couple moves away.

Gabriella cannot feel a thing inside. At least nothing she can name. Her thoughts are these: *I don't know what just happened. What just happened? Why would he do that for me? Literally, no one does that. For anyone! We aren't even that close.*

"Jack," she whispers because this situation calls for quiet. "I don't *hate* you now."

"Good to know," Jack says lightly as the elevator doors open.

There is a brief silence. Sweet silence. Gabriella doesn't usually like a complete absence of sound, other people find it comforting, but her mind supplies the necessary noise to make even the quiet loud. But not right now. Right now, her thoughts drift in comfortably; they are curious and confused but...lovely. They are these: *I don't think I've ever felt this numb. It's quiet inside. I feel like I'm curled up on my couch with a cup of cocoa and a favorite movie, and the storm is outside, far away from me.*

What if it works? What if it doesn't work, and because he's given me permission, I've done this awful thing to him? And he's the one left hating me.

What if I can only stop— if I stop now?

"I won't release the clip," Gabriella says firmly, starting to feel again but unsure what she is feeling. The only thing she is sure about is that she cannot intentionally hurt someone who would make an offer like this for her. It would be wrong.

"Eh," Jack says easily. "Wait a few days, see how it goes. I'll probably do something really childish again."

He will. Childish is something he does with great ease and frequency.

But rather miraculously, Gabriella has found herself understood by someone who is not family, and it has a euphoric effect on her. It is bound to wear off, but in this moment, Gabriella is quite sure that there is nothing Jack could ever do to annoy her again. And Jack likewise is convinced that now that he understands her better, there is nothing she can do that will hurt him.

Gonna Get To Know Her Better

Upon peering at Terrance's laptop screen, one sees Jack Drummer sitting on a chair in the break room, staring directly at the camera. The doc crew managed to grab Jack after the contest for another quick interview. Now Terrance watches alone. Surprised to no longer actively dislike Jack Drummer.

JACK

I definitely don't want that damned clip floating around again. I can just imagine the auto-tuning and memes and (shakes head) general hilarity guys like Cory and Angelo would have with it. I hope it never comes out. (Beat) I hope my apology and voluntarily submitting to retribution brings about a more comfortable ending. But if not (heavy beat), When she was talking about not being 'normal' and 'proportional' like either of those things is fixed. Or even real. And I could see her trying so hard to shove herself into someone else's box of what is normal. I couldn't stand it.

Jack shakes head, cracks knuckles.

She's sweet and smart, and a little bit devious. (grins) Why is she the one trying to fit in? (Long silence) We look at proportion from a place of all things being equal, and they just aren't. Maybe this is proportional for her. She's going to feel it forever, so I should have to relive my greatest embarrassment.

It's not (tilts head from side to side) unreasonable. (Beat) I can bend a bit for her.

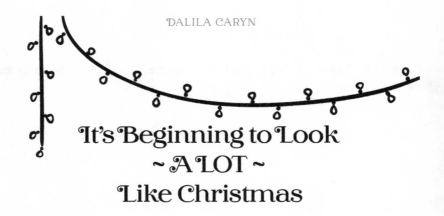

It's Beginning to Look
~ A LOT ~
Like Christmas

We find Jack and Gabriella again sometime later as she opens the door to her apartment and invites him inside. No, not for anything sexy. Sorry. They are here to work on the plans for the party.

It was Jack who made this suggestion; Gabriella was surprised to hear him suggest working on something for the office after office hours. She wouldn't have thought he was that committed. But almost the instant the thought occurred to her she felt bad for having thought it. He is being kind; she really must stop thinking rude things about him.

Were she privy to Jack's thoughts, she might have known that he does not find an unwillingness to take his work home with him to be an insult on any level. He does what work fits into his job description, and only during the hours he is paid. He takes full advantage of all of his breaks and really sees nothing wrong with the fact that if the servers crashed and he'd just begun his fifteen-minute break, he wouldn't go and look at it until after his break was over.

The reason he suggested going to Gabriella's house, or his own, to work on the party was really to spend more time with her. She's been very quiet since she shared her evil plotting with him. Plotting which the longer he gets from the initial shock, begins to seem sort of funny and cute. She would make an adorable evil villain. Likely a much more successful evil villain than most that television invents. Although, maybe not. Her nice side does rear up on her in the strangest moments. *She probably never would have used the clip,* he thinks, willfully ignoring the vengeful side of Gabriella's personality.

Jack suggested working because he wanted to know more about her. He wants to see her in her space, away from camera crews and cubicles. He wants to know everything about this mystery woman. As he followed her here in his car, it occurred to him that he really should have noticed before today that her neatness was not that mild type of compulsive behavior that is considered socially acceptable to tease. He's seen her in the past, come in early so she could clean down her desk. He's noticed that she carries wet wipes and that her trash was always neatly put into her can, it never overflows, and she flatly refuses to use the break room fridge or microwave because they were too dirty. He literally saw her shudder once when Cory took his chili out of the microwave and didn't clean off the explosive gunk. She always tries to pretend things don't bother her or to hide the bits of herself society might mock.

The more he thought about it, the more he wondered why it's socially acceptable to make fun of *any* compulsive behavior. Isn't that bound to make it worse? But he very quickly shoved this thought aside because it was going to make him feel very badly. And, like most people, Jack does not enjoy feeling bad about himself or his mistakes. So he won't look back. He'll go on from here, and try to be more considerate.

As Gabriella opens the door, but before she is inside, her sister's voice emerges from down the hall.

"Great, you're back; I thought I would miss you. How did the contest go? Did you win?"

Gabriella motions Jack inside, standing aside to give him the space. She can still feel the warm echo of his fingers closed around her own from when they held hands earlier. But she moves out of the way so as not to brush him. She is in an odd sort of middle between tense and comfortable.

As she drove here with him following, she changed her mind a hundred times. Maybe they should work at a coffee shop or something. But she relishes her time at home, in her own space, where she can shut out the world. That was always the case, but it is only so much stronger a feeling since the film crew started working at the Doll company. She'll be better in her space. But she is still nervous to see what he will make of it. If he thought her desk was over-decorated, what will he think of her home? People who like Christmas have accused her of over-decorating.

"Pam won," Gabriella calls out, a bit absentminded as Jack enters and wanders the room. "She only used white and yellow paint, but she made a snowman."

Jack's initial thought on viewing the apartment is: *She lives in a Christmas store.*

"Yep." Maria's voice grows closer as she makes her way down the hall with a bag slung over her shoulder and a sweater draped over the bag. "That would do...it." Her voice falls away as she catches sight of Jack. She glances at her sister, brow raised.

Maria immediately recognizes Jack; for a few reasons:

One: when Gabriella first got the job at My Best Friend Doll Company, she secretly took a picture of him and showed her sister, saying, "See. I told you there are hunky techs."

Two: because in the last two weeks of Gabriella's research, Maria has been forced to look at any number of pictures of him on his mother's Facebook page, with Gabriella exclaiming such things as "He's in a softball league" as if it were some sort of Satanic cult, or "Ugh! He would be an only child." And "What does he think he is a GQ model or something?" over a picture of him in swim trunks holding a volleyball. A picture she'd seen Gabriella go back and look at *several* times, but Maria generously didn't point out that Gabriella clearly to thinks he is a model *or something*.

And finally, three: because when she made her sketches on the Naughty-and-Nice list, she used the volleyball photo as the basis for her drumming/decapitated toy soldier.

With all this recognition, it is not at all strange that the expression she gives her sister, behind the back of the man examining their seven-foot Christmas tree and the fake fireplace beside it, is one of absolute disbelief and a raised brow asking if violence is necessary. And should she skip class.

Gabriella can usually interpret her sister's looks without thought. But right now, as simultaneously numb from Jack's earlier offer and nervy as she is with him in her space, she cannot focus on Maria's face enough even to know that she has eyebrows, much less interpret the meaning of the particular angle they are tilted to.

Jack can feel silent goings-on behind him, and as much as he would usually bask in such chaos from his mere presence, he is currently distracted. This home is so...homey. It's not a very large living room, and the kitchen is barely separated from it, with no room for a dining room. Every corner has something in it. The area under the window is fully enveloped by a Christmas tree and a heater that doubles as a fireplace. Well, a fake fireplace with a heater function, but though there are flames dancing on it, it is producing no heat. There is a paper chain hung in bows along the window. Atop the fake fireplace sits a fake bow of holly, and in front of it are the figurines of Santa and his *nine* tiny reindeer that used to sit on Gabriella's desk.

This does look like the North Pole, Jack thinks, remembering that Gabriella said that was where Santa went. He also spots her elves attached to the cord for the Christmas lights. He laughs quietly, realizing she's arranged it so it will look like they are decorating the tree.

Only Gabriella.

"This is Jack," Gabriella explains to her sister unnecessarily.

Jack turns around at his name and smiles. Holding out a hand for Maria. She does not take his hand, observing it as the trojans should have examined their gift horse. Jack, rather than being offended by this rejection, simply slips his hands into his pockets and continues his examination of the room.

"I work with him," Gabriella continues to offer unnecessary

information. "We're supposed to plan a Christmas party. Jack, this is my sister Maria. Jack, you can…" Gabriella waves her hand awkwardly, "make yourself comfortable."

It is at this moment that Jack spots the easel with the Naughty-and-Nice list. A list that has only one name on the Naughty side. He walks forward, chuckling.

"Yes, come in," Maria waves at the couch, her voice cold and suspicious. "So you're *Jack*, was it?"

"Yep. Jack." He nods at the easel with a laugh, pointing at the drawing beside his name. "The hunky broken piece of tin. Did you do this, Gabriella?"

"I did it." Maria pipes up.

"Maria is studying design and animation at CalArts. She is incredibly talented."

"Gee, thanks Mom," Maria says sarcastically. But it is worth noting that her heart burns brighter every time her sister praises her work. She simply does not feel that she should encourage this behavior.

"Right, Give me a second, Jack, I'll get my laptop, and we can get to work. Do you want any snacks or something to drink? Maria." Gabriella points at the kitchen as she walks out, clearly ordering her sister to be a proper hostess.

It is an order that Maria fully comprehends. And flatly ignores. As any sister would when faced with the man whose been picking at their sister. Manners have their time and place. So as Gabriella disappears down the hall where the two bedrooms and one bath are located, Maria crosses to the easel beside Jack to make some not-so-subtle remarks.

"Tin doesn't handle cold especially well, so it was a mistake for the soldier to also have an icy heart," Maria says with a pointed smile. "Our society is so inundated with depictions of violence that I feel we're largely desensitized to it. However, the juxtaposition of innately innocent images, i.e., a Christmas toy soldier with graphic death, should still leave the viewer with a startling, visceral impact."

"You know I get this vibe from your family." Jack chuckles.

"Is it warm and welcoming?"

"That's not exactly how I'd describe it," Jack says lightly.

"Great, sounds like you're picking up what I'm putting down. Try not to *break* anything *else*." Maria smiles all friendliness now her point is made. And trails her sister down the hall.

"Like my fragile tin neck?" Jack mutters, still grinning at the cartoon.

Maria stops at her sister's door, as Gabriella is already headed out, laptop in hand.

"What is he doing here? Did you get in trouble or something?" Maria hisses, leaning in near her sister.

Gabriella stops, darting a look down the hall to see if Jack is looking, listening. She shakes her head slowly, dazed still.

"No. Everything is fine." Gabriella's words just stop. She reaches out and latches onto her sister's arm. "I told him about feeling everything under my skin. And about level twelve punishment, and," she breaks off, still shaking her head, "he said to do it. He said to do my worst because he'd rather be embarrassed than have me hate him."

Maria Estrella Cruz is not a woman who startles easily. She's made a point not to be. But she stares open-mouthed at her sister for fully ten seconds without a thought in her head. She is entirely stunned. Her first thought, upon recovering any brain function at all, is, *damn, sis, nice pull!*

She does not, however, say this, as she feels Gabriella might rightly be somewhat insulted that Maria didn't think she could attract the casual, Chris Evan's looking, GQ model in the next room. But really...Maria assumes his type goes only for airheads who will let them get away with anything, and that doesn't describe her sister.

Her second and third thoughts are ones of suspicion. Specifically: *he is up to something*, and *he ought to be watched*.

It has now been seventeen seconds since Gabriella said what she said, and Maria knows her sister is counting the moments as they pass but hasn't yet worked her way around to having something intelligent to say. She needs to get a move on before Gabriella gets so nervous that she starts babbling. But... it's weird, isn't it? For a guy to offer up something like that. Either he has hidden depths, which seems unlikely. Or he likes her sister, which is not unlikely but... might not necessarily be good either. Or he is more evil than previously suspected and up to something.

"Okay, that's," Maria manages. By no means the most intelligent words she's ever strung together, but she is still in a slight state of shock. "Well, that's really sweet. Right? How do you feel?"

That's good; Maria congratulates herself. *Put it back on her.*

"I don't know," Gabriella responds, somewhat unnerved by this statement. "I've never not known. But I don't know."

"Okay. That's—" Maria puts a hand over Gabriella's on her arm and squeezes comfortingly. Though she as well is a bit lost. "Shit." She laughs. "I don't know either. That's *really* very sweet. Do you think he's into you?" Maria asks in her best approximation of a neutral tone.

"I don't know." Gabriella's eyes widen as if this is the last thing she has been thinking. That is not the case.

It would be more accurate to say it has been every other thought she's been thinking. Her thoughts go something like this: *There is something wrong with him. Maybe he likes me. He's playing some kind of trick on me. But what if he* does *like me? He's bluffing, trying to startle me out of doing it. Or...maybe he actually cares how I feel about him. No, he's just screwing with me.*

"Maybe," she says aloud. Shrugging.

"Are you into him?" Maria whispers.

Gabriella is entirely still for thirteen seconds. Thirteen seconds is a long time. And it's only followed by a slight downward tilt of her head and a shaking shrug. Maria takes this to mean Gabriella at least likes him a little. She's already known her sister finds him attractive, but that isn't the same as liking him, even a little. And a little isn't enough for Maria.

"Were you into him before he said that? Because it's awesome and sweet and not to be ignored. But just because he feels a certain way about you doesn't mean you have to reciprocate."

Gabriella rolls her eyes. "What do you think I'm in high school or something?" Gabriella leans in to whisper-yell at her sister in Spanish, lest Jack overhear. "No lo traje aquí para dormir con él. We were assigned to plan the holiday party."

Calmly unperturbed by her sister's reaction, Maria smiles sagely as she replies. "Everyone needs reminding sometimes that their feelings are important. Everyone."

Gabriella tilts her head aside and smiles at her sister in return. Honestly touched by her caring.

"Look, I gotta get to class. I'll be late, but just—be in the moment, you know," Maria advises with a wicked sisterly smile. "If you aren't sure what you feel, try not to stress about that; just be for a bit." Maria grabs her sister's head and smacks a kiss on her cheek. "We'll talk later. Te amo."

Maria spins around and charges out of the hall at a near run. She really is running late, and whenever she runs late, traffic decides to play games with her and be even worse than usual.

"Bye, Jack. Nice to meet you," she calls out, not even looking his way as she exits.

"Yep! You too." Jack, still examining the room's many decorations, laughs the words at Maria's back. The door slams behind her, leaving Jack alone in the apartment with Gabriella. Exactly where he wants to be.

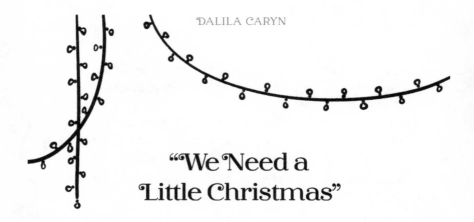

"We Need a Little Christmas"

Gabriella enters the room with her computer open, typing her password as she walks. Jack has taken a seat, mostly to hide the fact that he has been taking pictures of her room with his phone. He watches Gabriella closely as she moves.

"Okay, here's my computer." Gabriella sets it on the coffee table in front of him without really looking up. It is only as he's watching her that he realizes the table has a snowflake runner and Christmasy coasters.

"You can start looking at the notes I had on Secret Santa for inspiration while I grab us some snacks," Gabriella says and puts her back to him as quickly as she can.

"How long was that password?" Jack asks, laughter in his voice.

Gabriella pauses in the arch between the kitchen and living room and glances back at Jack with a brow raised. "Twenty-three characters."

"Letters and numbers?"

"What are you trying to do? Guess my code?" Gabriella demands a bit off balance.

"Definitely," Jack says flirtatiously.

Gabriella doesn't quite know what to do with this. It's not that she hasn't flirted before. She has. She's not altogether bad at it when she puts her mind to it. She has even, sort of, flirted with Jack before. But at the moment, her mind, and body, and commonsense and...well, she's a bunch of disparate parts at the moment. And Jack's overtly flirtatious attitude, right now, when he hasn't been so open with it before, is discombobulating. So she can only manage to answer with flat, awkward sentences.

"The computer is already unlocked. Just don't let it go to sleep." She moves into the kitchen, away from Jack's spreading grin.

Jack feels quite hopeful that Gabriella's sudden awkwardness when in the past she's been able to keep him on his toes verbally implies that she is shy of her massive attraction to him. He is aware that this is perhaps a bit more of a desire than a logical interpretation. But he has confidence enough not to quit flirting. Now more than ever, he thinks he has a chance. He lifts the computer into his lap, following her instructions with a smile.

"I have water, orange juice, tea, coffee, or hot chocolate," Gabriella calls out from the kitchen.

"Hot chocolate sounds good. Put us in the festive spirit," Jack says with an amused glance around the room again. He didn't realize adults without children got *this* into Christmas.

"You have seven different files about Secret Santa." Jack opens the files one after another, skimming through her notes.

"I'm intense," Gabriella says in a mildly defensive tone from in the kitchen.

"Yep," Jack agrees. "And thorough. And way too full of ideas: Build your own toboggan rides, snowman building contest, team gingerbread dollhouse building. Snowball fights, winter wonderland. Over half of these have to do with snow." He laughs. "How are you even planning to make the snowman contest work?"

"I don't know for certain." Gabriella pauses in the middle of filling a tray with cookies, brownies, nuts, and fruit. Absently she reaches out for plates. It is much easier for her to answer practical questions than to look at his face or respond to his flirting. "I had lots of ideas. Fake snow. Have actual snow brought in and do it first thing in the morning before it has time to melt. Or do it with food;

donut holes, frosting, and sprinkles could work. I may not even do it. I already did the paper snowmen. I thought people might like to decorate them themselves."

"Yeah. People have really gotten into your DIY Christmas stuff. It feels oddly unforced. Somehow it makes sense and takes away some of the stress of the year-end." Jack stares right at her as he replies, amused that she hasn't looked at him once. *Oh, she definitely has the hots for him;* he assures himself massively proud. *It's killing her.*

"I know. It's even gotten to me." As she begins to grow enthusiastic, Gabriella finds it easier to look at Jack, smiling back at him in a mixture of pride in her work thus far and excitement for its future. "It's like remembering the magic from when you were a child. When the whole world is getting lit up, and it feels like somehow it's all about you. Even though it definitely isn't. It makes you feel like magic is real." She breaks off, noticing Jack's wide, intent grin. Shyly, Gabriella glances away and forces a laugh. "Before you grow up and realize all the people running around are ridiculously stressed—"

Gabriella gulps and feels words desperate to get out as she hears Jack set aside the computer and stand. He is crossing toward her.

"And the lights and decorations and special drinks are just tricks to get you to spend more money," Gabriella says in a great rush.

Jack stops before her with a sad sort of smile. "Oh, Santa. Don't break my heart. You can't be a cynic. We cynics need you to keep the magic alive."

"Seeing the bad and the good isn't cynical. It's realistic," Gabriella says quietly.

"Maybe." Jack shrugs. "But the magic isn't in the realism, is it? It's in that childish belief that the holiday is all about you."

Gabriella stiffens as Jack reaches forward. He lifts the tray of snacks with a knowing smile. "Let me help you with these."

He walks away with the tray, and Gabriella is able to breathe out again. The kettle whistles, giving her something else to focus on, thank the steam gods. She pulls down a pair of Christmas mugs, one with a bunch of snowmen and the other with elves in a workshop, and fills them first with water, then scoops in chocolate. Only about double the number of scoops the package recommends. If she is going to have hot chocolate, she wants it rich. She reaches into the fridge for whipped cream and turns with a start. Jack is back. He came back silently. He smiles as he lifts both cups by the tiny plates they are resting on. They aren't real saucers, these cups don't have any, but using them that way, Jack carries them to the table without a word, only a slight smile.

Gabriella is ever so slightly weirded out. *He's being weird, right?* She wishes she could ask someone, but alas, she is alone in the apartment with him. Alone with him acting strange and solicitous. Maybe more than slightly weirded out.

Rather than dwell on it—which, let's face it, she actually will be doing in the back of her mind—Gabriella decides to just smile and carry out the can of whipped cream. They need to get to work. She *won't have time to dwell*, she assures herself. But of course, she will have time. Her mind, as if it is a supercomputer—which is technically not a bad description of it—is entirely able to obsess over Jack's odd behavior, play hostess, plan an office party, and also consider this unfamiliar numbness inside. While simultaneously pointing out that he has knocked the table runner askew, and catalog every time he accidentally brushes by her, keep a running count of how many minutes she's spent alone with him without fighting, and contemplate where they can possibly go from here, and consider what she wants for dinner tonight, and if she should invite him to share it, and even wonder over his words, and if he really means them and catalogue what objects could be used as weapons should his weirdness run deeper than she suspects.

Her mind can do it all.

"What's made you feel that way now?" She asks.

Do it all, except keep her mouth shut, apparently. She's followed him out of the kitchen and stands with the coffee table between them as he sets down the mugs of unstirred hot chocolate. He smirks at the table but hasn't replied yet. She watches as he stretches out a finger to dance across her laptop trackpad and keep the computer awake instead of trying to tease her into entering her password again or giving it to him. He should be teasing her.

"I mean, you were completely making fun of me for decorating early and 'believing in Christmas like a ten-year-old,'" Gabriella says, imitating Jack's voice snidely. "Why the turnaround?"

Jack takes a seat, lifting the laptop into his lap, and smiles up at her. "Your pranks."

Gabriella raises a disbelieving brow.

"Seriously. They were annoying, but—fun!" Jack grins, laughing at himself. "And I kept getting the group gifts. Now I'm getting weird impulses to decorate." He shrugs. "I guess you're a good Santa."

Completely lost, Gabriella shakes her head. "You're screwing with me somehow."

"Nope. I'm totally serious," Jack replies honestly. Though it must be noted that his expression is as incredulous as Gabriella's at the moment and thus not very serious in appearance. "It's like you believe enough for twenty people, and the rest of us needed it."

"Well," Gabriella has no idea what to do with praise of that kind. So she does the only practical thing and changes the subject; settling on her knees on the carpet, she begins stirring the powdered chocolate into the water with cinnamon sticks from her tray of goodies.

"I just hope I can figure out what to do about the last gifts. I can't think of anything I can get that will feel better than giving them the cash."

"So quit worrying about pleasing everyone."

"I take it you've given a lot of gifts in your life," Gabriella mocks Jack's sage advice, and not unfairly.

"Cute," Jack says, just shy of sarcastic. "I mean, don't make it a gift. Make it an experience like the rest have been. Something that ropes them in and helps them forget how cynical they feel because the world is so chaotic and scary."

Gabriella, with her eyes on the table, allows a smile to grow slowly from her lips. Leaving the cinnamon sticks sitting in the cups, she lifts the whipped cream and sprays it in a pleasing spiral. She admires the look of it before lifting the cup and holding it out to Jack.

He probably won't appreciate details like the drink's appearance. Or maybe he will. Maybe she's misjudged his antics in the past. He certainly seems to have noticed a lot since she started the Secret Santa mission. Honestly, now that she thinks about it, with all the teasing, he actually noticed a lot about her. He just made fun of it.

Jack carefully takes the cup in his hands, smiling at the cinnamon stick poking out the side and dipping into the beverage to give it an extra festive flavor. His eyes lift to Gabriella, and he pops his brows playfully.

Gabriella glances away to her own mug. Yeah, maybe he has noticed her before. When she was going to such effort to be unremarkable.

"It's like the song," Gabriella says. As previously mentioned, her mind can be in a few places at once. In this instance, its multiple places include, but are not limited to: *he's been really* noticing *me for a while. Jack is into me!* And considering his feelings about her work as Secret Santa thus far. And thinking about all the cynical people in the world and what they need.

"Which one?" Jack asks, taking a sip.

"'We Need A Little Christmas.' You probably grew up hearing it on the radio at Christmas time; I know I did. But it's actually from a play, "Mame." I didn't even know that until recently when Maria and I watched the movie musical   because it was by Jerry Herman." Gabriella pauses expectantly, but with no recognition from Jack, she goes on. She knows she is babbling, but she can't stop with Jack staring at her. It may seem silly to some people, but things like this song, adding cinnamon sticks to cocoa, and finding Mom's recipe mean the world to her. Even just those things alone would have felt like magic to her. And she wants Jack to understand.

"He wrote the music and lyrics for "Hello Dolly," it's our favorite musical. Anyway, the song is so jaunty it's easy to miss the lyrics, but it is all about someone feeling the world closing in around her and... needing Christmas to brighten her world and remind her that there is hope for things to get better." Gabriella's gaze is magnetically drawn to Jack's, and several moments pass in which they do nothing but gaze at one another, resting in their own thoughts. In the quiet, Gabriella realizes it isn't just the people she works with who have been needing this. It's her as well. Ever since Mom died, Christmas hasn't felt as special. But it's feeling very special this year.

Jack nods, smirking sideways. "Yeah, that's it exactly. It's like the pranks and the Secret Santa gifts have been combining to remind me that..." he chuckles shyly, his cheeks coloring slightly. "That magic can be real."

Gabriella's breath snags on her lungs a moment, a tiny jerk in her chest that ought to be a pain but is merely wonder and shock that he could be that moved by what she has been doing. The pair remain silent, unable to pull their eyes away from one another. And Gabriella is certain it will be her to put an end to it. She is usually the first to break awkward silences. But...this doesn't feel awkward. Just *charged*. It feels like a moment when silence is all that is needed. So when it is broken, it is by Jack, and with a soft smile.

"Do you know what's really torturing me?" Jack asks, his eyes sparkling, truly at ease now that he has her undivided attention.

Gabriella shakes her head.

"You've got a file labeled Jack's punishments, and I'm dying to click on it and see my future."

"Go ahead," Gabriella challenges. Well aware that this file is password protected. He might have noticed her more than she thought, but he most certainly hasn't guessed her code yet.

"I can't! Don't you get it?" Jack laughs. "It's killing me, but I can't spoil the surprise. Coming to work these past few days was the closest I felt to Christmas morning excitement since I was like— fourteen! I can't get enough of it."

Gabriella giggles, biting her lips as an unusually delightful burst of joy dances under her skin.

"Promise me you'll do something," Jack insists with a grin so powerful there truly should be inoculations against it.

Gabriella has received no such protection and cannot resist a slightly evil grin all her own. She will definitely do something. How could she not? He's asked so nicely, and anyway, he still deserves to be tortured, at least a little bit.

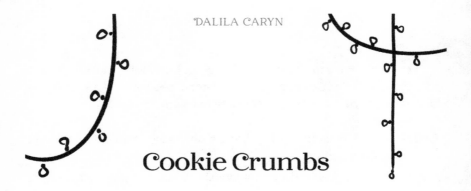

Cookie Crumbs

Persons of a gingerbread variety were found on the desks of every My Best Friend Doll Company employee when they arrived on Wednesday the twelfth of December. Indeed, they found three things waiting for them: A gingerbread person. A gingerbread conversation bubble with unique greetings. This took Gabriella most of the night and, after a brief rest (when she fell asleep waiting for frosting to set), part of the morning.

Although...she really feels like there were more finished cookies when she woke up than had been finished when she fell asleep, it must have been the magic because Maria swears she didn't do it.

"That would have been encouraging this reckless behavior," Maria said when Gabriella asked this morning.

Last night, at least fifteen times, Maria advised her sister that making conversation bubbles was a bad idea. And that she should maybe make the other events less involved. At the time, Gabriella heard Maria's voice in her head like a low buzzing noise. She had already started, and Maria ought to know her well enough to know Gabriella *cannot* stop until she finishes a thing. And anyway, she was still too thrown over all the events with Jack and her uncertainty with her own feelings to do something so ordinary as sleep intentionally. Today Gabriella is by no means as exhausted as she should be, but tired enough, and she can now hear her sister's voice as words. Maria had a point.

NICE TO BE SO NAUGHTY

From now on, any idea this big either gets cut from the list or she has to get some elves to help her out. If she doesn't have some already.

But back to the other employees, the ones with no clue how much work is going into all of their magical experiences. The third thing they found was a note which read:

Good morning Doll makers,
Today's winter challenge requires a team. All teams are assigned, no employee is required to participate, and teams have been arranged with the possibility of absences taken into account. That being said, we hope everyone in the office gets a chance to join in the fun. You will find your assignment at the bottom of this letter.

Teams of no less than three and no more than five will design, assemble and decorate a unique doll house, using the gingerbread and decoration provided in the break rooms. Each team will be given an assigned time of 45 minutes to discuss and assemble; additional time of one's breaks can be used but is in no way required.

The last half hour of the day is set aside for the display, voting and awarding of the event. The grand prize winners will receive unlimited copies for the year! Second prize winners will receive an extra toner cartridge each, and third runners up will receive a box each of the fancy pens that only executives are allowed to take from the supply closet. You can go ahead and call this the office supply challenge!

You have your assignments!
Let the games begin!

In the third-floor break room, Maya, Cory, Miriam and Ed are at the table working on a gingerbread house. Their design sketched out on a piece of paper beside Maya is of a long, single-story ranch-style home. The home sports an open back where Dolls can be moved about, as most doll houses do. There is a small forest of gum drop trees around it.

The walls have already been cut down to size. Maya is glueing the walls together with frosting while Ed decorates the finished bits. Cory is assembling the gumdrop trees. And Miriam is using extra bits of gingerbread to make stands for a trio of chocolate penguins.

"There is no way this is Coleman," Maya giggles as she accidentally squirts Cory with excess frosting. "I've never had this much fun at work before."

"I know! And everything is so organized, and weirdly... *team-buildy*." Ed says with an intensely focused expression as he pipes precisely spaced dots of different colors to create twinkle lights on the outside of the house.

"Are we just allowed to make up words now?" Cory asks, licking up the frosting on his wrist.

"Giff. Meme. Insta," Ed remarks without looking up.

"I didn't personally make any of those up, but point taken." Cory shrugs. "Hey, you know, what we really need are sugar cubes."

"Yes! We can make an igloo for the chocolate penguins!" Miriam agrees excitedly. "Are there any sugar cubes in the supplies?"

"No," Maya says. Then darting a furtive look around leans in to whisper. "But there are with the coffee."

Cory is up and headed to the coffee station at the counter before anyone else has a chance to comment.

"Isn't that cheating?" Miriam looks less convinced than cautious. The thing is, she really likes to win, and she has no intention of being disqualified over a bit of exterior decoration.

"I don't see a rule book," Cory remarks.

Miriam glances up at the camera crew and back to her teammates. "What if Ed is right? What if this is some team-building exercise, and we're being watched to see how we work together?"

"They'll admire our ingenuity!" Cory winks at the camera.

Everyone laughs; Miriam shakes her head, holding out a hand for the sugar cubes.

"Give them here. And finish up the forest," Miriam says. If she's going down for this, it's going to look good. "And I'm going to need a bit of frosting to hold them together."

"Ma'am, yes, ma'am," Cory says with a mock salute making everyone laugh.

Meanwhile, in other parts of the company, some people are not having nearly as much fun. The basement IT department is unusually busy. Well, *Jack Drummer* is unusually busy. There have been a few changes to his workstation, the addition of a pair of Christmas cards tacked up to the wall, and a mug with a Christmas sweater pattern sits on the desk, half full of coffee. Usually, by this hour, ten a.m., he has consumed an entire cup and is contemplating a second, but this morning he has been too busy even to finish one mug of what is now tepid coffee.

"Right, okay. Sounds like another email virus." Jack exhales, annoyed. He is on the phone and typing away on his own computer at the same time. "Third this morning. No! Don't turn it off, that's what I had Frank do and it got worse. We nearly lost all his files. I'm going to check out your hard drive remotely. Try working from someone else's station, and don't click on any emails." He instructs tersely, and that's before a question on the other end of the line *really* annoys him. "No. Not any! Not until I've had a look. I'm working on it. I'll try to save your life's work drawing dollies!"

He slams down his receiver after this, well-modulated response.

"Hey, Gabriella, can you give me—"

Before he can finish his request for help, his office phone rings again! Gabriella, scrunched up in her seat with a fist shoved into her mouth, stifles a chuckle.

"Damn it!" Jack mutters, lifting the receiver. "What? Okay, that's it. No, don't touch anything. Stand up and tell everyone around you not to open any emails! I think we've been hacked."

Gabriella makes a childishly tickled face at the camera crew behind her. Kristen is more entertained than she's been in years. Goodness, when she'd planned to pull out Gabriella's naughty side, she had no idea it was such a wickedly wild thing.

"No, I cannot send an email!" Jack shouts. "Because I don't want anyone opening emails! Gabriella!" Jack shouts as he slams down the receiver.

Giving herself a second to take a deep breath and hide her truly *immense* amusement Gabriella stands and peeks over to Jack's cubicle.

"Yep," she chirps sweetly.

"I need your help. I think we've been hacked." Jack is only half looking at Gabriella, typing as he speaks. "Could you get Stan and Michael to check the distribution, accounting and executive emails while I work back through design?"

"Are you asking me to be your secretary?" Gabriella demands in a sharp tone.

"What? No!" Jack looks up for the first time, annoyed and confused by Gabriella's attitude. This is the sort of thing she lives for. He is actually surprised to have to ask. Shouldn't she be volunteering, announcing that she's already repaired the whole thing because she's been eavesdropping?

"Look, I need a hand." Jack waves at his phone. "This is the fourth call I've gotten this morning. I need us to get on the most essential sectors before it gets worse. I'd have thought you would be all over this?"

"I didn't get any calls. Seems to me you're trying to play department manager before you've got the job!" Gabriella says as if bitter.

Jack looks utterly thrown and Gabriella is delighted. She's never taken part in any amateur theatrics, but now she thinks she should. This is fun! And much easier than she would have expected.

"What the hell is wrong with you? This is still your job," Jack shouts.

"I don't answer to you. They're your calls. You handle them." Putting on a snit, Gabriella spins around and marches towards the break room.

Jack is still staring after her, annoyed and confused, when his phone rings—again.

"What?" He demands at a yell.

Hot on the heels of the real story, Kristen and the camera crew follow Gabriella into the break room and pull the door shut. Gabriella still has her back to the crew when she releases a small torrent of giggles. When she turns around, Kristen has set up a chair for Gabriella and is pulling out one for herself, wearing a grin to match Gabriella's.

"So," Kristen prompts gleefully. "What have you got cooking today, Santa?"

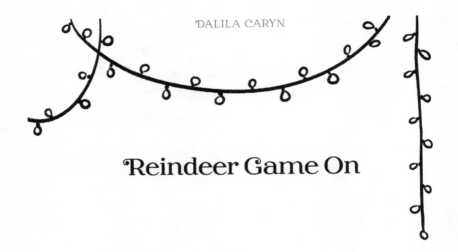

Reindeer Game On

"He asked to be pranked." Gabriella giggles to the camera crew. "This level was designed to make him work. And work hard. It was a lot easier than I expected to act annoyed and storm off."

It is worth noting that Gabriella has never had this level of fun at work before. Nor at school. Or really anywhere but at home with her family. Maybe not even there. There is a certain giddy euphoria to torturing Jack, to getting revenge when really, she's not sure she wants it any longer. She is playing with him and forcing him to dance to her tune, and it is *spectacular*.

She is well aware that, were she to share them with anyone, her thoughts might be called unkind. And she has never, that she can recall, been called unkind. But...well, she doesn't care. She isn't planning on sharing her thoughts with anyone deeply enough for them to know what joy she took in Jack's dumfounded look and the phone ringing as she walked away.

"And how *exactly* did you guarantee that he would have to work?" Kristen asks, loving Gabriella's wildness today.

A week ago, she thought this woman was the most boring woman in the world. She saw no reason why Santa should feel a need to give her a special gift. From what Kristen could see, Gabriella was one of those good people without a single bad thought. Without a single darker instinct. But that just isn't so.

Kristen gets it now. Why Gabriella deserves the magic. Gabriella has spent her whole life battling these instincts. Which, to Kristen's way of thinking, still aren't that bad but are in no way as gentle and passive as one might expect after meeting this woman. Gabriella literally fights down her angry, vengeful thoughts and goes through life treating her oppressors kindly. Yeah—she deserves the power of Claus. Maybe even more than the real Santa. But that is another story. The magic is letting Gabriella see the value, even in her darker feelings. Letting her see some of the power she's been holding inside and helping her embrace her fuller self. And it's a beautiful thing.

"On an average day, each tech gets about two calls. Usually with hours between them, and most problems can be fixed by say plugging in routers or turning off and on computers." Gabriella answers. "So usually we run system checks, make sure the security software is up to date, and maybe run usage checks. Occasionally we get to do something vaguely challenging, like make softwares work together that aren't designed to. But they really only need a few of us and they have seven because no one really gets tech. So, I just," Gabriella shrugs, "routed all the calls to Jack's phone."

"That's it? Really?" Kristen prompts, not about to let this woman shy away from the genius of her vengeance.

"Well...I needed to make sure there would be calls." Gabriella giggles looking like a cartoon squirrel that's hidden a nut. "I didn't exactly hack us. I just sent one tiny cookie crumb bug to a few people and didn't do the 'redundant' work Jack teases me about by flagging emails the software misses. The staff did the rest."

Here she breaks off, really smirking as she internally basks in the brilliance of her plan. So simple. So effective. "I only did it with the design department. They're useless right now, so they do the most web surfing and email checking. If he were paying attention, Jack would notice it was only them. But he's a bit distracted." She giggles hard, biting her lip and looking over Kristen's shoulder out the window in the break room door to Jack, hard at work.

A while later, having managed to rope in his fellow male coworkers, Jack is still hard at work trying to rid the company of the scourge of Gabriella's cookie crumb bug.

"Hey. We've checked all the other departments, and they're fine." Michael remarks, leaning into Jack's cubicle. "So somehow the bug is localized to design."

"That doesn't make any sense. Why target design?" Jack asks, looking up from his screen momentarily.

"Corporate espionage?"

"The company is doing fine for us. But it's not like we're Cabbage Patch Kids."

Michael laughs. "No one is hacking Cabbage Patch. Or any doll company for anything but fun."

"Fun?" Jack demands, and the next words to come out of his mouth are as much a surprise to him as to anyone else. "It's Christmas, and they're hacking a company that makes things for kids! Who does that? It's twisted."

"Trust me, it's a teenager playing Grinch." Michael, having delivered his news and done his job, simply nods and walks off without offering Jack any additional help. He is off to two, to join his dollhouse-making team.

Jack is shaking his head. Hunching over her computer and fuming internally. *A kid playing Grinch.* Ha. This is way too targeted.

As annoyed as he is by the work. He is more than a little distracted by Gabriella. What exactly did he do to offend her? Is she really still that upset not to have been offered the IT manager job? And even if she is, it's not like that is his fault. Why is she taking it out on him? He asked for her help, and she hasn't helped him. When she has always been willing to help anyone before! He thought they were getting past the whole broken nutcracker thing! He thought… she was starting to like him. He thought he was going to be pranked today, but she is acting weird and annoyed and not helping and he has too much work to do to chase her down and see what's going on!

This is the most frustrating day he's ever worked.

For a moment there, it seemed like Jack might pick up on a few clues; he was raised by mystery novels, after all. But to be fair to him, he is working hard to try and single-handedly beat back a system incursion as fast as possible so he can chase down Gabriella and see what's gone wrong; she has not been back to her desk once since he asked for her help.

The Gingerbread Wars

Elsewhere meanwhile—the second-floor break room to be specific— other workers are going along quite blissfully as they prepare to compete in the winter games.

This team of four, Carol, Angelo, Michael and Daniel Burns, are working to build a gingerbread "A" frame house. This elaborate two-story design sports two bedrooms, an attic, and on the ground floor, a dining room and living room.

Angelo is building a tiny table and chairs. Michael is decorating the exterior of the already assembled home. While Carol decorates the interior and the furniture pieces, Angelo has finished. Daniel is constructing a cobblestone walkway of Milk Duds and lining the walkway with candy canes.

"You know," Angelo says thoughtfully, examining the remains of the gingerbread. "If you cut six really narrow pieces of gingerbread and use those broken wedges—"

"We can make a gazebo! We are totally going to win this!" Carol says a bit fanatically. This is, by far, the most competitive team in the building.

"Who'd have thought this hodge-podge team would be the best? We're literally the only group with no one from design. But I actually think we can take this!" Angelo says, having finished his table, he begins to work on the gazebo he suggested.

"Oh yeah. I've seen a few of the others, very basic," Daniel Burns remarks.

"Should the HR director really be in competition with the workers?" Michael remarks dryly as he is piping a window onto the exterior of their home.

Daniel laughs, unperturbed and entirely unwilling to stop competing with the staff. "Are you kidding me? I've wanted extra copies all year. Debbie runs that machine like a dictator."

Everyone laughs. Debbie is easily the most frightening member of staff.

"Who keeps coming up with this stuff?" Carol says when the laughter has died down. "The games? The prizes? No offense, Daniel, but this isn't anyone in management. But I also don't buy that *Santa* email; this isn't Jack."

"Nah! Jack isn't doing this. But he got real bent out of shape with Gabby when that email went out. Could be her," Angelo says, his tone a bit doubtful.

"It's not Gabby," Michael says with great authority. "She can't even pull herself away from work long enough to participate. I wouldn't be surprised if she sent the email, though. They're flirting hard, and it's turned into pranking."

"Whoever is doing all of this has a massive operation set up." Carol comments. "It's some party planning group. There is no way one of us is doing all this."

"Maybe it's the real Santa and his elf slaves," Michael comments, and only Angelo laughs.

"Right. And tomorrow, the reindeer will deliver our mail," Carol says snidely. Everyone laughs, and their attention turns away from the mystery of Santa and back to what they are certain is an award-winning dollhouse.

Downstairs meanwhile, Secret Santa, A.K.A. Gabriella Cruz, has taken a break from work and is with her own assigned group of dollhouse builders. Jack was assigned to her group, but he has yet to pull himself away from *a tiny little bug* infesting the design department to come and play. Gabriella feels a happy hum inside in anticipation of Jack realizing the virus is a prank. But also...in anticipation of him getting to join them. Isn't that strange?

On her team is Frank from design and Hannah from accounting. Their gingerbread house is a two-story building of a long rectangular design, with a slope roof. Both floors have a single room style. Focusing the majority of their work on decoration. Hannah is building and individually decorating seven beds, seven chairs, and a long table, while Frank decorates the exterior of the completed building, adding exposed wood beams over neatly piped brick walls. And piping flower boxes under cut-out windows. Gabriella is decorating seven snowman candies to make them individual and one gingerbread-girl doll for the design that they are calling "Ginger and the Seven Snowmen." It is hard to say what Jack thinks of his team's design, as he has yet to see it.

"What do you suppose they plan to do with all this gingerbread at the end of the day?" Frank asks in a near whisper as he leans in near his building to lay a perfectly straight beam. "There are more than ten teams! Who is going to eat and judge it all?"

"There is a local youth group coming by this afternoon. Homeless children," Hannah remarks as she is painting holly onto the dried frosting bedcover with food colouring.

Gabriella looks around the very neat table before her and recognizes how free of tension her body feels. She didn't realize she was doing it, but she grouped herself with the two other most fastidious members of staff—and Jack. Jack could not be called fastidious by any stretch of the imagination.

Funny how that worked out. She glances backwards, to where Jack is still stuck at his desk. Not having Jack's chaotic work style at the table is certainly making it an easier work environment for her. But—Last night Gabriella found Jack's presence more of a help than expected. And though his company was unsettling it was not unpleasant. Part of her wants to explore that further.

"And we're giving homeless children cookies?" Frank snorts derisively.

"The company is giving dolls and backpacks, and there were emails all week asking for donations of clothes, toys and bedding," Hannah replies cautiously. Somewhere, somehow Frank has gotten a rather explosive reputation.

"Lots of people have been bringing stuff," Hannah finishes awkwardly.

"Emails from whom?"

"H.R.", Gabriella responds carefully, dragging her eyes back to her team.

Gabriella is very pleased with this particular event and all she has been able to get out of management for it. Every year the company donates toys to children's charities. So when Gabriella came up with the idea of having a local youth group judge the event, she sent emails to Debbie asking for her help getting Coleman onboard. Debbie was super helpful; she sent the email to Coleman herself and sent the email to H.R., asking them to get everyone to donate. Even coordinated with the charity. It was Debbie's suggestion to give unlimited copies as a prize, well aware of the reputation she gets, just for doing part of her job and keeping the copy number down.

It is not common knowledge, but Gabriella knows that Debbie spent a few months living out of her car with her kids after her husband emptied out their joint accounts and ran off with another woman. It was Gabriella's hope that the experience would give the woman a soft spot for the charity and the event. And it had.

It is little things like this that make Gabriella happiest about her tenure as Santa. She is involving people who usually don't join and acknowledging parts of people that they tend to keep hidden. It feels special. It feels like something she desperately needed and finally has. It feels like...like this magic is letting her really, truly love this time of year again. Since Mom died, she has been pretending and wishing she could feel like she used to. The feeling isn't quite the same as when Mom was alive; it will never be the same. But...it is beginning to feel like "The Most Wonderful Time of the Year" again.

But at the same time, she knows people like Frank are still angry enough with the company for even these events to feel a bit forced and annoying. And she understands that.

Frank grumbles a bit uncomfortably. "Oh. I never open those."

Gabriella laughs awkwardly. "I wouldn't worry about it; there will be plenty. I got other people in my building to donate, so I have bunches. You can have some of that to give if you want." Gabriella offers, not quite meeting Frank's eyes.

"Thanks." Frank stares at Gabriella for a long moment. He's never spent much time with her before. They don't work in the same department, and he's not much for socializing, and it seems neither is she, but she's nice. "That's...very sweet of you, Ga—"

"Gabriella!" Jack's shout echos around the basement, drowning out the sleigh bells Gabriella has started to hear. All heads swivel.

It is at this moment that Jack Hilary Drummer has, at last, discovered Gabriella's stunt. Gabriella is so entirely delighted by his annoyance that even as he is stomping giant-like into the break room, Gabriella is giggling like a teenager over a naughty word.

Jack Drummer is not amused. Jack Drummer has spent his entire day hard at work repairing a system incursion, frustrated, hungry, and impatient to get his work done so he can go fix things with Gabriella. And all along, it was her!

No. Jack Drummer is not amused. Not. At. All. Jack Drummer could better be described as— *livid*. He stomps into the break room, where Gabriella is sitting around, playing with cookies. He towers over her, just barely stopping himself from knocking aside the group's cookie creation. An impulse Frank seems to have noticed as he is protecting it with both his arms. Gabriella is hunched up like a turtle, laughing her head off. *He could kill her. Strangle her. Throttle her. Are those the same things? Maybe. He doesn't care. He'll do both, do it twice.*

She—Aaaaaargh!

"It's you, isn't it? All day I've been untangling that mess, and it was you the whole time! That's why it was only design."

Gabriella bites her lip. *She shouldn't reply, not with what she's thinking right now. No. It will be very bad. Look how angry he looks. She shouldn't. She won't.*

But of course, she will.

Notching her chin up slightly and with a smug expression she really ought to wipe away, Gabriella replies. "You said to do my worst."

"I...you—" It is not Jack's most articulate moment. But he is simultaneously too angry to think straight and too distracted to do so.

Gabriella is grinning, putting the full force of her considerable energy into a smile, and it does things to him. Makes him nearly forget that he is very angry with her. Makes him almost want to say she's being cute. But it isn't cute. *She isn't cute. This isn't cute! She is a menace!*

"I felt bad for offending you!" Jack hisses, leaning nearer, unnecessarily, as his voice raises with each word he says, too frustrated to relent. "I was trying to fix it so I could come talk to you. And it was all a prank! You're— I—I can't. Argh!!!"

At this point, full of rage and righteous indignation, Jack spins about and stomps back to his desk before he does something really ridiculous, like kiss her. *What? No! Why would he kiss her? She is a menace. A pest! He should be trying to kill her, not kiss her.* But in either event, he can't be around her one second more.

He knows he told her to do it! And he expected something, but— *is he reading too much into this?* Because today's prank feels a bit like she was calling him lazy. Lazy! And she has implied as much a few times already. It's beginning to feel insulting.

Sure he pokes the occasional fun at her for doing more work than she has to. But he's never said anything really hurtful, has he? When she sets her mind to it, Gabriella is *mean*.

Gabriella sinks into her seat, staring after Jack. She feels tingly all over, charged and cold at the same time. And she is beginning to feel like maybe she took things too far. But—this wasn't even that far. But she feels badly that he feels bad.

Frank and Hannah, who had front row seats today at the *Gabriella and Jack* show, are a bit flabbergasted. Hannah's eyes are still wide and her left-hand hovers over her lips, concealing a wide smile. Frank is starting at Gabriella as if he's only just seen her. This is a whole other side of IT.

"The crumbling cookie screen that erased all our files?" Frank asks, aghast. "That was you hacking us?"

Gabriella's reply is hesitant and quiet. "It didn't erase anything. Just hid it."

Hannah snorts, tickled by the reply.

"Why?" Frank demands.

Gabriella shrugs, feeling tension coiling up her muscles. She hadn't really considered what she would say if other people found out. And there is a camera crew. She told them literally everything. But earlier, it all felt like great fun; now, she is talking to coworkers and realizing how this would sound to executives. Shit. This was a *very bad idea*. Maybe naughty list level bad, and she doesn't think she's qualified for that list very often in life.

"Jack and the rest of the techs don't really respect the work I do. They treat it like a joke." Gabriella answers honestly but flatly. "So I showed him what a week of me not doing extra email sweeps looks like." She finishes with her hands forming slow fists, one on the table, the other on her thigh, wishing she is invisible.

Frank raises a brow. "Damn. Why am I the one in anger management?"

Hannah laughs. "Because Gabby is too cautious to ever do that with management."

Gabriella flinches at the nickname. She really hates that name.

But the thing that is bothering her most is herself. In the back of her mind, she can see the string of snowmen that came in her office mail today, five grinning guys with puffy paint and glitter clothing. The envelope had no name but hers, but she knows they were from Jack. She was so...*charmed*. Breathless, when she saw them. It was so sweet of him. She sinks a little inside.

"You're a bit of a dark horse, aren't you?" Frank smiles.

Gabriella glances over her shoulder towards Jack, seething at his desk. Her right fist drums a light one-three-one beat on her thigh. "I should go apologize."

"Don't you dare. I just started liking you." Frank reaches out as if to stop Gabriella, who has made no attempt to rise.

"Yeah. What did you really do but make him work?" Hannah points out with a laugh as she returns to her painting.

"Nothing, I suppose," Gabriella admits and turns away from the door to focus on what she's doing. This is a group project, and she's never respected people who don't give their all to group projects.

Anyway, Jack seems pretty mad. She should give him some space. She can apologize later. If he is willing to talk to her. If he is even willing to hear it. Drumming on her thigh one last time, she gets back to work. But in a far-off corner of her mind, she can see her Naughty-and-Nice list, and a check mark is forming in the naughty column, next to her own name.

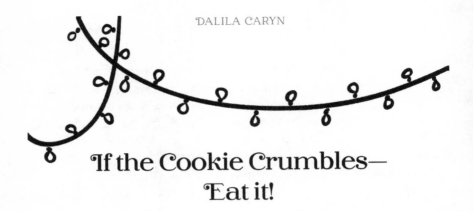

If the Cookie Crumbles— Eat it!

Some time later, Gabriella excuses herself from her group to use the restroom. But her plan is to go fix things with Jack. As soon as she approaches his desk, he turns his back and lifts the phone receiver dialing a number she doesn't manage to see.

With a sigh, Gabriella heads to the restroom. She told the others that's where she was going, and she is feeling like she might need a moment alone. She can't honestly believe she made Jack *this* angry this quickly. This isn't even level six torture. And he said to do her worst. Why did she believe him? Until yesterday she hadn't really thought he liked her —

"Gabriella," Kristen's voice invades Gabriella's thoughts. Only then does she realize the camera crew are following her to the restroom. A big invasion of privacy, and she knows they know it.

"What?"

Kristen laughs at Gabriella's sharp tone. "Could we grab you for a quick word?"

Gabriella nods, even as she's shaking her head and motioning towards the bathroom door with her thumb. Kristen, in usual only-child fashion, takes the response she is most pleased with. She leads Gabriella a bit further down the hall to the dead end, where there is a framed print of the first doll designed by the company, a blond-haired, blue-eyed sweetheart with more hair than body and a furry white dress: Nikki.

"So, a few follow-up questions about this bug you sent to the design department."

"I..." Gabriella opens and shuts her mouth, eyeing Kristen in fear. She thought they were becoming friendly, but this girl is the daughter of the CEO. And earlier today, on camera, Gabriella admitted with *great joy* to intentionally sabotaging an entire department.

"Explain to our audience how you've shown the company a flaw in its tech security. Could this have been prevented? And how?" Kristen winks, clearly leading Gabriella.

Gabriella could kiss this woman with gratitude, and generally speaking, her gratitude is *far less* demonstrative. But clearly, Kristen is trying to help Gabriella should this part of things make it into the final footage.

An odd thought occurs to Gabriella as she sees Kristen's smile: no one from Kristen's family has come by the office to see Kristen. If Gabriella had been making a film in a company where her mother worked, she would have had to fight to keep her away. Mom would have been there every day, telling people this was her daughter, talking about how proud she was, and yes, butting in and telling Gabriella what else she thought she should ask or include. But none of that is going on with Kristen.

Kristen is the sort of independent young woman who might have demanded her family stay away. But Gabriella's family would have interfered anyway. Even if just to watch or boast. Gabriella wonders if Kristen even expects her family to watch the finished product.

Gabriella has a weird impulse to reach out and hug the girl or to ask the entire film crew to participate in the events. Something to let them know they are seen.

But apparently, Gabriella has been quiet too long as Kristen says her name again like a prompt.

"Oh, well..." Gabriella clears her throat, standing straight and facing into the camera. "Our software catches most of the spam the average user gets. But if people go to certain sites or turn off cookie blockers, actual hackers or spam bots can get enough info to spoof the security. So I skim people's emails, not the content, just sources, frequencies, and subject lines for suspicious emails. Then I either spam or flag them with warning messages telling people not to click on any links. Since I've been doing it, it's cut down on the number of hard drive incursions we've seen by sixty percent," Gabriella says, unconsciously smiling a bit smug. "If we had an IT manager, they might have noticed. But as it is, I think even the other techs attribute it to software improvements. So by not doing my extra, self-assigned work and sending an email, I knew some people would click on...I sort of revealed the value of what I do. And no one's files are gone!" Gabriella rushes to explain.

But her mind doesn't stop with the explanation. And she doesn't entirely like what it shows her. This isn't like her. Not at all. She picks at her nails, unaware, pulling and pulling at the skin until they are bleeding.

"I knew I was bored here," she says after a long silent stretch. Glancing down at the strip of skin between her fingers. "But another time, I would never have done something like today's prank. It didn't just mess with Jack. It messed with the whole design department, and I didn't care. I was having fun. I...I...I knew they weren't really useful right now, so I made them useless. It's not like me. And as fun as it was in the moment, seeing him so upset. I don't know. He is *so upset*! I didn't expect that."

"Wasn't that the point?" Kristen asks softly.

"Yes, and no," Gabriella replies. "I definitely wanted him annoyed. And I wanted to make him work. I loved getting to pretend to be upset and walk away, leaving him to stew. But with the other pranks, I always gave him time to participate in the day's events, I didn't with this one."

"I spent most of my elementary years getting excluded from events that other kids were a part of and hating it. I didn't want anyone to feel that way about my Secret Santa mission. And so far, no one has!" Gabriella says fervently. "No one has opted out! I was so proud of that. Then I went and excluded Jack with my prank. I feel bad about that. I should have gone after him, right?"

Gabriella chews her lip. Digging a fingernail into the tear she made on her thumb by peeling away the skin. Realizing what she is doing, Gabriella shoves her arms behind her.

"Today, I was as excited about pranking him as I was nervous about his reaction. I don't want him to hate me. But he asked for my worst, and this isn't even close!" Gabriella says with a laugh that verges on sad. "It's probably for the best that he got upset because I was getting ahead of myself again. I was imagining what it would be like not to worry about my worst. Imagining feeling comfortable in my own skin." She laughs, bringing forward her bleeding thumb. Looking at what she's done unconsciously. "But I should worry."

Gabriella is staring at her hand still when she notices the camera crew moving away. Looking up, her eyes fall on Kristen, who has stayed behind. She smiles softly at Gabriella.

"Come on. Let's clean up that finger." She walks back down the hall to the bathroom, holding the door open for Gabriella.

Gabriella follows. Once they are both inside the unisex bathroom, Kristen pushes the door shut and locks it. Gabriella has already crossed to the sink and turned on the water, letting her finger linger under the stream.

"He overreacted. Give him some time, and he'll cool off. If he is anything like other men. Give him a week of never addressing it and he'll forget it ever happened," Kristen says, standing casually next to a paper-towel dispenser.

Gabriella laughs. "Yeah. That's true. I'm fine. You don't need to stop filming to take care of me," Gabriella says awkwardly.

"Oh No! Never," Kristen exclaims in horror. Reacting a bit strongly for so mild a statement. "That isn't even in my wheelhouse. Ask anyone. I just got what I needed for the moment and thought I'd take a break. I'm with boys all day."

Gabriella nods doubtfully. Switching off the water, she holds out a hand for the bundle of paper towels Kristen is holding. Kristen hands them over and looks into the mirror, pretending to check her pristine make-up.

"I used to pick at my nails like that," Kristen remarks. "Boarding school girls will cure you of a lot of outward displays." Noting Gabriella's confused expression in the mirror, she smirks. "Nope. I was not always the alpha girl I am today."

Crouching down to the wooden cabinet under the sink where extra toilet paper and paper towels are stored, Gabriella pulls out a first aid kit and rummages inside for a bandaid.

"I don't know if I'm supposed to congratulate you or say I'm sorry," Gabriella says awkwardly. "I have begun to quite like you. But I can't say it sounds like much fun, being *cured* of things by a boarding school."

Kristen shrugs. "Don't know that I was looking for either. Just… felt like sharing, I guess." Kristen can see that Gabriella is about to say more, and having shared far more with this stranger in those few sentences than she has shared with really anyone in years, she is certain she doesn't want to know what she will say, and thus changes the subject.

"For my two cents, I don't think you excluded Jack today. You just overestimated how good he was at his job."

"I…no." Gabriella shakes her head, wanting to protest harder, but thinking it will sound like she's defending her crush, which of course, it would. Anyway, the same thought had occurred to her, but— it felt mean.

Kristen, whether a fault or a strength, is much more comfortable than Gabriella is saying things that sound mean.

"Come on, let's get back before rumors start to fly that I like you best." Kristen teases because, of course, she does like Gabriella best, and it wouldn't do for Gabriella, of everyone, to know it.

Unfortunately for Kristen, though Gabriella nods and precedes Kristen through the door, Gabriella is quite aware that Kristen likes her best. What's more, she is certain that Kristen took her into the bathroom to comfort her, to try and take care of her, because she cares. Gabriella hears a jingle of bells and can picture her Naughty-and-Nice list; Kristen's name has a new note on the good side: *She's sweeter than she means to be.*

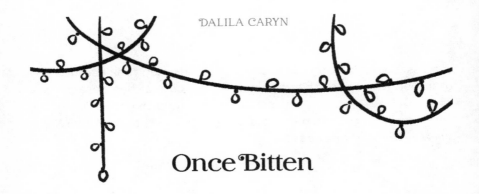

Once Bitten

Rather than even pretending to work today, Gabriella returns to the break room to finish her portion of her groups dollhouse. A fact that Jack observes from his desk. But upon noticing Frank walking his way, Jack looks away and pretends not to have been looking.

No one is deceived.

"Got you good, did she?" Frank inquires, casually amused. Perhaps more than casually. He is especially pleased to have found someone at this company nearly as high-strung as he is.

"I'm still unravelling her little joke, so yeah," Jack says petulantly.

"Good for her," Frank replies with a smirk.

Jack looks up, startled. Is this the same man who was chewing Jack's ear off hours ago about how he couldn't do any work without his designs?

Jack is prepared to launch into a speech with exactly those words when he hears Gabriella laughing. He glances towards the break room. He cannot hear what is going on, but Hannah and Gabriella seem to be having quite a good time. And Jack is struck again, his whole chest lifting, drawn towards her happiness. He is meant to be angry, but he feels *needy*—of her presence, her energy, her light.

"A bit of a shock, that girl," Frank remarks in an oddly bland tone. The sort of tone men use when they want to tease each other about liking someone.

"Yeah," Jack agrees, turning back to the computer. "And annoying as hell."

"What did the gingerbread she left you say? Everyone had a different air bubble."

Jack smirks at his keyboard. The cookie was hidden in his desk for half the day; he'd been planning to save it. But once he realized Gabriella sent the bug, he ate it out of spite. "It said: game on. Wait!" Jack exclaims, realizing what Frank has said. "She told you?"

Frank grins superiorly. "I figured it out. *I keep getting extra gifts for Linda. And in there, Gabriella offered me things for this donation drive, almost as if she knew I'd need them.*"

"She's too sweet for her own good?" Jack shakes his head fondly. "Does anyone else know?" He asks, feeling a protective urge rise up; he has to stop this getting around. She's having too much fun keeping it secret.

"I might not even have noticed if she hadn't worked with us today." Frank shakes his head. "This is the most time anyone has spent with her."

"Yeah. For a bubbly thing, she isn't that social," Jack says thoughtfully.

"Some of us have a harder time than others interacting with people. Trouble being ourselves and still being accepted," Frank says pointedly.

Jack smiles at the not-so-subtle rebuke. It is something he's heard from his own parents. Frank isn't nearly old enough to be Jack's father, but he is so serious he does give one the impression of being fatherly. It feels like his father admonishing him to be *the bigger man,* something he's heard often. Jack laughs, realizing that he has perhaps been a bit overly sensitive.

He did ask Gabriella to prank him, and after she had already stopped! And really...he does make fun of the extra work she puts in.

She is very pointedly picking at things he's mocked her about. If it feels like she is calling him lazy...maybe it is because watching her work makes him feel that way.

"Excuse me." Standing, Jack walks around Frank to the break room.

Gabriella and Hannah break off a conversation about what they should name their various snowmen. Both women look up silently as Jack leans over the table, his eyes intently locked on Gabriella.

"Do you want to know what I think of your little prank?" Jack asks tauntingly.

"Look, Jack." Gabriella begins, feeling a bit contrite. "I'm—" Gabriella breaks off as Jack lifts a nearly empty tube of frosting.

She stiffens, staring at the tube and Jack cautiously. *He's going to squirt her with it, isn't he? Ugh.* She hates food play. It's dirty and sticky, and wasteful.

Jack watches Gabriella closely. In this moment, he is as observant as he generally believes himself to be. Noting her stiffening shoulders and her eyes on the tube. Noticing her shallow breaths and her clenched fists. Noticing the bandaid on her thumb that wasn't there earlier and the way her pulse pounds the longer he waits. She expects to be squirted with the frosting, he can tell. He can also tell she hates the idea. But she is just going to sit there as still as a statue and let him do it rather than making a scene.

He laughs internally. Wasn't he sure she was a mean menace earlier? Why does he now feel like telling her she needs to get meaner still. Needs to get in people's faces and cause scenes rather than allowing herself to be this uncomfortable. There is something wrong with him. Or her. Or both of them.

Jack smiles wide, letting her be uncomfortable for one second more. Then he opens his mouth and squirts a big dollop of frosting onto his own tongue.

Gabriella gasps in shock, but her eyes never leave his. Their gazes hold, obscuring everything around them as heat builds. Hannah watches, devouring her grin to repress an embarrassed giggle as she enjoys the show like it's the best daytime drama ever. *Who knew work could be this entertaining?*

Dropping the tube back on the table, Jack swallows the frosting, grinning around the sticky remnants in his mouth. "I eat weak crap like that for breakfast. And I'm going to get you back," he says, low and enticing.

"Do your worst." Gabriella grins in delight, a bit shocked by how breathless she is from saying three tiny words.

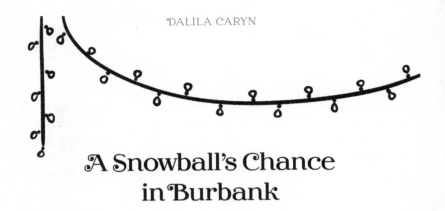

A Snowball's Chance in Burbank

My Best Friend Doll Company, in Burbank CA, was the site of a violent incident on Thursday, December the thirteenth, at four-thirty in the afternoon. The incident occurred in the parking lot and involved the majority of staff and a few managers, resulting in multiple scraped hands and knees and even several bruises—but most of all, a bright, colorful, sticky mess.

Authorities were not summoned. But it was a close thing.

"I like that graphic, but...I don't know, can we make it more... sinister?" Kristen asks. Without waiting for Terrance's reply, she pulls the laptop towards herself and begins to scroll through the available fonts.

"I don't know; I think the Christmasy font next to the *incident report* has a sort of sinister look all its own."

Kristen laughs. "Sure, but imagine the Law and Order font, with Christmas lights strung around it."

Laughing, Terrance yanks back the laptop. "You do realize, princess, that this is a student project, not a big budget movie. We can't afford to buy a new graphic for every scene."

Kristen smiles at the back of Terrance's head as he opens a window for free fonts and starts searching for something to suit her esthetic. She knows he's teasing. He's taken to calling her princess whenever he does what she asks him to. Or, more accurately, tells him to do. She can admit that she is a bit bossy. But only to herself.

Still, she tries to tease him with the game she suspects he's begun to enjoy.

"Mā hontōni?" She exclaims in Japanese, *no, really?*

Terrance doesn't even glance back. *Humph. He's grouchy*

She would have looked for the graphic herself. She already was. Hm. Now that she thinks of it, she leans back and takes out her phone, using it to search for free Christmasy clipart. She airdrops the first one she finds to the computer without a word and is rewarded by Terrance's slight laugh as he sees the snowball with a frightened face.

Andrew couldn't make this cut meeting. But neither Terrance nor Kristen seem to mind. This is the first time they've worked together entirely alone, but it feels natural.

"What language was that?" Terrance asks without glancing back.

Kristen beams. "Japanese."

"How many languages do you know?"

"I know bits from about eight. And only one of them is pretend." She winks. "When I came home from sixth year knowing *only three.* Grandpa told my father he'd chosen a second-rate school. So I branched out. I'm fluent in five."

Terrance glances back. The phrases "came home" and "sixth year stuck out to him. She'd attended junior high in another country? And her grandparents were offended by only three languages of fluency. *Damn.* Maybe he is too hard on her.

"So, what did you say to Gabriella in the bathroom the other day?" Terrance asks, changing the subject, but just as soon interrupts himself. "Hey, what about this one?"

"Oooh!" Kristen leans in and examines the *very* sinister font with drooping hooked lines and sharp angular tops. "Well, it's no Law and Order, but it's got something."

Terrance adds it to a folder for consideration but doesn't bother downloading it. Kristen likes that he knew without her actually having to say it that she wasn't sold on that font. She also likes that even as he was showing it to her, he was looking for more; he wasn't sold either. This film is starting to come together, and something of both their visions is affecting it, making it new.

Terrance glances back with a brow raised to let Kristen know he still wants an answer to his question.

"Not much. Just helped her clean up her hand and insulted boys for a few minutes."

Terrance laughs. "Ah yes, the true function of bathrooms, a place to insult boys."

"Oh modi!" Kristen exclaims playfully in Haitian Creole, *oh damn*. "Did I let that secret out? I'm going to get in so much trouble with the other girls."

They both laugh. And work silently for a few minutes. Once Terrance has a folder of several options and Kristen has found a few more fun bits of clipart, they start putting things together, trying out the composition. Settling for the time being on a less sinister but very austere font for the opening text to lay over a black and white shot of the dirty parking lot, and a blinking colorful strand of lights draped crookedly over the titles.

Sitting back, they watch the scene again from beginning to end. A black screen appears with the words:

A SNOWBALLS CHANCE IN BURBANK

Fade in on a black and white still of the parking lot of My Best Friend Doll Company, with the incident report text over it. A cartoon snowball flies across the screen. Jump to full color.

The chaos of an epic snowball fight unfolds. Employees wear sunglasses and the rain slickers they decorated for the ugly slicker contest. They run around throwing colorful snowballs. There is laughter and screaming, and people duck behind cars. More than one vehicle alarm goes off. The din of amusement is louder than the car alarms.

Cut to the front door of the company, with the logo in black on the glass doors. Carol stands laughing, wearing a slicker decorated with a giant teddy bear that's drooping forward, and now splashed with various colors of syrup.

CAROL(smiling wide)

I hate sticky. I hate messy. I won't even do water ballon fights, but (giggles)This is ridiculously fun!

Jump cut. Angelo stands before the company front doors in a rain slicker with a painted Santa smoking a 3D joint made from pipe cleaners.

ANGELO

We got emails yesterday telling us to bring our slickers back and today, on our desks were snowball-shaped invites listing our team assignments. (grins big) I love Santa!

Jump cut to Carol.

CAROL

We were put in teams, pitting everyone who signed the complaint last year against the HR department and most of the managers. (cackles hard) Guess who won?

Jump cut to Angelo.

ANGELO

It was a syrup bath! (chuckles, licking red syrup off hand) It was almost more fun watching that fight than being in mine with accounting.

Jump cut to Frank at the company's front door, wearing a nearly pristine slicker, decorated with teeshirt paint depicting a sweater-style pattern of elves flipping the bird.

FRANK

Oh, this Santa is an evil genius. (chuckles TV villain style) Who needs anger management when you can pelt your problem with balls of syrup?

Jump cut to a scene of the complainants of the prior Christmas pelting snowballs at the HR department. The complainants pelt so fast and hard that the HR slickers are thoroughly covered in colorful splats.

Jump cut to the front door of the building. Mr. Coleman stands centered between the doors, wearing a dark blue suit and tie and a slightly disapproving expression. No slicker.

MR. COLEMAN

The executive branch of the company isn't taking part in Secret Santa. It's strictly an employee moral-building event. And it's working out (beat examining the parking lot) Quite well. Exactly as planned.

Jump cut to fight between accounting and sales teams. One might assume, based on the enthusiastic aggression of the accounting team, that they have a little something against the sales department. The accountants employ a well-organized campaign involving two snipers and a screaming frontal assault that sends the sales team into disarray.

Jump cut to the front doors. Gabriella, in her bell slicker, spotted with purple, pink and blue spots of color stands shivering involuntarily but grinning broadly.

GABRIELLA

Today's prank on Jack was an elf widget that pops up on his screen whenever it's been idle for more than five minutes and starts singing, "All I want for Christmas is my two front teeth." (grins evilly) He hates that song. But I very generously accepted Jack's input on today's event.

Gabriella shakes her head, looking down at her colorful slicker in a cross between dismay and delight, and scratching her left arm with her right hand.

GABRIELLA

I'd just planned a snowball fight with teams. When I told him I was having my neighbor Leticia provide the snowballs courtesy of her shaved ice truck, he was *wildly* insistent that we had to use the syrup as well. (Gabriella shudders and scratches harder) It seemed too messy. For all of these gifts that involve a mess, I stay after to clean. It's not fair to put all this on the janitorial staff, who are outside contractors and aren't part of the fun. And *I didn't want to clean this up.* But Jack promised to help and—this is totally worth the extra work! (laughs, shocked and happy) Do you know I think all of us are just taller, really stressed-out kids. And this sort of thing *eviscerates* the stress.

Jump cut to another snowball fight between IT and shipping. The camera zooms in slowly on a pair of snowball fighters. Jack and Gabriella. Jack launches a purple snowball that catches Gabriella right in the shoulder. Laughing, she launches a blue ball of her own, that falls short of its mark. Dancing around superiorly, Jack throws another snowball that catches Gabriella in the gut. He throws up his arms triumphantly and immediately has to run away as Gabriella charges toward him with a snowball in hand.

Jump cut to the front door. Miriam and Hannah stand together. Hannah's slicker has sequins coming off and pipe cleaners hanging askew. It was once a twinkle light pattern, with dangling stars and dots of many colors hung from blue pipe cleaners. Miriam's slicker has spots of glue where there once were 3D noses for her trio of snowmen.

MIRIAM (smiling)

You wouldn't know Jack and Gabriella are on the same team.

HANNAH (giggling)

Oh, I know! They don't see anyone else, do they? (Wiggling eyebrows) You should have seen them the other day at the gingerbread building...Wow! (Fans self playfully) I may start taking my lunch in the basement to watch the Jack and Gabby show.

MIRIAM

I think they're a really cute couple.

HANNAH (excited)

I knoooow! And I never would have thought of it before.

Jump cut to Jack, licking syrup off of his fingers at the front door. He waves at his pristine Reindeer booger slicker.

JACK

Varsity short stop. (notches his head up proudly) And the undefeated champion of this snowball fight! Whoop! (incredulous) Can you believe I had to talk her into adding the syrup? She said it was "just for fun."(air quotes) And we (air quotes) "don't need winners and losers!"

From the right of the camera angle, a team of stealth attackers are creeping up. Gabriella Hannah, Frank, and Carol.

JACK

I think she was afraid to—Ack!

Stealth attackers strike out while Jack is defenseless and unaware.

JACK

Cheaters!

Jack runs out of the shot, pursued by coworkers.
Cut to Gabriella breathless and laughing in front of the office doors.

GABRIELLA

I don't think wearing the slickers is all that helpful. We're all sticky messes. (looks around smiling)(beat) No. Jack is not right. I am not afraid of losing (holds up colorful slicker). I was a little afraid of getting sticky or really being a part of the snowball fight at all. (Stiffens, smiling) Do you know how often you get touched without your consent on an average day. *I do.*

Gabriella rolls shoulders, hands fisted at her side, twisting every few seconds as if attacked by an electric current.

GABRIELLA

It used to make me seriously anxious. I didn't like to go out if I didn't have to. I would wear lots of layers even in the middle of summer to blunt the effect of people brushing me. Something like this, a snowball fight—everyone running around screaming, intentionally trying to hit you, it's a minefield of discomfort and triggering situations. (breathes deeply)(beat) I loved the idea of seeing one, but I hadn't meant to be a part of it. But, (shrugs) Jack dared me, and I *couldn't* let him think he had the upper hand, so I did it. And while I was doing it—I didn't feel the snowballs hit me at all. I mean, they ought to be painful, right? But it's like they just dissolve in puffs of magic when they hit me, so all I can feel are the ones I'm throwing. It's awesome! (laughs joyfully) It's like (voice softens) I was pummeling people with all the stress that ties me up most days. I'm sure when the adrenaline has worn off, I'll be an anxious mess. I'll probably take three showers tonight. But it was fun while it lasted. And a while ago, even knowing the fun to be had, I wouldn't have been able to risk the stress.

The film freezes on Gabriella's soft smile.
Cut to black.

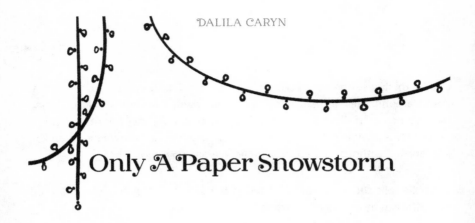

Only A Paper Snowstorm

Later that same evening, in the home of Gabriella and Maria Cruz, Jack Drummer is enjoying the display of sisterhood. Jack has once again invited himself to Gabriella's home, insisting that she will need help with all the snowflake making for tomorrow's event.

Since Gabriella was *very* insistent that he should not come over before seven-thirty, Jack offered to bring dinner. Some pizza and spicy potato wedges. Gabriella claimed to have errands she needed to run, but Jack has his own suspicions about what Gabriella really meant to do. And they are immediately confirmed when she opens the door with her hair still wet, braided down either side of her head and looking adorable in a reindeer onesie!

Kristen was right. He can't believe it. He also cannot believe how much he loves this oversized, fully zipped-up animal-headed outfit. He'd bet Gabriella wasn't concerned with adorableness when she put it on. Only covering every bit of her skin that she can, only with cushioning, only with feeling more comfortable in her skin.

One might think that Jack is rapidly developing some *impressive* observational skills. After all, he predicted that Gabriella wanted the extra time to shower and remove every last bit of stickiness from her person. And he was clever enough to put together that she had covered every bit of her skin to avoid having any of it touched. But his observations are so specifically restricted to one woman that it might be more appropriately termed—obsession—than skill.

Jack and Gabriella had stayed behind at the office after everyone left to hose down the parking lot with dish soap. The whole while, Jack had watched Gabriella, seemingly unaware of what she was doing, scratch angry red lines into her arms every few seconds. And before she'd been willing to get into her car, she'd laid down two layers of open garbage bags that she duct-taped into place. She'd thrown away her own colorful rain slicker, though many people saved theirs, and he kept seeing her reach up to scratch her hair and stop herself.

The poor thing, he thought with an internal smile. He knows she enjoyed the event while it was going on. But the further from it she gets, the more it all seems to bother her. He is simultaneously sorry that it is bothering her now and happy that she was able to enjoy it in the moment.

In a bid to...comfort her maybe, or just to make her smile Jack also stopped for some ice cream. And something for her arms.

Greeting him at the door, her right eyebrow arches and she smiles at him incredulously.

"That's a lot more than we discussed," she says, blocking the doorway.

"I felt like ice cream," Jack replies cautiously, watching her roll her shoulders. "I'm sorry, does that..."

Shaking her head, Gabriella reaches out for the grocery bag atop the pizza box and steps back into the apartment.

"It's great, thanks. Come in." She turns around, walking into the kitchen with the ice cream and leaving Jack in the doorway. He follows, smiling broadly at the shifting reindeer tail on her onesie. He really wants to make a bad joke. Really. But he is restraining—

"Someone's got an eye for tail." A voice calls out behind him, making Jack spin.

He knew Maria would be here. But...he'd forgotten to look. She throws him a smug, and not altogether welcoming smile.

Gabriella doesn't respond verbally to her sister's quip, but as she comes out of the kitchen, her face is so red that she's definitely heard.

"You forgot to take this out of the bag." Gabriella holds out a bottle of lotion without looking at him.

Jack shakes his head. "That's a gift. For your arms."

If it is possible, Gabriella blushes even harder, and an awkward silence descends on the room. Before her sister jumps in, demanding the pizza and doing her damnedest to cut all the tension hanging in the air. But Gabriella looks up silently, with her sister between them chattering, and catches Jack's eyes looking so warm and lovely that it is all he can do not to kiss her.

By nine, when they have been cutting snowflakes for nearly two hours snagging bites of pizza in between. The pile of paper snowflakes is quite large, and up until a few minutes ago, Gabriella still wore that focused look that says plainly she will be at this for hours. But her sister brought up a Christmas past, and Gabriella has gotten into the story, smiling easily and her fingers moving more slowly as she cuts. She even pushes up one of the sleeves of her onesie and the cotton shirt beneath it, revealing the scratches on her arms but not seeming to notice because she's relaxed enough to want to be cool, more than she wants to hide.

"I was not that bad! I just got a little upset," Maria is shouting defensively.

"She slammed the door like seven times," Gabriella insists, mercilessly laughing at her sister's expense. "And shouted that she hated our family. She kept sobbing about being poor."

Jack laughs, enjoying them together. It is fun and sweet. All night long, they've shifted fluidly between championing and insulting each other.

"In my defense, being poor was pretty dramatic when I was fifteen." Maria shrugs at her own comment. "Now it's fine."

"What did your mother do?" Jack asks, laughing at Gabriella's rolling eyes.

Gabriella smirks at the memory. "She shook her head and started praying in Spanish," Gabriella imitates her mother smirking superiorly at her little sister. "Padre celestial, ¿qué he hecho yo para merecer toda esta fe que pones en mi paciencia? Permita que otra madre tenga la oportunidad de demostrar que es digna de su fe."

Maria grins, translating for Jack. "Oh God, what have I done to deserve all this faith you put in my patience? Please allow some other mother a chance to prove worthy of your faith." Maria has always been annoyed when this story was trotted out for friends and neighbors, but she finds she quite likes it now. It is no longer a jabbing reminder of her childhood foibles, but rather a sweet memory of the mother she misses. She and Gabriella exchange loving smiles, sharing the sweet memory.

Jack, meanwhile, is simply enjoying the story with a bit of laughter. But the sisters are quite pleased with that reaction. Their mother was a funny woman. And kind and loving. She would appreciate that a stranger would find her response amusing.

"Then," Gabriella goes on with the story. "She grabbed me and said, 'okay, we can't send her skiing, so let's bring the snow to her.' All night Mom and I cut up newspaper and bills," she giggles at the irreverence of such supplies, "any paper we could find making snowflakes."

As she says it, Gabriella opens a finished paper snowflake and holds it wide. "There were so many. I remember feeling giddy." She lays the snowflake aside and begins another, unaware that she is being observed with a quiet pleasure.

"Mom knew the cure for everything," Maria says softly.

"She did. It was amazing." Gabriella says, with her eyes on the snowflake in hand. Then giggles and glances at her sister. "I had been annoyed with Maria over the whole thing. But a few minutes into cutting, I forgot all about it. It was definitely one of the top three of our Christmases ever. When Maria woke up the next morning, Mom made her put on sunglasses—"

"I was totally freaked out!" Maria interrupts dramatically. "I was sure it was some bizarre punishment. I demanded to know what she was doing and where she was taking me. She looked so serious. And she stops me and says, 'It can never disappoint you as much as it does me that I cannot give you everything you want. But do not forget that you do have everything you need.'"

The sisters regard each other again, caught up in the memory. And Jack is silent as well, watching them like a lovely work of art, unwilling to disrupt.

"Anyway." Gabriella shakes herself and gets back to the story. "She dragged Maria out, and I'm waiting there with the fan at full blast and a laundry basket full of snowflakes. As soon as Mom moved out of the way, I threw the snowflakes at the air stream."

Jack lets out a sudden bark of laughter.

Giggling, Maria continues the story. "I got like twenty paper cuts, but it was so much fun! I made them do it again and again. We kept gathering them up and taking turns standing in the snow storm."

"Sounds almost as dangerous as a real blizzard," Jack remarks, amused and perhaps even slightly jealous of the silly story and lovely bond it created between the sisters.

"Afterwards, we drank cocoa and hung the snowflakes all over the ceiling with string and scotch tape," Maria remembers. "When I got to go skiing with friends a few years later, I kept thinking about our hallway blizzard and how much fun we had."

Yeah. Jack thinks, *I would have been too.*

Snow Gifts

J ust before work hours on Friday, Gabriella makes her way to her desk. She and Jack have finished decorating the building. Each taking a few floors. Jack had the first floor and basement. Exiting the elevator, Gabriella looks around in wonder.

She is quite pleased now to have a helper. She was at first both annoyed and insulted. But Jack has added something special to the events and...it's fun getting to step off the elevator and feel some of the wonder the rest of the staff feel, seeing the decoration.

Snowflakes hang all around the room with pictures taped into their centers; pictures of children holding the dolls, and the employees enjoying the Secret Santa events. It's magical.

The camera crew, alerted to a need to be early by Jack, are in the break room, filming Gabriella and moving slowly towards her. Jack was meant to have been hidden as well, but he answered his office phone when it rang and was called away just before Gabriella finished her work on the third floor.

Gabriella stops cold at her cubicle. It has been wrapped in blue and white snowflake paper with a silver bow and a tag shaped like a Christmas tree hanging from the top. Gabriella holds her breath and lifts the tag.

Pull.
Trust me,
Santa's helper.

Gabriella holds her delight inside momentarily with her fizzing captive breath. She grips the ribbon and tugs. The wrapping paper falls apart, dropping away at either side of the cubicle to reveal a strand of snowflakes that hang across the entrance like a gate. She runs an airy finger along the chain of snowflakes wondrously.

Gabriella has felt the presence of the camera crew, quiet though they tried to be. She glances back now with an awed expression her sister would tease her mercilessly for, but the hopeless romantics of the doc crew quite enjoy.

"He didn't put a single snowflake or piece of wrapping paper *inside* my cubicle. He respected my space but still managed to give me this beautiful surprise." She breathes softly. "I didn't think guys were sweet this way."

Kristen takes this opportunity to interview Gabriella with a different background, showing off the snowflake-filled room.

"So, is the decoration the gift for today?"

Gabriella nods, then shakes her head. "It was supposed to be, that and instructions for how to make their own. But Jack was so enthused by one of the ideas I cut, so we added the toboggan ride."

"And Jack's punishment?" Kristen prompts coyly. "Or do sweet boys not get pranked?"

"Oh, Jack is getting pranked!" Gabriella giggles. "It's gonna be fun, just you wait. Trust me. I'll give you a heads up when it's time."

The interview ends there as the elevator opens and workers start filtering in. The other IT workers look around at the snowflakes. There are some admiring comments. But by and large, it's just a glance or a smile.

Gabriella takes the strand of snowflakes off the back of her desk and hangs them along the inside wall of her cubicle before settling in to work. Every once in a while, glancing at the snowflakes and the pictures inside, especially one. A picture of Jack caught with an annoyed expression right at the moment when he tries to toss Angelo off his lap. Every time she sees it, she grins. It's nice to have one's work admired.

When Jack manages to escape his boss, he races to the basement by way of the stairs and manages to flag down the camera crew without emerging into the basement where he can be seen.

He'd been called into Coleman's office to discuss actual business for once. But unfortunately, it was nothing Jack wanted to talk about. Coleman is after him to find out who hacked their system. Unaware that this really isn't what Jack's kind of tech does. Jack spent the better part of fifteen minutes attempting to explain that basically, he can fix bugs in the system he's trained for, tell you why your computer is running slowly, and maybe fix it if it's something simple. Basically, they are a troubleshooting menu brought to life. But they do not trace down hackers.

Somehow Jack came out smelling quite rosy indeed. After all, he was somehow both unqualified to seek out hackers and still managed to repel the attack so that no information was lost. Quite the impressive feat. Coleman is certainly impressed.

Phrases like *good management skills, nice delegating,* and *very impressive* were thrown around. In the back of his mind, Jack is sure he should feel bad for taking credit for fixing a prank that Gabriella would have fixed at the end of the day. But he doesn't. He did fix it. If he were to tell Coleman the truth, despite the fact that it didn't harm the company at all and the incredible skill it took to put the bug together, to begin with, Gabriella could easily be out of a job.

His taking credit is giving her credit. At least that's how he sees it. At the end of the meeting, when Coleman asked Jack to suggest some security companies to hunt down the hackers, Jack was able to use his new *impressive* reputation to suggest letting it go.

"It'll be much more expensive than it's worth to track them down. Since we didn't lose anything, I suggest we upgrade our security to make sure it doesn't happen again. I can suggest some programs," Jack said, striving for casual. What if Coleman pressed this? Would he find out it was Gabriella who hacked them? Would she get fired? Sued? Arrested?

"Well, if you think that's best."

"Definitely. It was probably some teenager showing off how clever they are." Jack grins because that last bit, at least, is very true.

Gabriella could have made it much easier on him, but while she does not do a lot of in-your-face boasting, she is in no way shy of proving her talents.

When Jack gets the film crew into the dim stairwell, all four of them are shoved together, so he has to stand a few stairs up to have room; he looks down at them eagerly.

"I could kill Coleman. Why did I even answer my phone? I can't believe I missed her seeing it. Did she like it? Can I see the tape?" He smiles in a flirtatious way he is well aware is quite effective on the average woman.

Kristen shakes her head, wearing an evil smile *she knows* quite annoys the average man. "When everyone else does," Kristen replies brightly. "You seem to have changed your tune about her. Doesn't her intensity annoy you anymore?"

Jack narrows his eyes slightly, but as ever certain that he is an easy-going man, he shrugs. "No, I suppose her intensity doesn't bother me anymore. I guess once you get to understand a person, their quirks become less annoying and more endearing. Unless getting to know them makes you hate them, of course." He laughs.

Hypothetically...
When Finally We Kiss

Quiet cozy fun is Gabriella's stated preference of entertainment, but it seems not to be the case for Jack Drummer, as the events he has taken the most pleasure in are the wild shouting rides. Like the toboggan ride contest of today's winter games. In teams of two, the staff build cardboard box toboggans, climb on and slide down the wheelchair ramp into the parking lot. It is not a very long ramp, but being as it was built some while in the past, it is a bit steeper than is strictly up to code, thus making it *quite* fun. To help things along, the ramp is lined with the large cardboard dowels left over from packing paper. And in the landing zone, blown up and waiting is an air mattress for safety. The event is timed, and winners receive a month of their choosing to splitting Coleman's coveted parking space right near the door and constantly shaded by the building. Ideal for those hot summer days.

Because of the close proximity required for the event, Gabriella allowed people to choose their own teams. She had intended to opt-out. But Jack asked her to be his teammate.

She should say no. She isn't overly fond of being touched. *She should say no.* But...her heart races at the thought of his arms sliding around her, and she has to think in order to breathe when he asks. Gabriella nods her agreement before she has even knows what she is doing.

They do not win. But neither Jack nor Gabriella is terribly upset by their failure. Indeed, they had both wished that the ride would go on a bit longer. Though neither one says this aloud. Jack relished the chance to hold Gabriella close and whisper in her ear.

"Is this alright?" He asks as he slides his arms around her waist.

Gabriella nods as her hands settle atop his arms, and a blush rushes tingling from her chest all the way into her hairline. Gabriella is breathless, her body brushed by whispers of electricity as Jack's arms close around her waist. She knows she will continue feeling the impression of him there for weeks. Maybe even months, but she is pleased with the prospect. She never wants it to end.

"I don't know if I liked him before," she admits to her sister on the phone, having snuck away after the event because she needed time alone. "But I know I do now. Is that...ridiculous?"

"No," Maria says softly. Though internally, she wants to say something snide and unromantic. But her sister sounds so happy. She can't ruin this for her. "Of course not. He's being very sweet; it would be ridiculous to hold a grudge against him. You're supposed to like people better the more you know them. Just enjoy it." She advises, thinking privately that she would keep an eye on Jack, a less lovesick and thus more observant eye.

Later in the afternoon, only about half an hour before it is time to go home, Jack steps around his own cubicle to lean over Gabriella's. Busy typing away, Gabriella manages to pretend she doesn't notice him for a full three seconds. The willpower is *strong* with this one. *Wink.

When she *finally* looks up, Jack stares at her for several seconds before blurting out. "Santa's evil little helper?"

"What?" Gabriella laughs, flabbergasted.

"With ones for all the I's?" He adds. When she only stares, he explains further. "Your computer password."

Gabriella laughs and shakes her head. "Not even close. Is that why you came over here?" She asks, feeling her skin prickle with a blush as her mind whispers that he came over because he wanted to see her.

Jack shakes his head, smiling because she is not entirely wrong. He did very much just want to look at her. But he also has a question.

"So there is something I've been wanting to do for a few days now," Jack says quietly when it begins to feel strange that he is not talking. "And I'm not sure how to go about it. It's something nice, but technically it would require invading your personal space again, and the point is to do something you'll enjoy, not to make you uncomfortable. But I don't know if it would be better to surprise you or—"

"Are you asking my permission to kiss me?" Gabriella demands in a shocked whisper, leaning near with her eyes wide and her posture secretive.

Shocked, Jack chuckles, slowly shaking his head and biting down on an utterly tickled smile.

Gabriella looks away, mortified. Ready to dig a hole straight to the earth's core so she can die in fiery oblivion. Ready to quit. Ready to change her name and enter witness protection, even if all she witnessed was her own humiliation, and she definitely doesn't want to have to testify to that. "No. That was—" she breaks off breathlessly, fighting off the infuriating urge to cry at the devastating shame that is her existence. "A weird thing to—"

"Should I be?" Jack interrupts with a grin, thoroughly enjoying her distress.

"Kissing me or asking?" She asks, snappish. Because focusing on self-rage and directing it outward, is the only way to beat back the shame tears. "Sorry. That's embarrassing. I wasn't saying—" she breaks off; *where are you going with this, Gabriella?* "I was just confused by the way you were—" *Aaaaargh!* "What had you wanted to ask me?"

"Oh no, you don't," Jack says playfully, leaning his head into the cubicle until she is forced to look at him, though she's been trying valiantly to avoid it. "I'm having an answer to that question. It's far more pressing than my original one. So let's say, hypothetically, that I am—*very*—interested in kissing you." He pauses, their eyes locking for a quiet fraught beat of the heart. "Should I *ask* first?" His tone has suddenly become *incredibly* seductive. It is smooth. Slow and *rich,* melted chocolate swirling invitingly as it's tempered. Though his questions are still quite simple, direct even. "Should I say the words? Would that be something *you* would like— *hypothetically*?"

How does he make the word hypothetically *sound seductive? It's a scientific term. It's...an SAT word, for crying out loud!* But he says it and she can't take her eyes off his lips. It is all she can do to keep from licking her own.

"I—" Gabriella breaks off. Her fingers keep tapping at the table and her feet keep shaking. *How the fuck am I supposed to answer this?* "It's not as though any other boyfriend, that is, any other guy," she rushes out, mortified again. *Did I just call him my boyfriend when literally nothing has happened between us?* "Has, you know, used the words to—I was—" She fumbles.

"But," Jack says with seductive precision, "do *you* find the idea of being asked more appealing than going with the moment without words?"

Gabriella is silent, just staring at Jack. And he waits. Patiently. Maybe even eagerly for her answer. She crushes the fingers of her left hand in her right fist and forces herself to be honest. She nods once.

"Yes. These past few days, it has been a lovely, appealing surprise having my space respected." She manages to say on the thread of air she was able to pull in. It escapes her with the last words, though, leaving her staring at Jack in entirely breathless anticipation.

"That is *excellent* information to have." Jack's eyes positively smolder at her. "Thank you."

Gabriella feels her hands relaxing. She doesn't know that she has ever felt this *warm* and this *electric* just from a discussion. An honest, uncomfortable, very close conversation. It's weirdly like a kiss. Their breaths are mingling, they are so close that the air between them tickles when either of them moves, and their eyes are bonfire hot as they gaze at one another.

It is a kiss. Though they haven't touched at all. She may need to cool down in a second.

Jack is experiencing similar thoughts. He is entirely shocked to find that he finds this asking, this open conversation about something as chaste as kissing, really very *hot!* He is considering all of the very promising things he can ask her as their relationship develops. Imagining her breathless replies and excited eyes. Her fiery intensity focused entirely on him and his requests. Very hot!

He's got to change the subject. Because now really isn't the time to ask to kiss her. Or run his hands up her body. Or—

"Well!" Jack clears his throat. "That also helps answer my first question. I think you'd prefer to be asked." He steps back and breathes out several times, looking around the room, reminding himself that there are other people here. And *cameras!* He'd forgotten all about the cameras. Yep. He needs to focus. "So, may I borrow your mother's nutcracker for a few days?" He asks bluntly.

Christmas Conspirators

Gabriella jerks upright, tensing at the sudden shift in conversation. And Jack's ice bucket of a statement doesn't only affect him and Gabriella. Jay, the tech seated closest to them, could not make out every word, but he was definitely leaning in excitedly and feeling that tension. Now he has to snap back to work before anyone realizes he was listening. And it surely startled you, not to mention the intrepid young film students diligently documenting the entire exchange.

Terrance is fighting off a chuckle at how quickly the moment went from sexual tension to dramatic tension. He's loving it; the longer he watches them together, the more he likes Gabriella and Jack as a couple. He wouldn't have thought Jack the type of guy to care, much less directly ask what Gabriella finds comfortable. He's not a bad guy. And Gabriella is certainly stuck on him.

Andrew, for once, is fully engaged in the moment. He'd found himself leaning forward the longer they talked, holding his breath, waiting for a kiss! Now that it hasn't come, he is a bit annoyed. Come on, that was the perfect moment for a kiss! But they aren't even touching. People are so annoying, when they aren't scripted!

But it is Kristen who is most...shaken. *Jingle Bells,* that was hot! And literally nothing happened. She needs to get out of here. This place is really lowering her bar for what is hot. But—at the same time—her mind keeps replaying Jack's words. *Do you find the idea of being asked more appealing.* No one has ever asked her anything like that, and not just in romantic relationships. Up to now, she wouldn't have pegged herself as someone who went along with other people's desires, but in this moment, she's hard pressed to say what she has ever done beyond pursuing a career in film that was exclusively her choice. But while she is caught up contemplating her life, the universe and everything, the universe keeps expanding.

"My dad used to teach shop," Jack says to Gabriella by way of an explanation. "I think he can help me fix it."

"Doesn't he still teach shop?" Gabriella's mind shoves out a thoroughly unimportant question to stall for time. That's a lot of trust he's asking for. A lot more than kissing. Maybe they should start with the kissing. She's game.

"Yeah." Jack rolls his eyes; *she always has to correct him, doesn't she?* Then he realizes what she's said. His eyes narrow. "How do you know that?"

Gabriella's shoulders bend in with the embarrassment. "Oh, your mom and I are—Facebook friends," she admits, talking rapidly in the hopes of explaining before he gets too upset. "I friended her looking for dirt to prank you with. But your mother is one of those people who actually look at everyone who friends her, and she realized I work with you and started messaging me."

Jack laughs incredulous. "This is too much. What excuse did you give for friending her?"

"The truth. I said you'd broken something precious of mine, and I was looking for revenge."

"And she still accepted your friend request?" Jack demands.

"Yes. I used her idea today because I was short of ideas."

Jack steps back, looking so appalled one might think this was the biggest betrayal of his life.

For those curious minds begging to be satisfied, let's rewind to earlier today and see that prank.

In this not-so-distant past, it is ten a.m., and the mail boy, August, enters the basement by way of the elevator, pushing a cart. Gabriella was on high alert already, and the moment the elevator opened, she poked up her curious head to be sure of who was coming before tapping away at her computer; really just one command, she set it up ahead of time. Then she leans in towards the screen no one else can make out because of her replaced privacy shield, rubbing her hands together.

The film crew were alerted to a need to be ready and were angled in from the break room, a much better view of Jack and Gabriella at the same time. What Gabriella can see that no one else can is the webcam footage from Jack's computer, which she has remotely turned on. Jack is leaning over his murder mystery *Brains on the Tile*. When August, a truly interesting young man of a bright future that shall not be covered and thus ought not to have been mentioned, leans in holding out a wrapped Christmas present addressed to Jack

"Wow. I've never gotten a present at work," August says, very nearly jealous. And moves off without waiting for the thanks that Jack shouts after him.

Jack flips over his novel to hold his place and leans back in his seat, opening the present wearing a secretive smile. He suspects it is something from Gabriella. He even suspects it will be a prank. What kind, he isn't sure. A scavenger hunt designed to make him defrag a bunch of computers. A Christmasy mug that will look normal, but the bottom will drop out and spill something all over his pants. A pair of trick headphones, so he plays his music for the whole office.

He is grinning, at the idea of having wet pants in front of the office, and thinking that Gabriella is going soft all of a sudden, and he thinks, quite fondly, that he knows why.

But the second the bow atop it is untied, the pressurized box explodes. It gives off a quiet pop. But it is the loudest noise in the basement, second only to Jack's scream of terror as he throws the box full of confetti away from him. Something clatters onto his desk as Jack leaps backwards, hitting the wall of his cubicle and shaking his and Gabriella's desks.

Gabriella watches it all from her cubicle scooting down in her seat and fully shoving her fist into her mouth to silence her laughter. *Oh no!* She hadn't thought he was *that* terrified. She is sure it says something awful about her that she is so delighted by his shock and fear, and she is not wrong. But that awful thing is generally known as —human nature. Shameful. *Wink.

"Damn it, Gabriella!" Jack calls out with a hand on his chest. "I could have been killed."

Gabriella snickers. Not just because of the dramatic words, but because of the still cautious way he is peering at his desk from behind his chair as if concerned the box will explode again.

When he finally works up the nerve to approach the desk, Jack retrieves the tiny Santa figurine that had clattered out of the box.

"Ho. Ho. Ho," it says the moment Jack lifts it. With an angry shock, Jack tosses the Santa hard against the back of his cubicle and stomps off towards the bathroom.

Gabriella watches him go, surprised but not nearly contrite enough to chase him down and comfort him. In fact, she snickers even more as she sees him go.

In the here and now, Gabriella continues her explanation. "Your mother said they gave you a Jack-in-the-box when you were little, and you," she giggles, "screamed and cried when it opened. She said she didn't think you cried anymore, but you still didn't like things that pop out at you." Gabriella admits, face to the floor, but by no means anymore contrite than earlier as she chews on a grin.

Jack shakes his head several times. Unable to speak for a few seconds. When he does, his tone has lost that lover-ish quality and has become quite annoyed. "I don't know if I should be offended by the gross invasion of my privacy and my mother's betrayal—"

Gabriella snorts. She should feel bad. She knows she should. But honestly, today's prank felt so good. Too good. She may need to get ahold of herself soon.

"Or oddly impressed by your ability to be simultaneously honest and duplicitous," Jack finishes. His tone is no longer annoyed because Gabriella is looking up now, smug and unrepentant, and her lips are swollen from where she's been chewing on them, and part of his brain is thinking very definitely about how it would feel to be the one enjoying that snack. But he really needs to stop thinking this way at work.

"Why did you even need help? I thought you had my whole punishment planned out from stage one to stage twelve?" Jack asks, striving for casual and missing quite widely, his voice sounding far too deep and breathy

"Oh," Gabriella shifts in her chair, looking for something to adjust on her table, but all is perfectly in place. She hadn't meant to say that. The truth was, after his reaction to the crumb bug, she got to thinking about how mean some of the later pranks were. She had already planned to do the pop box, but much more publicly. So she made some small adjustments. "Well, I did, yes. But...The later stages were more mean than funny. And once I knew you better," her voice drops to nearly a whisper as she rushes out the last words. "I didn't want to be mean to you."

Jack and Gabriella lock eyes for several fraught seconds, thinking very different things. Jack's mind is saying: *I knew she was a big softy at heart. She's developing a real thing for me. But I cannot believe she has been conspiring with my mother! I bet Mom's having the time of her life. They probably really like each other.*

Whilst Gabriella is busy thinking: *He probably thinks I'm a weird stalker now. Not just weird. He already thought that. And mean for using his insecurities to prank him. He probably doesn't want to kiss me anymore. Not that he did, to begin with, he was just having fun with my embarrassment, most likely.*

"Well, I guess I'll forgive your duplicity," Jack says playfully to break the growing silence. "But only if you let me have the nutcracker. I swear if I cannot fix it, I will not break it any further."

Carefully Gabriella swivels and lifts the nutcracker from its home at a right angle behind her computer screen. She holds it out to Jack with both hands. Looking into his eyes as she hands it over.

"I trust you."

Three Turtle Doves are a Crowd

Maria Estrella Cruz is not an unsocial individual. She has over the course of her life, been a member of several clubs. She was counted among the popular kids in junior high and high school, by no means at the top of the social hierarchy, but too cool and confident not to be adored by many. She is generally confident in any social situation and has, on more than one occasion, more than one hundred occasions more like, used her social savvy to drag her sometimes less-than-social sister into a group, into a party, into the light, and helped her shine.

So it is a new and somewhat unsettling development for her on this lovely Sunday afternoon to be standing in the kitchen of her apartment watching her sister and Jack glue pieces of felt together in mitten shapes, laughing and giggling and occasionally staring into one another's eyes as though they are the only two people in the room, or indeed the entire world.

It is not that she has never seen her sister with a boyfriend before, or even one she's been this *smitten* with and really, it's the best word for it. It's like an old-fashioned sort of cuteness they share. But she has never seen her sister so...simultaneously at ease and excited before. And Jack too. Not that she knew him before or anything, but his whole attention, every moment, is on Gabriella. His eyes don't leave her.

Maria has snuck into the kitchen to get away from all the —nauseating—*cuteness*. To breathe in air that is not romantically charged. And though she's been gone for a good two minutes, the pair don't seem to have noticed. So, to entertain herself, Maria leans on the counter and imagines that the documentary film crew have followed her sister home again tonight.

In her head, she talks to the crew, with her sister and Jack in the background, their voices muffled but their *intensity palpable*.

"It's like watching a Victorian romance over there," she would say to the crew in a light, mocking tone. "Oh, I wouldn't dare touch you, but let me get as close as I possibly can." She would pull a dramatic period piece style face before continuing and Jack and Gabriella would flirt on, entirely oblivious to the fact that anyone else was there.

"Don't get me wrong, they're cute. But I'm more of a, let's kiss already and get on with it, sort of girl. I was prepared for the worst with Jack, but he seems okay." Her mind shifts to a slightly more serious subject; it would make for a richer cutaway moment after all. "He is one of those *comfortable* guys. Like his life has never been extravagant, but it's never been difficult either. When Gabriella was looking for dirt on him, she got all bent out of shape when she told me he was an only child, that his parents were happily married and that *all four* of his grandparents are alive! That may well have been her biggest complaint. Not to be partial or anything, but she has a right to be jealous. Both of our parents were only children and are now dead. We have one living grandparent, but we've never met him. We don't have extended family. We don't have Mom anymore. It is *just us*. And Gabriella—" here she would pause, here even her mind pauses because this relationship is new and as sweet as it is to see, it is also scary. What happens if something this special to begin with goes wrong? Gabriella has never had anything quite this sweet. No boyfriend has ever been so cautious of invading her space that he made the not touching romantic. No boyfriend has ever pushed her out of her comfort zone and respected that there are boundaries he cannot nudge her past. What happens to someone like Gabriella, who *cares* so much about other people and what they think of her and does not let anyone down? What happens to her when something this sweet, sours?

"Gabriella has *never* been comfortable. But who knows, right? Maybe she can be comfortable now."

Maria abandons her make-believe camera crew with that last bit of forced positivity. She walks back into the living room, settling on the floor beside her sister, silently resuming her task of cutting out felt.

Jack is smiling all for Gabriella, poking fun at her. "So we had the snowball fight for our A.D.D. staff, and now we're having the ultimate game of cleanliness for our O.C.D. staff?"

"Well, technically," Gabriella replies, with a slightly instructive, bite to her words. "The last D in both those acronyms stands for disorder, so when referring to the people who *live with* those disorders, as the disorder, you can go ahead and leave off the last D." She raises a brow, which quickly turns into a blush and a glance away when Jack smiles his sheepish *don't you love me anyway* grin. "And... I'm not sure the snowball fight was technically good for anyone with A.D.D. the trouble is an inability to filter things out enough to maintain focus, I think. It might actually have been very bad for them." Gabriella thinks aloud, her eyes unfocused and thus unaware of Jack rolling his eyes in amusement. "But...well...it's over now. And anyway," Gabriella shakes herself, "I'm sure anyone who wants to, can make this game equally as messy as the snowball fight and have a great time of it."

"They just can't win that way." Jack grins.

"They've all seemed to love the competitive aspects of the events. And mitten cocoa making is a classic game," Gabriella says defensively.

"I've never heard of it," Jack says in a blatantly flirtatious tone, slow and smooth and intent. "*I* think it's *all you*, and you're trying to trick us into playing neatly."

Maria drops a mitten half onto Gabriella's pile unnoticed and lifts another piece of felt.

"It's one of those 'games' boys are never expected to play," Gabriella says with air quotes. "But they'll play in my world. I'm making it worth their while. Two months of never getting break room clean-up is a better prize than the day off."

"That's because you actually *clean* when it's your turn. The rest of us just wipe up crumbs and make sure the fridge is closed." Jack teases, reaching out for a mitten Gabriella has finished glueing together and adding precut felt stickers to decorate.

"Ugh! No wonder the microwave looks like a war zone." Gabriella shudders in disgust, reaching out for more felt pieces without even glancing her sister's way.

"You're kind of adorable when you're annoyed," Jack says softly.

"You should see her when she's intently plotting your destruction," Maria says, intentionally bright, a startling pop to their bubble of cuteness. They glance over, remembering Maria's existence. "Super adorable!"

"I bet." Jack agrees, clearing his throat.

Maria cackles briefly while Jack casts about for a new subject, and Gabriella pretends not to have been startled at all.

The Baggage is Hung by the Chimney

"**I** can't believe you guys have a fake fireplace." Jack lands on a neutral subject. "It's a heater too, right? How often do you use that function?"

"Never." The sisters say in disgusted unison, glancing at each other and shaking heads as if to say, 'who would ask such a thing?'

Jack laughs.

"How do you decorate for Christmas? Or are you too cool?" Gabriella inquires.

"I usually spend Christmas with my parents, sometimes even my grandparents and cousins," Jack says with a shrug in his voice as well as on his shoulders. "So I don't do much at home. But I have a potted pine tree that I put lights on."

"Just lights? You don't have a favorite ornament that makes you think of the past? Or makes you smile?" Gabriella asks.

"Well, my parents have all of my childhood ornaments. I used to have some other stuff—" Jack breaks off awkwardly.

"When you were with Lauren?" Gabriella asks, sounding casual. Though her mind is screaming, *shut up! Let it go. It's none of your business. Why are you bringing up the woman he wanted to marry? The woman that made him run away. The woman he's clearly still hung up on.*

"Yes," Jack says lightly, though his mind is cautioning. *Oooo. Don't say too much. Exs are always touchy, and you're talking about her with a girl you want to date but haven't even made out with. Dangerous. Keep it casual, it's over, but if you aren't casual, she's gonna think something is still there.* "Well, we lived together for a while, and we got stuff together. But I gave it all to her or threw it away when we split."

There is a rather long silence following these words. An awkward silence. The sort that is hard to break when one is involved in the wealth of unsaid words between the two main players in this play. Luckily for them, they have once again forgotten their audience.

"Oh, what a trial it is being a single man, so lonely." Maria remarks in a dramatically creepy voice.

Gabriella glances at her sister and snorts. Almost a giggle, but it stops short. "Cute, but not nearly catchy enough." She shakes her head at Maria, though she is grateful for the distraction. Her mind was ready to run away with all the implications of Jack not having bought a single decoration since his split with his girlfriend. Four years ago. Or wanting to delve into why he hadn't kept a single one. Were they that painful a reminder of her? Or had he done that boy thing where he handed over a box full of things he hadn't even looked through?

"Am I missing something?" Jack asks, striving for light and playful when he is *very* grateful! *Rescued.* Maria is a real sport because he can tell from Gabriella's expression that she wasn't going to let his answer go at face value.

"It's a game we play, referencing this line from an old movie we love to...not hate-watch, but watch and mock certainly, *Thoroughly Modern Milly.* There is this landlady who repeats a catchphrase over and over when she is picking her next orphaned kidnapping victim. We used to quote it back and forth to each other whenever one of us was saying something maudlin. Now we compete to see who can change the line enough to slip it past the other."

"It's a really ridiculous movie, spoof level!" Maria adds helpfully.

"But so fun!" Gabriella laughs. "Maybe it was meant to be a spoof." Gabriella glances at her sister curiously.

Maria bobs her head thoughtfully. "Could be, but even spoofing doesn't explain away the racism and sexism."

"But you love it anyway?" Jack asks unnecessarily.

"It has its moments," Gabriella says.

"Like the elevator that only works if you dance in it. And the landlady's catchphrase." Maria provides enthusiastically. "My joke was funny," she laughs, "because you've got all this family, and we're the orphans, but you're the one with the pathetically lonely Christmas season."

Jack laughs along. He is beginning to quite like Gabriella's little sister. But Gabriella isn't laughing, and when he glances over, she is wearing a serious expression.

"You should get your own things. Not a ton, and not with anyone else. Just...*one* ornament or decoration. Something that makes you smile. Something you'd want to take with you if you ever run away again."

Jack forces a laugh. "Is that my warning that the clip is coming out?"

"No. I—" Gabriella breaks off awkwardly. "You shouldn't just *be* in an apartment, or house or wherever you live. Whether you're alone or in a relationship," her intensity begins to grow, as she worries her for him. It sinks her heart, thinking of him in a home as bare as his cubicle. Like he doesn't realize he deserves silly, hopeful things. "You should make your space into your safe space. A place where nothing that is wrong with you is ever *wrong*."

Another beat of awkward silence follows, but Maria doesn't break this one. Cannot. Here she is again watching her sister, who has never been comfortable and cares way too much about seeing that everyone around her is. She wishes she could help her care less. Life would be so much easier for Gabriella if she didn't care.

"I've hung up the slicker I made in my entryway. Does that count?"

"Entryway?" Maria begins incredulous at the choice of words. But Gabriella talks right over her.

"No. Not something to do with work or me, or —" Gabriella breaks off. She has been squeezing the bottle of glue so hard some has spilled out onto her hands. She glances around the room, noticing the awkward silence that has descended once more.

Very precisely, she sets down the glue bottle, using the mitten she's messed up to clean the spilled glue first off her hands, and then off the bottle. Breathing deeply, she trains her eyes unshakably on her task and forces words out without seeing anyone.

"I suppose it should be whatever you want. I just think if you're defining your happiness, it shouldn't be something contingent on other people."

Gabriella doesn't wait on a response. Standing, she takes the very gluey mitten into the kitchen. With her back to Jack and Maria, she washes the felt out with soap and water, laying it over her dish rack to dry as she tries to chew up every bit of intensity inside. Chew it up, grind it down. Kill it. She needs to kill it. That was way too intense for something so...frivolous. She's letting her real, loud, nosey, intense self show. She used to know better.

Jack is staring after her awestruck by her intensity, yes, but also in shock at her insights. He hadn't really thought of himself as defining his happiness by other people. He can't say that he's tried to define it at all since Lauren. He just went along and did what he did. Worked. Hung out with friends. Dated. But never with much thought to the future, because the last time he thought about the future, the future ripped the rug out from under him, spilled champagne down his back, leapt up in horror and went viral, rejecting him.

It is sort of shocking that Gabriella, of everyone in his life, is the one to notice it. Or at least the one to point it out. He hasn't really tried to...move on, has he? He is still hiding.

Or he has been.

Jack smiles into the kitchen, watching Gabriella work. She is something else. But he doesn't think now is the time to address it. And someone has to break this silence.

"Throw those out; they're ruined," Jack calls out, knowing full well Gabriella will do no such thing. Too thrifty and too determined.

"It's only glue; it will wash out. And once they're dry, I can glue them again." Gabriella replies. With her back to him, she crosses to the fridge. "Want anything to drink?"

By unspoken agreement, they return to casual subjects, leaving all the moments of intensity behind. Even as he's leaving, Jack plays light, teasing Gabriella about her computer password again. "Santa's #1 very best friend."

Gabriella shakes her head, smiling softly. "Would it help to know that Santa is not a part of my password?"

"Wow, and here I thought you were his super-fan." He teases. "How will you ever live down the shame?"

Gabriella watches him go, smiling and pretending she is someone else, someone who is never so intense that it startles people into silence. She pretends until the moment he is down the stairs, and she has shut the door behind him.

Maria waits for her sister to shut the door. She can feel Gabriella holding her emotions back, so she waits watching her without words. When Gabriella turns around, she slumps against the door. Almost teary-eyed already, and the words come pouring out.

"I know. I know. I know." She says, and her right-hand worries at the padlock, locking and unlocking it once, three times fast, once again. She shoves off the door, pacing forward. "I got too intense about the whole ornament thing. It's not really about an ornament. But...when he told me that he was willing to run away if I released the clip, at first I was so caught up in being touched and shocked that I didn't really pay attention."

Maria lets her sister speak, waiting for her to wring out like a rag and fall, limp with all the expelled emotions she's been holding in check to make everyone else comfortable. Maria longs to tell her sister to *say these things in the moment!* But she knows it isn't that easy. Even for Maria, it isn't that easy.

"But it keeps playing in my head over and over again now. And then I'll see his desk with just that one picture and his mystery novels and nothing else that's his." Gabriella shakes her head silently, and Maria just waits. She knows Gabriella isn't finished.

"Tonight, I kept thinking about it, and that maybe it's what makes him seem...I don't know; it isn't lazy, maybe not even unmotivated, but you know he's not living up to his potential. And if he seemed happy, like really happy, otherwise, that would be fine. But he doesn't. He's not invested in his job or his life. He could literally take or leave a life he's had for *four years*, and that's not good enough for him." She breaks off, wiping tears from her face and clearing her throat. "He deserves to love his life and to know he belongs. Picking an ornament," she scoffs at herself. "It just became a symbol of that in my head, and I couldn't let it go. But I need to... let him be him. He was really quiet after. And I don't know if I hurt his feelings or exhausted him." She nods her head sideways with a tear-soaked voice. "I've been known to do that."

Now Maria crosses to her sister, very gently pressing her forehead right up beside her sisters, but not quite touching, waiting. Gabriella eases her own head forward to press against Maria's, and her arms slip around her shoulders. Both sisters hold tight to one another.

"No, you don't. I don't think he was angry or hurt. I think you did that thing you have a superpower for, and made him think. He was just taking it all in. And that's okay. It's okay that you make him thoughtful. And it's lovely that you care about him enough to want him to love his life. You just have to...learn to embrace the mystery of his silent thoughts. And trust that he'll let you know if you ever push him too far. The way you let him know when he did."

"What, with pranks?" Gabriella mutters snidely into her sister's shoulder.

Maria laughs. "Absolutely. So...watch your back come Monday."

They laugh together. And Gabriella's tears dry up. And just because they are in the mood, they round out the Sunday night with a viewing of *Thoroughly Modern Milly.* Laughing their way through it. Glad, as always, to have each other.

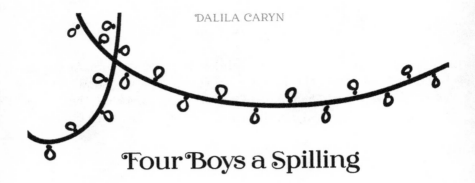

Four Boys a Spilling

Bright and early Monday morning, Gabriella is in the basement break room laying out supplies for today's contest. While talking to the film crew behind her. Jack is upstairs working in other departments. They were friendly and flirtatious in the parking lot. Not one word has been spoken about Gabriella's intensity over Jack's lack of Christmas spirit— kidding!—over Jack's lack of commitment to his own life. Gabriella is attempting to be someone totally foreign to her. A chill girl. A girl who does not watch every twitch of his eye or tilt of his smile and catalogue them for cross-referencing in a valiant attempt to decode the mystery that is Jack Drummer.

She wouldn't have called herself a mystery sort of girl before Jack. To be honest, few and far between are the mysteries that can stump her in books or movies. But in reality, people can flat-out shock her. And she wouldn't have claimed to be very interested in figuring people out before. But she is very interested in figuring Jack out. Now that she knows her original assessment of him wasn't quite right.

However, right now, she has other things to focus on. Like the camera crew and answering their questions. And she's using that distraction for all it is worth.

"Today's *gift* is a contest; everyone has to make a full cup of hot chocolate and deliver it to their desk, staying as clean as possible and wearing a pair of white felt mittens." She holds up a pair for the camera. "If there is a tie, we will move on to making a plate of cookies, then a final stage of eating and drinking while staying clean and having to dunk the cookies at least once. The winner gets out of cleaning their floor's break room for two months." Gabriella says brightly in reply to Kristen's question about how this week is shaping up.

"On Tuesday, I'm bringing in a bunch of plastic photo frames and those snow spray bottles, and there will be a window frosting contest. The winner will escape the staff meeting of their choosing. Wednesday, there is a snowflake-making contest. They get five minutes, and the person who makes the most wins, one winner per floor. The winners get to be exempt from office *spirit days* for three months." Gabriella says, with all the enthusiasm forced spirit days deserve. None.

"And Thursday there will be a resolutions in reverse guessing game; everyone writes down—based on what they have done this year—what their resolution should have been, and people guess. There is a prize for the person who guesses the most correctly and one for anyone who stumps everyone. And Friday's event is the party, so no gifts or games until then." Gabriella grins.

"A lot of these events have to do with your party plans now?" Kristen remarks. "And you seem almost okay with planning it."

Gabriella shrugs. "The party will be decorated using things everyone will have made this week, as well as the snowflakes and pictures of the activities from last week. Sort of like a grand...closing ceremony for our winter games." Gabriella says, only realizing as she's saying it that Kristen is right; she isn't just forcing enthusiasm. She was offended to be asked to plan a party. Even more so to be asked to hand all of the hard work to Jack. And her anger with Mr. Coleman isn't gone. But once she embraced the task and made it her own, she found joy in it. It's not just an office Christmas party; it's closing out of the year with your coworkers on a positive note. It's a celebration of all the fun she's helped them to have together.

"So, Mr. Coleman approved your party ideas?" Kristen presses when Gabriella gets lost in thought.

"Yep. Mr. Coleman approved our party ideas. No meeting this time. I think he's afraid I'll press for bonuses again. We emailed our plans, and he okayed them. Literally." Gabriella shakes her head. "He only wrote the one word: OKAY. I seem to be developing a reputation for being difficult. Can't seem to care, though." She walks out to the main room, laying mittens on desks with a smile on her face.

"And what is Jack's prank of the day?" Kristen asks.

"Nothing too dramatic. I got a friend from my building to record a few things in a *very creepy* Santa voice. He'll get calls off and on all day from different lines in the building, and Rex will be asking him things like: 'Jack, are you being a good boy today?'" She says in her best imitation of a creepy Jack Nicolson voice. "Or: 'Jack, this is Santa again. Should you really be reading right now?'" She giggles. "And: 'Jack, you already have one checkmark against you on the naughty list; what should you be doing?'" She laughs. "I had five unique phrases, but Rex suggested a couple, and Maria suggested a few, so we ended up with about twelve. It should be fun!"

Laughing, Kristen asks, "who came up with the funniest ones?"

"Oh, Maria came up with some of the best," Gabriella says brightly. "I mean, mine was more personal and specific. But she had things like 'Jack, I hear you've been passing yourself off as me to get girls on your lap. Instead of coal, I may send you to therapy for Christmas.'"

The film crew get a good laugh at that, and Gabriella smirks, quite pleased with the prank. She can't wait to see his reaction.

By lunchtime, Gabriella's smile has slipped. She sits stiffly at her desk, on a call with the accounting department about printers that won't print out a specific report. Everything else prints out fine, just not this report. She's given two suggestions over the phone and will probably have to get up and go see for herself, but she's distracted and not pleasantly so.

The contest is well underway, and every time one of these oversized boys walks by her desk, she can feel her body bunching up. She has a splitting headache and these *loud* boys are so determined to be dirty. Why does she have to work with boys?

Cory and Stan are outside the break room intermittently taunting and laughing at Michael as he attempts to carry his paper cup of hot chocolate. So far, his mittens are clean. But the more the boys shout and laugh, the more Gabriella's mind plays out horror scenarios with him tripping and dumping the whole mess on her desk. Or spraying it all over the carpet. Or up the walls!

Why did she let Jack convince her to have them carry the drinks to their desks? The original plan was only from the kitchen counter to the table.

"That's not much of an obstacle course," Jack had argued. "Anyone can do that."

"I don't want to risk them messing up the carpet. It will be us who gets into trouble."

"No one will get in trouble." Jack laughed. "Before you started working here, Jay shook up and sprayed a whole bottle of soda all over the room because the Lakers won *a* championship game."

Now Gabriella can't stop picturing the hot chocolate spraying everywhere. Intentionally. This was all Jack's fault. Ugh. She can't look anymore. She scrunches herself against her desk and focuses on the phone call.

"This isn't a new report, is it? You've run it before?" She asks, trying hard to focus.

"Yes, plenty. Only...I don't usually print it. I just email it, but today they want a physical copy, and it keeps coming out tiny and in the middle of the page."

"Right," Gabriella says, flinching as she hears another shout from the boys. She knows there are things to suggest to Gloria. Changing the way the page prints, she just can't find the words, page orientation, landscape or portrait. She could suggest she make sure the printer is set to the right size paper, but again the logistics and the literal words have left her brain. Her thoughts are fully occupied with hot chocolate spraying all over the room, spilling all over the floor. Men spraying hot chocolate like they're marking their territory.

Gabriella removes every pen from her rainbow array and replaces them one at a time, touching their page clips to get each at the right angle. *Red, orange, green, blue, purple, pink*, she says to herself. Once—as she removes them. Twice—as she replaces them. Three times—as she adjusts their angles.

This is all Jack's fault.

A few feet away, meanwhile, Jack returns from the bathroom, oblivious both to Gabriella bunched up in a nervous crouch in her cubicle and the men competing around him. He's in a great mood.

He knows he is not supposed to enjoy today's prank, and some of the calls were annoying. Especially when they interrupted his reading. But this last one—he'd been so determined not to get annoyed that he took a sip of his coffee when he answered and wound up spitting it out in amused shock. "Hey Jack, man to man, how do you stay so fit sitting at a desk all day? Asking for a friend." He still finds it so funny that he is humming: "It's Beginning to Look a lot like Christmas."

He is so twitterpated that he nearly runs into Michael. Jack manages to jump back before they touch, but Michael startles so badly that he drops his cup of hot chocolate, spilling every last drop!

NICE TO BE SO NAUGHTY

Luckily he was at the edge of the break room and dropped it inside. Were Gabriella looking up, she would count it a huge favor, but despite hearing the loud whoops and cheers or rather, *because of them,* she is crouched down, trying her hardest to hear Gloria and not the room she is in.

"Whoop! Whoop! Whoop!" Cory shouts, waving his fist in the air.

"Another one down!" Stan shouts enthusiastically. "You are all going down."

"Damn it, Jack!" Michael shouts, turning his rage at his failure onto Jack. "That's cheating. I call cheating."

"And cheating answers: Only losers whine, *loser!*" Cory shouts playfully and yet loud enough to wake the dead. On Mars!

Hunched down in her cubicle with both hands over her ears, Gabriella finally gives in. "Do you know what, Gloria...it's too loud down here. I'll come up to you and give it a look. Bye." She hangs up without even waiting for a response. Too tense to be that polite. Honestly, she imagines this is exactly what Gloria wanted. No one wants the problem explained to them over the phone. They want someone to come and fix it. And not to explain it then either. Just to make the problem go away.

Why is that bothering Gabriella today? That's the job at a company like this. Reorienting the printer settings, so a page comes out the right size. Plugging in wires people accidentally knock out. That was always the job here. Mindless work. That's why she took it. But now, maybe since starting secret Santa, since being challenged at work. Now she is finding herself annoyed with her job. And these mindless, loud, dirty *boys* aren't helping anything!

Gabriella sits at her desk squinting her eyes as the headache splits her head open (not literally, *wink) giving herself a moment to just breathe. Why did she choose this game? It is so annoying. She never liked it even in the after-school daycare program where she'd learned it. So of course today is the day she has a headache. Ugh. Gabriella sighs, because there is nothing to be done about it now.

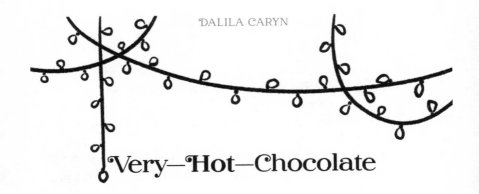

Very—Hot—Chocolate

Being a fly on the wall is very easy for Terrance Pine; he is the middle of five children, all of whom are louder and more demanding than him. He is used to fading into the background, grabbing what he needs, and slipping away. So the documentary medium came quite naturally to him. But there are moments when he finds it very uncomfortable, and now is one.

It's not so much that anything going on is so terrible, but watching Gabriella sink into her desk and massage her temples is disturbing. She is usually so positive and energetic. Seeing her this way reminds him of a solo documentary he shot at an animal shelter and this one puppy that would flinch and cower every time its cage was opened, or another dog would bark. He feels like he should be shutting off the camera and going to comfort her. But he isn't, because this is his job, to show life, not to take part in it. He's never been uncomfortable with that before now. And he didn't realize it was apparent to anyone until Kristen settled her hand on his shoulder.

Kristen can feel Terrance's unease. She can see that Gabriella is upset too, but she isn't punching her leg; she hasn't left; Gabriella seems to know her limits. Terrance, on the other hand, thinks he's good at fading into the background because he is used to doing it, but his heart is always reaching out, and that is a dangerous thing.

"She's alright," Kristen whispers. "Every day can't be easy, but she'll make it through."

Terrance glances back in shock, both because Kristen thought to try and comfort him and because...it is working. He breathes out, and Kristen's hand stays with him, and his tension starts to ease. Who would have thought Kristen would have that in her? To answer his question, almost no one thought Kristen had that in her. But the few people to have long suspected it, her cousin Misty, and her great grandmother, five times removed. And their belief in her softer side is the reason Santa gave Kristen this mission. And it appears to be paying off.

Across the room, Jack is busy apologizing to Michael. "My bad, I wasn't thinking. Let's just clean this up, and you can start over."

"No way. He had his shot, and he failed," Stan argues.

"I did cut him off." Jack points out.

"And he's a competitor," Michael yells. "That's cheating!"

"Loser. Loser," Cory chants in a sing-song voice. "Loser, loser." He only drifts off when it becomes apparent no one is going to join him.

"Maybe we should get an impartial ruling. Ask Gabby; she isn't entering," Stan suggests.

Jack glances back at Gabriella's cubicle. Only now, noticing that she does not seem to be enjoying today's entertainment. "She isn't? Why?" He asks though he knows it's unlikely these men know the actual answer.

"She said she would definitely win and the break room would become a disgusting mess for two months, and she didn't want that," Cory says with a laugh.

All of the men, including Jack, exchange varying looks of agreement. A few chuckle. Jack rubs the back of his neck. Why didn't he see this coming? He knew she hated the idea of the snowball fight. But she'd had fun when she joined in! Well, shit. He shouldn't have pressed her to make it more challenging.

"Let's just—" Jack begins to suggest cleaning up, but before he can get through the words, Gabriella stands with frightening suddenness, tosses aside her headphones and marches towards the gathering.

"Are any of you planning to clean that up?" She demands, more snappish than she's been since the day Jack broke her nutcracker.

That doesn't bode well, Jack thinks.

Gabriella has not managed to fully shut out her anxiety, her annoyance, or her headache. It may have something to do with hearing her name or rather her truly annoying "nickname," which she has asked people *not* to use! So she is frustrated but fighting hard not to descend to the level of squabbling her coworkers are displaying.

"We were about to look for you," Michael says eagerly.

"To clean up your mess?" Gabriella demands in an acidic tone that really should have stripped the skins off the backs of these men.

"No! No!" The men assure her at once and in *terrified* unison.

Kristen grins evilly. Her hand is still on Terrance's shoulder, making it easy to lean next to his ear without taking her eyes off of Gabriella. "See?"

"For an impartial ruling," Michael continues to press, oblivious to Jack shaking his head. "Jack cut me off, and I spilled."

Gabriella's eyes shoot to Jack. He makes a hissing face, edging backwards. He mouths "sorry" when her eyes don't leave him.

"Don't you think I should get a do-over?" Michael finishes entirely unaware of the by-play, so focused is he on the win he feels he was assured.

Gabriella is still largely focused on the spreading spill. She knows she has to go up and fix Gloria's printer. She knows Jack is looking at her like she's about to bite off his head, but she can't think why. And she can see all the expectant faces of the men around her, and she knows her ears have heard what they are saying. But really! *Is no one going to clean up that mess?* She asked that, right? When she first showed up. Why haven't they answered? Why haven't they cleaned it? Why did she choose this game? Just because hot chocolate and mittens are winter things but not specifically Christmas things? Because it had a competitive element? Because it was cheap and easy to set up?

"Well?" Michael presses intensely. Making Gabriella want to shout at all of these men because if she were that intense about a game, they would all call her emotional, but they are just laughing at Michael.

"Did he physically touch you?" Gabriella demands, her toes curled up inside her shoes and her rigid pointer finger jabbing against her thigh.

"No, but—" Michael prepares to launch into a defensive argument, but Gabriella will hear none of it.

"Then my opinion is no." *And that's only partially because I want this game over and done with.* She adds mentally. "It's called a hot cocoa obstacle course."

"No one else had people jump out at them," Michael shouts.

"I did have to jump over the tacks you *dropped* as I passed," Stan jumps into the conversation, heavy on the sarcasm.

"And my phone started vibrating in my pocket as I was setting the cup down," Cory adds.

As the men argue, Gabriella's eyes are drawn magnetically back to the spreading puddle of hot chocolate.

"Seriously, are none of you going to clean that up?" Gabriella demands again, nearly shouting. "It is going to dry and get sticky soon."

"Not me." Michael, great sport that he is, shoves past Jack to stomp to his cubicle.

Gabriella narrows her eyes angrily as he leaves. *That's strike two,* she thinks, mentally adding a second check mark against him on her list. He may need punishing shortly.

Jack and Cory both laugh a little at Michael's response.

"You'd think a man of his age would be a better loser," Stan remarks.

"He ought to have had enough practice." Cory cracks up. "Last week alone!"

Cory and Stan laugh hard. Frustrated, Gabriella steps widely around the spill; walking fully into the break room, she retrieves several paper towels and flips on the faucet. She wets half before realizing Jack has followed her.

He reaches out for the dry paper towels. "Let me. It was partially my fault."

"I told you this would end in a mess," Gabriella says under her breath. She feels herself relaxing a tiny bit as Jack begins to help her. She knows he thinks she's mad at him, but she's not. She's mad at herself. At this sticky mess. At—

"What are you doing?" Gabriella crouches down, shoving Jack's foot aside as he uses it to push the paper towel around to dry up the mess. "You are spreading it. You have to pull the spill together. Haven't you ever cleaned a spill before?"

"Apparently not the proper way." Jack laughs incredulous.

Gabriella sighs. She stares down at the puddle. Using the paper towels to pull it together like she was explaining. When most of it has been soaked up and the towels are beginning to make her hands sticky, she stands, cradling the wet bundle, so it won't drip. She takes it to the trash can and dumps it in.

Her shoulders have tightened that little loose bit up again. She's offended him, hasn't she?

"I wasn't trying to insult you," Gabriella says low, hoping the others won't hear her.

"I'm not insulted," Jack says with his voice at a regular volume, unconcerned with Cory and Stan still in the doorway. "I learn so much from you. Who'd have known there a proper way to clean?"

Gabriella takes the clean, wet towels back to the spill. Watching Jack surreptitiously trying to gauge his sincerity. He seems truly unconcerned. Maybe she is feeling that tiny bit of tension for no reason.

"Don't worry about that," Cory says when he sees Gabriella crouch down to clean up the remnants of the spill and the stickiness. "The wetness is up anything more the janitors will get tonight."

Gabriella does not stop. "Hot chocolate is sticky. If it isn't cleaned properly, it will be tracked all over this office in an hour. And the janitorial staff are paid to empty the trash, do light dusting, and sweep nightly. They only mop once a week. And it is *never* their job to clean up our inconsiderate messes."

"What were you a janitor in a past life?" Cory jokes.

"No. I did bus tables through high school and part of college. And one of my mother's two jobs was for a janitorial service. Why? That a problem?" She demands sharply as she pushes to her feet.

"Of course, it's not a problem," Stan says stiffly, jumping in to defend his friend. "Cory didn't mean anything. Anyway, the janitors must be getting extra because clearly, they've been cleaning up after these messes for a while, Gabby."

"It's Gabriella," Jack snaps.

Stan looks between the pair stiffly.

"Oooooo!" Cory taunts.

"What are you twelve?" Gabriella snaps, back on her feet and is annoyed that they are making fun of Jack.

Jack had sounded almost angry when he spoke. But he looks normal. Is he...defending her...well, not her honor, but her name! Is he annoyed at them for using the wrong name? Or for the whole picking at her for cleaning thing?

Cory strikes back when Jack and Stan snicker at Gabriella's remark. "Do you need your *boyfriend* to tell people what to call you?"

"No. So how about you listen to me?" Gabriella takes an

unintentionally threatening step forward. "I've asked everyone not to call me Gabby."

"You have?" Stan startles as much as the comments intended target.

"Oh. Sorry, Ga—" Cory breaks off. "I didn't remember. I'd be happy to call you Gabriella."

"Of course. We'll call you whatever you like," Stan says. There are a few moments of awkward silence, no one knowing quite how to end this little dust-up. "So I guess it's down to you and me, Jack. Unless you're entering, *Gabriella*?" Stan asks.

"No, I'm good." Gabriella moves off to throw out the trash.

Stan and Cory use her turned back like an end of the conversation and duck out. Jack crosses to the sink and leans in next to Gabriella as she washes her hands.

"Sorry about them. I can tell them we aren't together."

"If it would make you more comfortable," Gabriella sounds snappish to her own ears and begins to wish she'd never woken up this morning.

"I meant to make *you* more comfortable," Jack says in his low, warm voice. Hot chocolate. That's what his voice reminds her of when he turns all seductive. *Very hot* chocolate. "I'm good. When you asked Cory if he was twelve, I had to literally bite my tongue to keep from asking to kiss you."

Gabriella bites her lip, fighting the urge to giggle. Wasn't she a tense mess a moment ago? How does he do that?

"I might have said yes," she whispers.

Jack just stares at her, his eyes so intent that Gabriella feels as if her skin is being incinerated. She has to glance away, only then noticing that Jack has been splashed with the hot chocolate. His shirt is splattered with it. Gabriella's fingers itch to reach out, to... offer to clean it, she decides. Her brain pretending to be quite innocent. Then it begins to whisper, a bit more honestly. *If this were a romance novel*, she thinks, *this would be the scene where Jack's shirt would come off. He would pull it over his head, his eyes never once leaving her, and her breath would catch as she resisted reaching out to feel him. They would both resist the wild pull between them— Or maybe not. Maybe they would be overcome by it! Maybe they would kiss and set the room on fire with only the kindling of their mutual passions.*

Alas, this is not a romance novel.

*Wink.

If only the writer creating this world wasn't an evil goddess. Oh well, since she is, Jack's shirt is staying on in this public workspace— weird.

"I suppose it's not the best idea at work." Jack swallows uncomfortably, ending yet another bout of intense silence, though he is entirely unaware of exactly how far Gabriella's mind wandered from a mere kiss.

"Probably not." Gabriella agrees breathlessly.

"So how would you feel about having an adventure with me after work? There's this place that does sleigh rides. We can ditch the camera crews and coworkers and—be alone."

Gabriella can't quite bring herself to speak, so she nods, smiling into his eyes and reveling in the feeling of her body relaxing one degree after another.

"Excellent. I can't wait." He grins at Gabriella walking backwards out of the break room to keep his eyes on her as long as he can.

Gabriella watches him go. Suddenly very glad that she got up this morning, spill and all. She's just not at all sure what to do about it. She may be getting a little too hooked on him. This could end very badly, but—what a lovely ride it will be. And goodness knows she can't stop a thing once she's started.

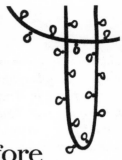

Not Eight Days Before Christmas

Having given her what he considers to be plenty of time to change, Jack arrives at Gabriella's apartment very eagerly, at six-forty-five in the evening. He is more excited about this date than he would have expected. They're going to a Christmas Village, for goodness sake.

But he found it! And it's exactly the sort of place Gabriella will love! It is a Christmas tree farm with a collection of shops. A Santa for kids and pictures. And fake snow for snowman building and tube rides. And best of all, for Jack's purposes, romantic sleigh rides for two under twinkle light decorated trees.

Entry to the place alone is fifteen dollars per person, and he's gonna bet everything from a cup of hot cocoa to a picture with Santa has a serious mark-up over market value. The sleigh ride is *thirty* bucks a pop. But it's going to be great. There is even a romantic restaurant in the "village." *She'll love it.*

Gabriella steps out of her apartment, having gone out of her way to look very special indeed in the only forty-five minutes he gave her to change. She is wearing a red cocktail length dress, with a soft white cardigan over her arm, she definitely doesn't need it now, but it will complement the look should she need it on the sleigh ride. And a pair of adorable lace-backed short boots because she is not about to wear a plain heel at a Christmas tree farm. She also has a pair of drop snowflake earrings and her reddest lipstick on. She looks very Christmasy and very cute indeed, and she is well aware of it.

Nevertheless, she chews on the inside of her cheek as she steps out, blushing slightly at the way Jack smiles at her without much to say. As they are walking down the hall to the stairs, Maria pops out of the apartment, pulling the door shut behind her and locking it.

"Oh, are you guys headed out?" She mocks playfully. "I hadn't realized. I'll walk with you, shall I? Pretend I'm not here. You do that really well."

Gabriella glares at her sister, barely resisting the urge to laugh. Maria is so annoying but simultaneously very good at setting people at ease. Jack winks at Maria.

"Who are you again? You look vaguely familiar."

Maria nods playfully and runs around them, racing down the stairs on her way out to meet friends. Gabriella feels a lovely sort of ease settle around her. Very slowly, she slips her arm through Jack's, not quite touching, just that little bit nearer to him that makes her feel so warm and comfortable...no, cozy. All wrapped up, safe and happy beside her artificial fireplace.

As they drive out to the Christmas tree farm, they chat easily about the secret Santa event at work and a bit about the party. Jack pretends great offense to today's prank, and she pretends to believe him.

She didn't think today's prank would offend him just annoy him. And it did. She was there to see it! But Gabriella is not about to interrupt the performance. She loves his false indignation and the crinkling at the side of his eyes when he resists laughing. She enjoys a lot of things about him. This is shaping up to be a lovely evening.

But fate or Santa or...the greater Los Angeles area school districts may have a bit more havoc in mind for this couple, headed to a Christmas Village only a week before the big day.

It takes seven-and-a-half minutes to park. In a dirt lot. At the end of a dirt road. In a residential neighborhood near the hills. *Not good.* Jack is already looking around at the mass of bodies, moving—

entirely unconcerned by cars—through the parking *field*. It is almost exclusively families. *Large* families, with screaming babies and children running everywhere. Even the well-behaved children are in mobs of really no less than five people. Jack feels threatened. He can see the entrance to the village and there is a line, or more accurately, a corral of people at least twenty deep that don't appear to be moving.

He should leave, right? He should change plans. But look at Gabriella! Her eyes are alight, taking everything in and she's all dressed up in Christmasy things and he promised her a sleigh ride. *Shit*. He has a feeling this is not going to be the romantic evening he had planned. But...the sleigh ride, he just has to get her to the sleigh ride. It's getting late, surely, people will take their screaming children home soon. It's a school night!

Gabriella wears a smile as she eyes the crowds of children in matching Christmas sweaters or carrying hot cocoa and cookies, but inside she's concerned. That is a lot of bodies. Like Disneyland level. Instinctually she puts on her sweater for extra protection. She wonders if Jack ordered sleigh ride tickets ahead or if they will have to stand, as they are now, in a fifteen-minute line.

It doesn't matter. She's here with him. And this is so sweet. Exactly the sort of place she loves. Just not, eight days before Christmas. But it's fine. It's lovely. Gabriella presses herself closer to Jack and decides to embrace the moment. It will be like the snowball fight. Loud and startling, and nothing she would have expected to enjoy, but with Jack beside her, the excitement will hide enough of her anxiety for her to live in the moment. Maybe *just* for a moment.

By the time they make it through the entry line, twenty minutes after parking, and have found the line for the sleigh rides, Jack is annoyed. Why are there so many people here? He says something aloud about school nights only to have a very loud, very rude parent behind him in line jump into the conversation uninvited.

"Schools out! You don't have any kids."

"No—"

"It wasn't a question," the man laughs, slightly spilling his hot beverage, coffee based on the smell, as the toddler in his arms shifts positions, pulling her father's head sideways, nearly out of joint to find herself a more comfortable position in his other arm. "The week before Christmas through the first of January. Single people like you should come to these places earlier; this shit is all—argh!"

Thankfully, in Jack's opinion, he is spared the rest of the man's rant because the toddler in his arms chose that moment to climb her father like a mountain and kneed him in the jaw. Gabriella turns away, knotting her hands together in front of her and biting down hard on her tongue to keep from laughing. *There is nothing funny about this,* she tells herself. There are people everywhere. Jack is quickly growing as frustrated as he did when she had everyone sit on his lap for a prank. And that father got kneed in the jaw by the universe for not embracing the joy of spending time with his children. Gabriella chuckles inside of her mouth, a sensation that, while lovely in its humor also feels slightly like she is about to vomit.

This is a *terrible* date. So why is she enjoying it so much?

Though Gabriella doesn't know she is doing it, far away north, through the mist of the arctic ocean, an extra checkmark is added to the good side of *Santa's* list for a little girl by the name of Whitney Hall. In thanks for climbing her father in just that way, at just that moment. It is a growth in power not even Santa saw coming, and it is just strong enough to attract the attention of some nearby elves despite the limits Santa put on her gift. All that energy Gabriella shoves down had to go somewhere.

"Would you like some hot chocolate or something?" Jack asks between his teeth, though it's clear he is trying to sound solicitous. "It looks like we'll be in this line a while."

"That one doesn't seem much shorter." Gabriella points out. "I'm fine. Everything is lovely here. How did you find it?" She tries to draw him into the moment.

"Um, my parents got their tree here. Give me a second, hold our place. I'm going to go make sure we're in the right line."

Gabriella opens her mouth to argue, but Jack is already moving off.

"Probably gonna get in his car and bolt," the man behind Gabriella says, but she maintains the pretense of not hearing, staring straight forward. "Lucky bastard."

"Bastard!" The child in his arm screams. It seems, based on the father's shocked and proud expression, to be the child's first word, but Gabriella finds that unlikely; she looks about two. Still, it might have been.

Bastard was not, in fact, the child's first word. That honor went to "no", something she heard a great deal of in her formative years. But from formative years on through to adulthood, Whitney Hall, rarely heeds that order. She will wind up on Santa's naughty list about as much as one would expect from a headstrong future competitive snowboarder.

But Gabriella will never know that the snowboarder she cheers on during the twenty-thirty-four winter Olympic games was the toddler in line behind her on her first date with Jack. She will all but forget the girl. As she is at this very moment as she stands stiffly holding their place in the unmoving line and watches Jack argue with the ticket man.

At this exact moment, Jack regrets his every decision in life. Most strongly, his refusal to allow his mother to purchase the tickets to the sleigh ride and indeed the Christmas Village itself for him ahead of time. She'd been so excited when Jack had asked her about the family Christmas tree and where she got it that she'd gushed about the village and Jack unthinkingly remarked.

"Gabriella would love a place like that. I should take her."

"Ooooh, you should!" Mom had effervesced, only too thrilled to finally hear about her son going out with someone again after his last girlfriend. "I could get you some tickets online right now. When do you want to go?"

"Mom," he'd laughed confidently. "I'm not a kid. I don't need you to buy me and my date tickets to the skating rink."

"But it is a date, though? With Gabriella, who you work with?" She'd sounded so sly, but Jack already knew about their conspiracy, so he'd just let her stew refusing to answer.

Now he feels like an ass. If she'd bought the tickets ahead, or if *he* had, he might have known how crowded the place would be. And he might have known that all the lovely pictures on the website of happy couples alone on sleigh rides under the night stars and twinkle lights were clever advertising.

"What do you mean we can't ride alone?" Jack demands of the very harried-looking sleigh ride bouncer drunk on his own power.

"Look, it says it on the website. No individual sleigh rides between December fifteenth and January first. Schools out. We don't have time. The minimum occupancy of a sleigh now is ten. And you'll be lucky tonight to get on with less than fifteen people. Don't like it; get out of line."

"Individual rides would be one person, not two!"

"Minimum occupancy of ten people!" The man shouts in Jack's face. He turns away as a sleigh returns with a cart full of people, in time to save him from more arguments from Jack.

False advertising! Asking for a manager. Making a scene. Really, Jack offered to buy out an entire sleigh! Why couldn't he do that?

Not that he wants to. Damn. Minimum occupancy is ten people at thirty dollars a piece. He'd be paying three hundred dollars for a sleigh ride in southern California with no real snow, while it basically goes about half a mile around a loop. Barely ten minutes. It's ridiculous. Another time, a little less annoyed with himself and thus the world, Jack might actually have thanked the guy for turning down that ridiculous offer. What is he, a Rockefeller?

Jack returns to the line, silently fuming but trying not to let it show. He sidles up alongside Gabriella, dodging a superior smirk from the man behind them.

"It's the right line," Jack mutters. "I'm sorry about all of this."

"About what?" Gabriella says with laughter in her voice and eyes dancing happily. "There is Christmas music playing. I'm in line for a sleigh ride, and I'm with you. This is great!"

Ugh!!! What is wrong with you? Gabriella thinks the moment the words are out of her mouth. *That sounds so corny and weird and he's going to...*

He smiles his *I could charm an executioner* smile. "Is it just possible that you are *very* easy?" Jack teases.

Don't say it. Don't say it. Don't say it. Gabriella thinks to herself. But of course, she is going to say it.

"It might be," Gabriella teases back.

It's not true. There is no way he doesn't know it's not true. You are incredibly high maintenance, and while you might be easy to entertain, that doesn't mean you're going home with him. And he probably thinks you—

The line moves, graciously cutting off Gabriella's internal ramblings. She needn't have worried though. Jack is well aware that she is just flirting. And more than that. He has also been enjoying the very charged moments and the gradual development of their relationship. He has no plans to rush any part of this.

Except maybe the line.

Eleven Interlopers Singing

Jack is *not* having the time of his life, nor is he having the sweet private, romantic date he had pictured. They do not make it onto the first sleigh, and the line is too noisy for them to talk much. But Gabriella is making friends with the children in the line, talking to them about cookie flavors and favorite Christmas songs. The wife and three small children of the man behind them have returned, making things quite noisy.

It is actually sweet watching Gabriella interact with the children. He would have thought someone so rigid with herself would be so with children as well, but she is playful and positive. She doesn't take herself so seriously that she can't say silly things that embarrass her in front of the adults in the line to entertain the children. So Jack tries to give up his grumps and joins in.

"Gabriella knows Santa personally. I heard her call him on the phone to try and put me on the naughty list." Jack says.

A few of the adults laugh. While the littlest of the children grow wide-eyed with excitement. But it is the older children to whom Jack relates best. They roll their eyes and look away, well aware their parents would punish them for spoiling the magic so publicly but unwilling to let such lies pass without everyone knowing they are far too cool to believe it.

"I met Santa today, but he looks different from last year," a girl of about seven is saying to Gabriella. "Do you think he gets younger sometimes?"

"Well, he is magic." Gabriella widens her eyes and nods along as the girl talks.

"He didn't give *me* his phone number. Can we go back and ask, Mommy?" Bright Cindy Lu asks. A future journalist, she always knows the perfect questions to most devastate those around her.

Gabriella chuckles, intercepting that one for the mother. "I don't have Santa's personal number; it's just an answering machine where you can report people being very good or very naughty."

"What did he do that was naughty?" The girl eyes Jack suspiciously.

"He took something off of my desk without asking."

"That's stealing!" Another child pipes in, ready to call the police. Gabriella would bet he's been punished a time or two for stealing himself.

"Yes. It was very naughty," Gabriella agrees.

"Did he get *punished*?" The boy demands with zeal. His name is Jerold Hall, and he is not, as one might imagine, destined to be a corrections officer. But rather the future author of a mildly successful series of children's books. For money, he will manage a Home Depot until the company is seized by the government as a ration distribution center for survivors of the third world war. But that is another story altogether.

Gabriella shrugs. Yes, she supposes, Jack has been punished. Maybe too much. But the kids don't need to know that. "He gave it back. And he said he was sorry. You know, we all make bad choices sometimes, but if we say we are sorry and really try to do better, then we are still good," Gabriella says, and her tone grows slowly heavier. She looks at all of these little faces and shares secrets she usually wouldn't. "That's what Santa told me. He sent me a letter when I was very young because I was doing a lot of naughty things after my father died. The letter said that my father had chosen a special Christmas present before he died and that Santa was going to give it to me, even though I had been on the naughty list that year because he wanted me to remember how much my daddy loved me. And to remember that, my daddy always thought I was a good girl. It made me so sad and so happy at the same time. I think about that letter a lot when I start to do things I know I shouldn't, and it helps me try to be better."

"What was the present?" Another boy demands. He is almost a teenager and has been listening to the whole story like he knows it is a lecture. Now he looks intrigued.

His name is Ben Lu and he is well used to hearing lectures and frequenting the naughty list. He was even destined to be on it this year—until this story dug into his mind and made him work to earn forgiveness for a few naughty deeds. It so moved him that though he will not specifically remember the rest of the evening or much of where he'd been, Ben will, several years in the future, still recall this particular lecture and the kind lady who gave it. So much so that when he becomes an elementary school teacher, he always pays close attention to the children being naughty, trying to help them all find ways to remember they are good children underneath.

"Well, I was only six, so not something most grown-ups want." Gabriella laughs at herself. "It was a teddy bear that we'd seen in a store together. She was wearing a pink tutu and ballet slippers. I named her Clara Bear, after Clara from The Nutcracker. My father had taken me to see a children's ballet perform it only a few days before he died." Gabriella can feel the parents around her getting uncomfortable with all the death talk. But she knows that the unthinkable can happen at any moment and as scary as that is, it is important for kids to know that they can go on after it.

Jack's mind is very definitely engaged; he has seen that bear. It sits atop a bookshelf in Gabriella's living room. Right next to a copy of The Nutcracker. He wonders if she wanted to be a ballerina. Or if she loved the story from childhood. He's never asked about her parents. But he knew already that her mother was dead. Her father too, apparently, and when she was so young. He wonders how it happened. How it has changed her. Because even with her pranking him, shouting at him, or being really too intense for most merely mortal men to bear, he can't imagine her ever being on the naughty list. She is too sweet. And that letter sounds like quite the intense thing to give to a six-year-old.

Gabriella doesn't see the letter that way. Gabriella holds onto that letter with love because it truly reminds her of how much her father loved her.

Gabriella's mother, however, felt very differently about the letter. She wrote it one teary, sleepless night before Christmas after Gabriella had spent hours screaming and breaking things and throwing things at her baby sister. In the moment, it felt like the thing that would reach her suddenly furious child. But after, for the rest of her life, she regretted that letter. If she could have, she would have gone back in time and handled things differently. It put too much on Gabriella. But as Gabriella said to the children and her mother wrote in the letter, we all make bad choices. And contrary to the guilt she placed on herself, that letter didn't cause Gabriella's anxieties. It certainly didn't help them, but that mistake was merely one serving of extra pressure she put on her daughter out of years of lifting as much weight as she could off her shoulders. And most importantly, years of boundless love.

"But it wasn't about the present," Gabriella continues, unaware of Jack's deeper thoughts or her mother's regrets. "It was knowing my father had been thinking about me before he died and that he would want me to be happy. And realizing that...I wasn't happy when I was doing naughty things. I never am," Gabriella admits out loud. She is sure she's said it before, known it before. But the realization is different now.

She is *never* happy when she is doing bad things, even when exacting revenge on Jack. It didn't make her happy. It was just so bright and fiery that it distracted her from the pain for a time. But since the pranks became more playful, she actually has been happy. She is *happy*. It is a startling realization. But she keeps talking because it is so startling that she isn't ready yet to know what to do with that feeling. "But sometimes I felt so angry that doing something naughty felt powerful when it was really just sad."

The youngest children all nod as if they understand, but it is only Ben and Jack who are truly affected by the words. Them and Gabriella herself.

Their group is loaded into the next sleigh. Jack, Gabriella, seven children ranging in age from twelve to two and two sets of parents. Gabriella leads the children through a pair of carols, "Here Comes Santa Clause" and "Jingle Bells."

This is the least date like of any date Jack has had since he was thirteen. When his parents came along with him and Courtney Blake to Roller City and kept skating between them or making them race. But when Gabriella begins to shiver, Jack asks in her ear if he can put his arm around her, and she looks up at him, her eyes locked warmly onto his, and nods.

When his arm slides around her back, she snuggles into him and leans her head against his shoulder. She keeps singing, but her arm slides around him as well, holding him close.

Honestly, the evening might have ended differently were it not for a pair of playful elves who have been following the couple. Elves, you recall, are possessed of very playful impulses and a unique sense of fair play. So when they spot a mother burping her child in line near the couple, they nudge Jack forward at just the right moment to get a face full of spit-up. It is retribution for his grouchy behavior at the beginning of the night, and they are quite pleased with the results as Gabriella laughs her head off in shocked amusement.

All in all, this date was simultaneously the worst of Jack's life and the best. There is something magical about Gabriella; even as she is laughing uncontrollably at the spit-up on his face, he can't stay mad at her.

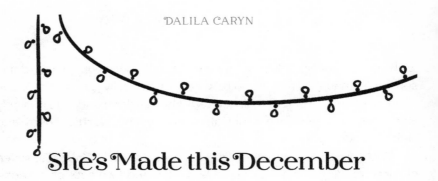

She's Made this December

Kristen asked Terrance and Andrew to keep filming until the company closes for the last two weeks of the year, even though technically the project should be done shooting at this point, and neither of the boys pushed back at all. They should be focusing entirely on editing now; they have enough for something decent. But they are all enjoying the project, and it doesn't feel finished.

Terrance originally expected the project to be a bit of fluffy reality tv set at a doll company. After seeing Kristen at it, he was certain it would be a propaganda piece. But it is changing. All of those things are still a part of it, but at its heart is the thing Terrance loves best about the documentary medium: a peek into another world. The sort of thing that helps you understand and relate to a part of life you are sure you know everything about. Or that you are sure you don't want to know anything about.

Terrance likes these people. He likes the interactions that the cameras catch when no one is looking. He even likes the few interviews he conducted himself, at Kristen's suggestion. As he waits now for Kristen and Andrew to show up for another editing session, he reviews footage from Monday and Tuesday, marking things that might prove useful to the story the film seems to be taking on. A story of bonding with unexpected people.

On his laptop screen, Gabriella is seated in the break room for an interview, beaming. He hits the space bar.

GABRIELLA

It was raining this morning, and I saw some people come in wearing the slickers they made. Carol was one of them! Yes. (hands fisted, triumphant dance) I know it's not the most important thing in the world, but it makes me happy when usually excluded people feel included and have fun.

Terrance pauses the feed. Gabriella has her head tilted sideways, wearing a soft, self-deprecating smile. Warm and inviting. It is moments like these that have made her stand out in this piece. Not her role as Secret Santa, but the genuine pleasure she takes in it.

Terrance hits the space bar again and hears his own voice.

TERRANCE

So how was your date?

GABRIELLA (snickers)

Oh, the sleigh ride was lovely. But not as romantic as Jack had hoped. Turns out he hadn't realized they hold fifteen people at a time. (chuckles) But I loved it! We sat together and sang carols, and after, we had cider and cookies and wandered around looking at lights. And went through Christmasy shops. I bought ornaments, washcloths, and a mug, and even Jack bought a few things. It was a really great night (laughing hard), But poor Jack, I'm not at all sure he felt that way. When we were in line for the cider, this woman in front of us was burping her baby, and it spit up right on Jack's face.

Seven seconds of giggles.

GABRIELLA(smiling softly)

There was a Christmas bag outside of my cubicle this morning. It wasn't big enough to hold my nutcracker, so I knew right away that wasn't it. I'm surprised how calm I feel without it. It's been five days, and I want it back.

Very much! But it feels safe with Jack. (beat) Anyway, in the gift bag were all these tiny plastic elves. They weren't even all Christmas elves. One was Legolas! The note said he'd pick a decoration if I'd fill out your elf forces. Jack can be really sweet. I lined the elves up on my monitor this morning.

Cut to Jack in the interview seat.

TERRANCE

So Jack, how was the date?

JACK (seeking commiseration)

Man, (shakes head)The sleigh ride was (beat) a lot more people than I like to have with me on a date. I can't believe I didn't check first. I bet she would have. It seemed like such a fun, spontaneous adventure, all Christmasy and right up her alley. Oh well. The sleigh ride itself was actually pretty nice. She doesn't like touching strangers, so she was huddling into me pretty close, and she was smiling massively. So I think she enjoyed the night. I know she did, but I can't really count it as a good date when I got spit up on by a baby! Though, Gabriella really seemed to love that. (snorts)(grins helplessly) She is so mean! It's too weird that I like it, but I do. Today—after this date that she seemed to love—she's got half the office interrupting me all day with crap "I" (air quotes) *had* asked them to bring me in emails. Everyone was getting annoyed with me for nothing! I took an extra fifteen in my car to get away from it. And she was just smirking as I walked away, looking so (beat) *Smug*. Like the other day in the break room (imitates Gabriella), Are you twelve? (laughing)She looked so untouchable and confident. I loved it. And what with her instructing on the right way to clean and decorate, she has this real Mary Poppins thing going for her that I am *way too* into. I guess it was a good date, her smile when she saw me with the vomit on my face was priceless. We'll just have to work out a romantic date where she can't have all her fun at my expense.

The recording breaks off with Jack wearing that affable grin that Terrance honestly disliked in the beginning. But at least Jack can laugh at himself. Not everyone can do that.

Shifting away from the interview portion of the recordings, Terrance switches to the footage from one of the stationary cameras in the third-floor break room.

Miriam, Carol, and Frank decorate plastic rectangle inserts from picture frames. Miriam sketches her design. Frank sprays free hand. Carol with coffee, chats.

CAROL

I'm so glad they invited families to the end-of-the-year party! I've been telling Jewel about our winter games, and she's made me repeat a few of them with her. I hope they have more games there.

FRANK (focused zeal)

Oh, they definitely will.

CAROL (cautiously)

Will Linda be able to make it?

FRANK

She's looking forward to it (pauses spraying to smile at Carol). Even John's excited, which is a real feat with a fifteen-year-old.

MIRIAM

I hope Santa is there. (Long silent beat) What? (Chuckling at other's shocked faces) The man gives out gifts to the well-behaved. Do you know how much crap I took from Ed this year? I'm raking in *all the presents*.

All chuckle.

CAROL

Well, personally, I hope he isn't there. These games have been enough fun without him. But...presents do sound nice!

All exchange smiles and fall into an easy quiet.

A week before, Frank would have been enraged just by Carol entering the room. And Carol would have been too cautious about offending people to even comment on her own preferences. But now they're laughing together. Terrance scrolls back a bit to the moment Frank smiled at Carol and freezes the image.

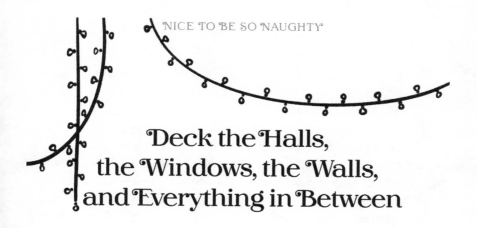

Deck the Halls, the Windows, the Walls, and Everything in Between

That same Tuesday evening, across town in a two-bedroom apartment, on the living room floor sorting through photos on Gabriella's computer, Jack, Maria, and Gabriella are laughing and working.

"So is there a single, super old, really obscure movie musical that you two haven't seen?" Jack asks after the sisters have described the plot of yet another musical he's never heard of, *Summer Stock*.

The sisters exchange questioning looks.

"Probably," Gabriella admits with a shrug. "But, just to be clear, *Summer Stock* is not *obscure*! It has Judy Garland and Gene Kelly and one of Judy's most famous songs!"

"What my sister is saying is, do you want her to put it on right now, so you can stop being such a low-brow, film history, known nothing?" Maria says with a laugh.

"I'm good." Jack holds up his hands in surrender. "It seems so strange that you guys would even have watched all of these movies from like ancient history."

"Ancient?" Maria shakes her head.

"How did you even hear of them?"

"Cable!" Gabriella chuckles.

Even as Maria is shouting, "TCM baby!"

"And a really hot summer in an apartment building," Gabriella adds.

"2005," Maria shudders.

"The summer of musicals!" Gabriella grins at her sister.

Maria returns the nostalgic expression. "We discovered Turner Classic Movies, watched a ton of musicals and screwball comedies. We only really turned it off when they aired dramas or war films."

"Citizen Kane," they say in disgusted unison and laugh.

Jack loves it. Not so much the story. It isn't important. But them, together sharing history and favorite things even though they are very different women. He also loves how easy it feels to be with them, hanging out, working together.

"So, your turn," Maria says. "What are you obsessed with?"

"Oh," Jack shrugs. "I'm not really obsessed with anything."

He is. Her name is Gabriella Anjelica Cruz. But while she isn't saying this because she wouldn't believe it even if she were told, the object of Jack's obsession isn't letting him off the hook either.

"Murder mysteries," Gabriella answers for him. "He keeps at minimum two with him at all times. Since I've been at the company, he's gone through at least twenty."

"Oh, way more than that," Jack admits with a laugh. "I also read at home."

"Damn, that is obsessive," Maria teases. "How embarrassing for you. Ooo! We should watch *Murder on the Orient Express*, or *And Then There Were None!* We watched the murder mysteries too."

"*Thin Man!*" Gabriella exclaims. "That's the best, hands down."

Jack laughs. "I've actually seen *The Thin Man*. And *The Maltese Falcon*. I really like Dashiell Hammett's books, so I watched the films."

"Just the first." Maria leaps to her feet and goes digging under the couch. "There are a whole series of *Thin Man* movies, you know?"

"Um, I saw the first two," Jack says with a shrug.

"You're missing out!" Maria says with her face shoved under the couch.

Jack looks at Gabriella in question. She grins.

"We loved *The Thin Man* movies. But it took us forever to see the last two; they don't air them as often. I mean...they aren't *as* good because the writers were no longer the wife and husband team from the first three. But the others are still pretty great. So..."

"Found it!" Maria yells, yanking her arm out from under the couch, dislodging a few DVDs that go sliding across the floor. She holds up a box of DVDs.

"We bought the box set," Gabriella finishes with a laugh. "We binge them at least once a year. Wanna watch one?"

Jack nods, amused. "Is that where you keep your DVDs, under the couch?"

"Only during Christmas." Gabriella shrugs, her face heating with shame. "We need the space for decoration."

Jack chuckles hard, and the trio settles in to watch a classic movie they can all agree on. They shift around their seating so everyone can see the tv, Maria stretching out across the couch, and Jack and Gabriella settling against the couch legs beside each other. The later into the film it gets, the less space exists between them until eventually, Jack has his arm around her waist, and Gabriella's head rests on his shoulder.

When the film ends, Gabriella shyly offers to put on another, but Jack says he has to leave.

"Maybe we can finish the whole set some time," he says quietly as he walks to the door.

Maria has fallen asleep on the couch.

Gabriella follows him to the door, nodding. "I'd like that."

"Hey, I've been meaning to ask you." Jack pauses in the open doorway, holding onto the door to turn back and look at Gabriella. "That stuff you said to the kids at the tree farm, was it true?"

Gabriella is startled by the question; she'd sort of thought he was going to ask to kiss her. Now her shoulders shift with unease. "About the letter?" She asks. At Jack's nod, she shrugs. "Well, yes, I got the letter. But I mean, I don't think it was from Santa anymore. I was six."

Jack laughs at the defensive tone. "That's not why I was asking. You never mention your father. I sort of assumed your mom was a single mom."

Gabriella bobs her head back and forth. "Well, she was for most of my life. Almost all of Maria's, she was only two. I don't talk about him much because I don't remember a lot of things about him. Mostly his smile and how well he loved us. But Maria doesn't remember any of it. And I don't like to make her sad."

Jack nods. "I'm sorry. You must miss them both a lot. But..." he smiles as Maria rolls over on the couch, whining in a sleepy voice.

"In or out, come on. Shut the door."

Gabriella and Jack laugh; Jack pulls the door further shut, but not all the way, stepping outside. He grins at Gabriella.

"All I was going to say is, when you said it, it made me really sad for both of you. And I am sorry for the pain and all of that, but," he notches his head towards the house. "You two are great together. No one who knows either of you could ever believe that you're lonely. Goodnight," he whispers to Gabriella's stunned smile and ducks out, pulling the door shut behind him.

Gabriella stands there with her heart on fire staring at the closed door for several long moments.

Groaning and pulling a throw blanket over her shoulders, Maria turns towards her sister with a soft smile. "I like your boy. And he is really hooked on you."

Gabriella leans against the door, beaming. Pretty hooked herself.

'Tis the Season...

Wednesday, December the nineteenth, sees Jack in an excellent mood. He hasn't slept much, kept up by a fun, silly idea for a Christmas present for Gabriella. It is a combination of things he loves and things she loves. He knows she is going to adore it. He can't wait to watch her open it, and hear her laugh as she reads it. It's going to be great.

He is so excited about it that when they meet in the parking lot a half hour before work, it is all he can think of. He is grinning and fighting the urge to show her now. Gabriella has waited in her car for Jack to arrive, waited until nearly the last minute; she would have run out of time to set up if she had waited a minute more. But neither she nor Jack seem to notice once they are out of the cars and walking together into the building, apparently in no rush at all. With their twitterpated eyes locked, they walk in, discussing innocuous things like the weather and how they slept. Jack takes two of the bags full of paper, scissors, and the remaining craft supplies from the slicker decorating contest and still tries to grab the door for her, which ends in laughter for the pair when he can't manage. All the while, he is thinking of his secret. And Gabriella is watching his smile, thinking, correctly, that it is all for her.

Rather than divide the floors as they usually would, Jack and Gabriella work together, setting out the day's surprise, unwilling to be away from one another for very long. When nine o'clock hits and other workers start heading in, Jack and Gabriella force themselves to separate as far as their cubicles require. Gabriella, for once sitting at her desk with nothing to do and no thoughts in her head but of the sweet boy on the other side of her wall. And Jack, ever her opposite, is hard at work. Not the work he is paid for, naturally, but work nonetheless. He is putting the finishing touches on his quick, Nate the Great style mystery—a Christmas mystery—when his phone rings at nine-forty, and he is summoned to Coleman's office for the third time this month, making it just the...hm...oh yes, *third* time in the nearly four years he has worked here. But Jack doesn't mind. The full-color copier is on the corporate floor. Carefully, Jack takes his snowmen off the wall of his cubicle and slips them, folded up, into a notepad, headed upstairs.

Coleman sits miserly behind his black slate desk displaying the bare minimum of emotion so he might build up his reserves. With as little as he expresses himself, one must assume he has built quite the reserve indeed. Jack has no idea why he's been summoned, and Mr. Coleman's lack of expression leaves Jack few clues, but to be honest, most of his thoughts are on his Christmas story.

He'd thought he could charm Debbie into helping him, and he wasn't wrong. Once he told her it was a gift for Gabriella, she took over the cover designing herself. Printing out several versions of the title page on blue paper and copying the snowmen onto each to see which she liked best, then settling in with tape, a stapler, and an array of other supplies to make sure the book came out neatly. He can't wait to see it, but right now, he needs to focus, Mr. Coleman is observing him very closely.

"Jack, I've been watching you for a while now. I think you're the right man for the manager job," Mr. Coleman remarks, by no means showing any great enthusiasm but some curiosity. "So, why haven't I received your resume yet?"

"To be honest, I forgot about it when you gave Gabriella and me the party assignment. I'll get it to you." Jack replies brightly, a bit relieved. He'd worried he was here about the hacking again.

But he is surprised to realize he had entirely forgotten about the manager position. Apparently, some things, some *people,* are more engaging.

"Good. I think you have a bright future here. How are the party arrangements coming along?" Coleman asks as an afterthought.

"The family invites went out over the weekend and today's Secret Santa activity was to have people make and decorate snowflakes and we'll use those to decorate at the party as well as some of the stuff from the other events."

"Nice money-saving technique. Great idea."

"I can't take the credit. Gabriella is full of thrifty ideas."

"Good for her. But don't sell yourself short. It's a sign of a true leader that he knows when to listen to ideas and when to ignore them."

Jack shifts in his seat, growing uncomfortable. "I understood this to be Gabriella's assignment, and I just…help where needed."

"And your help has been invaluable. I haven't been receiving her token ten emails a day since I added you to the team. It's a great improvement. Half of her emails were to press for bonuses; the fact that you've talked her out of that shows real management potential. Good work."

Keep your mouth shut. Jack's mind warns him. Coleman clearly dismissed him. And the guy's opinion shouldn't really matter to anyone. He's not that invested in his work, just in keeping as much money as possible. Yet as Jack stands, crossing to the door, he feels an uncomfortable knot growing between his shoulders. He's watched Gabriella for the last few weeks working around the clock to make these special surprises for the staff. To bring people together when they don't really like each other. She's stayed after and cleaned to make sure the janitorial staff doesn't have extra to do. And stressed about finding the right balance between her "Christmas" assignment and respecting everyone's beliefs. She's done her job and the job of a small team-building firm, but Coleman doesn't see any of it. More than that, he's basically insulting her and giving Jack credit for reining her in.

Keep your mouth shut, he thinks again, nearly at the door now. But his mouth isn't listening to his brain.

"I understand how handing out bonuses might set a precedent you don't want to repeat," Jack says, pausing at the doorway and turning back to face Mr. Coleman. "But I think you may be missing Gabriella's point. A lot of your employees live from paycheck to paycheck. They're happy to take overtime, even though it means less time with family because they need the money. And with this being Christmas, a lot of them would probably be thrilled with even the extra fifty. It's a small gesture, but it could build a lot of goodwill."

Mr. Coleman says nothing, folding his hands atop the desk as he raises his eyes to watch Jack coolly.

"If it's a sign of a good manager to listen, perhaps you should listen to Gabriella in any of those ten emails." Jack immediately regrets his words. He regretted them before he even spoke. His mind has always known that his mouth is a serious liability. When Mr. Coleman continues to stare silently, Jack excuses himself. Something he probably should have done before.

Jack nearly runs to the elevator, furious with himself. "Shit," he says aloud.

"Jack! Jack." Debbie leaps up from her desk, trailing him to the elevator with the book Jack had forgotten about in hand. She holds it out. The cover is just the title *Clara Claus, Christmas Detective, and the Case of the Murdered Snow-folk,* with the murdered snowmen Gabriella gave him all lined up underneath. It's cute; it should make him smile, but all Jack can think now is: *will you ever learn to shut up?*

But Debbie is still talking. "Oh, Jack, it's such a sweet story. She is going to love it. Umm. I read it through, sorry, but I found a few typos. I marked them with post-its. If you want to fix them up and email it to me, I'll put it all together again. But I'm sure she'll love it even with the typos if you don't want to fix it." She remarks after he says nothing. The truth is she is *certain* Jack should fix the typos. It would be one thing if he had missed them, but now that they have been pointed out, to leave them would be silly.

Jack, however, is barely listening. "Thanks." He takes everything Debbie is holding out, his snowmen and notepad, and the *book*, just a few pages bound together with staples and a blue tape spine.

Shit, he thinks again as he walks into the elevator, *go into his office to talk about a promotion, and talk yourself right out of the job you have.*

"You were fired? I didn't notice." Jack hears Kristen's taunting voice in his mind as if she is actually here.

He knows he is overreacting, but all he can think is: *I'm going to get fired over bonuses Coleman was never going to give out.*

Jack tries to shut down the part of him that wants nothing but to scream. He's said he can walk away from this job, no problem. So being fired shouldn't be any different. But it is! His eyes drift again to the book in his hands; he's not even sure he'd be at all able to walk away now. All he knows is his system is running on overdrive, afraid to lose this job all because—

The elevator doors slide open and Jack shuts off his brain. He rushes to his desk and settles in, shoving the book into a drawer. He picks up a murder mystery, burying his nose inside so he doesn't even notice Gabriella wave hello from the break room. But he isn't reading. Isn't seeing a single word.

He's calling himself an ass. He's realizing that even if he didn't lose this job, he might have lost the promotion that he would have been happy with. And realizing that the why of it all is really more of a problem than the loss.

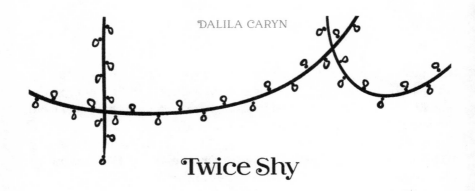

Twice Shy

By eleven fifteen in the afternoon, Gabriella is a little concerned. Jack has been behaving oddly since he came back from upstairs. He has said all of two words to her. *Hello* and *yep,* in that order and both in response to multiple words from her. After that, he just nodded and grunted. Not his style. Now he's reading. Like he has been all day. Just reading, nothing else.

But she shouldn't read too much into it. She shouldn't read *anything* into it. But as has been observed by many a person, that is far easier said than done.

At the moment, though, she has the help of a tech call. "Okay, I can't access your desktop. Could you do me a favor and check how many cords are plugged into it?" Gabriella asks pleasantly.

On the other side of her cubicle wall, Jack, who is very much so not reading and might actually be obsessing over a small disturbance of his own, rolls his eyes and shakes his head over the people at this company. And how truly pointless his job is. He wonders how Gabriella isn't bored out of her mind already. Why doesn't she have a stack of books at her desk?

"I can't find the tower," Matt says on the other end of Gabriella's phone call.

"It doesn't have a tower. It'll be plugged directly into the back of the monitor. You should have two cords."

NICE TO BE SO NAUGHTY

"Oh, okay. At home, I just have a laptop."

"No problem, I can wait," Gabriella replies pleasantly. Michael walks by her desk, rolling his eyes in commiseration to Gabriella over the silly things their coworkers need help with.

Gabriella forces a smile. But as she sees Michael stop at Jack's desk with a confrontational posture, her interest in the tech call diminishes. She leans near to eavesdrop.

"It has a power cord and nothing else that I can see," Matt says on the phone.

As Michael is confronting Jack at his desk, "What's this I hear about you arranging the end of the year party?"

"Okay," Gabriella says quietly. "Look around and see if you—"

"There is nothing here," Matt says before Gabriella has even completed her sentence.

"Dunno," Jack responds to Michael disinterestedly. "What is it you hear?"

"It should be around you," Gabriella whispers discomforted by Jack's tone. Something really is wrong with him. "Try under the desk. Maybe it was kicked out. It should be a basic USB cord."

"Did you ask for this assignment as some sort of trial for the position?" Michael demands. It seems at least one person has *not* benefited from Gabriella's team-building winter events. He's too competitive to do well, especially since he hasn't won any of the events. Maybe she should give him some sort of edge tomorrow. "Everyone should have the same chances!" Michael snaps at Jack angrily, unaware of the pity coming his way from Gabriella's side of the cubicle wall.

"Take it up with Daniel. I do the work I'm assigned." Jack says, sounding like he pities Michael not at all.

"Should it look like a phone cord?" Matt asks Gabriella.

"What?" Gabriella shakes her head though Matt has no hope of seeing it. "No. It's not an internet cable. It's a tie-in to the company servers."

"You know if you want to apply for the job, you should," Michael says, leaning into Jack's cubicle angrily. "But be careful who you piss off along the way, *Santa*."

"The thing is, I'm still online, so I really think the problem is something at your end," Matt remarks on the phone.

"You know what—" Gabriella breathes in deeply, holding it for ten seconds with her fists clenched. "I'll be right up to check it out. Hold tight."

Gabriella sighs, removes her headset, and sits back a second. This thing between Jack and Michael is her fault. If she'd never sent that prank email, no one would think Jack was the Secret Santa. She's just not sure how to fix it. And she knows it isn't all that's bothering Jack, but something definitely is.

Standing, she tugs down her Christmas llama sweater and takes an extra deep breath before exiting her cubicle. She stops beside Jack on her way out.

"Hey, are you alright?" She leans near to whisper.

Jack, displaying the usual self-indulgent behavior of his species when feeling frightened and embarrassed, pretends that the other person has lost their mind by caring.

He waves at his book and shows off a slightly unpleasant smile. "Why wouldn't I be?"

"I don't know. But it is okay if you're not. And if I can help with it, I'd be happy to. Or even happy to listen." Gabriella offers.

"I'm all good. Don't you have a call to get to?" He asks, clearly a dismissal.

Gabriella straightens. Now she knows she's not reading something into nothing. Even when they weren't friends, he didn't talk to her like that. Just trying to get rid of her. The thing is, now she worries that it is her he is upset with.

And Gabriella, predictably, and in the long-honored tradition of her gender, when feeling unwanted or feeling a partner's anger, but having no clue whence it came, pretends nothing is going on.

"Yep. Okay." She nods, smiling brightly. "Talk later then?"

"You bet." Jack doesn't even look her way, turning the page in his book pointlessly. Pointlessly because he hasn't read that page, he hasn't even opened the book he was reading yesterday, so great is his distraction, pouting about things he shouldn't have said to his boss. And the reasons he said them.

Kristen watches Gabriella walk away from the back of the room. Her hands are fisting at her sides. Kristen's hands, not Gabriella's. No, Gabriella is wearing her fake smile, the one she wore when Jack was first messing with her deer, the one that covers her pain, rage, and struggle. And the calmer Gabriella looks, the more Kristen knows she is shoving all of that stress and that worry inside, hurting herself more to make Jack comfortable, and the more Kristen wants to march across the room and punch Jack; right in the face!

Why are men such shits?

Look at him pouting. She'd bet, and be right, that this is at least fifteen percent Uncle Coleman's fault. He has that effect on people. She feels like keying his Tesla or something because retribution and vengeance sound so good. But...she is supposed to be hanging back! Kristen is very quickly growing to hate the documentary film medium. She knows how to fix things or, failing that, she knows how to make grown men thoroughly miserable. But she isn't doing any of that, and it is so frustrating. Gabriella better as hell get Jack back for this, or Kristen may give up on film and start a new career.

Male Bashing, she'll call it, she decides, resting in the fantasy to resist violence in reality. She'll put her number on bathroom stalls and alley walls. And free of charge, paid only in the joy of it, she'll bash the bones of the men who've wronged the people who call. *Yeah, that's her new plan.* Kristen comforts herself.

Needless to say, *Male Bashing* the company is not to be part of her future. A good verbal bashing, however, will remain a frequent aspect of her life.

The tech call takes Gabriella all of twenty-four seconds once she reaches Matt's desk. Once he's plugged back in, Gabriella briefly considers going to her car to stew a bit about Jack.

She is well aware that she and Jack have done nothing so formal as define their relationship. She doesn't know if they are dating, flirting, or nothing at all. Right now, it feels like nothing at all. But she's worried about him. Even when they weren't friends, he tried to make it better when she was feeling low and angry and embarrassed. That's all she wants to do for him. So instead of stewing, she darts into the third-floor break room and buys a full-size KitKat for him.

"Hey, is now an okay time to ask you something?" Gabriella asks, smiling softly, as she stops outside Jack's cubicle.

Jack flips his book over. "I'm free as a bird."

"Of course, but that doesn't mean you have to be..." already Gabriella wishes she were curled up in a ball under her desk, invisible, forgotten, allowed to stay curled up there for the rest of time. "Never mind," she presses on with forced cheer. "Look, I know you say you're not upset. And maybe you actually aren't, but if you are and it is because of something I've done, please let me know. Because," she leans close and whispers, "I don't want you to hate me either. I'm really sorry if today's prank took things too far."

"What prank?" Jack laughs bitterly. Don't worry, he hears it. He sounds *very* whiny. *Why the hell am I upset not to have been pranked?* But he is. "You didn't do anything today."

"I did," she says slowly. "I guess I overestimated how quickly you read."

Jack raises a brow, intrigued. Now he wants to yank up his book and see what she's done to it.

"Right, well, I got you this," she holds out the candy. Jack takes it wordlessly, and Gabriella backs up. "I guess I'm reading something into nothing. Sorry." She says, giving in to her generous nature and being gaslit in the process. And *gaslighting* is something she is well acquainted with, one of her favorite Ingrid Bergman films was "Gaslight," whence came the term.

Yet, in this instance, her familiarity with the phenomena escapes her as she tries to accept Jack's words, despite the distance, she feels him building between them. After all, she does occasionally feel things that other people do not. Or feel things stronger than other people do. *Maybe now is one of those times.*

Nope. It's not. She should trust her instincts.

"Gabriella. Wait." Jack drops the candy. "I'm not upset with you."

That's it.

That is all he says.

Gabriella stares at him as incredulous as you.

"Are you sure about that?"

"Yes. I'm just..." Jack breaks off, searching for the words to say to simultaneously make this better and still give him the space he needs to pout. The words he's looking for are: *I'm upset about a work thing, but I need time before I'm ready to talk about it.* What he chooses to say is: "In a bad mood."

At that revelation, Gabriella has nothing to do but nod. A bad mood. *Interesting.*

It is not as though she, the camera crew, the rest of the staff, and even virus microbes floating in the air couldn't pick up on that. But as it seems that no further explanation, nor even any request for space, is forthcoming, Gabriella simply nods again.

She smiles unconvincingly. "Then I'd skip page one-eighty-four." Gabriella turns her back and walks to the break room.

Jack watches her for all of four seconds before diving back into his seat and yanking up his novel. He flips to the page and realizes he is looking at his backup novel. Tossing it aside, he grabs his current read, *Brains on the Tile*. When he finds the page in question, he skims the prose until he spots Gabriella's alteration. Chuckling hard, Jack looks up, hoping to spot Gabriella in the break room, but she has apparently left the basement altogether.

Damn.

The Little Girl That Santa Claus Forgot

Kristen Kringle watches Jack laugh as Gabriella disappears upstairs. "Why don't you boys set up in the break room? I think it's time for some interviews," she says, sharp and bright.

"Hey, wait a second." Sighing, Terrance turns off the camera and sets it aside. "Look, I know you're going to do what you want to do."

"C'est vrai." She agrees in French.

"But," Terrance says slowly, raising a smirking brow at her. "Look, I didn't give you much credit for being good at this when we started, but you were. Accidentally."

Kristen laughs at the insult. And it was an insult.

"You were good because you keep yourself so separate. Now you're getting good intentionally, but...the longer we're here, the more we feel involved, and we're not. We're going to leave in two days and likely never see any of these people again."

"Your point?" Kristen asks snidely.

Terrance hesitates. "I don't know," he lies. He knows. He's starting to understand Kristen, and the reason she is so bossy and confident. She didn't care before. But she does now. All he really wants to say is *don't get so close that it messes you up* because he's worried about what will become of her after...when she has no one else's problems to solve.

Kristen smirks. "Javajin," she taunts in a language he has no way of knowing.

The word means *fear baby* in Maltuban, an invented language from a fantasy novel series whose first book will not be published until the year twenty-twenty-two, and its associated language guide long after that. But Kristen knows it. Being a Claus is great for getting early editions.

*Wink.

Kristen smugly thinks that fear baby is an appropriate description of Terrance at the moment. And while she is perhaps not entirely wrong because he is resisting what he wants to say in fear of her reaction, Terrance would not be entirely wrong either in thinking the same of her. Kristen does launch into other people's problems in a bid to avoid her own. But neither of these *fear babies* is ready to express their deeper concerns, so it seems nothing will come of it.

When Jack is seated in the break room facing the camera, he wears a broad smile, still delighted by Gabriella's prank. And Kristen allows him to discuss the things he is enjoying. She has plans to rip him up soon enough.

"She is seriously evil, and I love it." Jack grins excitably. "Look at this." He holds up the mystery novel, pages out, opened to page one-hundred-and-eighty-four, the facing page is number two-hundred-and-seventy-nine.

"It looks totally normal. And it's right in the middle of the action. I would have been halfway through it before I realized she'd spoiled the ending. I would have been livid!" He laughs. *Everything Gabriella does is so fun, so unique, so...* "It's twisted. She doesn't pull her punches, does she? She's awesome." Here he breaks off his facial expression drooping pathetically.

Kristen smiles, prepared to pounce, but Jack opens his mouth again.

"And I literally cannot explain to her why I'm upset," Jack admits, and his stomach drops. He knows he fucked up earlier. He watched Gabriella's face as she walked away, stiff and cold. Nothing about her is ever cold, but she was because he was a shit. But he didn't know what to do. "How do I say, 'hey, I know we've only been out once, haven't kissed, and you have an annoying habit of making me more self-aware. But I don't want to stop seeing you every day. And I've either screwed myself out of a job that would have proven to you I'm not lacking in ambition. Or I've gotten myself fired altogether in an attempt to get you what you want. To get you the recognition you deserve, but   you don't fight for with anyone but me." Jack shakes his head heavily.

Kristen is struck by the words. He is right; Gabriella doesn't fight for the recognition she deserves. She gives and gives and gives. Look at all she's been doing, work that would cost him an arm and a leg from the elves union if Santa wanted to be done in the North. But Gabriella does it basically on her own, and the few things she's asked for have been flatly ignored.

"When I was talking to Coleman earlier," Jack goes on, interrupting Kristen's thoughts. "I kept thinking about all she's done to make this place better and how hard she works at everything. *Everything.* It made me think about weird things like what she said to Cory about her mother working two jobs and how invested she got when she realized what Frank was going through. I wanted to get Gabriella recognition, but I also wanted to...help out the other pains in the ass that work here. It felt like I was investing more in this place, trying to make it more than just a job. But now I might get fired, and half the reason that is upsetting me has nothing to do with the job and everything to do with being near her. And this is all —*really* fast. And I think you know I've been known to get ahead of myself. How do I tell her any of that without scaring her off? I can't say any of that to her."

On that point, Kristen disagrees. Gabriella is the only person he should be telling. But as Kristen watches Jack sitting there, all morose and pouty unwilling to voice his fear. She wonders about other people and why it is that people never can say the words they need to say to the people who need to hear them.

Gabriella has found a spot of relative calm when Kristen and the doc crew find her in the second-floor break room, decorating snowflakes with Maya. Gabriella has been having fun, but as soon as she sees them round the corner, she feels tired, knowing what is to come.

Maya had been sharing about the changes she's made to her Christmas plans, how she called her family and told them she was bringing a bunch of Christmas games to play with the kids and the adults, but mostly the kids. Sharing how much she's looking forward to it now, even without her boyfriend. And it made Gabriella feel *peaceful* and happy. She's making a difference.

But she sees the doc crew, and she knows all they want to talk about is Jack, and while she was here, she put his total reversal of attitude out of her mind. She doesn't want to go backward. All the same, Gabriella Anjelica Cruz does not do things halfway. So she agrees.

Kristen is still angry. Kristen is usually angry. She was angry when her mother died, angry and scared when she first went to boarding school, then totally enraged when she came home, and it seemed that no one had missed her. She is always angry, but it is mostly on Gabriella's behalf today. But her anger burns ever wilder, seeing how little rage Gabriella expresses.

"Why are you working up here?" Kristen prompts when everything is set up.

Gabriella smirks sideways, without much humor. "I'm not sure if I upset him. Or work did. Or the phases of the moon!" Growing agitated, Gabriella shifts in her seat. "But something upset him. And...*I* need for it not to upset me, and he probably needs that too. So I'm trying not to feel hurt, worried, or responsible. Not until I *know* what the problem is. But that isn't easy. Particularly not with him on the opposite side of my cubical wall. So I came up here where I wouldn't see him constantly." Her hands fist now. And Kristen realizes she had been looking calmer before they started talking.

"Maybe it really was the prank." Gabriella goes on. "Though he seemed genuinely unaware of it. I suppose this one was more invasive than my usual pranks. People can get really bent out of shape when you mess with their books. That's why I bought a replacement. It's hidden in his desk. I probably should have bought a new copy, but I found the used one and planned to leave his original copy alone, but it had this funny note written inside the cover." Gabriella breaks off, smiling over the silly threatening note. She had found the book before Jack apologized, and the inscription seemed so fitting.

Retribution shall be taken by—The Goddess of War—
should any unworthy hands fuck with this book.
This isn't a threat. It's a curse.

The note was signed with a doodle of rams horns, and it had called to her like magic. So she'd chosen it. And today, when she'd hidden it in Jack's desk, she'd imagined him laughing about it later. Now, who knows? Something quiet comes over Gabriella, not quite sad but heavy.

"If it was the prank, wouldn't he just say something? He's been reading all day. He should have seen it! I'm obsessing." Gabriella stares intently into the cameras.

Her hand is raised, poised to punch her thigh, and she feels her chest seize, holding onto the air inside it for dear life. She came up here because she needed it because she needed space, and she had that for a few minutes, but now the anxiety is following her. It probably always will. It definitely always will. Not always the same, but always there. Gabriella stops fighting it. She breathes out. Her fingers uncurl. Her right index finger taps against her thigh in that same old rhythm, gently, comfortingly, not attacking, not right now.

"Do you know?" She shakes her head and smiles softly as she breathes in the rhythm of her tapping finger. "I begin to think you guys are really disruptive to my ability to manage my anxieties. The whole nature of these interviews has me obsessing over every little detail. So," she breathes out softly, one more time. "Yeah. I'm just gonna go now."

Gabriella stands and begins to remove the microphone clipped onto her Christmas sweater. Andrew rushes to help her, but Kristen is frozen, staring at Gabriella, at the chair she just vacated. Staring at the empty space and Gabriella's open hand. Staring as something new floats through her, shock maybe. Gabriella is still stressed and disturbed, but she also looks much more confident than Kristen has ever seen her. And Kristen wonders for the first time, despite years of ignored admonishments and well-meaning nudges to consider exactly what she is thinking now. *What would happen if she were to just...let the anger go?*

Hard Candy Christmas

Late into the evening of Thursday, December twentieth, Gabriella and Maria sit in the living room diligently folding and stuffing party crackers with paper crowns, some candy, and...fifty dollars in cash. There is a movie playing in the background *White Christmas,* but they are barely paying it any attention as they talk. It is almost nine o'clock. The work is nearly done, but the energy is not high tonight.

"So what happens when the boss finds out you gave money even though he said no?" Maria asks, stuffing another fifty into a cracker.

Her sister is such a rebel. Not that you would know it to talk to or look at her. She dresses like a quirky best friend in a romcom circa nineteen-ninety. With her different Christmas sweaters for every day of the week, and her cheap, multicolored, sleigh bell earrings.

Maria laughs at herself, only partially listening to her sister's response because her inner monologue is so entertaining.

Gabriella is on a role. Not an excited or happy role, but not a bad one either. An energetic, take no prisoners, not gonna let this shit bother me sort of role.

"Don't know. Don't care," she replies.

This is, of course, more of an aspirational statement than a factual one. She cares. She wishes she could believe she won't get into trouble for having slightly overstated the cost of a few items for the winter games to hold back money for this final gift. The only thing she is certain of is that this choice, her choice, is the right one. If she hadn't made things like felt mittens, cookies, building gingerbread, and so many snowflakes, it would have cost far more than the extra fifty dollars per employee she's held onto. But it was dishonest to pad the figures. Some might call it theft. Embezzlement seems a bit of a stretch because she was giving it back to the staff, but she supposes she will get fifty herself. Not that she doesn't deserve it. She is an hourly employee who's been working twelve-hour days and getting paid for eight for the last two weeks. So...she deserves it. And if Coleman had been willing to listen to what she was saying even once, or to let her bring in one of the accountants to show him what was possible, she wouldn't have needed to steal.

Not that she is admitting that this is theft. She isn't. Not even internally.

"Well, good for you!" Maria tosses a finished cracker into a basket. "Who needs a job anyway?"

Aggravated, Gabriella stops folding her cracker and glares at her sister. Maria smirks back. Both sisters are well aware that the larger part of Gabriella's frustration has nothing to do with Coleman, slightly embezzled funds, or anything other than Jack.

Jack, who was supposed to be here helping them but is not. Jack, who was supposed to be at work today but was not. Jack, who was supposed to have stayed after work with her to help with the early setup for the party, but did not.

Jack, who was grouchy on Wednesday and now missing on Thursday. Jack, who went from sweet and flirty Tuesday night to cold and annoyed on Wednesday.

Jack is the main source of Gabriella's anxiety turned *don't give a crap* attitude. They could have been done hours ago if he had been here to help. They could actually be watching *White Christmas,* and damn it. She wasn't paying attention and missed "Love, You Didn't Do Right By Me." She loves that number.

Her annoyance is all Jack's fault. Everyone knows it. But it is really rather annoying that Maria won't pretend *not* to know it. They glare at one another. Well, Gabriella glares, and Maria smiles until Gabriella gives in.

"Look, I know it shouldn't upset me that he's upset and won't tell me why. But it does. He skipped work today rather than seeing me."

"I thought he texted you."

"He did!" Gabriella snaps, annoyed at Maria for being so reasonable when she doesn't feel like being so herself. "But all it said was he was sick, and maybe that was why he was so grouchy Wednesday."

"Maybe it was." Maria pops a brow.

"I think he's lying. I think he's upset." Gabriella has to drop the cracker she's been folding as her fingers clench up, threatening to crush it. "I'm trying to be an easygoing girl." She waves at her sister very nearly venomously.

"No one is easy going about things they are emotionally invested in." Maria shakes her head. "I'm not easygoing. I'm just better able than you to cover it up."

Annoyed with herself, Gabriella flops back against the couch. "I liked our flirty days. So," she throws her hands up, "big deal, he didn't flirt with me for one day. Why am I so neurotic that I can't let it go?"

Maria smiles wryly into her lap. Lifting Gabriella's unfinished cracker, she takes over the task.

"You know, at first, I didn't like Jack because he'd hurt you in the past," Maria admits with her eyes on the cracker. "Then I didn't like that he was helping you in ways I hadn't figured out."

Captivated by her playful sister's unusually serious tone, Gabriella leans forward to listen.

"But I can cover with smiles and sarcastic comments. I think you're a lot more *normal*," she says with great emphasis and a raised brow. "Than you give yourself credit for. You just can't hide from things the way the rest of us do. I think you're pretty brave too." She adds, giving her sister a warm smile. "You confronted him about it. You always confront your weaknesses. Maybe you should acknowledge your strengths the same way."

"Like what?" Gabriella challenges, a touched smile slowly stretching her lips and a fire of love burning in her heart.

"Like this, you pain!" She waves at the crackers. "You never give up. You always do what *you* think is right. And you care *way* too deeply about other people."

"I think that last one had a backhanded insult hidden inside."

"Might've."

Gabriella beams at her sister. This time, fully aware of what she's doing and the magic inside her, Gabriella latches onto that magic and sends out a burst of power. Sending a demand far away to the offices of a very different Santa Claus, demanding something very special for the sister who is always here to lift her up.

Gabriella feels more relaxed for the spent magic, and her sister's love. "I know that what Mr. Coleman said about not getting ahead of myself was meant to stop me from applying for the job," she breathes in, "but I've been updating my resume in my spare time anyway."

"Tell me something surprising."

"I don't think I'm going to use it," Gabriella says lightly.

Maria glares. "Because Jack is up for the same job?"

"No. I was offended when Mr. Burns asked for Jack's resume and not mine, not because Jack isn't capable of the job, but because I've proven myself more than any man who works there. I *am* a more valuable employee." Gabriella says forcefully, so much so one might think she was trying to convince someone other than Maria, who is already agreeing. "But as I was working up my resume, I realized half the reason I was doing it was to prove to them how wrong they were to overlook me. But I don't really give a shit about that job." She says, slouching her shoulders and leaning her head sideways.

Maria cracks up.

"I don't." Gabriella pauses, watching her sister intently. "I want something more challenging than the job I have. More challenging than that promotion. I want...more," she says softly.

"Wow." Maria's every humorous expression dissolves, and she watches Gabriella blankly a moment before quirking a brow and grinning. "Finally."

"This Secret Santa thing has reminded me of the things I used to dream of doing. Getting to help people who are otherwise left out find a place to be comfortable and productive. I want to do that. I'm not sure exactly what that will look like, but I know I can do it." She laughs, waving at the crackers. Reawakened to the need to work, she resumes folding.

"For a while now I've been sort of just...going along."

"Really," Maria mutters sarcastically. "I hadn't noticed."

"I was bored at the job, but I didn't care because it paid the bills and I didn't have to think about anything, and when I got home I could...shut it out of my thoughts. I don't think I realized really how sad I still was."

Maria drops a finished cracker into the pile and leans forward, reaching a hand out for her sister's. She knew. Maria is still grieving too, but in a different way, her grief was always angrier than Gabriella's. But she knew. It's just good to see that Gabriella finally recognizes it, that she is finally ready to do something to change it.

"I wasn't giving any thoughts to what I wanted. I wasn't happy. But this Secret Santa thing has reminded me of ways I can enjoy myself with work. Even sometimes with too much work. I've felt charged and excited and *useful*. I really love that feeling. And I want more of it."

"Good." Maria smiles, full of fire and delight. "Then you have to find it. You deserve to be happy." She squeezes Gabriella's hand. "I'm glad you've realized it. Just promise me that you will take as much care of yourself as you are of whoever you are *being useful* to."

"I will," Gabriella says more easily than she would have thought possible before now. "I've actually gotten better at that lately. Much better. Like this," she tosses another cracker on the pile. "I'm sticking to the things I think are right, no matter what anyone else tells me. I'm expressing myself more forcefully. Jack's helped with that." Gabriella says thoughtfully, wondering if there is weakness in that. Wondering if she would have come to it on her own. "Giving me permission to do my worst."

"Well, that's great," Maria says just shy of sharply. "But before you go giving Jack all the credit, answer me this. Are you doing your worst? Or did he show you a path, and you took it? Because if you take the road, the work is still your own. Your choices equal your successes," Maria says with a forceful sort of sageness that makes her seem almost mad that Gabriella would imagine Jack has anything to do with it.

It reminds Gabriella of Mom. She laughs.

"Did Mom give you that speech at some point? Because it has a very Mom, sage, sort of feel to it, and that's not really you."

"I'm an artist. We're basically philosophers who prefer a visual medium." Maria rolls her eyes at her sister.

"Yeah, right. Copy-cat. Admit it. You stole the whole thing from Mom."

"You are such a pain." Maria shakes her head.

"And you love it."

Embarrassed but fond, Maria sticks her tongue out at her sister.

Gabriella considers Maria's point quietly. She supposes she has not really been doing her worst. And she has been enjoying herself much more than usual. And a lot of that had to do with Jack. But it that doesn't make it his doing. Some of it even started before he made that offer.

"You're right, you know," Gabriella admits as she tosses aside the finished popper and picks up another. "It is my doing. I almost never verbally address my boundaries with people, and ask them to respect them. But I did that with him and with the film crew. I opened the door. I walked through it. But I like having him around." She admits.

"I think I might have even before this. It's why I got so angry when I felt like he was picking at me. Because I'd thought we were friends. I like being around him. He...puts me at ease a bit, lets me be myself." She says, then her eyes narrow and her tone darkens slightly. "But if he doesn't feel the same, for whatever reason, that's fine."

Maria rolls her eyes annoyed to be put in the position of defending Jack, but knowing it's what her sister needs to hear. "The guy is obsessed with you. Something might be bothering him, but it isn't you. Maybe he is sick! You're a real pain when you're sick."

"He isn't sick," Gabriella says, with absolute certainty that she has no facts to back up, but in this instance, she is entirely correct, so...score one, Gabriella. "But that isn't the point. If he wants me to treat him like he's not angry, that's what I'm going to do."

"What does that cryptic comment mean?" Maria laughs cautiously.

"It means I'm pulling one last prank on him whether he is there or not tomorrow. And we'll see how much of a coward he is by how far he runs."

Christmas Through Your Eyes

In another apartment, in another part of town, all alone for the evening, Kristen Klaus watches the last seventeen seconds of Gabriella's interview Wednesday on repeat. It has already been cut into what is building into the final segment. She had to argue for it, though.

Terrance was determined to protect his crush. To protect her fragile feelings from everyone, knowing that something in the world, something external and thus entirely out of her command, might affect Gabriella. Might cause her added stress and make her symptoms harder to bear.

But Gabriella doesn't need protection. It isn't coldness on Kristen's part. It isn't her wanting to create the most compelling piece she can. It isn't even envy, though she feels it as she watches those seconds on a loop.

It is...inspiration.

GABRIELLA

I begin to think you guys are really disruptive to my ability to manage my anxieties. The whole nature of these interviews has me obsessing over every little detail. So (breathes deeply), Yeah. I'm just gonna go now.

Kristen doesn't know that she has ever seen a thing like it. Certainly not in her family. No one says what they mean. No one says what they need. No one looks everyone in the face and acknowledges when they aren't healthy for one another.

GABRIELLA
So (breathes deeply), Yeah. I'm just gonna go now.

It's breathtaking, incredibly strong, and quite honestly, Kristen feels like it should be the final shot of the piece. But the boys are pushing for something traditionally uplifting, like a montage of the employees laughing. Or overlapping interviews with people talking about how Secret Santa worked last year versus this year. Because this is a group project, she has promised to listen and to see what they can all come up with. But if this were Kristen's piece alone, it would end on this shot.

GABRIELLA
So (breathes deeply), Yeah. I'm just gonna go now.

Kristen hits the space bar.

GABRIELLA
So (breathes deeply), Yeah. I'm just gonna go now.

She hits the space bar again.

GABRIELLA
I'm just gonna go now.

Blue Christmas

Elsewhere in a town nearby, entirely unaware of Kristen's moment of epiphany or Gabriella's pranking plans, Jack, who is indeed not sick at all, is still sitting in his parent's living room. He has finished the project for which he took off the day of work hours ago. He could easily have finished the project after work, say, or having taken the day off, finished the project, then called Gabriella and popped over to help with the party he is meant to be sharing in the work for.

They never arranged a time to set up the party—he doesn't think—he thinks wrong. She talked about *maybe* doing it after work today. He hopes she didn't go ahead with that. He should have checked. Maybe she is going in early tomorrow. He can definitely get there early and help out. But he hasn't left his parent's house yet, and his entire slouchy posture implies he won't be doing so any time soon.

Earlier his parents were full of advice and commiseration when he walked in, in what his mother called "a pout," but the hours have gone by and they are now sitting on the couch watching a reality tv show they know he hates, in what he assumes is an attempt to get him to leave. Or otherwise simply a complete disregard for his feelings.

He was right on the first guess. Louise and Matthew Drummer adore their son. He was their only child and thus doted on far more than he really should have been. Nevertheless, they raised him to be a strong, independent, intelligent human being, so they think. And they are of the opinion that he knows what to do but wants to be pitied. Since that isn't either of their styles of parenting, they are quite pointedly trying to get him to leave. It isn't working. Some children will hang onto their parent's ankles forever, waiting for a pity party. *Wink.

Jack isn't waiting for a pity party. He just...he doesn't want to leave. He feels like if he leaves before it is so late that he can't do anything but make it home to bed, it would be as if he didn't need to spend his whole day here. And...he did.

All last week he hung out with Gabriella and Maria, enjoying their *sister world* and all their sweet holiday traditions, and it made him miss doing things with his family. He hangs out with cousins, aunts, uncles, and grandparents for most major holidays, but those are single days. With Gabriella and Maria, Christmas really is a whole *season* a build-up, not just a single loud, sometimes fun, sometimes annoying day.

It has been so long since he's spent time doing Christmasy things with his parents. After he finished the project, he talked about all of Gabriella's winter games, and his mom dug out an old album. Laughing, she showed Jack a picture of him and his cousin Mark when they were about seven, wearing mittens and covered in hot chocolate. Turns out he had played the game before. He just didn't remember it. Both his parents laughed over his awful/wonderful date and the sea of small children out of school. And his parents let him go through some of the family ornaments and choose some to take home. His father practically dumped a whole box of old lights, tangled and different styles, on Jack. It felt a bit like being handed a box of trash he wanted to get rid of because it was, but it also made Jack a bit happy to have them. He needed to spend the day here. But that doesn't mean he needs to be there still. But he doesn't know how to leave.

Jack is slowly but surely beginning to grow invested in the reality tv show. A man among the contestants keeps picking on this one girl, stealing her things, embarrassing her, and making faces about her to the camera. Jack's mother hates him, and his father thinks he's a jerk. And honestly, Jack can't say he's fond of the guy. But the longer he watches, the more he relates it to the documentary being shot in the office and wonders how he's going to come off in the film, what with stealing Gabriella's things, and fighting with her, embarrassing her.

Shit. He's been a jerk to her over and over. And today, he avoided her after being cold on Wednesday. She's got every right to get annoyed with him and decide she wants nothing to do with him.

As he's thinking, his phone dings.

Jack digs it out of his pocket and reads the text message. Super formal and entirely devoid of emoji, which is not what he would expect of Gabriella. And yet, it reads exactly like her.

Gabriella
Hi Jack,
I hope this doesn't wake you. I wanted you to
know I was thinking of you and wishing you
well. Missed you around here. Feel better.

Missed you around here. Jack is smiling softly as some of the tension unwinds inside him. His fingers scuttle away, responding.

Louise Drummer glances up, watching her son smile, totally absorbed in the text message. She is grinning as she elbows her husband two times to get his attention, *really, this man*. They both watch their son, Matthew, shrugging and rolling his eyes because it looks like he's lost the bet they made when Gabriella first friended Louise. Damnit, he's going to have to *pay* someone to do the gutters. Not that he really minds, but he's going to grumble all the same.

Jack
Who were today's winners? Did you
stump everyone?

Gabriella
Cory won the highest number of correct
guesses. And Michael won for stumping
people. Turns out he is a red belt in karate.
Everyone thought that was me. Weird?

Jack
Not weird at all. You are super scary. Hey,
you haven't set up the conference room
yet, have you?

Gabriella
Yeah. After work today, like we planned. Maria
helped me.

Jack
Sorry. I should have been there.

Gabriella
Hey, if you're sick. You're sick. It's better
that you take care of yourself.

Jack is a long time responding to that one. He has a feeling she knows perfectly well that he isn't sick. And that...*it's better that you take care of yourself,* that was a jab at him. Trying to make him feel like the dick he's being by not telling her what's wrong. He should apologize. He should explain why he wasn't there. Then the bubble of dots appears, and he has to wait to see what she'll say.

Gabriella
I am sorry if I made Wednesday harder for you.
I should have believed you when you said you
weren't feeling well. I thought you were angry.
And I couldn't tell if it was with me or
someone else. And I...fixated a little.
Sorry.

Well, fuck him. The first comment would have been a dig if it were him. But he has a feeling Gabriella is just nicer than him. She is literally texting to make him feel better. Apologizing for upsetting him when his unwillingness to talk to her about what was bothering him could possibly be called playing mind games.

Jack

You have no reason to be sorry.

I was upset. But NOT with you. I should have explained. You shouldn't have had to do the last few events without me.

Gabriella

Don't worry about it. It was supposed to be my assignment originally.

Jack

I'll worry if I want to.

I missed being pranked. What was today's prank?

Now it is Gabriella's turn to take her time answering. She is lying on the couch in her apartment, curled up in front of her Christmas tree alone, enjoying the lights and the memories. Maria encouraged her to text Jack earlier. Encouraged her not to let his being upset rule her moods. And she's glad she is texting and that he's responding. But it still bugs her that she's shared deep embarrassing, painful truths with him, but he won't share what is upsetting him. She knows he isn't sick. He hasn't even tried to lie about it again, which is something she supposes. But she doesn't want to pretend she isn't bothered and flirt with him about the pranks.

For the last half an hour, Gabriella has watched and rewatched the footage of Jack's failed proposal. She spent the first bit of time freezing over and over on the woman's face, zooming as best she could in the low-quality video. She's quite pretty. A big part of

Gabriella watches her in this clip and sort of despises her. She's pretty, and she's clearly loved by a guy Gabriella is, sort of, dating.

She didn't mean to. In fact, she quite specifically meant not to, but Gabriella has, over the last week, done a deep dive on the woman, finding out everything she can. And a number of things bother her now as she texts with Jack.

1. *Lauren* had worked at the same company as Jack when they dated. In different departments, he was IT, and she was a sort of middle management position overseeing a sales department. But still the same company. *Does Jack just like conveniently located women?*

2. They had lived together for a year before he proposed and dated for a while. So his proposal didn't come out of nowhere. He'd seriously planned a life with this woman. Gabriella had never been that serious with anyone. How long would it really take to get over something like that? *Was he over it?*

3. She was more similar to Jack. They shared social hobbies. They had all kinds of shared excursions like camping, hiking, a co-ed softball team, and parties. So many parties. She seemed fun and social, and basically everything Gabriella is not.

Gabriella and Jack don't make sense. Not the way Jack and Lauren had made sense. At least on paper. And if one watched the video closely, as Gabriella had several times. You could see that Lauren had felt terrible. She really cared for Jack. She was just a coward. As soon as the ring had shown up on her dessert plate, she'd looked shocked and sad. She reached out for Jack, whispering something, shaking her head. And...well, Gabriella didn't want to, but she got that. *Ugh.* The mere idea of a public proposal had every fiber of her being quivering in discomfort. He shouldn't have done it that way. Honestly, Gabriella wondered what would have happened if he had asked her privately. Would she have said no? Would she have said she needed a bit more time? Would he have listened and given it? Would Gabriella have met Jack at all?

Because Lauren didn't even leave at first, she looked horrified, but she smiled slightly, glancing around at everyone. Gabriella felt she might have said yes, were it not for a champagne cork popping somewhere out of shot and Lauren jumping. She hit the table and spilled drinks and a chocolate cake down Jack's back. And he fell back looking utterly lost and reached out for Lauren, and people started laughing so loud you couldn't hear what she was saying, and then she ran. Like really ran, and in high heels!

Gabriella would have tripped. Or, more likely, she would have frozen like a grandma in the blinking red light of Rudolph's nose, just frozen until someone found her body and called the paramedics.

The first few times watching the video all Gabriella thought about was Lauren. This other woman who Jack had cared about maybe still did. Then she'd started watching Jack. How cheerful and excited he'd looked. He'd laughed when Lauren's eyes had gone big and startled. He thought she was happy. He thought it was going to be the best night of his life. He'd been a believer. And she didn't think he was now. But he was still the nice guy who picked up the pair of champagne glasses that had fallen on him and sat down at the table staring out the open door where his girlfriend had run away.

When she'd started watching it, she was trying to decide if she should send it out. If she *wanted* to. She didn't think it was nearly as humiliating as she'd thought it was when she found it two weeks ago. But she supposed that was because she'd watched it so much, and other people would still find it hilarious and humiliating and never let Jack live it down. A nicer person wouldn't even consider sending it out.

But he is hiding again. And this time from her and she doesn't know why. She is trying not to press him. But here they are texting, and he is still hiding, and she can't see that she's done anything to alienate and embarrass him. If she is being punished for something, she wants it to at least be something that deserves punishment. So even as she texts, she clicks on the video again. She watches his humiliation and wonders if it might be good for him to face it. To have to see it again. He just runs and hides when things get uncomfortable, just like his not-fiancee had. Maybe if he has to face it, he will come out stronger.

Here he is asking about being pranked. Asking for her to play a game with him. But it isn't just a game for her. It was always about teaching him a lesson. Gabriella *isn't* fun. She isn't easy-going. She is intense and unable to avoid the darkness in life. It isn't just a game. But—she *wants* it to be. Taking a deep breath, she tries to find a middle ground between demanding an explanation and pretending everything is fine.

Jack is waiting for that bubble to appear. Maybe she fell asleep. Or got distracted or doesn't want to respond at all. The bubbles appear.

It should be something scathing about wanting to know why he was angry. Something about him messing with her mind by lying and saying nothing is wrong. Something...

Gabriella
You snooze. You lose.
Don't snooze tomorrow, or you'll miss
the big finish.

Jack smiles. That may be the meanest she gets. She's such a softy. There is a lot more to say. And he's not entirely sure how, but he has a feeling he's been forgiven. When he didn't even do anything to deserve her forgiveness. His mother was right, he should have talked to her from the beginning.

Jack
Won't snooze. I promise. I'll be there.

She seems to have nothing to say to that. Not even thought bubbles. But he has a feeling she is thinking. If there is one thing Gabriella can be counted on to do all day, every day, it's think.

Jack
I'm serious. I'll be there.

I missed you today, Gabriella.

Three little dots. Seven little heartbeats and one held breath later—Gabriella replies—with exactly the words he wanted to see.

Gabriella
I missed you too.

Jack
Night, Gabriella.

Gabriella
Goodnight, Jack.

O' Christmas Lights Like Memories Aglow

O n the twelfth day of Christmas, well, the twelfth day of the My Best Friend Doll Company's Secret Santa events that is, and more specifically, Friday, December twenty-first, Gabriella finds herself bright and early in the conference room that will be used for the party, putting the finishing touches on the decorations. It is a huge room on the corporate floor. If she does say so herself, it looks spectacular. It is not just the decorations. There is a special twinkle to the lights and a very un-SoCal-like chill in the air, and the lovely scent of hot cocoa and cookies though none of the food has arrived. It is magical, exactly how Gabriella imagined it.

Kristen emailed her the night before and asked to get some footage in the room before the party and interview her a bit about the end of the event. Gabriella was oddly touched by the respectfulness of Kristen's request. A few weeks ago, Kristen would have demanded or steamrolled Gabriella's feelings, but Gabriella supposes the way she broke off their last interview has left the whole documentary crew worried for her. She hasn't sat for an interview since Wednesday. But the thing is, as uncomfortable as she felt at that moment, it wasn't weakness that had her leaving that chair. It was the boundaries she's spent years learning to develop.

It was the certainty that staying in the chair and fixating on... anything would be the weakness. Not standing up and walking out of the room and addressing her issues herself in her way.

Still and all, she can't expect everyone to understand that. It's good enough that she knows it herself.

So here she stands, under the array of paper snowflakes and frosted windowpanes with twinkle lights or painted decorations strung from the ceiling. And bouquets made out of the hot chocolate-stained mittens on the different tables. There are blown-up photos of the gingerbread houses and different contests on the walls. A few tables are set up with crafting supplies. One of particularly creepy interest to the camera crew is an array of doll parts and clothes, as well as a bit of crafting supplies, with a sign that reads, Misfit Doll Making Contest: no ordinary dolls shall win. Another table has boxes of donut holes, toothpicks, and tubes of colorful frosting. Its sign reads Snowman Building Contest. There is a table with supplies to make snowflakes and a toddler pool full of pillow stuffing with a sign that instructs one to: Find the White Ribbon in the Snowbank.

When Terrance finishes getting B roll, they line up a shot of Gabriella underneath the snow, with a snowball fight photo on the wall behind her. Gabriella is all decked out in her wintery finest. A blue dress with silver snowflake patterned stalkings, and a white cardigan dotted with fake pearls. She is also wearing a pair of elf ears, a red and white Santa hat, and jingling bell earrings.

"So, everything is looking good, Gabriella. Tell us about the party, any last-minute needs? Do you feel confident about it? Your general mood." Kristen prompts.

"Everything is set up and ready for the party!" Gabriella says brightly. "The food arrives at two-thirty and the guests a half an hour later. Then the magic starts!" Her eyes twinkle, and for a moment, even the most cynical of hearts might truly believe in magic, especially when observing her wonder as she looks around and all she's done.

"I fell asleep last night in front of my Christmas tree. And something about going to sleep and waking up with those lights glowing like memories of Christmases past," she shrugs, smiling, "it made me wake up happy. I don't know how to explain it. Whenever I sit alone in front of our Christmas tree, I feel the love, fun, and safety of our past Christmases flooding back to me. We struggled financially when I was younger. But at Christmas, something magical happened. The world got slower, and everything was lit up, and against all odds, there were always presents under the tree." She smiles, caught up in her bright, peaceful thoughts.

Her own laughter breaks the silent bubble. "When I got older, I solved that magical mystery." She quirks a brow. "The presents came from charity or Mom's friends, or her skimping on bills. For a while, after I realized that, I felt really bad about it. Sorry for even asking for presents and embarrassed for her and me, and sad for how she must have felt about it. But recently, I realized there was nothing to feel bad about. My mother gave me this amazing gift, and it wasn't anything under that tree. It was giving me faith in the impossible and the magical in the world. I have that. I'll always have that."

The doc crew is silent, but their brains are all uniquely inspired by Gabriella's words. Two weeks ago, Kristen would have vomited. One week ago, she would at least have rolled her eyes. But today she feels tempted to try it. To fall asleep in front of her own tree and see if it revives happy memories for her as well. Terrance isn't quite that moved, but he is touched by Gabriella's journey. He is certain any viewer of their piece would be too. On the other hand, Andrew has been contemplating Gabriella's tiny apartment and that giant tree taking up so much space and coming to life as she sleeps, with arms of needles and ornaments for eyes and a mouth of glowing lights to devour helpless Gabriella.

Kristen, entirely unaware of Andrews's truly disturbing musings, smiles calmly and professionally. "Would now be an okay time to ask you about Jack?" At Gabriella's nod, Kristen continues. "You seemed a bit upset with him Wednesday, and he wasn't at work yesterday. How do you feel about that?"

"I'm not angry with Jack. I'm still a bit worried about him. We texted some yesterday, and I am still very sure there is something bothering him. But I have to trust him to tell me what it is in his own time. And anyway, I believe in the impossible enough for twenty people, apparently. So I can give him the space he needs. I didn't really see how nice of a guy he was until these past two weeks. Now that I have, I can't abandon that new understanding because he's being grouchy. Even if our relationship never goes beyond this, I'll be lucky to have met him. Mom was a big believer in people coming into your life at the right moment and helping you change things for the better. I hope we can be that for each other. Not just him for me. Because he deserves to believe in magic."

"So what does that mean about his pranking? And level twelve? Is he safe from pranks today? Or are we finally going to see that video?"

"Oh, he's still getting pranked!" Gabriella laughs, rolling her eyes. "I'm just not going to be angry with him while I'm doing it. He needs to be pranked if for no reason but the pouting. No. He's not getting off that easy. I've told you already. I'm no pushover."

The Little Drummer Boy

By the time Jack Drummer arrives at the office, Gabriella is already hard at work at her desk with her headphones on, dancing to the beat and singing along under her breath to "Run, Run Rudolph."

She sings, oblivious to her audience, as Jack stops just outside of his cubicle to watch and smile. He is carrying a large package, gift-wrapped, and wearing an unusually cheery sweater. A red and white number with knitted reindeer and snowflakes. He is tempted to walk to her and make her open the present right now, in front of him.

But as he watches her bobbing and typing away, though what she can possibly have found to do he cannot say, he realizes that the gift would be so much more fun for her if it arrived magically.

He is all set to go hide the gift when he spots a small bag outside of his desk. Ducking into the cubicle, before Gabriella can see him, Jack sets down his package and reaches around the cubicle wall for the bag.

There is a cute note with a smiling snowman drawn onto it that he can tell from the style was not done by Maria. This is all Gabriella.

He made me think of you.

The note says. Nothing else, not even her name. But Jack knows who this is from. He reaches in, pulling away tissue paper to find a wind-up tin soldier with a drum.

Jack chuckles quietly and sets it in a place of honor, on his desk, right beside the phone where he'll see it most. Jack smiles at it briefly before grabbing his box, glancing around like a thief in a children's cartoon, and sneaking out of his cubicle in a crouch.

He doesn't think he can wait for the elevator and not be seen, so he darts away to the stairwell, unaware that the camera crew is following him in a much less circumspect manner.

Everyone makes it into the stairwell unnoticed by Gabriella, who is not working at all, but putting the final touches on an email she is about to send out company-wide. She has a weird little shiver race down her spine like she is being watched and looks up. She sees only Michael on his way out of the break room with a cup of coffee in hand. They nod at one another. No words are exchanged, and they return to their respective tasks.

Meanwhile, in the stairwell, Jack has been caught by the film crew and trapped in a quick interview.

"Jack, don't you look well," Kristen says with a very meaningful smile. "Much recovered, are you?"

"I took a personal day, not a sick day. I had a project to finish," Jack returns just short of snidely. "Now that it's ready, all it needs is a magical delivery suited to Santa out there."

"Did Gabriella know you weren't sick?" Kristen asks coyly.

Jack shrugs. "Don't know."

Kristen chuckles. "Oh, you don't know, hmmm? Don't the two of you talk outside of work? Or was your one date all the dates you're going to have?"

Jack raises a brow. He is weirdly disturbed now by the invasion into his private life when he wasn't bothered by Kristen before. But she looks so smug. Like she thinks she knows something he doesn't know.

"We talk. And we date. But not for cameras."

Kristen chuckles softly. "So, today is the big day. Are you scared?"

"About what?" Jack asks obliviously.

"This is when she is supposed to release the video of you, right? The one you said she could release. Are you prepared for your coworker's reactions? Have you sent out resumes? What's your plan?"

Jack laughs, shaking his head. "She's not going to release that video."

"Are you sure? I know she plans to prank you today. And the last time you two were together, it wasn't looking exactly friendly."

"She's not going to release that video. She's...too nice. You've been following her around with that camera for weeks. How have you failed to understand her? She would never."

"So confident? Good for you." Kristen says with those sly eyes like she's trying to instigate something. It reminds Jack of his parents' annoying reality show last night. He'd bet Kristen could get a job producing for that tomorrow if she wanted. "So, what do you think the prank will be?"

Jack shrugs. Suddenly a bit uncomfortable. He doesn't think Gabriella will release it. He didn't even believe it when she first said it. She's too nice to do that. But...what if he is wrong? No. This is just Kristen trying to instigate a fight to add drama to her film. He knows Gabriella.

"I don't know," he says bravely. "That's the fun of it, isn't it? The surprise."

Little does he know that Gabriella has a wide cruel streak and that Kristen really does know something he doesn't know.

"We'll see." Kristen grins.

When Jack has left the film crew behind and climbed a flight of stairs to take the elevator from the ground floor, Terrance finds himself turning the camera on Kristen for the first time. She looks different through the lens. Or maybe she looks different today. Still confident, still composed, still smug, but today there is an extra something. Tension, he realizes as she arches a brow but doesn't move another muscle. She's uncomfortable. Is it because the camera is pointed her way? Or something else?

"Why did you do that?" Terrance asks slowly. "You know as well as anyone she won't release that clip?"

Kristen notches her head aside for half a second, then grins.

"Guys like him are always *so* confident, so *at ease*. He was a dick on Wednesday, and he walks in today, is given a gift, and has *no doubt* in his mind that he's *safe*." Kristen shakes her head, and her eyes narrow as the coldness that tends to characterize her transforms into a blade of rage. "Gabriella might not be a pushover, but she isn't a ball-buster either. And he deserved to have his jingle balls busted. Now he'll be uncomfortable, if only for a while. And anyway, it will make for such a better drama." She says the last bit in a tone Terrance used to find annoyingly smug. Now he realizes it was always covering for something. She isn't smug at all, is she?

Terrance is being a bit dramatic in his turnaround. Because Kristen is indeed *quite* smug, that doesn't mean she lacks vulnerabilities. She is confident, and she is brash. She is in-your-face style smug. But yes, underneath it all, she is just a bit uncomfortable, every minute of every day.

"Why don't I believe it has anything to do with the film?" Terrance asks softly.

Kristen laughs, about to hit the nail on the head with her comeback as usual. "Because you're a bit of a sentimentalist, and you don't *want* to believe it. Go on, boys," she says confidently, exiting the stairwell and waving the boys up the stairs. "I'm not our story. I teed him up for you. Go follow the little drummer boy."

One Lord A Leaping

At just exactly nine a.m. and eleven minutes, an email went out from the Secret Santa account to all My Best Friend Doll Company employees in Burbank, California. It was a short end-of-the-year email reminding employees of the time and location of the office party, with an attached video file. By the time Jack Drummer exits the elevator on the third floor, at nine-nineteen, the video has been viewed by about half the staff. Jokes are loudly being exchanged on every floor, and there is much joy and merrymaking to be had by all.

Jack notices the commotion upon exiting the elevator but does not immediately connect it with himself or his pranks with Gabriella.

"Who's the sender?" Hannah shouts from her desk. Immediately followed by, "Oh! I got it."

As Ed is answering, "the Secret Santa account."

"This is hilarious! I want this to be my new screen saver," Angelo comments with a laugh as he is watching the video for the fourth time.

Jack is headed toward the wrong conference room, unaware. He glances around curiously, but with all computers in the office having privacy screens, he cannot say what is so entertaining and is only mildly curious. Playing in the back of his mind, over and over, is Kristen's smug smile as she asked if he was sure Gabriella wouldn't release the clip.

He is sure! He assures himself, again and again. Something he would not need to do if that assertion entirely true.

There is a wild burst of laughter from Ed. Followed by, "poor Jack. It kills me every time! He's never going to live this down."

Jack freezes, staring at a small group crowded around Hannah's desk. He moves closer.

"Poor guy," Hannah remarks, with a bit of amusement in her voice. "He has that whole strong sil—Oh!" She startles, spotting Jack behind her. "Jack! Hi!"

Angelo hops up from his desk and crosses to Jack. "Hey, man. That is hilarious. You've got to have a good sense of humor to send out a clip like that yourself. Good one! It's by far my favorite Secret Santa gift."

"I didn't send you anything," Jack snaps. "I was never secret Santa."

"No? Oh!" Angelo glances around awkwardly. "Well, it's not so bad." He laughs slightly.

"Yeah. I love it when—"

But Jack doesn't wait around to hear what Hannah loves. Spinning away, he heads towards the stairwell at a rapid pace. He has a sort of angry buzzing in his ears. And he can't quite seem to form thoughts. All he really knows is that he's shocked and angry.

He feels even angrier when he opens the stairwell door to find Terrance and Andrew waiting for him. They had something to do with this. They knew it was going to happen. Even if Gabriella decided to release the video, Jack can't believe she would tell the documentary crew about it. Why would she?

The door to the stairwell hits Jack in the ass, not quite closing as he isn't fully over the threshold. Jack steps forward, glancing around, but smug Kristen is nowhere to be found. It's just the boys.

"I...I can't believe she released the clip," Jack says without meaning to. Looking at Terrance, who he is sure would agree Gabriella is too nice to have done this. "If she still felt that upset,

NICE TO BE SO NAUGHTY

what was the gift for? I know I told her to do it if she needed to."
Jack says, and the buzzing quiets in his ears. "I told her to do it if she
needed to." He repeats.

Maybe Kristen had nothing to do with it. Maybe it was Gabriella.
On Wednesday, when he hadn't talked to her about how upset he
was, she seemed pretty disturbed herself. He hadn't seen her clean
or organize so many files since the company first announced the
documentary crew was coming. He'd known she was upset. And
then he skipped work Thursday without really explaining. Maybe she
is that angry. It didn't seem like it, but...he told her she could release
the clip if she needed to. Can he really take that back because he
feels uncomfortable now?

Jack shifts his gaze directly into the camera lens. "I was so sure
she wouldn't." Jack breathes deeply, fiddling with the bow on his
present. "Maybe there really is no killing the ghosts. Sort of hoped
this would, though, but...I guess I should have gotten it to her
sooner."

Jack Drummer is not a man well accustomed to displeasure. He
has certainly experienced it from time to time. When Lauren
refused his proposal, knocked her drink onto him, and ran out of the
restaurant, leaving him with the mess and the embarrassment, Jack
experienced quite a bit of discomfort. He was angry and humiliated
in front of the staff, one of his friends who had been hiding at the
bar to record their proposal video, and by noon the next day,
everyone who had seen it on Facebook including strangers who his
so-called *friends* had shared the video with. By the end of the next
week, he was too embarrassed to go to work. Living in a hotel to
avoid Lauren and refusing to speak to anyone but his parents.

Looking back now, Jack was glad of three things from that day.
One that Lauren had said no. She hadn't dumped him. Just said no
to the proposal and ran out when she saw people recording. She'd
called right away, begged him to come home and talk to her, and told
him how sorry she was that she'd reacted so wildly. She hadn't
dumped him. He'd done that in the two weeks that followed, and all

without ever really listening to what she had been saying, that she wasn't ready. He should have listened. Standing in the stairwell holding the present he's made for Gabriella, Jack feels a bit bad for not hearing Lauren out, not because he wishes they were still together, but because he realizes that she very likely had ghosts of her own, that were roused by Jack's public, and apparently to her, surprise proposal.

The second thing he is glad of from that night are the words his mother said that he most certainly did not appreciate at the time. "If you were ready to marry her, then you should be ready to give her the chance to explain why she ran away. Even if it was humiliating and irked your pride." He hadn't talked to his mother for days after that. It was why he hadn't stayed at his parent's house. But she had a point. If you really care about someone, even when they hurt you, you at least hear them out. Not let them trample you or hurt you again and again, but give them enough faith to understand that everyone makes mistakes.

The third thing he's grateful for is the seven minutes he had to wait, with champagne on his suit, in a restaurant full of people on Valentine's dates, as the waiter got him his check and brought back his credit card. Seven minutes of humiliation, waiting. With his camera-wielding friend hiding at the bar, as if it was he who had been rejected. Whatever people think of the video now, it cannot be worse than it was then.

He is older. He is not the same oblivious optimist who thought he wanted to spend his life with a woman but hadn't discussed that with her at all! He knows he can face this day because that ghost, his ghost, while it has not been fully laid to rest, doesn't haunt him either.

As the initial anger passes, Jack realizes what he is feeling now is just sadness. And not for himself. He is embarrassed for himself. And sad that Gabriella doesn't like him more than she needs revenge. But he is more saddened by the idea that Gabriella might be right and there is no killing the ghost inside of her. She deserves to be free of them.

"Right," Jack says, to get himself moving. He needs to go hide this gift.

Jack climbs the next set of stairs, taking him to the corporate level. When he exits the stairwell, the usually fairly empty floor has three bodies crowded around a desk. Miriam and Daniel Burns are leaning around Mr. Coleman's secretary Debbie and laughing at something on her computer.

What is wrong with everyone anyway? It isn't a funny video. It should be a source of pity. Pity he doesn't want it, but why is it such a source of amusement?

Jack doesn't acknowledge any of them. Walking straight towards the conference room with the *Do Not Enter* sign on its door.

"Jack," Daniel calls out, laughing. "Great joke. That was epic!"

"Thanks," Jack says without slowing his pace at all and without his usual easy attitude.

"I loved that jump!" Miriam looks up from the screen, winking at him, playfully flirtatious. "You got a lot of height coming out of a chair that way."

Jack pauses. "What jump?"

"When you—" Daniel breaks off, imitating Jack jumping, and throws a file full of papers across Debbie's desk.

"Daniel!" Debbie exclaims, annoyed with the mess.

But Jack is too flummoxed to pay attention to the by-play. He didn't jump or throw anything in the proposal video.

"What the hell video is this?" Jack demands, crossing to them.

"May I?" Miriam asks Debbie and is ignored as the other woman continues gathering up Daniel's mess. Miriam takes the mouse anyway and motions Jack nearer. "Come have a look. I take it your pranks with Gabriella have taken on a new level of fun."

Jack notices that Debbie's computer, unlike every other he's seen today, has no privacy screen. He hasn't really been paying attention to what Miriam is saying, but a bit of it catches in his brain as he nears.

"You don't call her Gabby?"

"She asked us not to." Miriam shrugs and then grins lopsidedly. "Both when she first started working here and yesterday in a generally distributed email."

"My bet is there was a Gabby in her past she didn't like," Debbie remarks, making it clear she's at least partially paying attention to the conversation.

"How do you even know about the pranking?" Jack asks.

"Are you kidding? Aside from the Secret Santa games, it's literally all anyone will talk about. The *will they won't they* of it all."

Jack thinks he might be blushing. He is. Sparing him any more embarrassment, Miriam nods at the screen and clicks on the video.

As the video begins, without sound, it shows Jack looking up from his murder mystery to accept a package.

"Wait, she recorded that?" Jack says in shock. Surprised to hear a bit of laughter escape with the words.

Words scroll across the screen:

It's our last day together until 2019

In the video, Jack unwraps the present. When the lid flies off, he jumps away with a look that can only be described as pure terror on his face. It freezes with a terrified Jack in the air, and more words scroll across the screen.

But don't panic. Our work family will be together again soon.

It cuts to black, then photos from the various winter games float on and off the screen. Finally, it fades once more to a black screen with the company logo and the words: *Happy New Year!* And confetti rains across the screen.

Stepping back, Jack laughs. Really laughs. A suddenly released and slightly vindicated laugh. *She is too much.*

Honestly, this video might be more embarrassing than the proposal fail, so why isn't he bothered? He almost wants to hit play and watch it again. Gabriella Angelica Cruz is diabolical. How did she time her recording that well? How did he fail to notice his computer's camera turning itself on? How does she make him want to kiss her by embarrassing him in front of his coworkers?

But she does. There is no one like her.

"I ought to kill her," Jack tries to sound threatening but only laughs harder.

"Sure, *kill* her," Miriam says doubtfully. "That's what you want to do."

Jack laughs even more, winking at Miriam. He heads towards the closed conference room. "Thanks."

"Oh, Jack...um," Debbie begins, looking awkward. "Did you have a chance to work on that...file you needed my help with."

Jack smiles at Debbie's attempt to conceal that she is helping him print out a personal gift using the company printers while at the same time, not that subtly, encouraging him to fix the typos she found. Jack has indeed fixed the typos and made a few small adjustments to the story, so he nods.

"Yep, thank you. I will email it to you when I get back to my desk if that is okay."

"Um-hm," she says, nodding as if nothing unusual is happening. "I'll have August bring it down to you before the end of the day." She hides a delighted smile, pointing her face straight down at her desk. She is quite enjoying the intrigue of this secret project and getting to be a part of the cute office romance.

When Jack enters the conference room, with the camera crew close at his heels, he stops and looks around in wonder. It really looks magical. Wintery but warm. Childish and nostalgic. He could never have come up with something like this. Wouldn't have even thought to, but it's amazing. Jack glances over his shoulder at Terrance and nods at the ceiling. "I know I should feel bad for not helping her set all this up, but it's really amazing to see it all put together. She has a *next-level* brain. But it's hard to be jealous when she's always using it to do nice things for people."

Jack hides the package behind a blown-up picture of Carol, wild-eyed, throwing a bright pink snowball through the air. Only to realize he hasn't put any note on the box. He shouts out the open door.

"Hey, Daniel, bring me a sharpie and some post-its."

Daniel enters as instructed. "Wow. Did you do all this?" He demands in shock.

"*I'm not Santa,*" Jack says for what he is sure must be the hundredth time—math is not his forte—it is only the sixth time. "I never was. But I know who is."

Jack quickly scribbles a note and attaches the post-it to the package. As Daniel wanders around the room, looking at everything.

—*To Santa*
From the Christmas Ghosts

"You know— this has all been really special. Whoever planned all of this did a great job," Daniel remarks.

"She literally can't help herself," Jack mutters under his breath before crossing to Daniel to shoe him out of the room. "Come on. Out. You'll ruin the magic."

What are you doing New Year's Eve?

Fifteen minutes after ten o'clock, Gabriella looks around the basement to confirm that Jack has *still* not arrived. She is beginning to give up on his coming at all. She is tempted to take out her phone and text him. Maybe she should be worried. Maybe he is very ill. Maybe she's being a real dick assuming he was making it up. But she doesn't text. She is about to. Her phone is literally in her hand when she leans around her cubicle wall and spots the missing gift bag.

He must have come in at some point without her seeing. Where is he? Because he isn't at his desk when she stands to peek over their shared wall. Did he leave? Did he see the prank video and bale? She hadn't thought he would. It wasn't that embarrassing. And it wasn't as if she released the proposal video.

She knows he isn't exactly proud of being startled like that, but everyone gets startled, and...well, she wasn't thinking about embarrassing him when she released the clip. She was thinking about how cute Jack looked, leaping out of his chair. Wondering whether or not he would grin when he saw it. His grin that makes her pulse race and her mind empty. She'd been wondering when he would ask her out on another date or if she should do it. And where he would want to go on a date. He'd tried to make the perfect date for her. She should do the same for him.

But now, she stares at the empty spot where the bag once was and worries that she should text him. Maybe the video hurt him. Maybe he is really sensitive about jumping at sudden sounds. He has a right to be sensitive. She should text him.

But she doesn't. She sits at her desk, with her headphones blaring Christmas music, holding her phone and wondering if there is any point in texting him, if something as small as this sent him away without even confronting her. She sits at her desk, wondering if she should start bringing a book to work. But the answer to that was an obvious no.

Not only would it be a waste of company work hours. She also knows herself well enough to know that if she got really into the plot, even if she managed to put it down to answer tech calls, she would be only thirty percent focused, she would probably be snippy with people, and she might start actively rushing through tasks that required her attention just to get back to reading.

In short, she would obsess. As she is trying not to do now over Jack. And where Jack is. And if Jack hates her. And how she should fix things with Jack.

While she is morosely staring at her screen saver, the man on her mind has stepped off of the elevator with two-thirds of the doc crew at his heels. He crosses to her desk unnoticed, leans in so his head is beside hers, and even though he knows he probably shouldn't, he can't help it. He blows a puff of air against the side of her cheek, exposed by the headphones pushing her hair back.

Gabriella jumps out of her seat, screaming in shock, and throws off her headphones. Mariah Carey can be heard hitting an impossibly high note as the headphones strike the desk. Jack leans back and grins as she throws a hand over her chest.

"Jack!"

"I should have made a video of that and sent it to everyone."

Gabriella takes an extra set of seconds to calm her breathing. And swivels her mouse, turning off her music. Then she notches up her head challengingly. "Shoulda'. Woulda'. Coulda'. Didn't," she says and has to bite her tongue briefly to avoid apologizing. She isn't sorry. She isn't sorry. She *isn't*. She's just too conditioned to be nice to people.

"You going to pout about that now?" She asks.

Jack snorts, grinning. "You are a seriously mean woman, *Santa Claus*. No. I'm not going to pout. I actually thought it was cute if a bit embarrassing. People keep leapfrogging out of their desks when I walk by."

"So run away," Gabriella challenges softly, not wanting that at all but not sure if now is the moment to say that.

"You know tin is really heavy, and I couldn't leave without that guy." Jack nods playfully towards the tin soldier on his desk.

Gabriella doesn't move, watching Jack the way he is watching her. She's missed him being around, and it was only one day. And here he is, as playful as ever, and she wants to slide right back into the flirtation and live there, but she can't.

"Look, you don't have to tell me everything just because I did with you," Gabriella begins.

"Oh, you haven't even begun to tell me everything," Jack interrupts playfully.

Briefly thrown, Gabriella straightens. "The point is," she tries again slowly. "If you need space, I'll give it to you. But *please* say it. Maybe I'll be offended or disappointed, but I won't die from it. And I won't hound you if I know that's what is going on. I'm not fragile. I just have some... hang-ups," she finishes uncomfortably.

"Cute ones." Jack's smile is creating its own radiation. Waves of heat, light, and electricity drift off his lips to sink into Gabriella, killing her every thought. He gazes at her for several seconds until Gabriella feels a bit too breathless for comfort.

Then he drags his gaze away, his own breathing a bit forced, and his expression turns serious. "Look, I didn't know how to tell you how I felt until I worked it out myself. And I do want to talk to you about it. Later. When we aren't at work with a hundred monitor cameras that you could be sneakily using to record me."

"Then maybe we should do it at your place," Gabriella says, ever so slightly breathy but determined to return his teasing as good as it's been dished out. "I have lots of cameras in my apartment. You should see the stuff I have on you already."

"Do you really?" Jack takes a step back, his voice going up an octave, utterly appalled by the thought.

Gabriella giggles at Jack's horrified expression.

Off in the distance, watching, as usual, Kristen grins wide. *That a girl,* she thinks. Throwing a quick wink at Andrew since Terrance is all focused on the scene before them. Andrew bobs his head sideways, agreeing that Gabriella indeed got Jack good.

"I'm just messing with you," Gabriella says quietly.

"I sort of love it when you mess with me. I must have some hang-ups too." Jack quirks his head to the side.

"Cute ones," Gabriella mutters, grinning into her lap.

Jack lingers there, staring at Gabriella, staring into her lap, unsure how to end this. Why do they have to be at work anyway? He is contemplating some great ways to end this conversion, but none of them is appropriate for work.

"I should probably get some work done before the day is over."

"Probably."

"But we'll talk later."

"I'd like that," Gabriella agrees.

"Hey!" Jack smirks, not willing to leave yet. "What are you doing new years eve?"

Gabriella quirks a brow, her lips lifting into a tiny half grin. "Are you actually asking? Or throwing out song references?"

"I can do both."

Gabriella shrugs. "Not a thing. I'm usually in bed by nine-thirty."

Jack shakes his head. "Terrible. We'll have to come up with something to keep you awake."

Gabriella smiles with a tingle racing beneath her skin and holds her breath until he is out of sight, ducking back into his cubicle. Jack has been holding his breath as well. When he settles down in his seat, he's wearing a broad grin and humming to himself.

He really ought to work. If nothing else, he could update his resume. But he feels literally no motivation to do anything at all but run around his cubicle and grab Gabriella and drag her somewhere private to make out. But he also likes being here, on the opposite side of the cubicle wall, listening to her, trying to force her breathing back into a stable rhythm. He just needs to...do something to pull his focus. He emails his revised story to Debbie, but that takes a few seconds; as soon as it's done, Jack thinks of Gabriella again, her grin, her lips, the possibility of dragging her away. Ugh. He'll never make it through the day like this.

Entirely forgetting Wednesday's prank, Jack opens his altered murder mystery and forces his eyes to read.

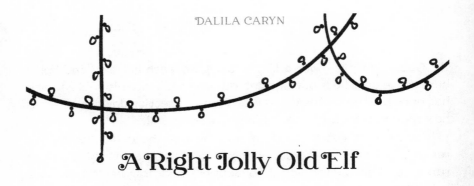

A Right Jolly Old Elf

The party later that evening is hands down the *best* Christmas party My Best Friend Doll Company ever had. Everyone agrees. Though...there was no mention of Christmas. The room is decorated as a winter wonderland. The memo inviting employees called it an end-of-the-year party, and all of the games, gifts, and decorations are merely winter-themed. It isn't until the end of the evening, as people are wandering out that anyone notices that there is no Christmas tree.

Kristen Kringle looks around the gathered employees and family members, the laughter and music, and can't think of a Christmas party she's liked better since she was a child. When a glance around the room shows her a surprise visitor, she doesn't feel her shoulders stiffening as she usually would, doesn't feel her smile glint with a touch of malice as it has in recent years. She feels oddly peaceful.

Her father, spotting her from across the room, walks over, stepping to the left of Terrance and Andrew recording from a corner to take in as much of the room at once as they can. Her father has his girlfriend of two years on his arm, looking about as engaged as a cat when petted. Not at all.

"Kristen," he says by way of greeting.

"Hello. Good to see you, June." Kristen lies. She can't imagine that anyone ever finds it good to see June. This June. Kristen is sure there are other Junes, worth knowing, the month at the very least.

But this June seems not to add anything to the air around her. So while it is never good to see her, it is never a great imposition either.

"I believe your film was supposed to have been done by now," Kristen's father, Don Kringle, remarks, eyeing the boys with camera equipment. He does hate to be caught on film. One would almost suspect him of being a vampire. In reality, the mere idea that someone might record him, or honestly, see him, is what has him stiffening.

Kristen has spent her life observing this phenomenon from her father. The stiff way he greets any part of the world but his own personal home. It used to enrage her. She used to fight with all her might to shake his cool just a little. But today, as she looks at him, she hears Gabriella's voice: *I begin to think you guys are really disruptive to my ability to manage my anxieties... I'm just gonna go now.* She doubts anyone else will find it the same sort of credo she does. Well, that's not true. She can think of a cousin or two who could really use the same motivation that Kristen feels inside when she hears the words. The same comfort allows her to observe her father dispassionately and understand that while he is nothing she has ever wanted from him, he isn't evil. He's hiding from some demon of his own. It isn't her job to fix it for him, but nor does it need to rule her passions any longer.

"We are, for the most part," Kristen answers pleasantly. "But this was too lovely not to add to the footage, don't you think?" She doesn't wait for a response. "Terrance, Andrew, meet my father, Don Kringle, and his girlfriend June."

"Hello, sir." Terrance nods. Lowering the camera, he holds out his hand to shake the other man's.

Andrew, uninterested and unimpressed, just nods.

As Terrance glances away, he casts Kristen a look and mouths the word "father" with something akin to shock. She grins. She has a feeling she knows exactly what Terrance is thinking. It disturbs him to find her so formal with a family member. That he is appalled by how equally cold her father is. That his family is nothing like that, So few families are like any part of hers that she is well used to seeing these thoughts in the eyes of those around her. But usually, seeing them sets her off. And today, it merely amuses her.

"Have you met the woman responsible for all of this?" Kristen asks.

"Not as yet. About her." Father removes June's hand from his arm and merely nods away to dismiss her. Not for the first time, Kristen wonders if the woman is less of a girlfriend and more of a paid arm-piece because she just walks away without a word or a visible expression.

June Stringer is not a prostitute, as Kristen imagines. Nor is she Don Kringle's girlfriend. She is simply a long-time friend. Neither she nor Don are very fond of social occasions, and even less so of other people's questions and expectations. So they choose more often than not to spend time in the company of those who have no demands for emotional expression, each other. They can be very pleasant company when not in rooms like this, full of bodies and expectations and disappointments. But when they are here, they always afford the other the respect of asking nothing of one another. She does not mind at all being dismissed so he can chat with his daughter. Who she knows he loves, even if he cannot ever give her the expressions of love she seems so badly to need.

June has always felt a bit sorry for that, internally. It is unfortunate, she feels, that people who need physical expression and verbal affirmation are not all born into the same families, and people who require quiet support and nothing draining on them are not born into the same families.

Hers is an old lament and one never to be solved. But really, were everyone to keep strictly to people exactly like them, how dull this world would be.

Don Kringle leads his daughter away from the camera crew and out into the hall away from the party.

"There was a suggestion that you might be...unduly influencing the young lady."

Kristen laughs. She nods into the room at the families building snowmen out of donut holes and the toddlers searching piles of fluff or just throwing it in the air. And the teenagers make truly ugly dolls

"You think *I* inspired that?"

"I think your subject wound up with a check *against* her on grandpa's list for the first time in years. And some people are saying it is your influence."

"Grandpa?" Kristen asks, looking away from her father and feeling rather smug inside when she is meant to feel chastened. She is sure she knows the answer to her question: if Santa is the one saying such things. And anyway, Kristen has been watching Gabriella *very* closely, and that woman hasn't done a thing that Grandpa Claus would hold against her. If her father were a betting man, Kristen would wager him—and win— that it was Gabriella who made the mark against herself. She is still too hard on herself. But, she is also very powerful.

Don Kringle makes no response, which is a clear enough no for Kristen.

Kristen grins ever wider. "Let me guess, Uncle Coleman? He doesn't like that she was right and he isn't allowed to contradict her while she has the magic. He kept playing mind games with her to keep her from pushing."

Her father draws a deep breath through his nose. Don Kringle has never known how to handle his daughter. When she was little, her mother wrangled Kristen's wild moods. She used to joke that Kristen had to be a storm of energy and disaster as a balance for Don's calm. But the older Kristen gets, the less he understands her. Now it seems she is angry with him every time they meet before he says a word. And she always wants more of his energy than he is able to give. He hates it, but he has no idea how to repair it.

"Well, be sure you take the magic back before the party is over. We cannot have mortals running around with that sort of power for long."

"Naturally." Kristen smiles politely and moves around her father to rejoin the party. If she was in charge Kristen would let Gabriella keep the power all the time. More of the power even. After all, Kristen has never enjoyed the Christmas season more, never believed more in its magic and worth.

Christmas could use more Gabriella-type Santas.

Christmas Wrapping Up

The end-of-the-year party was not a dramatic affair. Just a bunch of families and friends playing weird winter-themed games. Over the course of the late afternoon and early evening party, the most rambunctious moments came in bursts and passed as quickly.

Jack Drummer garnered shouts of laughter from several spouses and coworkers when he reenacted his jump from the wildly popular new year email.

The five-year-old snowman judge made many hearts stop when he stuffed the winning snowman into his mouth without removing the toothpicks. He found all their reactions quite entertaining as he drew the pick out of his mouth without being injured. His family will want to keep an eye on it because he is not the first little boy to find nearly causing heart attacks in others to be a source of personal entertainment, and it rarely ends well.

Throughout much of the evening, Gabriella hung back at walls, just watching. Not because she feels uncomfortable joining in but because she almost prefers this.

"You gonna mingle at all?" Her sister pesters from her side.

"I like looking at them all from back here like a special new Christmas movie, just for me." Gabriella watches the smiles and the laughter and looks around at all she's helped to create and feels incredibly light, peaceful, and the tiniest bit vain. But she thinks it might be earned tonight.

"Wow." Maria rolls her eyes dramatically. "At least come make a donut hole snowman with me."

"You just wanna eat the donuts and frosting," Gabriella mutters.

"Yeah!" Maria confirms. "The whole reason they're here is that you want to too. Come on."

Gabriella lets her sister drag her away, laughing.

At the same moment, outside the conference room, standing in front of the company logo, Frank magnanimously submits himself to one more interview.

"How are Carol and I now?" He repeats Kristen's question and rolls his eyes, but without any anger fueling his response for once. "We're fine. New year, new attitude." He glances over his shoulder towards the party. "I haven't done fun things like this with Linda since she got sick. We should do more of it. She's really enjoying herself. All thanks to a weird genius Santa."

Before he rejoins the party, but after Terrance has turned off the camera, Frank approaches Kristen.

"I...I didn't put together who you were until I saw you with your father tonight." Frank says a bit hesitantly. Kristen smiles blandly, waiting to see what is so special about being Don Kringle's daughter.

"Your mother always called you Poppy when she brought you to work with her," Frank says with a softer smile than usual. Kristen's breath catches.

"Come on, Poppy the pest, help Mommy makes some dolls today."

"Not everyone in there was here when your mother was COO. But everyone who worked with her remembers her well. Your mother was a lovely woman, and we miss her."

"Me too," Kristen admits quietly, with a nearly teary laugh. "I'm surprised you remember me. Poppy the pest is what Mom would call me when I'd gotten in trouble, and she brought me with her to keep me out of my father's way."

Frank laughs. "You know, it's changed a great deal from the original design, but your mother wanted Krissy designed after you. You should go to the museum if you haven't. Her original design is framed at the far end. I think...she would be very proud of you for pursuing your dreams. Anyway..." Frank says awkwardly, unsure how to end this conversation. "I'm glad I got to see you all grown up." He nods once and heads back into the party, leaving Kristen alone with the boys.

"Krissy, the Christmas doll is designed after you?" Terrance asks playfully because he sees Kristen is ready to cry and knows she hates that.

"I was an adorable child." She winks, flatly ignoring the heavier subject. But inside her heart is warm with tears and memories.

Back at the party, Carol watches horrified as her daughter Jewel, with great zeal and rather frightening instincts, builds a doll from random discarded doll bits. It has two heads and, so far, three arms. Also four random fingers, one toe decorating its bald head like a crown, and thus far, no legs. This is the least Christmasy thing Carol has ever seen, and if it weren't for the fact that her daughter seems to be having the time of her life, laughing with John, Frank's son, who is making an equally grotesque monstrosity, she would drag her away.

"Ohhh. You're gonna sleep with both eyes open tonight if that thing comes home with her," Maya remarks over Carol's shoulder with a chuckle.

"No, that thing isn't getting into my house. It wasn't like that, the holes where the eyes should be. When she picked that doll's head up, it had eyes. Jewel plucked them out. I may never sleep again."

"Eh. She's just flirting with John, seeing who can make theirs the creepiest. I wouldn't worry...much!" The women, who have never been close, and really are not now either, exchange glances and crack up.

Her daughter may be flirting, but Carol thinks she'll keep the lights on in her room tonight just the same. Maybe for the next several nights.

A little later, the doc crew urges Angelo outside for his last interview.

"How did Secret Santa work this year?" Angelo repeats the question he's been asked. "It was terrific. The games were great, and everyone was nicer. I don't think there will be any topping it next year." He pauses for a laugh. "Although I still maintain Ed and I deserved thanks for those awesome supplies we stole for everyone."

Even bah humbug himself, Mr. Coleman, makes an appearance at the party. His eyes trail around the room, taking in the decor with inner delight. Being Santa's younger brother *Mr. Coleman* has been forced to endure too many Christmases to care about them any longer. And running his great, great, great, great, not so great to hang out with, nephew's doll company has never made that any less apparent. Christmas isn't a day for him; it isn't even a season. It's an unfortunate, year-round focus. But he has to admit (to himself and only himself) that he quite liked this year's office function. It almost makes him happy that his plan to get the family sued last year didn't work.

Ah well, he'll have to find another way to get fired from the doll company. Why can't they make something bland and entirely un-Christmasy, like dish soap or plastic wrap? Nevertheless, he must maintain appearances, walking among the underlings, pretending distaste for the festivities, although he really wants to make one of those *demon dolls* all the teenagers are making. They crossed out the misfit dolls sign and made it their own.

A group of employees tries to engage him in a conversation about this year's Secret Santa. Trying to thank him for it and only slightly pulling his attention from the doll that boy is making with a head at each end of its body and limbs stuck into holes, he's clearly cut himself. Mr. Coleman pretends to be listening. Nodding along to something about this being a real team-building experience. Who cares?

"Yes. Wonderful. Don't think we've gotten complaints about anything at all this year," he says, barely managing to conceal his displeasure.

"No!" Daniel Burns says in an unusually high voice. "None at all. Your Secret Santa strategy has been a real hit."

There is a chorus of agreement from the staff members Mr. Coleman hasn't looked at and likely wouldn't have recognized anyway. And he nods kindly to show he is listening when he is quite engaged watching that teenager cut a hole in the back of the doll's body to give it an additional head. *Hideous!* Maybe if he suggests a line of demon dolls, he'll get the boot from this company.

Daniel Burns, having noticed a number of other people being pulled outside for interviews. And not wanting to be left out as it seems they intended, invites himself out. Kristen is not there to ask questions, having slipped away to the museum, but Daniel is undeterred. After all, he has something worth saying, he thinks.

"We got a few complaints. We always get a few complaints. Mostly petty stuff. A few people were having their lunches stolen out of office fridges. And there were three anonymous complaints about an employee's body odor. And one employee complained about another getting more management opportunities when they were both up for the same position. But overall, this year was much better than last, in my opinion. I can't say I loved being viciously pelted with syrupy snowballs, but it was in the name of fun, right?" He asks about the void that is the film crew.

Not one of them is going to answer. And certainly not, honestly. They couldn't tell the man that they knew a few people who were pelting him out of something more accurately described as resentment or total lack of respect.

The Woman with the Bag

The closest to explosive the party ever gets is while Kristen is away, having slipped off to explore the museum. Jack is entertaining Gabriella, Maria, Hannah, and Jay with the story of his second pranking of the day!

"So, I'm going along, caught up in the cat and mouse game with this serial killer—halfway convinced that it is this person who disappeared and stared the whole mystery— when Bam!" Jack claps his hands together dramatically. "Right in the middle of a murder, I'm reading the killer's confession. Because this diabolical monster," Jack says with wildfire eyes, all for Gabriella. "Has very precisely cut out a page and glued it into another's place.

Gabriella cannot repress either her giggles or her blush. "I told you about the prank on Wednesday," Gabriella says without an ounce of regret.

"I forgot!" You made me—"

"Hey, there are party crackers in here!" Matt exclaims from across the room.

Damnit. Gabriella flinches, and her whole attention shifts. It would be Matt if there is a bigger pest at this company she doesn't want to meet them. She specifically planned the party so the gift bags would be taken home to prevent management from being in the same room with her when people find the cash in the poppers.

Genius. But—apparently—not Matt-proof. A bunch of people have now grabbed their bags and are starting to open them, and

Coleman is still in the room, breathing down the necks of the teenagers at the demon doll station. And the CEO is here!

Jack watches Gabriella start forward tensely and begins to worry. He's stopped talking and can tell the others have noticed, but he's too focused on Gabriella to address it. What the hell did she put in those bags? He never even asked what the last gift would be, but he has a growing suspicion.

"Oh, but...they say to open at home," Gabriella tries to calm the crowd in a way that would make her secret identity quite obvious if anyone in her office were paying attention.

"No way! They're party poppers! The fun is in opening them at the party!" Cory says.

Angelo seems to agree as he's passing out bags to anyone who hasn't grabbed one. There is no slowing down this train.

Morosely Gabriella takes her own bag when it's handed to her and sinks back towards the wall. Jack notices Maria petting her sister's shoulder comfortingly as he takes his own. *Well, shit. It's the money, isn't it?*

Would you look at that—for perhaps the first time in this tale, Jack solved the mystery before it was laid out in front of him! He may be improving.

Following Gabriella, and even though he already thinks he knows and is correct in this instance, Jack asks, "what did you do?"

Gabriella shakes her head, watching her coworkers toss their bags to their feet and prepare to pop their crackers, and with them Gabriella's hold on her anxiety. Someone starts a countdown from five. Four. Three. Two. One! Poppers explode with tiny pops individually, but altogether quite the din. There is laughter and cheering, so it isn't strange that it takes a moment before anyone spots the—

"Cash!" Maya exclaims.

People all stoop for their own share, and the buoyancy of three seconds ago has dampened into shock. People look around at a loss, no one even pretending to steal anyone else's fifty. Carol is the first to find her voice.

"Wow. Mr. Coleman, this is...great! This year's whole event has been lovely."

"Absolutely, Thanks!" "Happy New Year!" All around the room, different people chime in, happy to spread their cheer. But a few sets of eyes do not look quite as pleased. Coleman looks positively glacial, his great nephew Mr. Kringle looks far from jolly, and Jack looks worried.

"Fuck, this isn't going to be good," Jack mutters.

"It's fine," Gabriella hisses in response, already on high alert. She doesn't need his fretting. "It was my decision. It will be my problem. I won't let it come back on you."

Mr. Coleman is shooting Gabriella, and Jack glares from across the room but is so inundated by well-wishers that he cannot get to them.

"They didn't *need* the money," Jack hisses. "And it isn't just your problem."

"They were supposed to open them at home." Gabriella defends herself. Though why she should need to, she can't say.

"That isn't the point; and you know it," Jack snaps. His brain is scrambling to think of a way to protect Gabriella since she clearly needs it. *Why couldn't she let this go?*

"Excuse me," a woman interrupts the pair softly. "Are you Gabriella? Mr. Kringle would like to speak to you in the hall."

"Oh." Gabriella nods. Well, if she's going to get fired, it is better to know it now. "Okay."

"I was a part of the party planning team!" Jack rushes out.

June Stringer patiently waits out Jack's hysterics. She nods softly. "Of course. But he only asked for Gabriella. Don't worry. He's house trained." She laughs at her own joke softly. "You know, *he doesn't bite*," she explains unnecessarily. They had failed to be amused because of fear, not a lack of understanding.

Jack swallows his fear watching Gabriella walk away. He wants to go with her, but Maria grabs his wrist, shaking her head.

"She's got this."

June leads Gabriella to the hall outside the conference room silently, which Gabriella appreciates. It gives her a chance to calm her racing heart. June is a very calming presence.

Okay, so she is going to have to defend herself. But Gabriella is prepared for that. She made the right call. And if they want to fire her for that, so be it. She is only slightly discomforted coming face to face with the company CEO. Don Kringle is not a warm sort of man. But, nor does he seem as austere as Mr. Coleman. He has the same sparkling skin and hooked ears as his daughter but does not seem to possess the light Gabriella has begun to see in her. Don seems unmoved by the world. *This is Kristen's father? That explains a lot, poor girl.*

"I understood that Mr. Coleman had rejected the idea of bonuses," Mr. Kringle begins. "Do you frequently decide you know better than your superiors?"

"He did reject my initial idea of bonuses," Gabriella agrees. "But I hadn't really considered that anyone would see giving people the last fifty I was to spend on gifts as a bonus. The value is the same as a gift."

"Ah, I see," Don Kringle remarks entirely without inflection, while internally, he thinks this is clearly Kristen's fault. That sounds exactly like something she would say.

And were he privy to Gabriella's thoughts, he might discover that she was indeed channeling his daughter's brash confidence. She doesn't need to defend her decision. It was the right one!

"Well, it went over well with the staff and was in the budget, so..." He stops speaking briefly, bobbing his head to the side. "My daughter sent several emails this past week about the amount of time, energy, and unpaid hours you spent on your special project. There were even threats of a report to OSHA with video evidence."

"I..." Gabriella is flummoxed. On the one hand, Kristen is so sweet, she could kiss the girl! On the other what the hell is she supposed to say to that? *Yes, I did work a ton of extra hours. Or, sir, I would never ask her to do that? Or...nothing.* Not a thing seems to be coming out of her mouth.

Don Kringle holds out an envelope before he is beset by this woman's flurry of emotions. "It's double time for all the extra hours, plus a small bonus. Kristen was right to demand it. You should have demanded it. Time has value."

June leans in to whisper as Gabriella is fighting her every instinct, which are all saying the same thing: *peek at the check. Peek at the check. Why the hell aren't you peeking at the check?*

"Oh, yes," Don Kringle sighs, put-upon. "And Mr. Drummer will be receiving a small bonus as well. You should—" he waves away dismissively, "—go enjoy the party."

Gabriella nods and goes away in a daze, finally peeking into the envelope.

Damn! Gabriella stops halfway into the room in shock. *Little bonus,* he'd said. She has to restrain her happy dance.

Jack crosses to her. "What happened? Are you in trouble?"

Gabriella shakes her head but cannot force out another word.

"What the hell?" Jack asks.

Gabriella looks up and grins, leaning near him. She whispers, "we got bonuses! I'll explain later, but...it's good. It's all good. Let's go get some cider."

Gabriella leads Jack to the refreshment table, but he still isn't convinced everything is okay. Coleman looks fairly grouchy. But Gabriella has slipped her hand in Jack's, and he follows where she leads. They pass Mr. Coleman on their way to refreshments. He pauses in front of them, making Jack nervous. Then he cracks a genuine smile and winks at Gabriella.

"Nice work, Miss Cruz." He nods and walks away.

Gabriella watches him go feeling weirdly tingly. He wore a rather jolly grin just then, almost Santa-like, and his skin sparkled, nearly glowed. As if he's been touched by— magic.

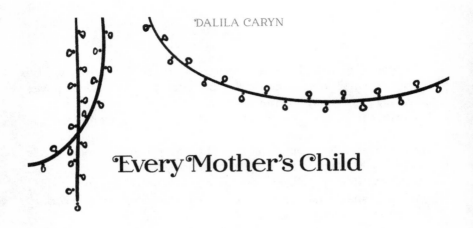

Every Mother's Child

Meanwhile, on the first floor, in the company's museum, Kristen wanders around the room, looking at the various designs. She remembers playing here with her mother and telling her the dolls needed better shoes. All of them with their fancy shoes. As a child, Kristen had loved galoshes best, loved to splash in a puddle and get dirty. Loved to be loud. Mom had started out as a doll designer, it's how she met Kristen's father, but he hated this company as much as Uncle Coleman, so he gave the day-to-day running over to Mom, and she loved it. She loved working with every department and loved continuing to put in her two cents about design while solving a problem in shipping. Mom was so happy here, and the company thrived. Now it is stalled, not bad, not good, just stuck.

Kristen could say the same about herself. Or she could have before she met Gabriella. When she makes it across the room to the original design for what is now Krissy the Christmas doll, she smiles, and a few tears slip down her cheeks.

She'd called her Poppy at first. The doll is wearing a bright orange dress like the color of her namesake flowers and red galoshes, holding a butterfly net in one hand and a camera in the other, with short messy hair under a baseball cap. Exactly how Kristen tried to dress for her first day of second grade, and the picture is right there in the frame to prove it, and...she doesn't remember doing it, but Kristen's name is signed at the bottom. Krissy Poppy Kringle, in wobbly letters and with backward s's. She sort of wishes they made that doll instead. But...as she runs a finger around the frame, she's glad this is still here. A memory of Mom even she had forgotten, but someone saved. A magical Christmas gift.

As she makes her way back to the elevator, Kristen wonders if Frank would have ever recognized her if not for this party. She wonders if she would ever have gone into the museum at all. She wonders if that magical power Gabriella was gifted with is really the magic she has or if there was something even more special inside her, fate-like in its power, that the Claus magic simply illuminated.

Kristen slips back into the party, unnoticed, or almost so. Terrance has set up a few cameras around the room but puts down the one he's carried up to now, crossing to the corner where Kristen is watching the party. He bumps shoulders with her as he settles in beside her.

"Where did your *father* get to?" Terrance asks, employing a sophisticated accent to properly mock Kristen.

The Kristen of two weeks ago would probably have returned the comment with a cool smile or total disregard. This Kristen chuckles.

"Ik heb geen idee," Kristen replies in Dutch with a sideways smile. "What's wrong with the word father?" She asks, still laughing.

"Nothing." Terrance shrugs. "But is it really what you call him?"

Kristen thinks about it, smirks and shrugs. "I don't usually give him a familial distinction at all. I just say hello. But yes, I suppose I call him father or my father if I refer to him."

"So when you called him up to ask for access to his company for the documentary, you said what? *Hello, I want you to use your company. This is Kristen Kringle, by the way?*"

Kristen bites her lip, unwillingly amused by the question. It should hurt. It would have in the past, but she keeps hearing Gabriella in her head, and it's a comfort.

"I sent an email." Kristen snorts. "But I do believe I signed it, Kristen Kringle."

Terrance laughs as if it is all just a story she is telling him to entertain. She is pleased that he doesn't try to comfort her or sympathize. He is a good friend, and she is glad she's gotten a chance to know him.

"Well..." Terrance stretches out the word after a few moments, then actually turns to face Kristen. "I didn't want to admit it before, but...you have good instincts. The piece is really coming together. You know, after you left the other night, I looked over that footage again."

Kristen raises a questioning brow. They reviewed a lot of footage, on a lot of nights. He needs to be more specific.

"Your idea of the empty chair for the ending, instead of something more uplifting."

Kristen straightens slightly, aware that her interest in his words is now physically apparent but unable to change that.

"I still don't know for sure. It feels like we'd need to recut some of the older stuff. Like we maybe have two fully separate films in this footage."

Kristen shakes her head, grinning smugly. "We have a hundred different films in this footage. It's all about choosing which part of it we frame. The inept company. The bickering employees. The people who feel excluded. The sweet romance. An office Secret Santa event. Or the lovely, good, quirky woman struggling to fit. We can tell any story we choose."

"How about the spoiled princess, finding a way to connect with the world."

Kristen chuckles hard. "Nah. Princess stuff, poor little rich girl stuff, it's all been done and done, and done to death."

"The point I was trying to make is...I like your idea. I just don't know that it's the safest path to that A you want."

"A we want." Kristen corrects Terrance with an eyebrow in the air. "And...maybe integrity and art and following where the lens leads us are more important."

"Who are you?" Terrance asks, utterly thrown by this new Kristen.

"I could tell you, but..."

"Then you'd have to kill me." Terrance rolls his eyes. But Kristen is already shaking her head.

"But puzzles are more rewarding when you solve them yourself." She winks when her flirty words leave him staring after her. Pleased with herself Kristen picks up the camera Terrance has left behind and follows the lens where it leads.

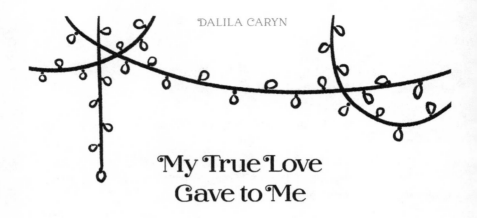

My True Love Gave to Me

As the party is winding down, everyone seems relaxed and happy. Gabriella is standing off in a corner watching the festivities, fully aware that she could join in more if she tried but very happy right where she is. She glances over to a side table as Angelo knocks a blown-up picture askew. It slides down the table onto the floor, and she notices a gift box she most certainly didn't put there when she set up the room.

She crosses silently to the table, avoiding touching anyone or disturbing their fun. She notices that Angelo has retrieved the fallen photo and *tossed* it *face-down* on the table. Well, at least no one will step on it now. When she reaches the table, Gabriella pulls the box towards her. A post-it note is stuck to the top with her name on it. Well, her nom de plume: Santa.

With a quiet mind, she carefully replaces the blown-up picture of a fury-eyed Carol throwing a snowball. She lifts the box and, with as much care as she crossed to the table, exits the conference room, heading to a table by the window between a pair of corporate offices.

Kristen notices Gabriella leaving, and so does Jack. Jack follows Gabriella. Kristen follows Jack, slipping silently into the hall and behind a desk with her camera like a good voyeur.

Gabriella, meanwhile, is oblivious to the parade of followers behind her. She sets the box down carefully and lifts the post-it.

Setting it gently aside so it won't get lost when she removes the paper. She supposes a to-from note isn't really the sort of thing most people feel a need to save—and she is right, most people do not. But as has been well established, Gabriella Anjelica Cruz isn't like most people, and that is a very good thing.

She removes the ribbon, lays it in a neat pile beside her, and lifts the lid to reveal *her nutcracker!*

Her nutcracker with a brand new, attached cracker arm. But there is something on the arm. She pulls it closer to examine it. Pictures! There are three little pictures on the arm. Two of her and mom, and one in the middle of Gabriella, Mom, and Maria in front of their Christmas tree. And under the arm, fancy scrolling gold letters spell out Christmas Past.

Gabriella is crying before she even realizes it. Her chest is burning, and she feels light. So light. As if the burning in her chest is a helium tank, her body has been transformed into a hot air balloon. She is lifting off the ground and floating into the sky. Every part of her hums with....peace.

She is so caught up in the beauty of the gift, and the feeling, which could really only be described as love, blooming inside her that she doesn't notice at all that she is being watched.

Behind her moving slowly, with his breath held, waiting, is Jack Drummer. His heart is tapping a frantic building rhythm. If Gabriella hadn't found the gift soon, he would have shoved it in her face. When the whole fiasco of the poppers happened, he was so stressed thinking they would get fired, and it would lessen the impact of the gift...he was annoyed and stressed out. But as the evening wore on and she still didn't find it, he got impatient in a different way. He is sure he never knew one could feel impatient for this part of Christmas morning, for watching someone else open the gift you've chosen for them. This is not, in fact, true. He has known this feeling at different moments in his life, but most of them, having been in his very young childhood, have long since faded into the back corners of his mind, where he allows the dust of living to collect. He has felt that joy over gifts to his parents and some to his grandparents. And once, not for a Christmas gift, but for a birthday present for his friend Reggie. But even were these dusty memories to be at the forefront of his mind, they would not, at this moment, eclipse the burning excitement and hope as he watches Gabriella's back.

This is special. It isn't only a gift. It's a beginning. A wildly important promise, an offer to see the beauty in ordinary things, to fix the things he breaks, and to accept the ghosts, good and bad, into his life. Gabriella might not see all of that in what he's done, but he hopes she will feel it as he does. It's fiery and bright, like a SoCal Christmas afternoon.

He hopes she can feel it.

When he finally makes it to her side, Gabriella tears her gaze off of the most beautiful thing she has ever been given and looks at Jack with tear streaks down her cheeks and an expression of awe and wonder on her lips. Her lips move to say something, but no sound comes out, and a few more tears crowd up her eyes. But Jack isn't worried. He knows these tears aren't sadness.

"I tried to age the photos a little so they'd fit in with the nutcracker's *well-loved sweater esthetic*," Jack says, his words an apology for the way he referred to the nutcracker in the past.

She gasps and makes what sounds like a word but might not have been. Her brain isn't functioning quite right. She is floating, on fire, yet entirely at peace. What use are words? Jack seems to understand, or at least pretends to do so.

"How did I get the pictures?" He says like he is asking for her, but there is a smile on his lips, and Gabriella's brain has departed, so it is quite clear this question is rhetorical.

"My mother is your Facebook friend."

At this, Gabriella manages a watery laugh.

"I tested it out with walnuts and pecans, so I know it works," Jack says a bit nervously. She won't speak. Gabriella is rarely this quiet. He can tell she likes it, but...he doesn't know what. Something is making him nervous. A knot is growing inside of his gut.

NICE TO BE SO NAUGHTY

"It's perfect," she finally manages to choke out, hugging the nutcracker to her chest. "Better than perfect."

"There is nothing better than perfect." Jack points out playfully.

Gabriella sets the nutcracker gently back into the box and turns fully to face Jack, already speaking. "I know you want to talk later, but," she steps even closer, "if you don't object, I think I really need to kiss you right now."

Jack beams. "No object—"

Gabriella's lips cut off the words as she grabs the back of his head and pulls their lips together, unable to go one moment more without touching him, without sharing some of the love inside her. She presses near and feels his arms slide around her back, holding her tight, as desperate as she is to be together. His arms around her ease some of that incendiary desperation and the kiss becomes a softer promise. She can't recall when a first kiss has ever felt this sweet.

Jack is thinking along similar lines. That this is the first first-kiss, he's ever had that hasn't felt awkward at all.

They are both a little breathless when they separate, but Jack is ready with a silly comment as usual.

"You stole my line."

Gabriella smirks, wildly confident and enticing. "You can ask me next time," she says in a kiss-warmed voice. "I promise to say yes." She bites her lip, nibbling on her grin as her mind is already laughing at the joke tickling the tip of her tongue. "I assume fear of rejection was why you haven't asked before now."

Jack laughs deep, shaking both their bodies as they are still held in each other's arms. "It was terrifying," he agrees. Jack loosens his arms around her back and slides his hand into hers.

"Let's go tell everyone who their Secret Santa was," Jack says excitedly, proud of all Gabriella's done and hungry to watch her bask in the praise.

"Don't you dare!" Gabriella yanks him back. "You'll ruin the magic. They didn't know who it was, so they embraced it. They made

377

friends and healed wounds. Leave it a magical mystery. They just needed a little magic to lighten their years."

Jack is dazed for fully nine seconds. He must be getting used to her; a few days ago, she would have shocked him for nearly twice that long. "You really are the sappiest girl in the world," Jack says in a tone that implies something is wrong with this, but his grin belies the tone. His face drifts slowly closer as if their eyes are magnets, and the pull simply cannot be resisted. "May I kiss you," he whispers.

Gabriella begins to nod, but before she's done more than dip her head, Jack's lips nip quickly at her own. They both laugh slightly, breathless for no reason but delight...and desire.

"Alright." Jack takes a deep breath, dragging himself away from Gabriella because this really isn't the moment to gobble her up. "At least join in the fun, Santa." He smirks and drags her away, laughing.

Gabriella manages to snag the nutcracker tight against her chest as they run off. And Jack is right. She is the sappiest girl in the world because as they run off, she is thinking how lovely it is that her Christmas present is named Christmas past and is very much a promise for something lovely waiting in Christmases future.

Epilogue
Which, for symmetry's sake, should be a few chapters back and about non-essential characters.
But it is what it is. *Wink.

As was stated at the start of this tale: this is the story of Gabriella Anjelica Cruz and the twenty-one days in which she became Santa Claus. But it is also the story of what that brief brush between magic and evil genius brought about in the world. So, for this pocket at the end of someone else's story, this moment is all about Kristen Poppy Kringle, or K-Pop as her cousin Misty had started calling her just before Misty's disappearance.

At this exact moment, seven-thirty p.m. on December twenty-third, Christmas Eve eve, Kristen is all alone in her apartment. She has been rewatching the final cut of her project. She still wanted to end with Gabriella walking away from their interview. But...she will admit now that she is alone, that she actually quite likes the magical, Christmasy ending they went with. Just a bunch of interviews cut together, some voicing over silent images of the staff laughing and working together through the different Secret Santa events. She has reached the final scene now and watches with a smile. It's such a sappy ending. She can't think why she likes it.

Miriam stands in front of the conference room.

MIRIAM(smirking)

How did Secret Santa work this year? It was lovely, really. I don't know when I've had this much fun at work. I was disappointed not to meet Santa Claus, but if this post-it I found is right. I(sing-song)saw Jack Drummer kissing Santa Claus. (laughs) How many people get to say that? (grins)

Cut to Jack standing outside the conference room.

JACK

How did secret Santa work out this year? Pretty fucking magical. (shakes head) I don't know yet if we managed to kill the ghosts, but I know I had a lot of fun being on the naughty list. I would definitely steal those reindeer again, given a chance. (winks) I love living on the wild side, so I'm going to have to keep finding ways to annoy Gabriella. I have a feeling I'm up to the challenge.

Cut to Gabriella outside the conference room.

GABRIELLA (smugly)

Does the clip still exist? Of course, the clip still exists. Nothing is ever erased from the internet. But as soon as I mentioned it, I knew you'd look for it, and that's *my* leverage. (winks) So I changed some keywords and titles and (beat) lost it a little. Now I've got it in the bank the next time he annoys me. And let's face it, he will.

Montage of Jack and Gabriella fighting over their cubicle wall.
Fade in on Gabriella in front of the conference room, cradling a nutcracker.

GABRIELLA

Did we kill the ghosts? I don't know. (Looks at nutcracker) I know I can still feel it breaking. But now (beat) *so much stronger than* I feel the break. I feel it healing. Maybe it was never a matter of killing the ghosts. Maybe it was about finding them a place to feel at home. And if they pop back up a while down the line and need retribution (shrugs), Jack has given me permission to do my worst.

Montage of Gabriella laughing maniacally over pranks.
Montage fades to silent clips of the Secret Santa event with Gabriella's voice overlayed.

GABRIELLA (Voice Over)

How did Secret Santa work this year? (Beat) I am really quite pleased with my tenure as Santa. I know I did my best to include everyone. I know not everybody got as much out of it as some people, but I don't think anyone felt excluded! And that was my gift to me. Getting to watch them all. Getting to make people happy. Getting to make the end of their year (beat) a little more magical.

The final shot slowly zooms in on Gabriella's smile as she watches her coworker at the party laughing and chatting together.

Fade out

It is now about half an hour after the film ended, and Kristen has assured herself, for the seventh time, that this is indeed an A-worthy assignment. But right now, she has other things on her mind. A confession, and a declaration in one, also if she can manage it, and let's face it, she can, also a sort of Christmas card.

Kristen Kringle sits forward on her couch, examining the angle she's set up for her recording. Her laptop camera is pointed at her ice blue walls and sheer white designer curtains held back at the side of her bay window, looking out over a flowering tree. Kristen sits on the window seat built into her bay window with on foot pulled up before her. She is wearing something her family has surely never seen her in, a pair of blue jeans and a tee shirt with a cartoon reindeer raising a brow and the word "sleigher" beneath her. The teeshirt was a gift from "Secret Santa." Gabriella left gifts for each of the film crew in their bags, so they didn't have to face her to say thank you. Kristen is rather fond of this tee shirt.

The setting is the perfect combination of her usual precision and her new ease. She's never imagined that ease might suit her, but it does. It doesn't make her any less bold or precise. Everything about this video is precise. It just isn't war any longer. It's a Christmas card. Not once in her life has she spent Christmas somewhere warm. The very idea was once offensive. She has always left whatever campus she was living on, returned to the frigid icy lands of home, and felt refreshed. But this year is different. This year will have no snow. No family. Nothing familiar. And she thinks she may have needed this for years.

Satisfied with the setup, Kristen clicks the record button and sits back, smiling at the camera.

"Merry Christmas, family!" She says brightly. "I am sending this video in leu of my person. Sorry, I won't make it home this year. I have sent gifts for everyone, and in a rare, perhaps never to be repeated exercise, they are all handmade," she pulls a shocked face and laughs slightly at the screen.

"I wanted to take this opportunity to say a few things. Firstly, Grandpa Claus, I want to thank you for this assignment truly. I know I wasn't positive about it to begin with. I didn't like your Gabriella Cruz when I read her file, and I saw no reason whatsoever for this gift. But I was wrong. She truly deserved it. I have never met someone who so fully embodies the spirit of Christmas, the hope, the joy, the warmth of gathering together and sharing love. So, thank you, she taught me a lot.

"Father and Uncle Coleman, I want to thank you again for how generous you were in helping me film my documentary in your company. I am certain to receive an A, but I will let you know when the grade comes through in the new year. One small note: if the true spirit of Christmas is wanting others to be happy, and that is our family business, don't you think that should include our family? Uncle Coleman is not happy running the doll company. I noticed it as we filmed. He is quite capable of the job and will continue to do it if we ask him to, but perhaps we should seek out a COO who loves the work, someone who is filled with the Christmas spirit just knowing what joy those dolls will bring. Someone who loves it, the way Mom did. Let me know if anyone is interested in my suggestions in that realm. I am sure you will not be surprised to learn that I have a list of prospective candidates. But that's for the new year."

Kristen pauses to consider her next words. Everything she has said so far she intended to say. Even the bit about her uncle. The documentary is finished cutting, and Kristen's coup has been left behind. She is saving that footage, using it to inform her own decisions because she has never much been able to influence the leaders in her family. There will still be bits of what Kristen would have highlighted apparent in the film. But by and large, it is now a love story. And not the one anyone, would expect. The blooming love between Jack and Gabriella has taken a back seat to the love between Gabriella and the role of Santa.

But now, Kristen is in uncharted territory. She could say a sweet farewell and share nothing else, but her tongue longs to share more of what she's learned and how she's changed. Maybe it won't affect the old guard in the family, but her generation will understand, and maybe even a few from the generation before hers.

"I won't make it home for Christmas because I was invited to a Christmas party, and I've decided to attend. You won't believe me," she chuckles. "But I am going to a party in the tiny two-bedroom apartment of Gabriella Cruz. She and her sister do their Christmas alone every year, and this year decided to invite some people over in the evening. They said there would be no gifts, just games, movies, and tamales. And it sounded lovely. If you'd told me two weeks ago that I would be accepting an invite from Santa's favorite, I would have rightly laughed in your face. But now it sounds like quite possibly the best Christmas of my adult life.

"Please do not take this poorly. I love you all. But I do think perhaps we are at times too close to the magic of Christmas and therefore fail to see that it is *magic*. I feel it near Gabriella, so I will embrace it this year, and embrace what we all tend to shun, a bright, sunny green and blue, and possibly purple too—Christmas.

"Merry Christmas, everyone." She leans forward, reaching out a hand to turn off the camera but stops suddenly, sitting up straight and pulling up her shoulders. "Oh, and Grandpa Claus, I didn't take it back. The magic. And...I won't be." She is quiet for a moment, then she smiles, looking fiery, intense, and joyful. "It belongs with her, with them. When Gabriella was gifted the magic, it didn't make her a monster of power. She glorified the power, spread it around, and *she made* that gift magic. It belongs with them because they can see the true power of Claus, the power to come together and make a brighter world. Please, leave it with her. See what the magic becomes in her hands."

"Right," she laughs. "Love you. See you in the new year."

There is not much to tell about the party a day later. Terrance and Kristen make it, along with Jack and Maria's school friends Rory and Alexandria. There is plenty of good food, a board game or two, and lots of laughter. The group watches *After The Thin Man,* the second movie in the series, because, as Maria put it, "you don't need to see them in the proper order to appreciate them."

"Except for the last two," Gabriella had argued.

Rather than admit her sister is right, Maria rolls her eyes and puts in the DVD. Kristen, who has actually seen all of the series, agrees with Gabriella, but she doesn't say anything, enjoying the sibling squabble.

Later, as the evening is winding down, Gabriella and Jack discuss co-creating a *Thin Man*-themed online interactive RPG murder mystery. Maria playfully teases her friends that it is time to leave before they are roped into the project as its artists, but nothing at all that definite is discussed, and most people just laugh at her comments.

There is really only one moment that needs to concern us. Just before she is about to leave, Kristen finds a tiny package sticking out of her purse and confronts Gabriella.

"You said no gifts!" Kristen says with her eyes narrowed into angry slits, offended to have been given a gift and not have one to give in return.

"That isn't from me," Gabriella insists, hands in the air. "Maybe Terrance."

Kristen shakes her head. They have already exchanged gift cards.

Gabriella smirks. "Maybe Santa left it."

Kristen rolls her eyes. About to say something quite snide about there being no way Grandpa would leave her gift here. Family gifts are all and only received at The North Pole.

"Well, go on. Open it, see what it is." Gabriella pushes.

Sighing, put-upon, as she is quite sure this is a gift from Gabriella and is trying in the back of her mind to think of anything in her purse she can give in exchange. The keys to her car, maybe.

But when she lifts the lid on the tiny box, she stares in absolute wonder. It's a golden medallion with the words North Pole Honor Roll engraved across it in scrolling letters.

Kristen has a sudden urge to hide the medallion, but Maria, having spotted it, comes over laughing before she can.

"Oh my gosh, you are so sappy. I can't believe you kept that." Maria rolls her eyes at Gabriella.

"Kept what?" Jack, who has been in the kitchen washing dishes, calls.

"I didn't," Gabriella insists. "I lost it, remember?"

"Right." Maria raises a brow.

"What is it?" Jack calls out again not one to be excluded, only child you recall. *Wink. Lest you think a miracle has occurred, Jack is only washing dishes in hopes of speeding along the evening to have alone time with Gabriella. He knows she will never relax enough to enjoy his company when there are dishes to be cleaned.

He and Gabriella exchanged gifts earlier, before the party. As suspected, she loved his murder mystery. Even suggested he pitch it as a companion to a doll. Jack is not exactly lacking in confidence, but he honestly thought she was teasing at first, but she is so insistent, and even Maria loved it, so Jack is now considering the idea. Gabriella's gift to him was a pair of tickets to one of those interactive dinner theater murder mysteries. When he asked if one of the tickets was for her, trying to playfully nudge her into asking him out, she blushed and stammered and assured him that he could take whoever he wanted. Though it seems Gabriella may still need some convincing, the answer to that is obvious. Jack wants Gabriella. He wants to spend all his time with her. He wants her to spend all her time with him. He is fully besotted.

He didn't even mind it when she totally embarrassed him, insisting on reading the story out loud, in front of everyone. And Gabriella roped Kristen into encouraging Jack to pitch the doll story companion idea at work. He would not have predicted Kristen and Gabriella being actual friends, but they seem to really like one another. It's sweet. Still, Jack is very impatient for everyone to be gone, so he can be alone with Gabriella.

Gabriella glances at Jack, blushing from embarrassment before she even sees the look in his eyes. "It's a pin. An honor roll pin." Gabriella mutters.

"Mom gave it to her one year, said Santa was *so proud,*" Maria says sarcastically. "Of how kind she was that she made the honor roll. Now she's passing it on to Kristen, sap."

"I didn't do it!" Gabriella shouts, with laughter in her voice. She drags her eyes away from Jack.

Kristen has remained silent, still in a state of shock. For one thing, she has seen these pins before. This is a genuine North Pole Honor Roll pin, formed from melted down sleigh bells and hand inspected by Santa. Holly wears hers around like a...*well, like an honor badge.* Which it is.

For another thing, Kristen knows that Gabriella has indeed received one. If this is hers, it should have the number twelve magically etched on the back to indicate how many years she's been on the honor roll. Kristen is itching to turn it over and see, but flipping it over to check with this audience would be weird.

But most of all, she is quiet because she can't think of a time in her life when she wanted one of these pins. But, with it in her palm, she realizes she may have always wanted one. And she doesn't know which would move her more, to have been given it by her great, great, great, great, great grandpa himself. Or to have been given it by this Santa Claus. But there really is only one way to end this poignant moment.

In a most uncharacteristic move, Kristen Poppy Kringle stretches her arms around Gabriella and pulls her into a tight hug. "Thank you," She whispers. "You really make an excellent and *much sexier* Santa Claus."

Maria laughs, Gabriella grins, Jack winks, and Kristen Kringle runs from the apartment in a moment of pure self-preservation. She flees with her heart burning in her chest and the pin held tight in her hand like the greatest treasure she's ever been given. Feeling changed and touched, and possibly nauseous. But also...happy. This has definitely been her best adult Christmas ever.

The Santa Claus of apartment three-hundred-and-seventeen, Gabriella Anjelica Cruz, watches Kristen go with a soft smile. She found the pin early this Christmas morning. It was on her dresser with a note beneath it, and next to a gift for Gabriella, the note read:

Thank you! I think you know where this belongs.
~ S.C.

And she did know. As soon as Gabriella held it, she knew this pin was for Kristen Poppy Kringle, who had at last learned to be kind to herself and, in the process, became kinder to others.

It was exciting, strange, and magical to feel with such certainty where that pin belonged and why. It was something she'd been feeling in smaller ways as she organized the Secret Santa events—and Jack's pranks. A kinship with people who were merely workmates in the past. Happiness that came from within.

Gabriella has always assumed that in order to be happy like other people, she would have to find a way to destroy those oh so different aspects of self that set her apart. Like her total recall of every time she has been touched, and the need to organize, clean, or punch her thigh in moments of stress. But these past two weeks have been full of punching, and cleaning. And these very new moments of noisily standing out. But she has been happy. It's magic.

And that extra special gift Santa left for her next to Kristen's is magic too. At first glance, it looked like an ordinary snow globe, aside from the bleeding snowman inside. But when she shook it up, the snow sparkled, and she could see different moments from the office Secret Santa in its light. And when she shook it a second time, she saw her sleigh ride with Jack. Shaking it a third time, she saw her hallway blizzard with Mom, and a forth showed when she got her own North Pole Honor Roll pin the first time. A magical orb of glowing memories.

It's lovely, but...she was even more pleased with the chance to give Kristen that pin. Or the letter that came for Maria offering her a job on the animation team for an upcoming movie, something Gabriella was certain Santa had sent to satisfy Gabriella's demand for something special for her sister. Magic, after all, is a gift that is best when shared.

Yes, indeed, Jack and Maria are right. Gabriella is *the sappiest girl in the world.* But she isn't bothered because she is also right. She has always been right. She always knew Santa was real.

Only this year, it seems, he needed a bit of Gabriella's sort of magic.

Thank you for reading
The first

Merely Mortal Men Myth

The series will continue.
Unless it doesn't.
*Wink!

ADDITIONAL (DEPRESSING) TITLES BY DALILA CARYN

The Forgotten Sister Series:
The Forgotten Sister
Future Queen
Armored Mage

The Liberator Saga:
Dust House And The West Wind

In The Shadow Of The Monster Trilogy:
The Battle For The Sky

Wait A Moment! Some Credit Where It's Due?

I would not be the author I am today if not for the movies, songs, and books that were directly referenced or paid homage in this novel. I thank them all!

A very special thank you goes to Turner Classic Movies and the fond memory of Robert Osborn for introducing me to a love for witty screwball comedy and the many hours of entertainment and aspiration during the sweltering SoCal summers of my youth.

Films, Movies, Television, and Plays:

And Then There Were None—Dudley Nichols (1945)

Call Me Claus—Sara Bernstein, Gregory Bernstein, and Brian Bird (2001)

Charade—Peter Stone and Marc Behm (1963)

Citizen Kane —Orson Welles, and Herman J. Mankiewicz (1941)

Family Matters— created by William Bickley and Michael Warren (1989)

Frosty the Snowman—Romeo Muller (1969)

Hamlet—William Shakespeare

Law & Order —created by Dick Wolf (1990)

Murder on the Orient Express—Paul Dehn (1974)

My Fair Lady —Alan Jay Lerner (1956, stage play)

My Favorite Wife— Leo McCarey, Samuel Spewack, Bella Spewack, Garson Kanin, and John *McClain* (1940)

Richard the Third—William Shakespeare

Scrooge—Noel Langley (1951)

Singing in the Rain— (1952) Adolph Green, and Betty Comden

Star Wars— George Lucas (1977)

Summer Stock—George Wells, and Sy Gomberg (1950)

The Nutcracker Ballet — adapted from short story *The Nutcracker and the Mouse King* - E.T.A. Hoffmann (1816)

The Thin Man (1934), *After The Thin Man* (1936), *Another Thin Man* (1939) — Albert Hackett and Frances Goodrich

Shadow of a Thin Man—Harry Kurnitz and Irving Brecher (1941)

The Thin Man Goes Home — Robert Riskin, and Dwight Taylor (1943)

Song of The Thin Man —Steve Fisher and Nat Perrin (1947)

Thoroughly Modern Milly —Richard Morris (adapted from the stage musical by Jeanine Tesori, lyrics by Dick Scanlan) (1967)

White Christmas—Norman Krasna, Norman Panama, and Melvin Frank, music and lyrics by Irving Berlin (1954)

It's A Wonderful Life—Frances Goodrich, Albert Hackett, and Frank Capra (1946)

Novels, literary characters, and children's stories:

A Christmas Carol— Charles Dickens

Alice's Adventures in Wonderland—Lewis Carroll

And Then There Were None—Agatha Christie

A Visit From St. Nicholas—Clement Moore

Encyclopedia Brown Mysteries—Donald J. Sobol

Harry Potter—J. K. Rowling

Hercule Poirot—Agatha Christie

How the Grinch Stole Christmas—Dr. Seuss

Life, The Universe, and Everything—Douglas Adams

Nate the Great—Marjorie Weinman Sharmat

Pierre: A Cautionary Tale in Five Chapters and a Prologue—Maurice Sendak

Pride and Prejudice —Jane Austen

Murder on the Orient Express —Agatha Christie

Sherlock Holmes Mysteries—Arthur Conan Doyle

The Hardy Boys—Edward Stratemeyer

The Lord of the Rings—J.R.R. Tolkien

The Maltese Falcon and Sam Spade—Dashiell Hammett

Thin Man—Dashiell Hammett

In the Bleak Midwinter —Christina Rossetti

The Polar Express—Chris Van Allsburg

The Works of Dalila Caryn—*Wink.

Songs:

"Alfie the Elf" — Wee Sing

"All I Want for Christmas is my Two Front Teeth"—Donald Yetter Gardner

"All I Want for Christmas is You" —Mariah Carey and Walter Afanasieff

"Blue Christmas"—Billy Hayes and Jay W. Johnson

"Chrissy the Christmas Mouse"—Filardi Louis S

"Christmas, Baby Please Come Home"— Jeff Barry, Ellie Greenwich, and Phil Spector.

"Christmas Wrapping" — Chris Butler

"Deck the Halls"—Thomas Oliphant

"(Everybody's Waitin' for) The Man with the Bag"—Irving Taylor, Dudley Brooks, and Hal Stanley

"Goody Goody Gumdrop" —Billy Carl, Jeffry Katz, Jerry Kasenetz, and Reid Whitelaw

"Hard Candy Christmas"—Carol Hall

"Have Yourself a Merry Little Christmas"—Hugh Martin and Ralph Blane

"Here Comes Santa Claus" —Gene Autry

"I Saw Mommy Kissing Santa Claus"—Tommie Connor

"It's a Marshmallow World" —Carl Sigman

"It's Beginning to look a lot like Christmas"—Meredith Wilson

"Happy Holiday" or "The Holiday Season"— Irving Berlin

"Jingle Bells" or "One Horse Open Sleigh" —James Lord Pierpont

"Last Christmas"—George Michael

"Let it Snow! Let it Snow! Let it Snow!"—Sammy Cahn

"Love, You Didn't Do Right By Me"—Irving Berlin

"It's Only A Paper Moon" or "If You Believed In Me" —Yip Harburg and Billy Rose.

"Rudolph the Red-Nosed Reindeer" —Johnny Marks

"Run Run Rudolph" —Chuck Berry, Johnny Marks, and M. Brodie

"Santa Baby"—Joan Javits and Philip Springer

"Santa Claus is Comin' to Town"—J. Fred Coots and Haven Gillespie

"Sisters"—Irving Berlin

"Sleigh Ride"—Mitchell Parish

"Snow"—Irving Berlin

"The Christmas Song"— Robert Wells and Mel Tormé.

"The Christmas Waltz"— Jule Styne / Sammy Cahn

"The Little Boy That Santa Claus Forgot"—Michael Carr, Tommie Connor, and Jimmy Leach

"The Little Drummer Boy"—Katherine Kennicott Davis

"The Twelve Days of Christmas" —Frederic Austin

"This Christmas" —Donny Hathaway and Nadine McKinnor

"Walking in a Winter Wonderland"—Richard Bernhard Smith

"We Need a Little Christmas"—Jerry Herman

"What Are You Doing New Year's Eve"—Frank Loesser

"Why Couldn't it be Christmas Every Day" —Jay Landers, and Walter Afanasieff

"You're a Mean one Mr. Grinch"—Theodor "Dr. Seuss" Geisel

"Kiss the Girl" —Howard Ashman

Several of these works were referenced more than once. Some are direct quotes, others were paraphrased, and a few are mere homages. Since I spent this book making up games, here is one I suggest to you, dear reader: find all of the references. I will post a key with page numbers of the specific references on my website, DalilaCaryn.com see how many answers you can get right. And if there is a film, song, or story you know nothing about, maybe check it out.

    *Wink.

Playlist:
The 25 Songs of Nice to be so Naughty

Songs referenced or quoted in the story:

1) **"It's Only A Paper Moon"** or "If You Believed In Me" —Natalie Cole

Okay this is not a Christmas song, but is one of my favorite songs of all time and is specifically referenced in the book. So if you haven't heard it I highly recommend it! There are lots of different versions but the Natalie Cole version is my favorite.

2) **"You're a Mean one Mr. Grinch"**—Lindsay Stirling

There are several great versions of this, but when I was writing I listened to the Lindsey Stirling version and wow!!! The violin adds so much! It's so fun. And was a huge inspiration when writing this book, I would frequently listen to it on a loop!

3) **"We Need a Little Christmas"**—Johnny Mathis

One of my favorite Christmas songs ever! I didn't know it was from a play until researching it for this book, so that is a tiny bit of my story that I added to Gabriella's. Cool, right? This is the first version I heard, so the one I go back to most.

4) **"Sleigh Ride"**—The Ronnettes

Another of my favorite Christmas songs! There are a million versions of this song but The Ronnettes have THE BEST version hands down. I will not hear any contradiction. *Wink.

5) **"(Everybody's Waitin' for) The Man with the Bag"**—Kay Starr

Big band fun! This song doesn't get enough love. I had to fight myself not to reference it more in the book but since it is not as well known as some Christmas songs I cut the chapter title "You'll Get Yours" which I thought was a lot of fun, but if one didn't know the song the title wouldn't sound at all Christmassy.

6) **"Let it Snow! Let it Snow! Let it Snow!"**—

Great song! Sweet song! Should be in more Christmas romances. Any version you like will do, but personally I tend to listen to either Dean Martin or Gloria Estefan. I love the trumpet riff in the middle of the Gloria Estefan version, and just her voice!

7) **"Walking in a Winter Wonderland"**—Darlene Love

This is a classic winter song. I sang it in school choir and I always loved that it isn't Christmas specific! I love any version of this song, but this is a particularly good one.

8) **"All I Want for Christmas is You"** —Mariah Carey
Her original mix is the best! But if you feel like arguing, fine, listen to your preferred (wrong) version.

9) **"Run Run Rudolph"** —Chuck Berry

Excellent song, high energy, lots of fun. I had this on my writing playlist twice, because I also love the Kelly Clarkson version. But all other versions can be ignored. *Wink.

10) **"Hard Candy Christmas"**—Dolly Parton

I actually never heard this song before writing this book, my sister recommended it to me and it grew into my heart and my story. Now I recommend it to you!

11) **"Christmas, Baby Please Come Home"**—Darlene Love

This is just generally a perfect song for a Christmas romance. And that voice—Wow! Love it.

12) **"Last Christmas"**—Wham!

I was not a fan of this song in the past, but when watching the movie, "Last Christmas" I developed an appreciation for a lot of Wham! songs. I really love it when that happens, and giving something (or someone) a second chance expands your world for the better.

13) **"Santa Baby"**—Ertha Kit

I have some very mixed feelings about this song. I love it, but...it also gives me some *ick!* vibes. But I can't stop listening. Also quite like the Arianna Grande version.

14)**"Sisters"**—Irving Berlin

I love the play this song comes from, "White Christmas." I watch the movie version every year with my family! It's one of the few classic musicals I can get my older sister into. If you haven't seen it, I highly recommend that you do. Love this song!!!

15) **"It's a Marshmallow World"** —Darlene Love

Fun winter song! There are a ton of great versions and all work, but this is the one I enjoy most!

16) **"It's Beginning to look a lot like Christmas"**— Perry Como and the Fontane Sisters with Mitchell Ayres & His Orchestra

This is the first version I heard and I love it. But any version you like will do.

17) **"The Twelve Days of Christmas"**—

Okay so...love to sing this song, but have rarely heard a recorded version that I like to hear more than once a year. That being said I do recommend the Natalie Cole version, she has a lot of fun with it, and pokes fun at the repetitive nature of the lyrics! It's great. If you know a version that you love, suggest it and I'll give it a shot!

18) **"This Christmas"** —Donny Hathaway

Perfect Christmas romance song!

19) **"Santa's Coming for Us"**—Sia

Love this song! So fun. I don't think it is intended to sound threatening, but that is definitely how I heard it. *Wink. So pleased that I found a way to reference it in the book.

Songs I suggest/ listened to while writing, that did not get specifically referenced:

20) **"Candy Cane Lane"**—Sia

"We'll eat candy caaaaaanes!" Such fun!

21) **"Wrapped in Red"**—Kelly Clarkson

Love this one it's a great taking a chance on love (at Christmas *wink) song. It is just perfect for a holiday romance!

22) **"Holly Jolly Christmas"** —Burl Ives

I suggest this version merely because it's the version I have heard the most.

23) **"Rockin' Around the Christmas Tree"**— Brenda Lee

Classic. You can't go wrong with this song. I love most versions, but this is a fun one that I've been hearing since I was a kid so it's the version I go to the most.

24) **"White Christmas"**—

Rarely heard a version I didn't like. Having said this, the versions I listen to the most are the Bing Crosby and Neil Diamond.

25) **"You Make It Feel Like Christmas"** — Neil Diamond

I love this song, it's a sweet loving song that goes so well with the themes of the book.

I hope you enjoyed the book, and the playlist. Much love and Merry Christmas!

Dalila Caryn

Dalila Caryn is not what anyone would call a mild lover of Christmas. Her urges to decorate, bake, and give gifts have been referred to as unstable. So it is unsurprising that her excessive love should be apparent when writing a Christmas novel. As should her boundless love of screwball comedies and a bit of witty banter. The author of fantasy novels from The Forgotten Sister series, The Liberator Saga, and the In The Shadow of a Monster trilogy, Caryn felt a deep need to faithfully present the magic of Christmas while still entertaining herself and, with any luck, her readers.
*Wink.
P.S. Caryn would like you to know that this reindeer in headlights shot is not her best photo, but she thought it might entertain.

p.p.s. are you interested in the fourteen-year-old witch in Oklahoma who was mentioned in passing? Or beautiful Kai? Or the random indie series with the two queens? Do you perhaps want to know more about the Maltuban language and the world it came from? Read about all of these things in the novels of Dalila Caryn. Go to DalilaCaryn.com today for more info! And eventually, you will even be able to read about the Goddess of War and her other curses. Adventure awaits!

Printed in the USA
CPSIA information can be obtained
at www.ICGtesting.com
JSHW082312180923
48389JS00004B/16